Praise for these other novels by
New York Times **bestselling author**
Allison Brennan

"If you haven't been reading Brennan's truly exceptional Lucy Kincaid/Sean Rogan series, then you have been missing out . . . In this mind-blowing installment, Brennan also gives readers a fascinating look into the mind-set of her epic villains. A chilling thrill-fest from beginning to end."
—*RT Book Reviews* (4½ stars, a Top Pick!)
on *No Good Deed*

"Allison Brennan reaches new heights in *Poisonous*, and this smart, sophisticated entry in the Maxine Revere series raises her to the level of Lisa Gardner and Harlan Coben."
—*Providence Journal*

"A fast-paced, suspenseful read with interesting characters and sinister twists that keep you turning the pages for more."
—Karin Slaughter

"Allison Brennan's *Poisonous* has it all . . . A twisty and compelling read."
—Lisa Unger

"Don't miss Max Revere's roller-coaster new thriller. Talk about grit and courage, Max never gives up."
—Catherine Coulter on *Compulsion*

"Packs in the thrills as investigative reporter Max confronts new murders and old family secrets in a suspense novel guaranteed to keep you up late at night!"

—Lisa Gardner on *Notorious*

"Amazing . . . The interconnectivity of Brennan's books allows her ensemble of characters to evolve, adding a rich flavor to the intense suspense."

—*RT Book Reviews* (4½ stars, Top Pick!)
on *Best Laid Plans*

"Gut-wrenching and chilling, this is a story you won't soon forget!"

—*RT Book Reviews* (4½ stars) on *Dead Heat*

"All the excitement and suspense I have come to expect from Allison Brennan."

—*Fresh Fiction* on *Stolen*

"Once again Brennan weaves a complex tale of murder, vengeance and treachery filled with knife-edged tension and clever twists. The Lucy Kincaid/Sean Rogan novels just keep getting better!"

—*RT Book Reviews* (4½ stars, Top Pick) on *Stalked*

Also by Allison Brennan

NOTHING TO HIDE

Allison Brennan

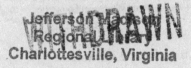

St. Martin's Paperbacks

This is a work of fiction. All of the characters, organizations, and events portrayed in this novel are either products of the author's imagination or are used fictitiously.

NOTHING TO HIDE

Copyright © 2019 by Allison Brennan.
Excerpt from *Abandoned* copyright © 2018 by Allison Brennan.

For information address St. Martin's Press, 175 Fifth Avenue, New York, NY 10010.

ISBN: 978-1-250-29765-5

Our books may be purchased in bulk for promotional, educational, or business use. Please contact your local bookseller or the Macmillan Corporate and Premium Sales Department at 1-800-221-7945, ext. 5442, or by e-mail at MacmillanSpecialMarkets@macmillan.com.

Printed in the United States of America

St. Martin's Paperbacks edition / May 2019

St. Martin's Paperbacks are published by St. Martin's Press, 175 Fifth Avenue, New York, NY 10010.

10 9 8 7 6 5 4 3 2 1

ACKNOWLEDGMENTS

Writing is a solitary profession, but writers need the help of others to make stories come alive. A special thank-you to all the people who helped bring this book to life: Wally Lind, the brains behind Crime Scene Writers, who always has answers to my many questions—or knows where to find them. The experts at Crime Scene Writers, who help me every time I post—especially Judy Melinek, M.D., without whom I would never have gotten these autopsies right. Martha Vasquez with the Bexar County Sheriff's Office, who helped with so many of the details in this book. And as always, my FBI go-to guy, Steve Dupre. If I got anything wrong—and I probably did—it was my own error.

As always the team at Minotaur Books and St. Martin's Press helped bring my book to the world, so thank you—and thanks especially to my editor Kelley Ragland and the brains behind Criminal Element, Joseph Brosnan. My agent Dan Conaway and the gang at Writer's House always keep me sane and focused. Well, at least they try! And lastly, thanks to my family for putting up with my odd hours and even odder commentary.

CHAPTER ONE

Saturday Morning

FBI Agent Lucy Kincaid squatted next to the latest victim of a possible serial killer. The victim had been identified as thirty-four-year-old Julio Garcia, the head chef of a convention hotel in downtown San Antonio.

Beaten then shot in the face. Fast, efficient, brutal. It was a gruesome sight, but Lucy was used to violence.

"I can give you five minutes," senior crime scene investigator Ash Dominguez said. "Until Walker gives me the thumbs-up, this is still his crime scene."

Lucy bristled. Ash was doing her a big favor, but the entire situation would have been a whole lot easier if the sheriff's deputy investigator Jerry Walker didn't have a chip on his shoulder about the FBI. She honestly hadn't expected the pushback. The FBI office had a terrific working relationship with both the sheriff's office and SAPD, but from the beginning of this investigation Walker had made everything more difficult than it had to be.

Besides, he knew she was coming to the scene, it had already been cleared by their mutual bosses. That he'd slipped away irritated her, but she wasn't surprised. The sheriff asked the FBI to assist shortly after the second murder three weeks ago, and the criminal investigations unit sent their office copies of the reports. But Walker hadn't followed up or returned her calls. It was clear he didn't like working with federal agents, but he didn't have a choice. The orders had come from higher up, and the three murders were almost identical. That fact put these deaths in a whole new category.

Don't blow it.

Her boss SSA Rachel Vaughn hadn't actually said those exact words, but she had lamented that there was no one she could send with Lucy to the crime scene, which was now an official joint investigation.

"It's not that you aren't capable of running solo with this, Lucy, but you're still a rookie and it's a touchy situation. As soon as I can juggle the workload of another agent, you'll have a partner."

Lucy shouldn't need an FBI partner—Walker was supposed to be working with her. She'd reached out to him this morning when she'd learned about the third victim, yet he'd disappeared from the crime scene before she arrived.

She pushed aside interoffice bullshit and visually inspected Garcia's body. The smashed hands. The gunshot to his face. If the MO from the previous two held, the autopsy would reveal that he'd been hit in the stomach and groin by the same object that shattered the bones in his hands—likely a small sledgehammer or mallet. There were conflicting interpretations of the murders and Lucy couldn't say exactly *what* they were looking at. On the one hand it seemed personal; on the other, sexual. Yet again, an act of revenge or retribution. Or even possibly a thrill killing, because the victims were beaten before they were murdered. In fact, they couldn't even confirm that the killer worked alone—each victim was a physically fit male with minimal or no defensive wounds.

The attention the killer paid to smashing his victim's hands suggested a thief, that the victims had taken something from the killer. But so far—at least between the first two victims—there was absolutely no connection that law enforcement could find.

This was the type of crime Lucy had the most experience with: violent. What that said about her, she didn't know—other than she was good at getting into the heads of both killers and victims.

Ash said, "It's not pretty."

"I read your other reports," she said. "Does this victim present the same way?"

"Damn near identical. The killer got up close and personal—several blows to the torso and groin, possibly one to the back of the head. Possible Taser burn on the victim's shirt"—he gestured—"but it was a contact stun, no cartridge and no confetti."

Virtually all personal Tasers now have AFID confetti to track to the owner. That put the killer in the smart category. Smart and confident.

But why the stun? It hurt like hell, but wouldn't keep the victim down. Was it before or after the initial blow? Had the victim tried to get up? Fought for the weapon so the killer used the jolt to stun him long enough to retrieve another weapon?

Except . . . there was little sign of a struggle. The victim had been found only a dozen feet from his car.

Ash said, "For some reason, the victim pulled over into this parking lot. He got out of his car, left his phone and keys. Then he was attacked. Though no way we can confirm this without an autopsy, he was likely attacked from behind because there don't appear to be any defensive wounds on his arms. Then *whack, whack, whack*, the killer used a blunt object similar to the first two murders. I should be able to confirm once I get trace from the autopsy. If it's consistent, I'm leaning toward a steel mallet with a diameter of between two and a half and three inches, but I can't tell you exactly what yet."

"It's unusual that the focus was on his hands," Lucy said. Extremely odd. "The groin suggests sexual, but the victims were all fully clothed, and the genitals weren't mutilated."

Ash shivered. "I don't know about you, but getting hit in the balls with a hammer would hurt like hell." He squatted across the body from Lucy. "You know, getting hit in the balls would bring most guys to their knees. Maybe that was the first hit. There just doesn't seem to be any reason. Nothing taken, no message, no purpose."

"You sound like a cop now," Lucy said. "And there's always a purpose. We just don't know why *yet*."

She swatted flies from the body and looked closely at the mouth, unable to avoid seeing the brain matter and blood from the close-range gunshot in the face. In the previous murders duct-tape residue had been found on and around the victim's mouth, but no tape was found at either scene. The killer had taken it with him, likely to avoid it being traced back to him. Tape is a terrific medium to obtain prints, trace evidence, or DNA. Here she could make out the rawness on the skin from the tape being pulled off. If they could find the tape—was it a souvenir? Did the killer dispose of it between the crime scene and his home? Destroy it? Why duct-tape the mouth at all? The kills had been quick. Not as efficient as they could have been—but was that part of the thrill? To beat a man down, then shoot him?

The killer was smart. Ruthless. Purposeful. Because even though these victims *appeared* random, there was a purpose. Killers almost always had a reason.

Once Lucy figured out how the victims connected, the

motive would be clear, she was certain of it. And if the killer was truly a serial murderer, there *would* be a connection. While the victims might *seem* random, there would be a commonality that made sense to the killer. She couldn't shake the feeling that this was retribution, which meant the killer may be done when he finished with his list. Who was on it? People who had done him wrong? Hurt him emotionally or physically? If that was the case, these three men would certainly be connected—even if it was long ago. Even if they hadn't communicated in years.

Ash jumped up. "Hey, Jerry."

Jerry said in a deep southern baritone, "Far as I know, this is still my crime scene."

Lucy slowly rose from her squat and turned to face BCSO investigator Jerry Walker. They hadn't met—he had been avoiding her calls—and she assessed him. Tall, broad-shouldered, all around a big guy, though not excessively overweight. Late forties, maybe fifty. He wore jeans and a white polo shirt with a sheriff's patch on the breast, his badge clipped to his belt next to his sidearm. But it was his well-worn black hat that stood out. He looked like he came from another era. The era where cops hated feds.

"Investigator Walker," Lucy said. "I've been trying to reach you. I'm Special Agent Lucy Kincaid."

"I've been working, ma'am. No time for chitchat."

She bit back a response that would have gotten her in trouble. Before she could form a more diplomatic comment, Walker continued. "Ashley, the coroner said he was ready to move the body twenty minutes ago but you told him to wait. It's not getting any cooler out here."

"Jeez, Jerry, call me Ash," he said.

"Nothing wrong with Ashley. Good southern name."

Ash rolled his eyes. "Maybe during the Civil War," he mumbled. He glanced at Lucy.

Walker noticed the look. "It's not her call, not yet at any rate," he said. "Agent Kincaid is simply assisting in this investigation."

Lucy could see Ash's wheels turning. He probably regretted letting her get close to the victim—except that she *was* authorized to work this case.

"Now, ma'am," Walker continued, "let's let the good folks from our crime scene unit take care of this poor guy, and we'll establish some ground rules."

She wanted to play nice—she *had* to play nice—and though Walker's tone was easygoing, his words were not. She'd been lucky in her career that most local law enforcement she worked with didn't have a problem with the FBI, and up until now she hadn't had any animosity from San Antonio LEOs. She'd learned from her sister-in-law who'd been an agent for nearly twenty years that such camaraderie hadn't always been the case, but in her time both working with her training partner in Washington, DC, and then here in San Antonio, she'd made many friends among local police. She really hoped she was wrong about Walker, but she felt like she was under a microscope.

She nodded curtly and forced a smile. "Ground rules."

He grinned back, though it didn't reach his eyes, then motioned for her to walk in front of him toward the staging area. She took a last look at the deceased. Julio Garcia. Early thirties, married, had the best part of his life ahead of him. Did he have kids? Had the killer left not only a widow but an orphan? She would find out why his life was cut short so tragically. While Walker flexed his authority, she wouldn't be chased away.

Though autumn officially started tomorrow and the

worst of the summer heat was over, it was still uncomfortable at ten in the morning and she was hot and now irri-
table. She walked to the staging area with Detective
Walker.

"Deputies," he said to the two first responders, "if you'd
be so kind as to finish the canvass. Check for surveillance
videos on the highway, if anyone heard or saw anything.
I'm right sure the gas station a mile down the road has one,
though it would be sheer luck if it caught cars passing on
the street, or if our killer or victim stopped there. No neighbors in the area, but check the closest homes for what
they saw and heard last night between eleven p.m. and
three in the morning."

"We're on it, Jerry."

He waited until they left, then turned back to Lucy. "I
understand you're a rookie."

She bristled. "Yes, I'll be here two years come January."

"I've been a Bexar County deputy for twenty-three
years, and an investigator for the criminal division for more
than half that time. I'll tell you this, every time the feds
have gotten involved in one of my cases, they've screwed it
up. I said as much to your boss. To be fair, I've only had to
work directly with your people twice over the years, so I'm
going to give you the benefit of the doubt. And the sheriff has a good working relationship with you folks and I
know he asked your boss personally to send someone in
to assist. He wants me to play nice. It's not my decision,
but I will live with it. However, just to be clear, our re-
spective bosses agreed that I'm the lead. I don't want
any misunderstanding about that, so if you have a problem taking direction, tell me now. Save us both time and
headache."

Lucy bit back her first sharp remark and said, "I have
no problem taking direction, Investigator Walker, as long

as you have no problem taking my assistance. I have a master's degree in criminal psychology, and have worked multiple serial killer cases."

"Psychology," he said with a hearty laugh. "Might as well consult a psychic to find out who killed these men."

"With all due respect, the FBI's Behavioral Science Unit has established clear guidelines based on evidence, victimology, and psychology to help narrow the suspect field."

He looked humored. "And what does your crystal ball tell you?"

Don't react. Stay professional. "I've read the autopsy reports, viewed the crime scene photos and reports, and read the case notes. I'm up to speed, except on one thing: witness statements."

"No witnesses. Each of the victims was killed at night in a remote area like this." He waved his hand around them. They were in the middle of a county park.

"I meant, the wives of the first two victims, the friends, neighbors, colleagues. Your notes were minimal." She shouldn't have said that, but she didn't backtrack. His notes *had* been basic. Just facts that the women knew about the days leading up to the murders of their husbands. When they left the house, what they were doing, when they planned to return. No known enemies. Ditto from their employers and colleagues. Nothing substantive, and she had more questions. "After reflection, the spouses may remember something else. These men got on the killer's radar somehow, and when we figure out how we'll know more. Plus, I want to go deeper into possible connections between the victims."

"They aren't connected, Agent Kincaid. It may surprise you, but I'm good at my job." He looked her up and down. "You have less than two years as an agent. And you're too young to have come from local law enforcement or the military."

"I don't think age has anything to do with competence."

"But it has everything to do with experience."

"Is your problem with me that I'm young or that I'm a federal agent?"

"Both, ma'am. Like I said, the feds I've worked with mucked up my cases and I have a long memory. But I'm willing to give you a shot."

"Sounds like I already have two strikes against me."

"I'm a man of my word, Agent Kincaid."

She sincerely hoped he was, because she was really tired of games and jumping through hoops with people who were supposed to be on her side—the side of justice.

"Then let me into this investigation. Don't push me aside as if I don't have anything to contribute."

"Well, you can repeat all the groundwork if you want, but I have dug around into the backgrounds of the first two victims and there is no connection between them—and no connection between their wives. Sometimes a crime is exactly what it seems to be: random."

"This killer has a reason."

"Could be he's getting his rocks off. Having fun."

"He picked these victims specifically. Knew they would be alone. Had the tools with him—stun gun, duct tape, hammer. Premeditated."

He nodded. "Yes, I'll give you that."

"He didn't stumble upon them and decide to kill them. He picked them out. *Maybe* initially at random, but he stalked them and *knew* when they would be alone. Knew their routine, and how to best approach them. He's smart; first two crime scenes we have no trace evidence to lead us to the killer. No prints, no DNA, no tire prints from another vehicle. I don't think that it was sheer luck that there were no security cameras at any of the crime scenes. Even the golf course where the second victim was killed, the security cameras were pointed toward the entrance, not the parking lot. I think the killer knew."

For the first time, Walker looked at her as if she had a brain. That angered her and relieved her.

More flies with honey.

She almost smiled when her brother Dillon's wise words popped into her head. She'd use the honey as long as it worked, but she wasn't going to be demoralized or dismissed.

"I pretty much came to the same conclusion, especially since the only thing Billy Joe Standish and Steven James had in common was that they were married, white, and under forty. And now Julio Garcia throws race out the window. He's Hispanic. They weren't even all born in Texas. Standish and Garcia are both from the San Antonio area—I did a quick run on him when we ID'd him—and James is from California, relocating here eight years ago to take a position with a large accountancy corporation. Standish is blue collar—in construction—and travels to find work. James is wealthy, works a white-collar job. Garcia was a chef, worked himself up from prep work to running the catering kitchen at a busy hotel."

"What about where they live? Go to church? School? Where their wives work? Truly random victims are rare. Men as victims of a serial killer are rare. *Something* connects them, maybe even a location where the killer picked up their scent. Or the killer knows all these victims and is killing them in an act of retribution."

"I base my conclusions on evidence, little lady. Facts."

She didn't comment; she wasn't going to take the bait.

He continued. "They all live in different areas. James upper middle class in Olmos Park, Standish barely holding on to his double-wide on a couple acres southwest of the city. Garcia here lives on some acres in Bulverde, about five, six miles up the road. Cheaper to live up there and find some land for elbow room."

"So he was on his way home."

Walker nodded. "He left his restaurant at eleven thirty last night. His wife was asleep—woke up at three thirty and realized he wasn't home. His body was found just after seven this morning by a park patrol officer."

She did a mental calculation. "It would take what, thirty, thirty-five minutes at night to get from downtown to Bulverde?"

"Thereabouts."

"These murders seem personal to me."

"Personal?"

"Why focus on the hands? Why beat the victim with a blunt object then shoot him? Why not simply shoot him in his car? Did the killer want information? But if the victims were interrogated, the killer wouldn't use duct tape on their mouths. Or did he beat the victims out of rage? Yet—there's no rage here. Not uncontrolled rage, at any rate. It was . . . methodical. Planned."

"Beating a guy to a pulp tells me there is plenty of rage in this killer."

"But they weren't."

"Excuse me?"

"Beaten to a pulp. The damage to their hands was extensive, but very specific. Focused."

Lucy was onto something, though she didn't know exactly where she was going with it. "I read the autopsy reports, but I want to talk to the ME for some clarification. The first victim was hit from behind, but the second victim was not. It's possible that one or more blows to the groin could have come from behind. It would definitely stun the victim, send him stumbling forward or to his knees. All three victims have electric burns to their shirt, indicating that at some point the killer used a close-contact device, likely a Taser without a cartridge in stun mode, either to hurt them—as part of his routine—or because the victim was fighting back. Only the first victim had clear defensive wounds on his forearms. Maybe the victim grabbed the killer and the stun gun was used to make him let go. But that wouldn't completely immobilize someone. As soon as the charge is extinguished, he can shake it off—especially, I'd think, if his adrenaline is pumping from the attack. Might think he's being carjacked or robbed, or maybe he knows the killer and suspects he's going to be killed. He's going to try to crawl away or fight back."

"So the killer hits him in the groin. I can tell you that would incapacitate any man, with enough force."

"And the first thing you would do is bring your hands down to protect yourself—unless they were restrained."

"*If* the killer hit the victims in the groin first. There was no duct-tape residue on the hands or wrists. Maybe our victim is trying to protect his privates and the killer smashes his hands instead, making this more sex-related than we think."

"We need to talk to Ash—he can look closer at the clothing. Maybe the wrists were bound over their shirts. Something to keep the hands on the ground—there was evidence of dirt and rocks embedded in the skin. The restraint wouldn't even need to be that secure—the killer didn't keep them alive long. Less than five minutes between first blow and the gunshot to the face. Or the first hit was to the groin, the victim reacted by protecting himself with his hands as you said, and the killer continued to attack that area, shattering the hands. But I would have to study the autopsy report in greater detail, because I would expect to find more damage to the surrounding area." She wanted to look at the photos, talk with Julie Peters the assistant ME, and run through some scenarios.

"Well, now, your theory makes sense, but that still doesn't tell us anything about these victims or the killer." He paused. "Or killers. Perhaps one guy held him down."

She nodded. "It's certainly possible. But this crime tells us everything about the killer."

"Well, unless you know his name, it doesn't. Guess your crystal ball didn't tell you that."

"Walker," she said as calmly as she could, "I am doing my best here to work with you, but this animosity has got to stop. I'm a good cop, and I read your service record—I know you're a good cop, too. You said you were a man of your word and would give me a real chance—so please start now."

He stared at her for a long moment, then nodded. "Very well. What now?"

"Talk to Garcia's widow, go back to the other two widows and re-interview now that we have more information. Ask the lab to reinspect clothing and any trace evidence. But something else is bugging me, and it slipped away." Likely because she was spending all her time battling this cop.

"Well, if the thing that's bugging you is bugging me, then we're on the same page."

"Excuse me?"

"Why did the victims stop? There was nothing mechanically wrong with their vehicles. They all pulled over right on the road—at least the first two—and this park is just off the road. And the victims all had the driver's-side window rolled down."

The blood drained from her face. "You're thinking a cop."

His face hardened. "Yes, I am, Agent Kincaid. But for now I'd like to keep this between you and me."

A cop. It made sense. Drivers would turn to the side of the road, or into a parking lot, if they were being pulled over.

She hoped and prayed that they were wrong.

"Maybe," she said slowly, "it's someone impersonating a cop. Or it's a driver who flagged them down."

"May just be that," Walker said. "But we have to look at the evidence wherever it takes us, and right now I don't like where it's leading."

"Still," Lucy said, "if it *is* a cop or someone with an official vehicle, there will be GPS tracking. We could discreetly look at the logs and determine who was in the area during the killing window."

"Perhaps, but something like that wouldn't stay secret for long." He paused and they watched the coroner load Julio Garcia's body into the back of the van. "I can probably do it discreetly."

"The killer could pretend to have car trouble. Waves him down."

"That's possible, too." He rubbed his eyes and said quietly, "I need to notify Garcia's widow." He wasn't a soft man, but she heard compassion in his voice and she pushed aside her earlier frustrations.

"I'll join you."

"You don't need to do that. Death notifications are never fun."

"Another thing we agree on. But I'll do it with you. It's not easy, but it's easier with a partner."

Walker looked at her. "You can call me Jerry."

"I'm Lucy."

"Short for Lucille?"

"Lucia. But I only respond to Lucia when it's my mother, so please call me Lucy."

He grinned. "If you want to leave your vehicle here, we

can go up to the Garcia spread together and I can fill you in on the rest of the details."

"Thank you."

Dillon was right. More flies with honey—honey and spine.

CHAPTER TWO

Saturday Mid-Morning

The first thing Lucy noticed when Marissa Garcia answered the door was that she was very, very pregnant. The second thing was the six-year-old boy pressed up against her legs.

This was the worst death notification of her career.

Walker took off his hat. "Mrs. Garcia? I'm BCSO investigator Jerry Walker and this is FBI Special Agent Lucy Kincaid. May we come in?"

Marissa's bottom lip quivered.

A voice with a thick Spanish accent called from the back of the house. "Marissa? Who is it? Is it Julio?"

"No, Mama," Marissa said, but her voice barely carried. "Please, please—no." She clutched her son.

Lucy stepped in first and put her hand on Marissa's elbow. "Marissa, let's sit down."

The woman allowed herself to be led to the back of the house to a comfortable, cluttered family room where an older woman sat in an easy chair, her leg in a cast. Two younger women immediately hopped up and went to Marissa's side.

"Sit, Issa," one of the women said. "I'm Sandra, Marissa's sister." She looked at the other girl and nodded toward the boy. "Anna." She tilted her head again.

"Dario, let's start lunch," Anna said, her eyes darting from Lucy to Jerry.

Dario clutched his mother tighter. "Mommy?"

Marissa didn't move. She stood there shaking with her spine as straight as it could be considering her condition.

"Just tell me," she whispered. "Just tell me."

Jerry said, "We regret to inform you that your husband was killed late last night."

"Dear Lord, no," the old woman sobbed loudly and crossed herself. "No, no, no! My Julio!"

Anna knelt next to the woman and took her hand.

"Wh-what. Ha-happened."

Sandra led her sister to the couch and urged her to sit. Sandra sat next to her and Dario climbed into his aunt's lap.

"He was so tired, so tired working to support his family!" Mrs. Garcia said. "Coming home so late at night, so late! Working overtime! I told you, Marissa! Too many hours."

Lucy cleared her throat. This situation could quickly get out of control. Jerry looked uncomfortable.

"May we sit?" Lucy asked.

"Of course," Marissa said, waving to a couch. "Just— what happened?"

"I told you!" Mrs. Garcia said.

Marissa rubbed her eyes. "Mama, I'm sorry."

"Marissa, you didn't do anything," Lucy said. "Julio was murdered."

"Julio worked so hard, six days a week," Marissa said, evidently not hearing what Lucy had said. "We were saving up for the kids. Dario's school. The house. College. We wanted them to have what we never had, we wanted our children to have a real education. Julio loved his job, but it was many hours and he was so tired. It was only until the baby starts school. Then I can go back to work."

She hadn't heard, but Sandra did. She said, "How?"

"We're still investigating," Lucy said cautiously. She wasn't going to give any of the details of the crime yet. Dario was old enough to understand, and she didn't want those images in his head.

Jerry said, "He was killed at a park off two eighty-one close to the interchange last night. We confirmed with his employer that he left at eleven thirty, and we suspect he was killed shortly after."

"Killed?" Mrs. Garcia said. "Murdered? Who would murder my son? Who, Marissa?"

"I don't know," Marissa said.

Because Jerry didn't suggest it, Lucy had to do something to prevent this situation from getting out of control.

"Anna, Mrs. Garcia, let's take Dario into the kitchen for a minute so Investigator Walker can talk to Marissa," Lucy said.

"No," Mrs. Garcia said firmly. "I want to hear exactly what happened to my son. I deserve that!"

Marissa was fighting not to cry, and Sandra stared at her sister's mother-in-law with fierce displeasure. Sandra glanced at Lucy, then stood, picking Dario up with her. "We leave them alone now, Beatrice. You're upsetting Marissa, and I won't have that."

Mrs. Garcia objected, but Sandra took charge and handed her a cane. "Don't do this," Sandra said quietly to the old woman, "not around Dario. Not now."

The woman grumbled and complained but went with Sandra and Anna.

Lucy was relieved, and it appeared Marissa was, too, as suddenly she started to cry. "I'm sorry," she said. "I'm sorry."

Lucy handed her a small package of tissues. "Nothing to be sorry about, Marissa."

"What happened to my Julio? I really don't understand why someone would kill him. We don't have a lot of money."

Jerry said, "We don't believe that this was a robbery. We are still investigating, but there are some similarities between Julio's murder and those of two other local men. Do you know Billy Joe Standish or Steven James? Standish works in construction and James is an accountant."

She seemed completely befuddled. "I don't know them. At least—I don't think so. I don't know the names. I don't know. Oh God." She clutched her stomach.

"Are you okay?" Lucy moved to sit next to Marissa. She took her hand. "How many months are you?"

"Thirty-four weeks. My baby—she'll never meet her papa."

Jerry stood and said, "We'll come back later, Mrs. Garcia. You should rest."

"Why would someone kill Julio? Everyone loves him. He would give you the shirt off his back. If he was mugged, he would give his car or wallet. He wouldn't fight back. He wouldn't risk being hurt. He was a good man. A great man. I—I don't know what to do."

"We'll find out what happened," Lucy said. "But you need to remain calm for your baby. She has a few more weeks she needs to grow."

"Mama—she will never believe me. She blames me."

"Blames you for what?" Lucy asked.

"Everything. That Julio works so many hours. She thinks it's because I want things, but I don't. I don't want anything. I just want my family. Julio and Dario and Baby Bump." She smiled through her tears. "Julio calls her Baby Bump because we don't want to name her until we see her."

"That's sweet," Lucy said.

"I just want my family. They are all I care about. And . . . he's gone. He's gone. Julio is my true love. My soul mate. My . . . my . . . I can't."

Lucy looked at Jerry and said quietly, "Tell the others what we told her, and ask her sister to come in." To Marissa she said, "Deputy Walker is right, we can return when you've had a chance to rest. I'm sure you didn't get much sleep last night."

She shook her head. "When I woke in the middle of the night and Julio wasn't home, I couldn't sleep. He called when he was leaving work, and I should have stayed up. I shouldn't have fallen asleep."

"There was nothing you could have done, Mrs. Garcia," Lucy said. "He was already dead when he was expected home."

Jerry stepped out of the family room and into the adjoining kitchen. He was clearly uncomfortable with the intense emotions and family conflict. Death notifications were hard, but this situation—the absolutely senseless act of violence that had ripped Julio from the people who loved him—was disturbing on multiple levels. Lucy didn't know how she remained calm, but she would pay for it tonight. When everything came crashing down and she felt the loss that rolled off Marissa in waves of grief as she processed her tragedy.

"I want you to think about your baby right now, your baby and your son," Lucy said. "I know this is not going to be easy for you or your family, but your children need you to be strong. Especially this little one." She rested her hand on Marissa's stomach. Almost immediately she felt the baby kick. She took a deep breath and held it. Then slowly let it out. It wouldn't help Marissa or the investigation if she became emotional.

"I—I don't know how to go on."

"Sandra and Anna are your sisters, right?"

She nodded.

"What about your parents?"

"My mom—she's been gone for a long time. A car accident when I was in high school. Sandra took over. She was in college and she left to take care of me and Anna."

"And your father?"

She shook her head. "We all believe he died of a broken heart." She stared at Lucy, anguish clouding her face.

"Why? You said it wasn't a robbery."

"We don't know why yet."

Sandra led the way back into the family room, and Mrs. Garcia hobbled behind her. Anna and Dario weren't with them, which was probably a good thing. "I'll take care of my sister," Sandra said. "If you need anything from us to find out who did this—call me." She handed both Jerry and Lucy a business card. ROBERT & SANDRA VALLEJO, REALTORS.

"We'll have more questions," Jerry said, "and I'll call before we come by."

"When can I bury my son?" Mrs. Garcia said.

"Mama," Marissa pleaded. "Not now."

"I need to call Father Paul. We have to make arrangements."

"The coroner will contact you when they release his body," Lucy said. She wrote the number on the back of her card and handed it to Sandra. "That's me, and the number on the back is the coroner's office. But it will be at least forty-eight hours. There is nothing you need to do today except relax."

"Thank you," Sandra said. "I need Marissa to lie down."

"We'll let ourselves out, ma'am," Jerry said with a nod to each of the women, then motioned for Lucy to go first.

They left. "Well, damn," Jerry said quietly as he climbed back into his car.

"There are few truly random killers out there—especially with weeks between murders," Lucy said. "But I don't see a motive. A loving family man, a close family? We need to dig into the pasts of these three men. Maybe . . . maybe it's something that connected them long ago. They may not have grown up in the same town, but maybe they were at the same place at the same time. An airport. A conference. A vacation. *Something* has to connect them."

"It would be more likely that *if* the murders aren't random, San Antonio is what they have in common. Meaning, perhaps it was an event or situation *here* that they were involved in. That narrows it down to the last eight years." He paused. "I really hate senseless violence."

"We need to make a list of ways these men *could* have known each other, over and above the obvious like church or employer or gym."

"Like if they all witnessed a crime. Or were on a jury together."

"Exactly. Maybe they went to the same concert, took a continuing education class. Or perhaps the wives are connected and that's how the killer is targeting his victims. Did the other two men have children?"

"Steven James has a daughter, freshman in high school. Standish has no kids."

Jerry pulled up next to Lucy's vehicle at the park. Nearly everyone was gone from the crime scene, though a two-person patrol remained to keep the park closed. CSI would release the scene as soon as they confirmed they had everything they needed.

"You know, Kincaid," Jerry said, "a random serial killer is not unheard of."

"I sincerely hope that's not what we're dealing with." Some serial killers might *seem* random, but most weren't.

They were generally organized and targeted a specific type of person—in this case married men. But *married men* was far too broad a category for a traditional serial killer. Maybe the killer didn't know these men were married. A killer driving around, looking for a male driving alone? That would lend to the theory that the killer was a cop or impersonating a cop—pulling over a vehicle. But if the victim was summoned by someone pretending to be in trouble, then the killer knew when and where the victim was going to be in order to set the trap.

Jerry concurred. "It's like the sniper in DC—if anyone can be a target, everyone panics."

"That, and a truly random killer is going to be much harder to find until he messes up. No fingerprints have been found at any scene, no weapon, no witness has come forward. Nothing that connects to the killer other than the MO. And the MO doesn't make sense right now. Is it sexually motivated or revenge? Targeting the hands indicates theft of some sort, stealing—targeting the groin indicates a sex crime. But both? It feels . . . unnecessary. Then the final gunshot? To ensure they are dead? I don't know." Lucy paused, thinking things through, but not seeing any answers. "I want to be there during the autopsy. Would you object?"

"We don't routinely observe autopsies, even homicides. The procedure is recorded."

"Still—I need to see exactly what was done to the bodies. It'll help me."

"Help you how?"

"Get inside the killer's head."

"Psych mumbo jumbo," he said.

Lucy shook her head. "And here I thought we were getting along."

"Sorry," he said, though he didn't sound like he meant

it. "You seem like a smart cop. I just don't really cotton to the whole *my daddy hit me so now I kill people it's not my fault* mentality."

Lucy almost smiled. "Well, it's a lot more complicated than that."

"And I don't want to give the defense any reason to get the guy off."

"Most serial killers are sane by legal standards."

"You want to watch the autopsy, go right ahead. Might even be this afternoon. I'll call over there and find out their timetable."

"Thank you. And in the meantime, I'd like to review the complete case files of the first two murders."

"And I'll get started on paperwork. I don't know about you feds, but we spend more time filling out forms than hitting the ground."

"Another thing we have in common," Lucy said.

CHAPTER THREE

Saturday Afternoon

The sheriff's office was in the city of San Antonio adjacent to the detention center. It was a sturdy brick multistory building in the middle of a light industrial area, right off the freeway. Lucy had been to the jail a few times to interview suspects, but she'd never had cause to go into the station.

The sheriff was responsible for the county jails and court security, but also maintained patrols and investigative units throughout the entire county, not just the unincorporated areas. The local FBI office worked with both the city police and the sheriff, and had a good relationship with each office, save for—apparently—Jerry Walker.

Jerry handed Lucy a visitor's pass and led her upstairs and down the hall to the homicide unit's small corner of the building. No other detectives were at their desks.

Jerry had his own small office, a sign of seniority. He could be the lead investigator—it wouldn't surprise her considering his years of service.

He flipped on the light and pointed to two tall, unorganized stacks of files. "Hardcopies. You've seen the important points in the information we sent over to the FBI."

"Which wasn't complete."

He didn't comment.

She glanced around. There was a chair for her, but no place to review the files. "Do you have access to a conference room that we can use for a couple of days? Just to spread out a bit. I've found that looking at the evidence side by side can help."

"To each his—or her—own," Jerry said. "I can grab a conference room, but I don't know how long I can keep it. We don't have the space around here."

"We can set up at the FBI, we have a room I can use for the duration of the investigation."

As soon as the words left her mouth, she wished she could take them back. Jerry stared at her, eyes narrowed, once again suspicious. "Not going to happen, Kincaid," he said. "I'll get permission to use a room for the duration of this investigation, if I have to. Grab those." He took one of the two stacks, gesturing toward the other.

She followed him down the hall. He looked into several rooms before pushing open the door of a small room with a lone narrow window and a table that could seat four people if they crammed. "We can use this." He dumped the files on the table.

She wasn't going to complain. There was a floor-to-ceiling whiteboard on one wall that would be useful.

"Since I already know what's in these files, I'm going to grab a sandwich. Can I get you something?"

She wasn't hungry, but she didn't know when she'd be able to get lunch, so she said, "That would be great, thank you."

"Anything specific?"

"I'll eat almost anything."

"I'll be back in a few." He stepped out, closing the door behind him.

She sighed. Back to square one. She hated walking on

eggshells around people, and she really wanted to know what had happened between Jerry and the FBI in the past. It might help her understand why he was so hostile toward her.

Lucy sat down with the files and in minutes forgot about Jerry and his issue with her and the FBI. She started mapping out the crime scenes and the assault on each victim and couldn't shake the belief that these three murders simply made no sense.

Jerry had already done an extensive amount of work. When the first victim turned up—Billy Joe Standish, also killed on a Friday night—the police thought it was a personal attack. Standish had been beaten by the side of the road and shot. They interviewed everyone he worked with, his wife, his family, his neighbors. Standish had a reputation for drinking on the weekends and had two misdemeanor charges for fighting. But there had been no brawls in the last year, and no one had any idea who would want him dead. He had no alcohol or drugs in his system. They interviewed people in the area, both residents and businesses, to see if there had been any recent break-ins—perhaps Standish had seen something. Because even though he had a reputation for being a weekend partier, he was a charitable guy—he'd spent a week in Houston after the flood helping rescue stranded families. So it wasn't a stretch to think that if he saw someone breaking into a business, he might do something about it.

Except, nothing. No break-ins in months, and he was killed nearly half a mile from any private residence. The quarry near where his body was found was empty at night and never had cash or unsecured equipment on the premises.

Jerry had made notes to talk to the wife again about any threats—he'd asked her once, she couldn't think of any, but he also noted that she became hysterical the two times he talked to her. When the second victim turned up, Jerry apparently hadn't followed up with Susan Standish again. The case took a different direction, and Jerry worked diligently to try to find a connection between Standish and James.

There was not one connection that he could find. They didn't go to the same church (James didn't go to church at all; Standish went sporadically); they didn't run in the same circles (James was white collar, upper middle class—Standish blue collar, barely making it). Not the same doctor, not the same dentist, not the same vet. (James had a cat; Standish had two yellow Labs). They lived in different communities. Susan worked at an elementary school, but not in the same district that the James kid attended, and they didn't drive the same type of car. Standish was Ford; James was Toyota. They had no friends in common.

And now a third victim, who seemingly had no connection with the first two.

The basement—which had high, ground-level windows so it didn't feel like you were buried—had a decent cafeteria set up like an old-fashioned diner with hamburgers, a soup of the day, a salad bar, and sandwiches. The specialty was a club sandwich, but Jerry's favorite was the seasonal turkey—from October 1 through New Year's, the cook offered a carved turkey, stuffing, and homemade cranberry sauce sandwich that was to die for. Ten more days, Jerry thought. The food was fresh and reasonably priced, and Jerry was all about good, cheap food.

He had a headache, so he dry-swallowed three aspirin while he waited in the short line—short since it was both Saturday and after the lunch rush.

Doris Jackson had worked in the cafeteria since before

Jerry became a cop, and considering he'd been here for twenty years, that was forever. She knew every cop by name, always had a smile, and while she didn't gossip, she knew everything that went on in the sheriff's office. If there was an officer down, she worried and fretted with the rest of them, always preparing sandwiches and snacks to take to the hospital. When the sheriff found out that Doris was spending her own money to feed grieving cops, he created a fund to cover the cost. Everyone had assumed that the cafeteria—which was run by the county—took care of the expense. Doris had shunned a tip jar for years, but the sheriff bolted one to the register. "You and your crew deserve it." Then he put the word out that everyone could spare a dollar a day.

"What are you feeling like today, Mr. Jerry?" Doris asked.

"Meatball sub." He needed something substantial because he'd eaten breakfast on the run.

He didn't know what to get Agent Kincaid.

"You need something else?"

"A fed I'm working with on this case. She said get her anything."

"Club is always a winner."

"One of those, then."

Doris smiled, called out the order to the chef, and Jerry paid her. He slipped two bucks in the tip jar.

He stood aside and waited, checking his phone. He texted Jeanie, his wife, that he didn't know when he'd be home, probably not before six, and he'd call later. It was Saturday and she was used to his erratic schedule.

He had to get out of this mood. Kincaid was young and a rookie, but she didn't seem like an idiot. He simply didn't want to work with the feds. He knew he had a bias, but at the same time he had a hard time forgiving the local FBI office for their screwup.

Kincaid wasn't even here. Hell, she was probably still in high school.

He'd told Kincaid that the FBI messed up two of his cases, and that wasn't a lie, but it was only the one—the kidnapping that ended in the death of two young boys—that soured him on his federal counterpart. The FBI had never admitted they made a critical and fatal error.

The agent in charge of that investigation had left the bureau, last Jerry heard, but that didn't make the situation any better. He'd had ten years to fume. The feds had dismissed his concerns about their approach. The whole case was a mess, but he had known they were going to get those boys killed. He knew it and he fought them and they'd removed him from the case. Just taken him out of the equation. Yes he lost his temper, but the lives of two kids were at stake. He couldn't sit back and let it happen.

He was removed and the FBI didn't truly understand the situation because they didn't listen to him—that *agent* didn't listen to him—and Jerry had never forgiven them. Never. Because had they realized the situation wasn't as it appeared to be, those boys might be alive today.

None of that was Kincaid's fault, and he was trying to separate the cases. But the whole psychology crap irritated him. That was exactly what the feds said ten years ago, that the kidnapper—a relative of the family—wouldn't hurt the boys. There had been no sign of violence, nothing in the kidnapper's psychology that suggested she would hurt her nephews. It was a family dispute, and the FBI was so damn confident in their theory, they made several missteps.

One thing Jerry knew was people. He may not have graduated from a prestigious university—got his AA at SAC, the oldest community college in Texas, right here in San Antonio—but he wasn't an idiot. He might not be able to throw around the latest terms of misbehavior, but he understood people. He knew criminals and victims. He understood motivations, maybe not able to articulate them like some folk, but he knew in his gut. And when he was first on the scene when those two boys were grabbed by their aunt on their way to school, he knew something was different about this case. Something wasn't adding up. But because he couldn't give the jerks at the FBI more than his gut impression based on years of police work and talking to thousands of people on the street as first a beat cop then an investigator, well, they completely dismissed him.

"Jerry," Doris called out, a bag packed with his order. He walked over to the pickup.

"You're a million miles away," Doris said.

"Thinking about a tough case."

"I heard about it."

"You did?"

"Three men, same killer."

"Looks that way."

"You'll get him. I know you will."

He smiled. "Glad for your confidence, Doris."

"But that ain't what put the frown on your face," she added. "You're thinking about those boys again."

Sometimes, Doris seemed downright psychic.

"The feds are all over this."

"Same one?"

"No."

"Well, that's your answer, ain't it?"

He didn't know that there had been a question, but Doris had a long memory. He hadn't been in a good place ten years ago after the kidnapping and murders. He nearly got himself fired. Started drinking heavily, was angry and temperamental and put himself and others at risk. He'd ended up taking a month off and got his life back together, thanks mostly to his boss, and his wife. His boss told him to get his act together or he was gone. First half of the wake-up call. So he took leave, and Jeanie was a rock. Firm when he was angry, sympathetic when he blubbered like a kid. She probably should have left him, he was so moody, but she pulled him out of his hole. He loved her more now than he did when they'd married twenty-seven years ago.

The thing was—he had mostly accepted the outcome of the Barton kidnapping. He'd done everything in his power to fix it, he knew—and they shut him out. That wasn't on him. But he couldn't put aside how the FBI had screwed everything up.

He was just waiting for Lucy Kincaid to do the same thing. Only now, because he maintained control of the case, she didn't have the final say. She didn't have the authority. And if she overstepped, he would cut her out so fast her little rookie head would spin.

Lucy jumped when the door opened. She felt foolish, but she was so immersed in reading the files and taking notes that she almost forgot where she was.

"Excuse me," a tall, lean female deputy in uniform said as she entered. "I'm Assistant Sheriff Maria Jimenez. I oversee the investigative unit. I spoke to your boss this morning, wanted to introduce myself since we haven't had the pleasure."

Lucy stood and shook her hand. "Lucy Kincaid. Nice to meet you."

"You've been busy," she said, waving her hand to the stacks of papers Lucy had set out. Lucy had rearranged the files to better help her see patterns.

"I'm visual," Lucy said.

Maria glanced down the hall, then shut the door. "I know that Jerry has been fighting sharing this investigation, but the sheriff and I agree that we need all hands with this, especially now after a third body dropped. Just so you know, Jerry Walker is hands down the best investigator we have in our office. The strongest combination of experience and instincts. I understand that he's been distant and nonresponsive the last two weeks, but I talked to him this morning and want to make sure you understand that the FBI is welcome in our investigation. My office has an outstanding relationship with your office, and your reputation precedes you. You have a lot of friends in SAPD. If you have any issues, please let me know."

"If I have any issues with Investigator Walker, I'll talk to him about it," Lucy said. She wasn't going to go running to Jerry's boss because he was a jerk. "It might help if I understood his animosity toward my office. He said the FBI messed with two of his investigations."

Maria hedged. "They may have, but only one affected him. It was before my time. I was in the military stationed overseas so all I know is rumor and innuendo, which I won't repeat. As far as Jerry is concerned, he felt that the FBI made a fatal tactical error on a kidnapping case. He recognizes that it was the agent in charge of the investigation, but he blamed everyone and the aftermath was difficult."

Lucy needed to know more about that case.

The door opened and Jerry walked in with a bag. He glanced at Lucy, then nodded to his boss. "Maria. I emailed you a preliminary report."

"Got it. Just wanted to introduce myself to Agent Kincaid. Let me know what you need, Jerry—the sheriff is getting press calls, wants to have a press conference on Monday with something."

"The press can just go pound salt for all I care," Jerry said.

Lucy refrained from grinning.

Jerry continued. "We're waiting on the autopsy. Talked

to the morgue, they can't fit him in tonight—they have a full house right now, and it's the weekend so they're short-staffed. Tomorrow afternoon, but might be Monday morning. Once we have the evidence processed we'll go back and review each of the cases to identify any commonalities. This guy is going to make a mistake, and he might have already."

"Let's hope it's before another body drops," Maria said. "The press haven't connected these murders, but it's only a matter of time, so the sheriff is taking a preemptive step. He's going to announce it's the same killer, unless you come up with something in the next thirty-six hours that says it's not."

"Yes, ma'am."

Maria left and Jerry sat in the chair across from Lucy. He stared at the papers laid out in front of her, then glanced up at the whiteboard where Lucy had created a time line.

"You've been busy in half an hour."

"The time line was easy," she said. "I had one already created from the information you'd sent earlier, and it was just a matter of adding the Garcia case."

"And did your magic ball tell you who the killer is?"

She ignored the comment. "There are a couple of things to add to the MO," she said. "The method used is consistent—pending Garcia's autopsy—and the target—male victims—but I don't think that we can now discount that each of the victims was married and under forty. All three were killed at night, between ten p.m. and two a.m., and their bodies were found within hours. The killer made no effort to conceal or move the bodies."

Jerry unwrapped his sandwich—it smelled real good—and said, "Just because the victims are married doesn't mean that they weren't random."

"But how are you defining random? Are they random because the killer picked them out at that moment, or random because the killer didn't personally know them when he chose to target them?"

He chewed, thinking about her comment. "Meaning, the killer either just decided to kill—which would mean whether they were married doesn't factor into it at all—or the killer picked the victim, then stalked him, learning about him and his habits before killing him?"

"It's the latter," she said.

"Why do you think that?"

He wasn't being antagonistic at this point, which was a relief. "At a minimum, the killer spent a little time studying each victim's routine." Lucy rose and went to the whiteboard. "First, the crimes were committed in three different areas—northwest, southeast, and north of San Antonio. All were committed when the victim was coming home from work or a business trip. If the killer was just looking for a lone male, he would likely have stuck to the same area, and out of all of the areas, the rural area where Standish was killed offers the best protection for the killer—very few people use those back roads that late at night."

Lucy glanced at her notes, but she already knew the case well. "Standish was killed coming back from Houston. According to his wife's statement, he'd been working in Houston Monday through Friday on a temporary construction job for the three weeks leading up to his murder. You confirmed with his employer that his shift ended at four thirty. He was staying at his brother's house while working the job, went there to shower, have dinner, and left Houston at approximately seven twenty that evening, according to his brother. He called his wife at nine thirty when he was at a gas station to tell her he'd be home in an hour. At eleven, when he still wasn't home, she called his cell phone and he didn't answer. He *could* have been followed from the gas station."

"We viewed all security cameras in the area and found nothing to help us."

"Right," she said. "His body was found two miles south of I-10 on a two-lane road he always took home, according to his wife." She looked at the map. "Farm to Market Road. Between the I-10 exit and where his body was found, there are a few light industrial businesses, an auto body shop, a couple houses set far apart. His body was found just south of a quarry that—based on the website and the street view maps—I suspect has cameras, but he was around a bend, right before a series of long driveways that lead to residences. The road is remote, not a major thoroughfare."

"Your point?"

"The killer had to specifically target him."

"He could have just have been the unlucky guy to get pulled over—if the cop theory is accurate—or was followed from the freeway."

"The killer targets *lone males*. At a minimum, he would have had to have spotted him at some point in order to follow him or . . . or stage something to force him to stop. Because though that road is not busy, especially at night, if the target was truly random, then was it just blind luck that the killer stumbled upon a male driving alone?"

"You don't want it to be random."

"No, I don't—because he'll be that much harder to catch. And in most random killing sprees, there isn't this much time between attacks. Truly random killers who are not sexually motivated are rare. The sniper on the East Coast terrorized residents for a short period of time before he was caught, and chose his victims apparently at random. Israel Keyes, who was arrested here in Texas, killed for more than a decade, picking his victims at random and moving from state to state to avoid detection, but he was sexually motivated. Son of Sam—Berkowitz—picked many of his victims at random, and there's a dispute whether they were sexually motivated because he didn't rape his female victims, and he killed both men and women."

"And so?" Jerry said. "You don't want him to be random, so what?"

"What I *want* means nothing. I just don't think that he's picking his victims spontaneously. Maybe that's a better word than *random*."

Lucy stared at her timeline, considering. Her analysis was falling into place, but there were still holes, and she needed to talk it out.

"Four weeks between the first two murders and three weeks between the second and third murders. Is he escalating? Did he want to make sure the police weren't onto him after the first murder, so waited longer for the second? And now . . . he's emboldened. Three dead, he's cocky and confident. If he has another target, he very well could speed up his time line."

Jerry didn't say anything for a minute. He chewed another bite of his sandwich and slid the bag over to Lucy. "I didn't know what you might like, and Doris who runs the shop downstairs said a turkey club is always a safe bet."

"Thank you," she said. Was he thinking about her comments or just eating?

She resisted the urge to keep talking, because she didn't have anything else substantive to go on—she'd reviewed the evidence reports when she first got them, reread them now, and there was little physical evidence at each crime scene. Partly because of the terrain—the first victim was on a gravel pullout next to the road, killed only feet from his car. The second victim was in a golf course parking lot between the airport and his house—it was only a fifteen-minute drive, but for some reason he'd stopped. It was after midnight, everything was closed except for the theater across a wide boulevard from the golf course entrance. Why had he stopped? Cop or someone needing help?

"Let me play devil's advocate for a minute," Jerry said.

"Please do."

She was relieved he spoke, because five minutes of silence was making her antsy.

"If the victims *aren't* random, then in all likelihood they knew their killer and weren't in fear for their lives. They exited their vehicle. If the killer isn't a cop, they knew him or weren't threatened by him."

"Agreed."

"Yet it could be that the killer followed them from their origin and when he suspected they were getting close to home—all three victims were found within a mile of getting off a major highway or thoroughfare—the killer acted."

"If it's a cop, he flashed his lights and pulled them over. I can see that. Yet in my experience, there is always a reason."

"Maybe the victims cut him off. Road rage."

"And he always carries a handgun, stun gun, sledgehammer, and duct tape in his car?"

"This is Texas. Those tools are good for a lot of things, not just murder."

She was about to argue, then realized that her husband always had a handgun, tools, and duct tape with him— Sean had a concealed carry permit for his gun, he'd once half joked that duct tape was the most useful resource created by man, and he had a tool chest in his trunk with anything he might need on the road.

"Road rage is generally immediate," Lucy said. "Maybe rear-ending the car, yelling, drawing attention."

"But not unheard of. You're the one who believes in the

psychology garbage. So what would make a person mad enough to kill?"

She fumed at the slight, but didn't respond. "First, I firmly believe that almost everyone is capable of killing another human being under the right circumstances. I'm not talking about cops and criminals, I'm talking about average people. A mother home alone with her baby when someone breaks into the house. A father who snaps when his son's child molester gets off on a technicality. A heat-of-the-moment argument. Sometimes it's rash and immediately regretted, sometimes it's not. But if these victims are because of road rage or a vehicular slight, that would mean the killer has the calm, ruthless patience to follow the victims for miles without tipping his hand—otherwise, the victims would have called nine-one-one, or they wouldn't have pulled over. That calm patience that ends in a violent, albeit brief, attack seems . . . at odds."

"I have no idea what you mean." Jerry finished his sandwich, crumbled the wrappings into a tight ball, and tossed it into the wastebasket in the corner.

"The murders were violent, but they weren't prolonged. There wasn't uncontrollable rage. Hit the victims, beat them, duct-tape their mouth, shatter the bones in their hands, then shoot them in the face—"

"I'm aware of the MO," he said dryly.

Lucy was getting angry. "Can I do a demonstration?"

He looked surprised, then shrugged.

Lucy walked out of the small office and down to the larger room filled with cubicles. She glanced at all the cops before she found one that matched the general build of the latest victim—Julio Garcia, five foot ten inches, 170 pounds. The other two victims were both six feet—the first a solid 200 pounds of muscle, the second a leaner 180. But Lucy wasn't sure she could drag a two-hundred-pound man. "Deputy?"

"Yes, ma'am. Deputy Bryce Hangstrom."

"May I borrow you for five minutes? And I need you to take off your utility belt." She didn't want it to get caught on anything when she dragged his body.

He looked skeptical. Jerry stepped behind Lucy. "Go ahead, Bryce, I want to see what Agent Kincaid plans on doing."

Bryce smiled, took off his belt, and handed it to another cop.

"We're going to reenact the first crime scene because there was less space, but all three victims were killed in roughly the same manner." The narrow space between the road and a gulley. She grabbed a stapler off a desk, then pulled a chair over to the large area in front of the elevator. "Bryce." She motioned for him to sit. "Now just do what I say, and I promise I won't hurt you."

He laughed and sat down.

"Jerry," Lucy said, trying to ignore the crowd of spectator cops who were watching her. "We know a few things. We know that the victim pulled over his car and there was no identifiable sign of malfunctioning. We know that the victim rolled down his window. And we know that the killer exited his vehicle without fear—the keys and phone were in each car, there was no attempt to call nine-one-one. I'll be the killer."

She leaned over Bryce, as if looking down and through a car window, two feet away. She had the stapler behind her back. As she worked through this in her head, she realized that the killer probably had a backpack or purse or something to carry the hammer in. "Thank you so much for stopping. My car isn't working, and the tow truck is an hour away."

"Maybe I can help," he said.

Lucy nodded and said to Jerry, "I think most people would help, especially if the person is clean-cut and doesn't appear to be a threat. Maybe there was a car with the hood up. And this is the South—honestly, in California most people would drive on by, but here I've found people more willing to help."

A few chuckles, then a, "You're from California?" in a derogatory tone.

"San Diego," she said, "the most beautiful beaches in the country."

She went back to her reenactment. "We know a few things about the attack, but the theory about the order of blows to the victim is based on the autopsy, and some of the findings are inconclusive. For example, you can often tell what blow was fatal, or which blow was first, either from the bruising or because of trace evidence from one part of the body to the other, and a good coroner will be able to count the actual blows based on tissue damage, but determining whether he was hit first in the chest then the groin, we don't know. With the first victim, the coroner was firm on a couple of facts." She had a thought and said, "Hey, can someone time this?"

"Got it," a female deputy said, holding out her phone.

Lucy waited ten seconds to allow for the time it took to convince the victim to get out of the car, then said, "Okay, Bryce, get out of the car and follow me to mine."

He did.

"What's the first thing you would do if someone has their hood up?"

"I'd be thinking they ran out of gas."

"With the hood up?"

He shrugged. "Well, it's dark, so I'd want a flashlight to see if something is obviously wrong."

"Or it could be a flat tire."

"That would be obvious."

"Not in the dark. You go around to check the tire you can't immediately see and what? Squat? Do that."

He did. She took the stapler and said, "This is a steel-headed sledgehammer. We know it can do extensive damage. I've now hit you hard at the top of your spine—there was severe bruising and a chipped vertebra in the autopsy, enough to know that it was the single greatest force used in the attack. But he was hit twice on the back, once at the top of the spine, and once in the lower back. I would argue that if he was standing at the engine, the blow to the lower back would be followed by the upper back; in reverse if he was squatting." She mimicked the two blows without actually hitting the cop. "Fall over," she said to Bryce.

He fell to the floor. "Even though I'm hurting, I'm going to fight back, because I know this guy is serious. Either rob me or kill me."

"I now sling the hammer—think a two-to-three-foot handle—into your groin. Are you fighting back now?"

He winced. "I'm dying at the thought."

Laughter.

"Standish was two hundred pounds, a solid guy, physically fit. The killer hit him multiple times." She motioned with the stapler four to five times. "We know from the autopsy that the victim died from the gunshot almost immediately after the beating—minutes. We know that all three victims were hit with a contact electricity charge, likely a Taser in stun mode. Standish had a burn pattern on his shirt and subsequent tissue damage on the lower left side, so if the killer was facing the victim, he used his right hand."

"Ninety percent of the people in the country are right-handed," Jerry said.

"Just an observation, because if he had the Taser in hand, he had to put down his hammer. Or is he left-handed, and used his nondominant hand to stun the victim? Did he use it because the victim was fighting back?"

"What about the duct tape?" Jerry asked. "We know the killer used it, but removed it before shooting him."

That made no sense, to take the time to tape his mouth. She frowned. She "stunned" Bryce, then pretended to duct-tape his mouth. Now she hammered his hands multiple times, beating them into the ground. "Standish had a minimum of eight hits on his hands, shattering virtually every bone in both hands. It's possible the killer targeted the hands first, but it makes more sense if the victim is incapacitated first with several serious blows to sensitive parts of his body. After the hands are smashed, he removes the duct tape and fires once, close range, directly into the victim's face." As she spoke, she held her fingers out like a gun standing over the victim. This felt right to her. It was dominate, finished. "Bang."

There was silence. "There was no robbery—nothing was taken off the body or the car except for the duct tape, which the killer brought with him." To the female deputy she said, "Time?"

"Three minutes, ten seconds."

More silence.

"No more than five minutes between the time the victim stopped and the killer drove off," Lucy said. "And probably closer to three. I spent time talking in the demonstration. This killer most likely didn't do a lot of talking."

She held her hand out to Deputy Bryce. "Thanks for being my dummy," she said to laughs.

"Anytime."

Lucy waited until she and Jerry were the last ones in the corridor. "I see what you mean," Jerry said. "Calm, but violent."

"This killer knew exactly what he—or she—was doing."

"She?"

"Do we have evidence that the killer was a man?"

"We don't have evidence that the killer was a woman."

"Historically, if we're dealing with a serial killer, and we have male victims who are not homosexual, fifty-fifty the killer is female. I'm not saying that here definitely—I'm just saying we can't make an assumption right now."

Jerry thought a long minute. She was getting used to his slow deliberation, but it made her antsy. "Well, I see your point," he finally said. "Would have to be a strong woman. Standish was two hundred pounds."

"The bodies weren't moved—Garcia was, but not far, and he was the smallest of the three victims. If I'm right, and the victim willingly got out of the car and was hit from behind—suggesting they *didn't* know their killer. Most physically fit women can use a hammer, and a mallet or sledgehammer like Ash is researching would provide far more force and damage to the body. I'm not saying the killer is a woman, but until we know more we can't rule it out."

"And the beating was a punishment? Why not just shoot him in the head and be done? Why not shoot him in his car and leave him? He's still dead."

"That's a really good question," Lucy said, "and it's bothered me from when I started looking at this case after the second murder. Cause of death on the first two victims was the gunshot to the head, not the beating, though it was severe. It looks like the beating was a message. Like you said, punishment of some sort. But still controlled, because there has been no evidence that the killer used his fists or feet on the victim. Just the hammer, in a controlled manner, on all three victims." Though she would definitely want to talk to the medical examiner about any inconsistencies, no matter how small. "The one thing that really doesn't make any sense is why the duct tape? Why take the time to put it on then remove it minutes later?"

"To stop the man from screaming? While Standish was

in a remote area, James was not—the golf course parking lot he was in was right across from a shopping center with a movie theater."

"Makes sense, at least for James."

"My big question, punishment for what?" Jerry mused. "Seems if we figure that out, we'll find the killer."

"Which brings me back to my theory. These victims were specifically targeted. They connect—maybe not to each other, but to the killer. A slight, a theft, an old grievance—and now that the killer has gotten away with three murders, he—or she—will be emboldened and want to try for four. And my guess? Sooner rather than later."

Jerry headed back to the conference room, and Lucy followed. "Well, Agent Kincaid," he said, "you make a compelling argument, and you sure know how to put on a show."

She wasn't positive he was giving a compliment, so she simply shut the door and waited.

"I can certainly buy into your theory," he said, "but I don't think we can make any assumptions at this point. There are too many unknowns."

"That's why we need to sit down with the first two wives again and not only go over what happened in the days and weeks leading up to the murders, but dig deeper. Look at any lawsuits these men may have been party to—or their families. Small claims on up. Accidents. Accusations. Anything is fair game."

Jerry sat down and looked at her time line on the whiteboard. "Married men under forty living in San Antonio," he mumbled. "That's a mighty big group."

"Looking at the Standish murder—it's hard to picture that it was the first time for the killer."

"You think there's another victim we haven't found?"

"Not with this MO. Something like this would have popped in one of the databases, it's too specific to miss.

Though maybe you can tag someone to look for similar, not identical, crimes in Texas and surrounding states."

He smiled. "I already have someone working on it."

Lucy wasn't surprised. "Good, because less than five minutes to beat a man half to death then shoot him in the face, then having the wherewithal to remove the duct tape and make sure you have all your weapons—is bold. Five minutes, then the killer leaves. A first-timer? Possible. But not likely."

"I agree with you there. To look a man in the eye and shoot him in the face? Yep, the killer had a purpose. Damn cold-blooded."

"Intentional. Planned. Cold and bold." He looked at her oddly, but Lucy ignored it and continued. "I read the ballistics report—it was clean."

"Yep. The gun hasn't been used in a crime. A thirty-eight, could be revolver or semi-auto. If it was a semi-auto, the killer was calm enough to collect his brass. Either way, both are very common handguns."

"When do we talk to the widows?" Lucy asked. "I want to give Marissa Garcia a day or two to process, because I don't think we'll get anything out of her right now. But the others—Susan Standish and Teri James—I have questions."

"Are they so pressing that we need the answers today?" He looked at his watch. "It's after four on a Saturday. I don't just want to show up at their homes without specific information to share. We need to wait until we have the autopsy, at a minimum, and officially connect Garcia to the others."

She didn't want to wait, but he was right—there was nothing pressing they needed to know today. "What time is the autopsy?"

"I'll find out and call you, fair?"

She nodded.

"Then Monday—Susan Standish is a teacher, so I don't want to disturb her until after classes. I'll reach out and suggest we meet at her house late afternoon Monday?"

"Okay. And James?"

"Teri James—she owns her own business, an accountant like her husband. I'll contact her Monday morning and find a good time to meet."

"What about the daughter? We should talk to her— she's a teenager, right?"

"Fourteen," Jerry said. "She was away that weekend at a sports clinic. Volleyball, I think. Left Friday afternoon. The wife said she and James were going to drive up to Austin watch her play Saturday morning. Poor kid—we had a deputy drive up and get her. The wife was in shock, didn't think it wise to let her drive."

Lucy felt for the young teen. "Losing family to violence is so damn hard."

"Did you lose someone?"

She hadn't been thinking of her own loss—her nephew Justin, who had been her best friend when they were little, had been killed when they were seven. It had impacted everyone in the Kincaid family, but as a young child Lucy had been partly shielded. In some ways it was worse because she knew that Justin was gone, that someone had killed him, but she didn't know the details for a long time because her family refused to talk about it.

Today she was thinking of Sean's son Jesse, who had lost his mother a little over two months ago and was still having a difficult time processing what had happened leading up to his mother's death, and the stress of the aftermath.

"Lucy, did I say something wrong?"

"We've all lost someone we love. My stepson's mother was killed this summer. Jesse's thirteen, it's been harder on him than he's admitted."

"I'm sorry," Jerry said with sincerity. "How about this—I'll reach out to the two widows, and we'll talk to them on Monday, at their convenience. Since you want to view the autopsy, I'll meet you at the ME's office tomorrow—" He held up his phone. "—they just sent me a message that Garcia is scheduled at noon."

"I'll be there." She looked the files and notes she'd spread out. "Is it okay that we leave this here?"

"Yeah, leave it. I'm going home, too. I'll walk you out."

CHAPTER FOUR

Saturday Evening

Lucy was glad to be home.

This was supposed to be her weekend off, but because this killer was her case, she had to respond to the crime scene. Last year she wouldn't have minded at all—she loved her job, and had a tendency to be a workaholic—but now that Jesse was living with them, and Sean was home so much of the time, Lucy wanted to be home, too. Even with everything that had happened over the summer, there was a sense of peace in their house that Lucy craved.

Bandit, the golden retriever she and Sean had adopted while on their honeymoon last year, bounded into the kitchen to greet her. He was two years old and still acted like a puppy half the time, though Sean had done a terrific job training him.

"What a good boy," she said and scratched him. He immediately turned and ran back down the hall.

Bandit was Sean's dog through and through, and when Sean was home Bandit stayed close.

She grabbed a bottle of water and walked down the hall. Sean was in his office. He immediately got up when he saw her and pulled her into a hug. "I missed you today," he said and kissed her.

"It's good to be home." The tension ebbed from her body. She sat down on the couch in his office. Sean sat next to her and played with her hair. "Where's Jess?"

"At the boys' home. He's staying for dinner, I'll pick him up at eight."

Sean had helped St. Catherine's Boys' Home since its inception to provide a safe place for a group of orphans Sean, Lucy, and Sean's brother Kane had rescued eighteen months ago from a violent drug cartel. Jesse had been spending a lot of time over there, and Lucy thought it was good for both him and the others.

"He seemed preoccupied last night, and then I left before he was awake. Is everything okay with school?" Jesse had started his eighth-grade year at a new school in a new city after losing his mother. Lucy didn't think he had fully grasped the magnitude of his loss.

"One day at a time," Sean said. "I don't want to push him too hard."

Both Lucy and Sean had dealt with loss and understood grief, and the one thing that they both knew was that everyone processed grief at a different pace. Losing a parent, like losing a child, was a particular minefield that took love and patience to navigate.

"Are you sure spending so much time with the boys is okay?" Sean asked.

"Of course," Lucy said. "Why do you think it wouldn't be?"

"He just seems to want to spend more time there than here."

"Maybe seeing how each of the boys dealt with their own traumas is helping him come to terms with what happened to him."

"He doesn't talk to me. I mean—he does, about school

and video games and soccer—but not about what happened, not about how he's doing, you know? He just says he's fine. And I know he's not."

"I haven't had a lot of one-on-one time with him since you both got back from California." Jesse's grandfather had done everything short of filing a lawsuit to claim custody of Jesse, and Sean and Jesse had spent two weeks in August working through whatever the powerful and wealthy Ronald McAllister tossed at them. "Maybe he thinks he needs to be tough around you, that he needs to pretend everything is fine. Put on a good front."

"You think he needs to be all macho tough guy around me?"

"The Rogans are all macho tough guys," Lucy said, trying to lighten Sean's mood. She put her hand on his face. She loved him so much and hated when he was in emotional pain. He harbored guilt about what had happened to Madison, even though none of it was his fault. He'd promised Madison and Jesse that they would be safe in this house, and the one place Sean felt safest had been breached. It had taken a dozen trained mercenaries to take the house, and only after the occupants had been drugged. But Sean didn't see it that way.

"Maybe I should ask Kane to talk to him."

"No," Lucy said emphatically.

That surprised Sean. "Did he say something to you? Do something?"

"Nothing like that. I love Kane, you know that, but your brother is black-and-white in everything. I know exactly what he'd say: *Jess, I'm sorry about your mom. She made some bad decisions and unfortunately, those decisions ended up getting her killed. That's not on you.* And then Jesse would feel like the very real grief he's experiencing makes him somehow weak or childish and he'd bury it deep, and that wouldn't be good, either."

"You certainly know my brother."

"Kane's a rare person who can compartmentalize his grief and pain. He deals with it the only way he knows how, and for him it works. But it doesn't work for most people, and it won't for Jesse. However, don't discount your concerns. Maybe there's something else going on with him that he's not talking about, at least with us. Maybe he feels like he can talk with one of the boys. He and Michael got off on the wrong foot when they first met, but last time I saw them together they were two peas in a pod. Michael lost his mother, too. All those boys did—either to death, to prison, or to addiction. If there's anyplace Jesse can heal, it's there." She leaned over and kissed Sean.

"Maybe you're right."

"I am—but we still need to be here for him, to let him know that he's safe and that he can tell us anything—when he's ready."

He pulled her into his lap and kissed her again. "I love you, Mrs. Rogan."

"Ditto, Mr. Rogan."

"You know, we don't have time like this much anymore."

"Time like . . . ?"

"Alone." He kissed her neck, then behind her ear. "Want to go upstairs and make out?"

She almost laughed, then adjusted her position, straddled him, and unbuttoned her shirt. "Like you said, we're alone."

Jesse looked at his watch. He'd never worn a watch before, but his uncle Kane gave him this totally cool military watch with a compass when he came to visit over Labor Day weekend and Jesse hadn't taken it off since. It was even waterproof.

"Michael, it's getting late."

It was nearly five thirty. They had to be back at St. Catherine's not a minute past six thirty for dinner. The last thing Jesse wanted was for Sister Ruth to tell his dad that he was late, because then Jesse would have to tell him what he and Michael had been doing all day.

"I told you to stay away."

"And I told you to shut up."

Michael glared at him, his expression hard and serious. If Jesse had met Michael two years ago, he would have avoided him at all costs. He looked mean and hardened, like he'd seen everything bad in the world. And he probably had. But Jesse knew him, and he wasn't scared.

Well, he was a little scared. Not of Michael, but of what Michael might be capable of when those he cared about were threatened. Lucy and Sean had told him some of what Michael had been through, and Jesse had picked up on a lot more over the last month. Michael would do anything to protect the boys at St. Catherine's, whom he called brothers. He was the oldest, and by far the strongest in every way—physically and emotionally. He was almost fifteen but seemed so much older and wiser than any kids Jesse knew.

They were both worried about Brian, another boy who lived at the boys' home, who like Michael was a freshman in high school. He'd been acting odd, though that in and of itself hadn't been much of anything. Everyone could get moody. But Jesse and Brian were on the same soccer team, and after practice this week Jesse had seen Brian talking to an older kid—*maybe* in high school, but he looked older. When Jesse asked him about it, Brian said he was a kid from school—but Jesse had the distinct impression that he was lying.

More than once, Jesse wished he'd gone to his dad instead of Michael, but now that they were in this, Jesse couldn't rat him out. Michael made a good point: If Brian was caught doing something illegal, he'd be kicked out of St. Catherine's. Father Mateo had a zero tolerance policy for drugs and alcohol.

"I'll find out what's going on and fix it," Michael had said. *"We keep this between us for now, okay?"*

Jesse had agreed, but still wondered if he'd done the right thing.

So far they didn't know what Brian was doing or if there was anything wrong, but he'd lied to Sister Ruth about a conditioning practice late that morning. Jesse covered for him—he almost wished he hadn't—and sought out Michael. They went to the practice field, but Brian wasn't there. It took them hours to track him down to this shit-hole neighborhood, and they still didn't know what he was doing here.

Jesse knew that if they didn't leave soon, they'd be late, and Jesse didn't want to lie to Sean. He was kind of worried about his dad because of what his grandfather did last month. All the games and manipulation and threats. In the end Grandfather gave in—but it was a battle, and Jesse had to promise to spend one month every summer in Orange County with him, and Sean agreed that his grandfather could visit with notice whenever he saw fit. Jesse loved his grandfather, but he was also angry with him for pressuring his mother into not telling Jesse anything about his father. And his reasons were stupid.

Sean said he was fine, but he always looked sad, even when he was smiling. Jesse didn't want to add anything to his plate right now, and trouble with one of the boys at St. Catherine's would be a heavy weight. He *could* talk to Lucy, and maybe he would, but one, she was an FBI agent, and two, she probably wouldn't keep it from Sean. Which would then add to his problems. The last thing Jesse wanted was to hurt his dad.

Jesse hoped he and Michael could figure this out and no one but them would have to know anything.

They were sitting in a sketchy park in the middle of the block surrounded by two-story apartments interspersed with tiny houses that had seen much, much better days. Michael was tense, on alert, watching everyone who walked through the park with a clear, narrow gaze. This was gang territory, and being here was dangerous.

"You really shouldn't have come," Michael said to Jesse. "You stick out."

"Because I'm white?"

"Because you're too clean."

Jesse looked down at his faded jeans and generic gray T-shirt. His mother would have had a coronary if she'd seen him dressed like this—she was the poster child for presentability.

Thinking about his mom made him shiver, and he tried to push her out of his mind. He was so angry about what she'd done . . . but he desperately wanted her to be alive. He missed her. He missed the way she cut the crusts off his sandwiches, the way she would come into his room in the middle of the night, when she was going to bed, and look at him. He always knew she was there. She'd put a hand on his arm, pull the blankets up if it was cold, or open the window if it was warm. She knew everything about history and proofread all his school papers for him. She never missed a soccer game, and even though she was always dressed impeccably and never socialized with the other parents, she cheered louder than anyone when he made a goal.

"Hey," Michael said.

"What?"

"I'm talking, you're not listening."

"I am."

"Right."

"Just—nothing."

Michael had suffered a lot more than Jesse ever had, and Jesse felt guilty for feeling crappy about his situation when Michael had actually risked his life to save all the boys who now lived at St. Catherine's. Like, he could have actually *died*.

Michael dropped it, and a minute later said, "I think I know what's going on with Brian."

"And you're only now telling me?"

"It took me a while to figure it out. This isn't just gang territory—it's Saints territory. Brian's dad was a member of the Saints. He was in prison for years, since Brian was a little kid, and got shivved last year. Probably because we escaped the general."

Jesse knew that "the general" was this guy who'd kidnapped, threatened, or bribed kids into working for him to move drugs across the border. He was dead. Michael had been with his uncle Kane in Mexico and they went to rescue a kidnapped DEA agent and the general's daughter, whom the general had taken from her mother. His dad was there, and Jesse thought Lucy was, too, though no one talked about it.

"Brian isn't like that," Jesse said. "He's not going to join a gang."

"Brian is weak," Michael said without any emotion. It seemed an odd comment. But before Jesse could ask what he meant, Michael continued. "Family makes us weak."

"You don't believe that," Jesse said. "Everyone at Saint Catherine's is your family."

"You don't get it."

"Don't talk to me like I'm an idiot."

"Family makes us do stupid things. I went to work for Jaime Sanchez because I loved Hector and Olive and I knew that Jaime would hurt them if I didn't go. That put me in a weak position."

"Who are Hector and Olive?"

"They were my foster parents. They wanted to adopt me . . ." His voice trailed off, and there was a deep sadness in his eyes.

"They know you're okay, right?"

He nodded. "Father Mateo has talked to them. They go to Saint Catherine's; I see them in church."

"Why didn't you go back to them? They wanted you, right?"

"Because."

"That's not an answer."

"You would never understand."

"God, you're an asshole."

"When you care about someone you are weak. They can be used against you."

"You care about Tito. And Frisco and Brian and . . ."

"You don't understand."

"Stop saying that! Shit, you're such a jerk." Jesse didn't know what was going on with Michael, but he couldn't possibly believe what he was saying. He did everything to take care of the boys at St. Catherine's, and both Father Mateo and Sean relied on him to be the leader. The role model. Maybe that's why Michael stayed instead of going back to Hector and Olive. Because the boys needed him more.

After what seemed like forever, Michael said, "Brian has an older brother. No one knows about Jose. He was probably mentioned in Brian's foster care records, but those were destroyed by the people who worked for the general. I never met Jose. He's twenty, twenty-one maybe. Brian believes in his heart that Jose would have come for him if he had known what was going on. That Jose would have rescued him. Brian convinced himself that Jose was lied to just like we all were, or that he was in danger himself. He was probably in jail or something—and really just didn't care about his little brother. But Brian hasn't talked about him in a long time, and I always thought he didn't want anything to do with him because Jose didn't help. But I can't think of another reason for Brian to lie to me, to be deceptive like this, to sneak around. This can't end well."

"We have to tell Sean," Jesse said.

"You promised, Jesse. First I have to try to help Brian."

"But you just said—"

"You should never have come here."

"Screw you." Jesse was tired of this shit. Michael had hated him the minute Sean introduced them, but he thought they'd worked through all that. Now, however, it was clear he didn't trust him.

"I'm glad you brought this to me," Michael said. "I won't forget it. But it would be safer for you if you let me handle this."

Maybe he didn't really understand Michael or what he was doing, but one thing he knew was that he couldn't let Michael do this alone. "We're in this together," Jesse said.

Michael stared at him. Jesse had no idea what he was thinking. Jesse stared back. Wished he could read minds or something because he felt he was way over his head.

Michael said, "Brian is weak because of Jose. He wants his brother to be someone I know he is not, certain he cannot be. If Jose is in the Saints, he will recruit Brian, and Brian will let himself be recruited . . . because he wants his family back. He won't realize the truth until it's too late, and there will be no turning back. There are initiations that no one can forgive. But I have to know for certain what is going on before we can fix this. I need to know how deep Brian has gone, if I can still save him."

"Okay," Jesse said, not really understanding what Michael wanted from him.

"I will watch him at school and home; you watch him at soccer. If you see the man Brian was talking to, get a picture. We'll figure out who he is, if he is in fact Jose, and then confront Brian before he gets hurt."

"We have a plan," Jesse said, relieved. "Now let's go before we're late."

CHAPTER FIVE

Saturday Night

Marissa Garcia went to bed more to avoid her mother-in-law than because she was tired. She didn't know how she would ever rest peacefully again, without Julio at her side.

It was too early to sleep, and she stared at the wall, her hand on her stomach. Tears came again, silent tears, as the impact of Julio's death hit her. Her baby would never know her father. Her baby would never know what an amazing, honorable, loyal, loving man Julio was.

Marissa didn't know how she was going to move on.

She may have dozed, because when she opened her eyes it wasn't light—but it was still only nine in the evening. Her face was sticky from her tears. She sat up and stared at the picture of her, Julio, and Dario on the wall—right next to their wedding picture. Marissa loved Julio with all her heart. Her heart that was now shattered into a million pieces. She would never be able to put it back together.

The baby rolled, then settled, and Marissa rubbed her large stomach. They hadn't planned to peek at the baby's gender, but she had some early complications, and when the doctor asked if they wanted to know boy or girl, she and Julio said yes. Then they could paint the small room to fit the baby. She chose a soft yellow, then her sister Anna painted one wall with yellow, blue, and pink flowers. Whimsical, happy flowers with a flying robin and a buzzing bee and a cheerful ladybug.

Julio and Anna had surprised her with the room only last month, and Marissa couldn't have been more tickled. She recognized then that she had been selfish for her frustration when Beatrice moved in after breaking her ankle. Julio's mother needed help, and Julio was the only one of her children who had stayed in San Antonio. The other six had moved far and wide—three went to Houston, two joined the military, and one went to Seattle for an important computer job. Sandra had said that it was because Beatrice was impossible and everyone had to get far from her. Marissa felt guilty that she had laughed, because it was true.

"*Julio is a saint, you know that,*" Sandra had said. "*But don't let that woman live here forever. She would drive Mother Teresa to drink.*"

The truth was that Julio was working extra hours, but not because Marissa wanted him to. He was earning money to put a manufactured house on the edge of their five-acre property for his mother. Beatrice didn't know that, Marissa suspected she planned on never leaving their house, but Julio wanted to help and support his mother while also making sure she didn't come between him and Marissa.

"*Mi madre is difficult. I will tell her to find an apartment.*"

"*No. She can't afford it. She's family.*"

"*My love, you are my family. She's too hard on you. I've told her to stop being critical, but she doesn't know better.*"

She did—Beatrice just chose to be obstinate. But Julio loved his mother. She *was* difficult, but she had raised seven children after her husband died in a construction accident. She had worked two jobs and they lived in a three-bedroom one-bath house in south San Antonio and not one of her children turned to crime or drugs. She favored Julio and didn't believe that Marissa—probably didn't believe that any woman—was good enough for him. But Marissa was the one who was pregnant before marriage. Beatrice had once told her that she trapped Julio.

Marissa had never told Julio that. He would have never spoken to his mother again.

And it wasn't like that at all. She and Julio were engaged. And Marissa didn't plan to get pregnant. She didn't want to get pregnant . . . it wasn't her fault.

But Dario was a gift, and she loved Julio more with every passing day.

"What about one of those trailers?" Julio said. *"The ones with a foundation, like Robert's parents live in. We have five acres here. She can have her own place, but still be close. When I go back to work, it would be good to have her nearby to watch the children."* Beatrice loved Dario with all her heart; she spoiled him, but was also strict. Though Marissa had problems with her mother-in-law, she appreciated that she wanted to babysit and help them save money.

Julio rubbed her stomach. *"Are you sure that wouldn't be too close?"*

"Well, truly, yes, but I can compromise."

He smiled at her, kissed her. *"How are you feeling this evening, my queen?"*

"I've missed you, my king." She kissed him warmly and they went to bed, never thinking that three months later Julio would be dead.

Marissa jumped when someone knocked lightly on her door. She wiped the new trail of tears from her face and said, "Come in."

Sandra entered. "Anna is going to sleep in Dario's room with him."

"Dario can come in here, with me."

"They're already asleep, Issa." Sandra sat next to her on the bed. "Did you sleep at all?"

"Some."

"You need to tell the police about Chris."

"What? No. No—you promised—no." The mention of that man's name turned her blood cold.

"Someone killed Julio. If Chris figured out—"

"No! Just—no. Please, Sandra, no." Christopher Smith was an awful man, but he wouldn't kill anyone. He wouldn't kill Julio. They had once been best friends.

"*I saw Chris at the hotel*," Julio had said many weeks ago, shortly after they found out Baby Bump was a girl. "*I wanted to hurt him.*"

"*He's b-back?*"

"*He won't be staying for long. I promise. I will never let him hurt you again, Marissa.*"

Sandra stared at her. "Is there something you're not telling me?"

She shook her head.

"We'll talk about this later, Marissa."

"There's nothing to talk about. Please, Sandra—not tonight. Not tonight." She started sobbing again, and her big sister held her tight.

"I am sorry, Issa. I am so, so sorry about Julio."

Marissa accepted Sandra's embrace, but just the mention of Chris instilled fear into her heart.

Could he have killed Julio?

Marissa didn't want to believe it.

But now that Sandra had opened Pandora's box, Marissa couldn't stop thinking about what might slither out.

CHAPTER SIX

Sunday Morning

Nothing pleased Lucy more than when Sean cooked—especially breakfast. He'd turned into an amazing chef, which Lucy appreciated since she didn't particularly like cooking, and when she did try something it never tasted right. Sean had learned to cook as a teenager, though just basics—including the most delicious spaghetti sauce Lucy had ever had. After he and Lucy moved in together, he started experimenting and discovered he enjoyed cooking—much to the satisfaction of Lucy's stomach.

Today it was basic, but still delicious. Eggs scrambled with cheese, tomatoes, and onions along with bacon and diced potatoes left over from a dinner earlier this week.

Jesse had been quiet last night after he came home from St. Catherine's, so Lucy was surprised when he said between bites of bacon, "Are you going to church today?"

"I was thinking about it," she said. She didn't go every Sunday, but since she had to meet Jerry Walker at the morgue at noon, she'd thought she'd swing by St. Catherine's beforehand.

"Can I come? Then go hang with Michael and Brian?"

"Sure," she said, glancing at Sean.

Sean said, "Want me to join you?"

Sean didn't like organized religion, and he wasn't Catholic, but he knew it was important to Lucy and he respected Father Mateo.

"You don't have to," Jesse said.

Lucy wasn't going to push religion on Jesse—she was brought up in the faith and it was a deep part of her that provided great comfort during times of trauma and stress. At the same time, she wasn't going to dissuade him. If Jesse wanted to go, she'd take him. He had been hanging out with the boys a lot, and maybe he felt that would give them another connection.

"I can pick you up after the autopsy—might be four or five," Lucy said.

"Great. I'll get changed." Jesse jumped up and ran upstairs.

Lucy helped Sean clear the table. "That's odd," she said.

"Why?"

"I don't know," she said. Maybe it was just that it wasn't expected. "At least it'll give me the opportunity to talk to him, one-on-one, and see what's on his mind."

Sean kissed her. "Thank you. I don't want to worry so much, but I can't seem to stop."

"I suspect that's part of parenthood." She smiled at him. "What are your plans for today?"

"I'm testing software for RCK. Once we get this down, Duke will install it and then I'll have to go out of town for a few days to test it on-site."

"That's your favorite part of the job," Lucy said. Duke's specialty was designing security systems; Sean's specialty was breaking into them.

"It is," he said, "but I'll miss you. Maybe you and Jess can come with me. We'll make a vacation of it."

"That might be fun," Lucy said. "Where?"

"New York."

She brightened. "I would love that. I can visit with Suzanne and maybe have dinner with Max and meet her new boyfriend."

"It would be fun. And we can take an extra day or two and go see a show. I'll let you know when as soon as I know, so you can ask for the time off."

On a Sunday morning the drive across town to St. Catherine's was much faster than during the week. Lucy asked questions about school, soccer practice, how Jesse was adjusting from beautiful California weather to the humidity in Texas. He answered everything, yet it was clear he was going through a mental checklist of what he thought she wanted him to say.

"You know," she said, "Sean and I are a little concerned because you seem preoccupied. We want to make sure you're doing okay."

"I'm fine," he said. "I don't want anyone worrying about me."

"It goes with the territory."

"Really, I'm fine." He didn't say anything for a minute. Then, "My dad seems kind of sad. Is he okay?"

There it was. Jesse was worried about Sean, and that Lucy understood.

"He will be."

"My grandfather was a jerk when we were out there. I knew it bothered Sean, but he just took it."

"I don't understand what you mean."

"Well, I could see that he wanted to tell my grandfather to fu—I mean knock it off when he started making all these ultimatums and threats. But he didn't. He just listened and let him be a jerk. But I know it really bugged him." He paused. "I'm not explaining this well."

"You mean Sean wasn't acting like himself."

"Exactly! He doesn't just let people treat him like that, and I don't know why he did it. But he's been sad since we came home, and I think the whole thing with my grandfather really bothered him. Is still bothering him."

"You know that has nothing to do with you, right? He is absolutely thrilled that you're living with us."

"I know, but—"

"There are no buts." Sean had a hard time expressing himself to Jesse, partly because he still harbored a lot of guilt about what happened to Jesse's mother. "You're Sean's son, and I am very happy to be your stepmother. We love you, and nothing will change that."

"Sean doesn't think I want to live with my grandfather, that's not why he's sad, is it? Because I don't. I made it clear that I want to be here."

"Of course we know you want to be here. If Sean thought for a minute that you wanted to be with your mother's family, he would have let you go—no matter how hard that would have been on him. He wants you to be happy, healthy—he wants what's best for you." She paused, thinking about what to tell Jesse, and decided that the truth was always best. "I think Sean blames himself for what happened in July. He promised you and your mom that you'd be safe and you were violently taken and your mom died."

"That wasn't his fault. My mom should never have come to San Antonio."

"It's not your mother's fault, either. It's wholly the fault of the people who put together the conspiracy to blackmail your stepfather."

"And it's *his* fault. You're not letting Carson off the hook, are you?"

She glanced at Jesse. His fists were clenched and he was looking at her as if daring her to argue with him about this.

There was a lot of anger there—anger that Sean would understand, and Lucy wished he and Jesse could talk about this more. But she wasn't lying about the guilt Sean felt deep down.

"Carson is being prosecuted to the fullest extent of the law. He's not going to be free for a long time."

"He started it!" Jesse shouted. Then, somewhat calmer, he said, "If he didn't hate my dad so much, he would never have hired someone to kill him, and Mr. Robertson would never have got the idea to kidnap me and my mom and blackmail him. It's *Carson's* fault my mom is dead."

"You know, it might help you and Sean to talk to someone about all this."

"I am. I'm talking to *you*. Oh." He paused, bit his lip. "I don't want to talk to a stranger."

"Psychologists are trained to help people work through situations like this. You were put in the middle of an awful situation. None of it was your fault. You didn't do anything wrong. When people you love and trust let you down, when they do things that hurt you, it's natural to be angry and conflicted. Plus, you're grieving. It's hard to work through all of that on your own."

"I don't want to talk to anyone," he said. "Do you not want to talk about it? Does it bother you to talk?"

"Not at all," she said, surprised at his empathy that she might have difficulty with any of this. "You want to talk to me about anything, I'm here. About anything, I mean that. Okay?"

"Okay." They were in the church parking lot, but Lucy left the car on for a minute.

She said, "Sean is working through his own feelings of anger and guilt right now, and that makes it seem like he's sad. Just knowing that you're adjusting to everything, that you're happy here, that's all that he cares about. If you want to talk about your mom, it's okay. It won't upset him. He cared about her at one time, and he loves you."

"Do you hate her?" he asked quietly.

"No."

"Why? After everything she did, why don't you hate her?"

Lucy wondered if Jesse was really thinking about Sean, and using her as a surrogate. Maybe that was why he was having a difficult time talking about his mother to them.

"Your mother loved you. You know she loved you more than anything. She made mistakes, there's no denying that, but she loved you and she did what she thought was the best thing for you—and for her—at the time. And honestly, I find it takes far too much energy to hate people."

"What about the people you put in prison? What about the people like the guy who forced Michael and the boys to work for him and kept them locked up? Or Carson who hired a guy to kill Sean? I hate Carson. And I don't feel bad that I hate him."

"Just because I don't hate them doesn't mean I *like* them. And I take great comfort in the fact that my job is to put people who commit crimes in prison. They're being punished, I don't need to waste emotions on them. You know, Jess, I'm not a saint. It took me a long time to learn how to forgive people. And I'll admit, sometimes it's much harder than other times. Sometimes, I reflect on the past and I get angry or upset all over again. That's why I work really hard not to live in the past."

"I'm *never* forgiving Carson."

"I understand why you feel that way now."

"I'm not going to change my mind."

It wouldn't do Lucy any good to tell Jesse that time would help. And with something like this . . . well, maybe it was better for him to put all the blame on his stepfather and none on his mother, though she thought part of Jesse's angst was that he had learned after his mother died that she had known about his stepfather's illegal activities and had—in some ways—condoned and helped him.

"You have to figure this out for yourself, but that doesn't mean you have to figure it out *by* yourself," she said. "I don't want you to harbor anger, because it's not good for you. Just because you forgive someone for things they did to you or someone you love doesn't mean you have to like them or even respect them. Forgiveness is about *you*, not them. It's about giving yourself peace, not granting peace to others."

"I know," he said, but in a tone that made her think he didn't agree with her. Which was fine. All she could do was give him advice that had once helped her—he would find his own path.

Deep down, she felt like a hypocrite. She had done some truly awful things and didn't regret them. She had killed her rapist in cold blood. And while she did believe that hate was exhausting, she still hated the man, even though he was long dead and buried. The difference now was that she could live a relatively normal life. She might never *be* normal—but she had a good life. A life filled with friends and family she loved. A life built on a solid career that she was proud of. The other stuff she had to keep locked up. Because that cold, dark rage nine years ago was at times just beneath the surface . . . and it wouldn't take much to bring it out.

She turned off the car. "Just know, Jess, Sean and I will always be here for you."

He spontaneously hugged her. She squeezed him, blinking back tears.

She wished with all her heart that Jesse was her son. But she didn't think she could love him more if he were.

CHAPTER SEVEN

Sunday Early Afternoon

Lucy arrived at the morgue a few minutes early because she came straight from church after clearing it with Sister Ruth that Jesse could stay for the afternoon.

"I'm here to observe the Julio Garcia homicide," she said as she showed her credentials to the clerk.

"One moment." She paged Julie Peters, an assistant ME who was also a friend of Lucy's. Lucy was glad Julie was working this weekend. She was smart and meticulous, the two best traits for someone in this field.

A minute later Julie came out. "Walker said you were coming. He's in the observation room—do you want to observe or be hands-on?"

Lucy had interned at the DC Medical Examiner's Office as an assistant pathologist. She couldn't perform an autopsy, but she was certified to assist.

"You know me. The closer the better." Not to mention that to keep her certification, she had to put in many hours of supervised practice, plus take a recertification test every two years.

Julie led the way to the main autopsy room, because it had the only observation platform. It was used by law enforcement if they wanted to watch—not a requirement because suspected homicides were always recorded by the ME, but some officers liked to ask questions—as well as for instruction since the ME's office was adjacent to a medical school.

"I offered for Jerry to come in, but he's chilling in the observation room. He doesn't come down here a lot."

"He didn't think it was necessary. He's humoring me."

They stopped in the locker room where Lucy left her sidearm and purse in a locker, slipped on a gown, and stepped into sterile booties that covered her low-heeled boots.

Julie's assistant was a quiet young intern named Ian Chen, whom Lucy had met before. He already had prepped the body on the table. Julie and Lucy washed up in the sink.

Through the speaker, Jerry said, "What are you doing, Kincaid?"

"Observing," she said. "But I'm authorized to assist."

No additional comment from Jerry, which was fine with Lucy. She still didn't know quite how to work with the seasoned investigator. She wanted everything to be smooth and easy, but feared it would be anything but.

Lucy had always felt most comfortable in the morgue. What that said about her personality, she didn't care to speculate, but there was comfort in working with the dead.

The dead didn't play games; the dead didn't lie. Their lives—and their deaths—could be readily observed through their autopsies, when performed by a competent and observant pathologist.

Julie said, "We've already taken pictures and prepped. I'm going to document the external injuries before I cut."

Lucy nodded.

Julie told Ian to start the video, then identified everyone in the room or observing. She confirmed that the victim had been identified both visually and from prints, and that BCSO had already done the death notification to next of kin.

Julie did a thorough visual examination of the body, noting the burn mark on his left side from the contact Taser, bruising on the arms, two distinctive blows to the abdomen, two to the groin, and a serious contusion on the back of his head. His hands, like those of the other two victims, had received the brunt of the killer's rage.

Julie motioned to the computer. "X-rays indicate multiple bones were shattered in each hand, likely from blunt force—a wide-head hammer or similar object. Trace has already been collected from the body and sent to the lab for analysis.

"The victim's groin is swollen and bruised, looks like one, possibly two blows," she continued. "The bruising on the forearms could be defensive wounds, though it's difficult to say definitively. They appear to be older injuries, perhaps an accident where he bumped hard into something."

Julie said for the record, "Clothing and personal effects have been sent to the county crime lab and logged as received by Ash Dominguez, assistant criminologist with Bexar County." That was a new protocol after evidence went missing over the summer. They had never recovered it and believed it had been destroyed.

Once Ian finished documenting external injuries, Julie proceeded with the autopsy. She chatted while she worked, interspersing commentary about local politics, bad jokes, and questions about Sean with observations about the victim.

Then she stopped the informal chatter. "Hmm," she said.

"Hmm what?" Lucy responded.

Julie didn't respond immediately. Lucy was used to that.

To Ian, she said, "Pull up the X-rays, locate all upper torso and the occipital lobe."

Lucy didn't know exactly what Julie was looking at, and she didn't want to overstep and get too close. Julie was specifically inspecting the gunshot wound. Did she think it was a different caliber? A different weapon?

"Ready," Ian said when he had the X-rays up on the computer.

"Wheel that over here, please."

He pushed the computer table as close as he could without pulling the plug. Julie enlarged a section of the base of the skull. Even Lucy could tell that the blow to the back of the head had been serious. The skull was fractured. But she couldn't read the soft tissue damage as well on the X-ray.

"Wow," Julie said.

"Julie," Lucy prompted. "What is wow?"

She didn't comment. Instead she turned back to the body and dissected the groin, then looked at tissue under a microscope. She called Ian over and they whispered together. Lucy grew increasingly impatient.

Julie returned. "Pending confirmation from the ME, I'm ruling cause of death blunt force trauma. He was probably dead before he hit the ground."

"What?" Lucy—and Jerry through the speaker—said simultaneously.

"Look here," Julie said and directed Lucy's attention to the gunshot wound. "This is by far the clearest indication that the gunshot was not fatal. He was already dead. What do you see?"

"I'm not in the mood for twenty questions," Lucy said.

"You're usually more fun," Julie said and frowned. "Okay, what do you *not* see? You don't see hemorrhaging. The heart was not beating when this bullet went into his head. I was suspicious when I inspected the X-rays of the abdomen because I didn't see extensive hemorrhaging, and looking carefully at a cross section of his tissue there definitely wasn't. He was dead before he was beaten."

"Then why the hell did the killer beat him?" Jerry said from the observation room. "Why shoot him if he was already dead?"

"That's your job, Detective," Julie said. "I just give you the facts as I see them."

"Would the killer have known that Garcia was already dead?" Jerry asked. "Maybe he thought he was unconscious, wanted to make sure he was dead."

"Garcia would have dropped immediately. The force and the angle combined to fracture the skull at the occipital and extended at a slight angle toward the foramen magnum. See this here?" She used a pointer to show a dark mass at the brain stem. "That is extensive bleeding, telling me that this was the fatal blow. And it was the first blow. The pattern is similar to the blow to the first victim, but Mr. Standish wasn't hit on the back of the head, he was attacked just below the head. The angle and force didn't break his neck or fracture his skull, but instead broke one of his vertebrae. He was in serious pain, but it wouldn't have been fatal. But Standish was taller and more muscular than Garcia."

"Are you saying the killer was shorter than Standish but taller than Garcia?"

"No, I'm not, because I don't know how Standish or Garcia were standing when they were hit."

Jerry asked, "Would the killer need a lot of upper-body strength to deliver a blow like that?"

"I don't know how you define *a lot*. I think any of us in this room could do it if we had enough momentum and the right weapon and hit at the right angle. Garcia is five foot ten—the killer would have to be much taller if he was standing straight. But if he was hunched over, or kneeling, the killer could be shorter than five ten."

"Can you send all this data and X-rays to Ash? I'm going to ask him to run a computer simulation."

"He'll love that. Any excuse to play with his toys."

"Anything else about this murder that is different than the first two?" Lucy asked.

Julie motioned for Ian to close the Y-incision, then went back to her computer. She brought up side-by-side images of the bodies. By the time she was done, Jerry had joined them. He stood behind Julie and looked over her head.

"Victim one—Standish. Blow to the upper back, blow to the lower back. Hands shattered with eight to ten blows. Virtually every bone was broken. Three serious blows to the chest and abdominal regions, and several glancing blows. Two hard blows to the groin. Cause of death was the gunshot to the head. Some defensive wounds on his arms—bruising from the same weapon, hard enough to fracture his radius. A Taser burn on the side, consistent with a close-contact Taser in stun mode."

She gestured to the second victim. "James. No injuries to the back—he wasn't attacked from behind. Two blows to his chest, two to his abdomen, and two to his groin. Hands shattered with six to eight blows."

"Standish was beaten more severely," Jerry said.

"Yeah, but he was bigger and might not have gone down as easily," Julie surmised. "I determined that the Taser burn to James was done postmortem."

"How can you tell that?" Lucy said.

"There was no bruising, which suggests the heart had already stopped pumping. But more, and this is where you can tell me I am a goddess and bow at my feet."

Lucy stared at her. "Okay, goddess, what did you find?"

Julie grinned. "I could get used to that. Ash will want to be called a god, too. When I realized after reviewing my notes and confirmed that the autopsy video showed no bruising, I asked Ash to spend more time on the clothing. He confirmed that there was brain matter on the shirt at the spot the Taser was used."

"How?" Lucy asked. "He was lying on the ground when he was shot. There shouldn't have been blowback in that direction."

"Our guess is that the killer was standing over him and the Taser was unsheathed and got blood and brain matter on it. It's not a lot, but it's there."

"It would have to be very close."

Julie shrugged. "Like you said, Ash loves his toys, maybe he can come up with a scenario. He has all my findings—there are absolute facts that you can't change, but there will likely be room for theories."

"This is good, thanks, Julie," Lucy said.

"It doesn't get us any closer to identifying the killer," Jerry said, sounding frustrated.

"Any other differences?" Lucy asked her.

Julie flipped through her files on the first two victims. "Standish is the only one who had grease on his hands, and Ash confirmed that it was oil from a vehicle and didn't match the oil from his own truck."

"Which lends to the theory that he helped someone with their car," Lucy said to Jerry.

He still didn't look happy.

"Neither James nor Garcia had grease on their hands?"

"No," Julie said. "Garcia's hands and nails were clean, other than from dirt at the scene. He also had trace of an industrial sanitizing soap that I looked up and it's used widely in restaurants. James's hands and nails were clean as well."

"What else?"

"Nothing—well, we know that they were all hit in the chest, but James was the only one who had two cracked ribs. The blows to Standish were severe, but they were all in the abdomen—one in the stomach under the rib cage and two lower."

"Same force?"

"More or less. I can't tell you that the same person killed all these people. I can tell you that the injuries are consistent, that the same or similar weapon was used to beat these men, and I know how they died. But that's it. Ash confirmed the ballistics, and I'll send Garcia's bullet over by courier. So we know James and Standish were killed with the same gun, and based on the bullet I recovered from Garcia it *appears* to be the same caliber, and Ash will have ballistics confirm."

Jerry asked, "Could there be two killers?"

"Hell if I know," Julie said. "But I don't see evidence on the bodies that there were two distinctively different forces, and I *can* confirm that the same weapon was used. I collected trace evidence from the wounds as well, and Garcia's can be matched with the others—see if there's anything else Ash can get from those tests. We have one of the best crime labs in the state, but even we are limited on some of the high-end testing. Might be the opportunity to play footsies with the FBI lab at Quantico and see if they get more."

Lucy inwardly winced. It was Julie's way, but she might not know that Jerry had issues with the FBI.

But to Lucy's surprise, Jerry said, "If Ash thinks the FBI lab can get more, he'll send it off. That's his call. Thanks, Julie. This was informative."

"I aim to please," she grinned. "Oh, one more thing—Ash and I were talking yesterday after I sent over the physical evidence. We concur that the killer fired directly at their face. Not at their forehead or back of the head, but the face. Don't know if that means anything from a psych point of view, but to me it stands out."

"How far away?" Jerry asked.

"At least two feet, not more than four," Julie said. "And from the angle, Ash and I concur that the killer was standing over the victim, one foot on either side of the body."

"You're sure?"

"Mostly sure. The trajectory would be different if the killer was anywhere else."

"The face, not head," Lucy muttered.

"Not much of a difference," Jerry said. "The face *is* his head."

"But the killer took away their identity. Like he wanted to obliterate their face. Hatred? Guilt? It seems so personal."

"That's your job," Julie said. "I'm just giving you the facts as I know them."

Lucy asked, "Can you send me the photos? The comparison of injuries? I want to study them in depth."

"No problem. I have some more work to do on Mr. Garcia here, and I'll send them off by tomorrow morning."

Jerry and Lucy met up for coffee at the university adjacent to the morgue. "I don't want to take up your Sunday," Lucy said, "but I think we should discuss what we learned."

"I never turn down coffee," he said. "I don't know that it's important that Garcia was dead before the beating."

"It's important because the killer had to finish the ritual. The beating—especially the hands—then the Taser, the shot to the face. It's a pattern. But even in the pattern, there are inconsistencies."

"Such as?"

"If Julie and Ash are right and James wasn't hit with the Taser until after he was dead, why use the Taser at all? We assumed the killer used it because Standish fought back, and the brief jolt of pain enabled the killer to regain the upper hand. With James he didn't need it. Was he holding it? Was it on the ground? These crime scenes make no sense."

"I'm not following you."

"The killer appears full of rage, but kills methodically. Standish was beaten more severely likely because he was larger and the only victim who fought back. The attack was a surprise, from behind, and there was no hesitation. Attack, pound, kill. Why smash the hands? Why stun the victims when they are already on the ground and hurting? To torture them? Then to stand over them, one foot on either side, and shoot their face. The killer looked his victims in the eye and shot them. That is *cold*. But with Garcia, there was no need. He was dead. The killer had to have known he was dead when he was beating on his body. If he didn't—I guess I don't see how the killer might just think he was unconscious. His head was at an odd angle, the body wouldn't feel the same when hit. Yet the killer still stood over the body and looked into his face and shot him."

"I'm open to suggestions," Jerry said.

"Maybe the killer wanted his face to be the last thing his victims saw. And the thing is—I don't think Standish, and maybe not Garcia, knew who the killer was. But James did."

"Because he wasn't hit from behind."

"Exactly. So either there are two people working together—one who lures the men to pull over, and the other who kills—or there is one person whom only Steven James *personally* knows. Because he didn't have his back turned to the killer, and he didn't have injuries on his back. Yet all the other violence to the bodies is nearly identical."

"So why?"

"We really have to talk to the wives again. Wives, friends, family, employers. These men made someone mad, and they may not even have known it."

"I'll make the calls." Jerry had a far-off look now, as if he was thinking about something specific.

"What do you think?" she asked.

He didn't say anything for a second, sipped his coffee, put it down. "Susan Standish is a kindergarten teacher. Sweet thing. I believed for a long time—until Steven James was killed four weeks later—that her husband was into something illegal. Didn't really know what, just fishing, really. But a beatdown like that tells me he was punished. Drugs, screwing around with his best friend's wife, maybe some corruption scandal with his employer. There were a lot of folks who were scammed after Harvey hit Houston. Contractors who came in, promised the moon, absconded with people's life savings. Scumbags, all of them, if you ask me." He sipped his coffee again. Lucy resisted pushing him to finish his thought. He was a slow and methodical cop, and she had to let him work it out.

Finally, Jerry said, "I asked Susan Standish if she thought her husband might have been having an affair. It wasn't the first angle I looked at—by all accounts they were happy, high school sweethearts, and he had a history of misdemeanors when he'd been drinking, but no accusations of fooling around. Bar fights and whatnot, nothing serious. Most people said he was a good guy and worked hard—good at his job. Quality work. Strong work ethic. I was looking more into the jobs he'd done, to see if someone sued him, or maybe he didn't do something he was supposed to, or it was shoddy work. Talked to everyone he'd ever been in a fight with. And nothing stuck. I looked at a gambling problem—he liked to bet on sporting events. But word was it was small bets, nothing over a hundred bucks, nothing that would get to serious payback. So I went back to the wife, asked about her husband having maybe an affair. She flat out said no."

"You think she was lying."

"Not at the time. At the time I'd say she was indignant, stunned, hurt that I would malign his name like that. But maybe now that she has thought about it, she might have some different thoughts."

"And that helps us how? We have two other victims who probably weren't having an affair with the same woman. And based on Garcia's schedule, I don't see how he would have the time."

"Just one more angle to look at."

Lucy nodded. "Let's look. Maybe you're right. And maybe these men aren't the upstanding citizens we think they are."

"Meaning?"

"Maybe this is a vigilante killer. Someone exacting their own brand of justice. I came up against one before. Justified every cold-blooded murder he committed because those he killed had hurt others." She didn't mention that they were sex crimes. "Or these men were a witness to something. Maybe they witnessed the same crime."

"We haven't put them together in the same place yet, but my people are looking."

"You need more manpower, let me know. The FBI has some great tools at our disposal."

He didn't respond, drained his coffee. Did he think that she was trying to take the case? Nothing was further from the truth. Today had been a good day working together, they'd learned so much more about the crime scenes and had agreed on an approach. "I'm going to light a fire under Ashley's butt tomorrow morning on ballistics—we need the confirmation, so at least the sheriff has something to tell the press. And I'll ask Ash to run through some scenarios on that fancy computer of his. I'll call the wives and let you know when we can talk to them."

"All right. I have a morning staff meeting, and then I'll head out to your office."

"You don't have to."

"Did we lose the conference room?"

"No."

"Good. I want to go over everything again, look at the differences of each crime scene again, and see if there is a pattern we're not seeing."

"I guess I can't stop you."

She tilted her head. "Why would you?"

He didn't respond.

She swallowed a confrontational comment and said, "See you tomorrow, Jerry."

After church, Jesse had lunch at the boys' home, then pulled Michael aside. "I heard Brian tell Ruth that he's going to the park for extra soccer practice. There is no extra practice."

"Shit," Michael said.

"Didn't you talk to him?"

"I tried—he told me I'm wrong. But I'm not."

"We need to find out what he's doing."

"Come on." Michael went downstairs and found Ruth. "Where'd Brian go?" he asked.

"Soccer again. Extra work, he said."

Michael glanced at Jesse, nodded. He wanted him to lie to the nun? Was that a sin? He wasn't Catholic, did it matter?

"Oh, I forgot that was today. We'll catch up with him."

"Back by five," Ruth called out.

They went outside and Jesse said, "I feel like shit lying to her."

"You didn't really lie."

"Feels like a lie," Jesse muttered.

They started walking toward the practice field, which was only a mile away. But Jesse saw a dark sedan drive by, and he recognized the driver. "That's the guy who was talking to Brian. I think Brian is in that car." They turned left at the corner—away from the park, but toward the neighborhood where the Saints hung out.

"Can we use your Uber app? We'll walk back, but if Brian is in trouble—I need to know."

Jesse agreed. They caught a ride to a Starbucks that was only a few blocks from the house where they'd staked out Brian and his brother before.

Sure enough, the dark-brown sedan was right out front.

They went to the park they'd been at yesterday, and watched the house. Gangbangers came and went. With each one, Michael grew more agitated.

"I don't understand what he's doing," Michael said. "He knows what kind of life this is. Why would he choose it?"

"You know, maybe you should just ask him. Maybe it's not as bad as it looks."

"The Saints were disbanded until recently. I heard a few were out of prison but I didn't think they could regroup so quickly, especially without a stable leadership."

Where had Michael heard about the gang? From Sean? Someone else?

"I need to know what's going on inside," Michael said.

"I can—"

"No, you don't fit into this neighborhood. I'm already worried that we're being watched here, that the Saints will know us."

"I was going to say, I can text Brian and ask him what he's doing. That we're at the soccer park but he's not there."

"Oh. That's a good idea. And then?"

"Get him away from Jose at least, right? Maybe he'll just come and meet us, then we can talk to him."

"Okay, text him, we'll see what he does."

Jesse sent Brian a text message.

Ruth said you went to the soccer park to run drills— where are you? I'm here, you're not.

He showed it to Michael, who nodded, then Jesse sent it. They waited.

A couple minutes later, Brian sent back one word: *later* That meant nothing.

"What's going on with him?" Jesse said, showing Michael the message. "Do you want to go in? Talk to him?"

"I can't."

"Why? Do these guys just kill people for no reason?"

"They would have a reason." Michael glanced at him. "What did Sean tell you about how we met?"

"I know about the general and the crappy prison in Mexico and how you helped Sean and Kane rescue Dad's friend the DEA agent. I mean, I know what you were forced to do and shit like that."

"One of the things that I did was steal information that helped the police and Kane shut down the Saints. Plus, one of their leaders was in Mexico and got dead."

"And they know it was you?"

"They know I stole the information."

"What are you doing even sitting out here?"

"Jose and his people don't know what I look like, I don't think. I'm not afraid of them, but I can't be sure that no one else knows. I need to talk to Brian, get him to come clean, and walk away. If he can't—if he wants to and can't—then we'll talk to Sean. Okay?"

Jesse liked this less than yesterday, but what else could he do?

"Fine."

Jesse's phone vibrated twenty minutes later. It was Brian.

I'll be there in thirty if you want to hang.

Jesse showed it to Michael. "We can walk it," Michael said.

"Too hot. Back to Starbucks and we'll get an Uber."

Brian wasn't at the soccer park in thirty minutes, and Michael grew increasingly frustrated. "Did he know? Did he see us?" Michael wondered out loud.

"I don't think so."

"I'm tired of this. His lies. His games."

"He could be in trouble. Maybe he walked. It would take thirty minutes to walk here."

Just then they saw Brian crossing the field to where they were sitting under a canopy of trees. He was alone. "Hey," he called out. "Sorry, I was meeting a friend from school, I didn't want Ruth to get all worried."

"You lied to her," Michael said.

"No."

"You lied to me."

Brian didn't look hot and sweaty—no way he'd walked from the Saints house. Jesse looked around—on the street, he saw the dark sedan. It was far away, he couldn't make out if anyone was in the car, but it was parked.

"I don't know what you're talking about."

"I know you've been with your brother."

Brian paled. "I—no."

"You lied to Ruth, you're lying to me." Michael was livid, and Jesse thought for a second that he was going to hit Brian.

The car pulled away from the curb and drove slowly off.

"Who was that, Brian?" Jesse asked.

"Stay out of this, Jess."

"You're going down a dark road," Michael said. "A road you've been on against your will. You think it's better when you're not in chains?"

"It's not like that. You have no idea what you're talking about."

"I know exactly what I'm talking about! You need to decide if you're one of them, or if you want to live."

"That's not the choice."

"That you can't see that after everything that happened, after what you saw. What you did. What we all had to do . . . you're not that blind."

"Just—leave me alone."

Brian started to walk away, and Michael spun him around, held him by the arm. "Is that what you want?"

Brian stared at him, obviously confused.

Jesse saw the same car drive by again.

"Michael, they're coming back."

"Do they know about me? About Saint Catherine's?"

"N-no. Of course not."

Jesse wasn't sure Brian was telling the truth, and it was clear that Michael didn't believe him, either.

"Let's go," Michael said. "The back way. I'm not leading anyone to our sanctuary. The only place any of us have *ever* felt safe. If you bring them to our doorstep, Brian, I will never forgive you."

"I wouldn't do that, I swear."

But in that admission, Brian realized that now he had outed himself: He had essentially confirmed that he was communicating with his brother.

"Jose has changed, Michael."

"People like him don't change."

"You're wrong."

"Follow me or go back to your brother and never return to Saint Catherine's."

"I—I'm coming," Brian said, and the three of them ran through the park to the opposite street.

The car was circling around, but they had the advantage of being on foot. Michael said, "We cut through those apartments. Follow me, don't look back, and don't slow down."

They ran.

CHAPTER EIGHT

Sunday Late Afternoon

Lucy drove to St. Catherine's to pick up Jesse. She was irritated by how the conversation had ended with Jerry. At first they were getting along, brainstorming, and then he was rude.

She rubbed her eyes. She didn't want to make something from nothing. It wasn't *nothing*, but maybe she was creating a bigger problem than there was.

Sitting in her car in front of the boys' home, she considered who she could ask about the case that Walker had worked on with the FBI—the one that had made him so hostile toward her. Well, she really couldn't call him *hostile*, because she thought they were developing a rapport, but he became irritated at things that made no sense to her—like her wanting to go through the files again. What was wrong with that? There was a lot of information, and as soon as they had the final results from Garcia's autopsy, they would need to go through everything again and compare. Investigations took time, they took diligence, they took reviewing evidence over and over in case something was missed. Especially in a situation like this where all three crime scenes were outdoors, at night, and brutal.

They would need to re-interview witnesses, ask different questions, make sure they had all relevant statements and then think bigger.

They were dealing with a serial killer just on the fact that there were three similar murders with a cooling-off period in between. Lucy had studied and investigated enough serial murders to know there was a reason the killer was targeting these men. It appeared random, but it wasn't. The victims might be chosen at random, but there was a specific reason the killer targeted men like them. He stalked his prey. Watched them. The killer knew they would be alone at the time of the attack.

How did the killer know Steven James's travel plans?

It was only twenty minutes from the airport to the James home. Steven James had parked his car in short-term parking, even though he had been gone since Monday. More expensive, but also more convenient. The killer most likely knew what flight he was on and tracked that information through the website, so knew when the plane landed. Knew what car he drove. Was able to steer him off the road, get him to pull over, *something* in order to kill him. But unlike Standish, which was in a remote area; or Garcia, which was adjacent to a closed park; James was killed in the suburbs, a stone's throw from a movie theater that still had people inside. On the edge of a golf course parking lot where there were no security cameras.

Which lent credence to Lucy's theory that James knew his killer.

How deep had Jerry dug into the accountancy firm? Did James know something serious about a client? About a colleague? If so, could the other victims simply be covering for the real target?

Or maybe Jerry's gut that there was something going on with Standish—he'd been the most violently beaten. It had been extensive and he fought back. Wouldn't that mean the killer had some evidence of a fight on his person? Bruises? Cuts? And wouldn't someone notice? Maybe they needed to go back to that time, re-interview everyone who knew Standish, and ask if they'd seen anyone with unexplained bruises on his face or hands. Julie was diligent in her combing for forensic evidence from the bodies, but maybe they needed to look at everything again to make sure they didn't have trace evidence from the killer.

Then why did the killer go through the motions of the beating, the Taser, and the gunshot to the face when Julio Garcia was dead from the first blow? You didn't have to be around dead bodies daily to know when a person was actually dead and not merely unconscious. Was it a ritual? For most serial killers, they'd want the ritual to unfold exactly as they planned it, and any deviation would anger them. Based on the ritual of these murders, if Garcia died at the first blow, that should enrage the killer.

How dare you die on me before I want you to! How dare you deny me my satisfaction!

The beating should be *more* severe, *more* violent. Even if the killer had the presence of mind and self-protection not to beat the body with his hands and feet, he would use his weapons more violently. Pummel the victim for having the audacity to die with one blow to the head.

She shook her head, pulling herself out of her analysis. She wanted this working relationship with Jerry Walker to be successful, not only to catch the killer, but because she wanted him to respect the FBI again. She put that weight on her shoulders, because as far as Jerry was concerned, she was now the face of the FBI.

A name popped into her head. Leo Proctor. He'd been in the FBI office ten years ago, he might know what case had turned Walker off. She called him, glad that she was parked under a tree because it was getting hot, even with her air conditioning running.

"Proctor."

"Leo, it's Lucy Kincaid."

"Hello, Ms. Lucy. What can I do for you? I have maybe ten minutes—working a complex case right now with counter-terrorism."

She hadn't heard. "Okay, quick question."

"Shoot."

"Do you know BCSO investigator Jerry Walker?"

"Yeah, we've crossed paths. Did some cross-training back when he was a beat cop. That was ten, fifteen years ago, I'd guess. I don't know him well. Seems like a good cop, calm and methodical I remember."

"I'm working with him on a case. The three men who were killed over the last seven weeks. His office requested our assistance after the second murder, but he put up roadblocks until yesterday when a third body dropped. He admitted that he has a problem with the FBI, and that they'd messed up more than one of his cases, but he hasn't given me any specifics. We've been working well together—but every once in a while he says something that makes me think he's still not happy. I want to know about the cases that he thinks we screwed up."

"Hmm. I haven't worked directly with him, but there have been some tensions in the past with the SO. Let me think on it, pull some files to refresh my memory. Might take a day or two—I don't know when I'll have time until we wrap up this other situation."

"That's fine, Leo, I appreciate it."

She was about to get out of the vehicle when she saw an old brown car with tricked-out rims driving slowly down the street. She'd seen the car before—it was hard to miss—driving through the neighborhood when she first pulled up, but she hadn't given it much attention.

St. Catherine's was in the center of an old neighborhood in San Antonio filled mostly with older folks on fixed incomes, and younger families who could afford to buy a fixer-upper. There were better areas to the north, and worse areas to the south—worse meaning more crime on the streets and poorly maintained apartments. The car stood out largely because she had never seen it before today and then she saw it twice in less than ten minutes. The two young men in the front seat seemed to be looking for someone, driving slowly, scanning both sides of the street. She put her phone to her ear and pretended to talk so they wouldn't think she was paying them undue attention, then she memorized their plates when they drove by.

She noticed a gang tattoo on the driver's left arm that hung out the open window. When he caught her looking at him he licked the air and made a kissing face.

She just stared. He was trying to intimidate her, and it almost worked. It would have, even a year ago. She steeled herself and watched as he turned to the passenger and laughed. Then they sped up and turned at the corner, running the stop sign.

Lucy took a deep breath. Let it out. Typed the license plate into her phone so she didn't forget it.

Didn't hurt to check them out. She was overprotective of the boys who lived here, and if a gang was moving into the area, they needed to prepare. Or if one of their fathers was out of prison and sent a gang to look for his son, it could spell danger for the whole group. That shouldn't happen without Father Mateo being notified by the prison system, but mistakes happened more often than she would like.

She decided that instead of going through her office—and having to justify the request with her boss—she'd send DEA Agent Brad Donnelly the request. He was temporarily in charge of the San Antonio office, and they had become friends when they worked together on her first major case after graduating from Quantico. Michael had helped save his life a year and a half ago when Brad had been kidnapped by a drug cartel, and Brad would help make sure the boys were safe.

Saw a brown sedan driving slow twice by St. Catherine's—an old Ford or Chevy, I think—with two males, Hispanic, early 20s. The driver had a gang tat—it looks familiar, but I don't remember which gang. I'm sending you the license plate—can you run for me?

She sent it off, then went up to the door of the boys' home, which was on the corner across the street from St. Catherine's Church and School, which took up the whole block. Sister Ruth opened the door.

"Lucy, so good to see you."

They made small talk—the house smelled amazing, and Lucy said as much.

"Call Sean, stay for dinner."

"I would, but it's been a long day and I still smell the morgue on me."

Her face fell, and Lucy wished she hadn't said that. Sometimes she didn't think.

"How awful to spend your Sunday working like that."

"It's better to get the results sooner rather than later so we can work it first thing in the morning." It sounded lame, but what else could she say? She'd put her foot in her mouth. "I'll track down Jesse."

"He's not here."

Lucy tensed. "He came here after Mass."

"Yes—and after lunch and chores, Brian, Michael, and Jesse went to the park to practice soccer drills. I told them back by five—the boys still have homework to finish, and I want it done before dinner. Come, help me with the empanadas while we wait."

It was quarter to five, so Lucy relaxed as she followed Sister Ruth into the kitchen and texted Jesse that she was at the house. Tito and Frisco were chattering away while cutting the dough for the empanadas. "Hi, Lucy!" Tito piped up. "Is Sean here? Are you staying for dinner?"

"Not tonight, but thank you."

"Good job," Sister Ruth told the boys. She had the filling already done. "Now set the table, and then finish your homework. We eat at six." She checked on a casserole in the oven, then started putting together the empanadas.

Lucy was glad the boys had left, and she asked Ruth, "You haven't had any problems with gang activity here, have you?" Lucy didn't like the idea that Jesse and the boys were out when a gang member was cruising the neighborhood—too many in that culture knew about the boys and their fate.

"At Saint Catherine's? No—not since that situation in June with those sweet boys, Mrs. Nocia's grandsons. Sean assured me that there was no more threat, and the family seems so much happier and healthy now."

"No, nothing to do with that. I just saw a young man with a gang tattoo driving slowly by the house, and I can be a little overprotective."

"Father doesn't tolerate gang activity at the church, but he will welcome anyone who wants to get right with God. Most of those involved in that culture either stay away from church or are on their best behavior at Mass."

"I'm acting like a cop, I'm sorry."

"A cop and a friend. I'll mention it to Father, but he hasn't told me of any trouble, and it's been quiet around here. The most excitement is when we pile in the van to watch Brian and Jesse play soccer. They had so much fun last week, and you must be proud—Jesse scored the game-winning goal."

"Only because Brian tied it up with his two goals." Lucy smiled. She was pleased that Jesse had made friends. Sean's fears that he was spending too much time with Brian and Michael were unfounded—the boys needed each other, and moving to San Antonio from California was a culture shock, but having ready-made friends was a small blessing.

Lucy then realized that she'd stuffed and folded five empanadas while Sister Ruth did more than thirty. Cooking was not in her skill set.

Jesse ran into the kitchen. "Sorry I'm late."

"You're not," Sister Ruth said. "It's one minute to five. Sometimes I think you all wait outside until the exact minute you need to be home. Where are the others?"

"Cleaning up," he said.

Jesse was overheated, as if they'd been running. Maybe they had—playing soccer all afternoon in the humidity could wear anyone out. But he also seemed . . . nervous? Why?

"Have fun?" she asked, watching his reaction.

"Yeah. Just tired."

"We should go," she said.

"One sec," he said, "I have to tell Michael something." He ran off.

There was something going on with Jesse, but Lucy didn't know if it was a problem. They'd had a great talk today, and she hoped that if something was bothering him, he would talk to her or Sean about it. Maybe he felt more comfortable with his peers. But Michael's world and Jesse's world were different. Lucy cared deeply for the young man who had been so grossly abused, physically and emotionally. She respected him, and some of the tough decisions he had made. He didn't always made the right decision, but that was because he had deep trust issues. They'd made great inroads with him, especially Sean, but he was still a young man who had seen far worse in the world than most Americans see in their lifetime.

"How's Michael doing in school?" Lucy asked Sister Ruth casually.

"Good. They have a web page at the high school where we can check his grades every week. They post on Thursday night. I check, make sure neither him nor Brian is having problems. The others are still at Saint Catherine's, so Father keeps an eye on their studies."

"I'm glad he's adapting to high school."

"His English grade could be better. He struggles with spelling and grammar, like many of the boys here, because their formal schooling has been sporadic. One of Father's altar boys has volunteered to tutor them weekly, but Michael doesn't take direction well from his peers."

"Maybe I can help," Lucy said.

"You already do a lot for the boys. And Michael needs to realize school is important. Even though he's talking about enlisting in the military when he graduates, he needs a solid education."

She hadn't heard that, but she wasn't surprised. Michael had bonded with Kane as much as Sean—but likely saw more of himself in the mercenary than in the computer genius.

Lucy tracked down Jesse, who was in the family room whispering with Michael. Michael saw her first and she knew for certain that they were up to something, but she didn't call them out on it. "We should go," she said. "Sister Ruth says that Michael and Brian have homework."

"Okay. See ya," Jesse said and followed Lucy out.

She didn't say anything for half the ride home, and neither did Jesse. He was texting on his phone.

"So what were you guys really doing this afternoon?"

"Just hanging out."

"So you lied to Sister Ruth about soccer drills?"

"Not really."

"That doesn't mean no."

"Brian just needed some advice, so we talked. I think he, um, feels like he has no privacy in the house. Tito follows him everywhere when he's home."

Maybe that was partly the truth, but it wasn't all of it. Lucy decided not to push. She didn't know if that was the right decision, and she hoped Jesse would come around and share more.

"How was the morgue? Did you learn anything cool?" He was fascinated by forensics, always asked questions, but she knew this was a plot to change the subject.

"It was very interesting. Cause of death was different than we thought, which puts another spin on the murders."

"You mean he wasn't shot?"

"He was shot—but he died of blunt force trauma before he was shot."

"They can tell that?"

She gave him a sanitized version of how Julie came to the conclusion, and Jesse seemed interested and asked smart questions.

Still, Lucy knew half his mind was elsewhere and she wondered exactly what he was thinking about.

CHAPTER NINE

Monday Morning

Lucy had sent her boss a report over the weekend about the investigation, but wanted to follow up before the weekly staff meeting to make sure Rachel didn't have any questions about the complex analysis of the three crime scenes. She found Rachel in her office.

Rachel immediately said, "I read your reports. Everything good with Walker?"

"Yes, for the most part." She wasn't going to share her concerns about Walker or how he viewed her and the FBI. "Do you know anything about the past cases he's worked with the FBI?"

"No," she said. "Did he say something?"

"Only that the two times he had to work with the FBI we screwed up."

Rachel snorted. "He could be old-school. Our office has an outstanding relationship with the sheriff's office, but there's always a few who grumble about 'damn feds.'"

"Maybe. I think there's something specific."

"Is it important? Because you don't want to go stirring anything up with your colleagues."

"I need him to trust me, and while I think we're okay, I have this feeling that he's waiting for me to mess up."

"Then don't mess up."

Sometimes it didn't take a mistake to cause friction. Lucy let the subject drop. She'd follow up with Leo later. She said to Rachel, "We're going to re-interview the first two victims' families, confirm that we have all the information about the night they died. Plus, we need to dig deeper into their pasts. I think these crimes are personal—the victims are either connected to each other, or they are connected to the killer. It just doesn't . . ." Damn. She didn't want to finish that sentence.

"What?"

It would be hard to backtrack, so she swallowed her pride and prepared for a tongue-lashing.

"It doesn't feel random to me. There are random serial killers, but even those killers have a pattern—it's just not always obvious." She felt like she was contradicting herself, showing that these murders had no apparent rhyme or reason. Except, they were planned, cold, and calculated. The killer was smart. Methodical.

"And you don't think this is a pattern?" Rachel furrowed her brows.

"There is, but it seems so basic. Married male under forty. Killed on a Friday night. Even *if* it's random, the killer stalked his victims. He had to, to know when they were alone. He's calculated, which seems the antithesis to the violence done to the bodies. Anyway, there's a good chance that one of the wives saw or sensed something that will help us."

Rachel nodded. "Let me know if Walker holds back information again."

"Okay," Lucy said, but realized she might not—she preferred to deal with any problems directly with Jerry. If she couldn't resolve it, and the situation impacted the case, then she'd go to Rachel.

She hoped it didn't come to that.

After the staff meeting, Lucy caught up on her emails, followed up on two outstanding cases where she was waiting for more information, then tried to talk to Leo about their conversation last night, but he was already out of the office. Lucy had been so out of the loop she hadn't realized that a huge task force had been put together for the counter-terrorism case Leo mentioned to her.

She grabbed an early lunch and headed over to the sheriff's office at noon. Several deputies gave her a high five for her demonstration yesterday. She smiled and continued on. She always felt nervous being recognized in an office environment. She did her job, though often wished she could stay in the background, unnoticed.

It hadn't always been like that. She used to bite her tongue all the time, fearing she'd be ridiculed or dismissed. It had taken training at Quantico coupled with the cases she'd worked to give her the confidence to recognize that she had much to contribute.

And it sure didn't hurt that she had someone at home who believed in her.

Lucy went up to Jerry's small office. He wasn't there. She walked down the hall to the conference room that they'd been using and it, too, was empty. She went in, sent Jerry a message that she was here, and looked through the files again to familiarize herself with the two women they were about to interview.

Susan Standish was twenty-six. She and Billy had been married for seven years and had known each other since high school. She was a kindergarten teacher at a local public school, and her family was local. Parents in San Antonio, two older sisters who moved to the suburbs with their families, a younger brother in medical school in Nebraska, and a brother still at home—a high school junior. She and Billy had bought several acres with a very small house outside of the city. Billy had an insurance policy that paid one hundred thousand dollars.

A lot of money to some people.

Lucy hated being cynical, but she'd too often seen people commit horrific crimes for money. She couldn't see someone planning and executing three murders for a life insurance policy, but she wouldn't discount it. She'd worked a case where the head of a drug cartel had killed the husband of his money launderer to keep his associate in line, and another case where a lobbyist ran a stable of call girls in order to blackmail members of Congress and judges in order to vote or rule her way.

Teri James was thirty-nine, the same age as her husband. This was not the first marriage for either of them. Steven James had been married for seven years to Bridget O'Connell, who was Abby's mother. Bridget died over ten years ago—their daughter had been three—though there was nothing in here about the cause of death. No life insurance policy on Steven James, though there was a note that he had a policy through his work that paid his family his salary for one year after his death, plus he had a retirement account with right of survivorship. They had a healthy bank account and small mortgage on their house—no obvious signs of economic hardship.

Teri James had divorced her husband Roger Abbott in Colorado nine years ago, and moved back to San Antonio where she was originally from, though there was no note as to whether she still had family in the area. Steven James moved to San Antonio from Southern California eight years ago for work, and they recently celebrated their sixth wedding anniversary. No other details.

Based on how hesitant Jerry was in talking again to the widows, Lucy realized she was going to have to play bad cop. It sounded cliché, but when necessary, cops often took different roles with witnesses. The *good cop, bad cop* routine might sound like it came from Hollywood, but many partners used the tactic to gather information from witnesses and suspects because it worked more often than not. Especially now, male cops didn't like being the aggressor when interviewing female suspects or witnesses, which left the job to Lucy.

She'd done both, but found that she had a knack for getting under the skin of people if she tried. She didn't want to run either Susan or Teri over the coals, but she would if she could learn more about their husbands and who might have been a threat to them. The two men had no criminal records, but that didn't mean they hadn't pissed someone off. Families didn't always want to reflect on the negatives in their loved ones' lives, negatives that might set a killer on their trail.

All they needed was one common name. One person whom both men knew would be a starting ground. Because right now, they had no direction to go. No witnesses. No known motive. No physical evidence linking the three victims to a killer. The minor differences in the physical evidence could simply be the killer adjusting. And there might be no real motive, other than the thrill of the kill—which gave weight to the serial killer angle. But even a serial killer started somewhere, and the first victim was likely the most personal. That meant they should look more closely at Billy Standish's life.

Maybe the killer *was* choosing victims purely at random. If that was the case, it wouldn't matter if the victims were married or not—maybe it was the thrill of targeting healthy men. A display of dominance from a physically weaker man. Or a woman, Lucy thought. But other than the attack to the groin, there was nothing that suggested this was a female crime.

Jerry came in as Lucy was putting her final questions together, based on the background information on each of the victims.

"No lawsuits naming Garcia or Standish as defendants or plaintiffs," he said. "Garcia, we have more work to do—your office was able to confirm federal records quickly, and we confirmed state because that's centralized, but local jurisdictions we have to put requests in by county because many counties don't have online archives. Nothing in Bexar, however."

"Good to know. But? You didn't mention James."

"The Los Angeles FBI office is working on any lawsuits from California and that will take a day or three. Locally, he's been named in two lawsuits jointly with his accountancy firm—one was an audit case where the individual they represented sued the firm for malfeasance and a bunch of other things—it was thrown out by the judge. The second was a bench trial, each side was said to be partly at fault for different things—I didn't read it, didn't seem relevant and it's very technical. Accountant issues. You probably have someone in your office who can understand it."

"We'll take a look. What was the final outcome?"

"The firm ended up paying a quarter of the original million the plaintiff was asking for."

Lucy made a note. "Do you have the name of the plaintiff in the first case?"

"Yes, but it was four years ago. And why kill the other two men?"

"If this plaintiff regularly files complaints or lawsuits, maybe he did the same with Standish and Garcia—maybe not them personally, but their employers. Standish is in construction, Garcia a chef. Food poisoning? A leaky roof?"

"That's dang crazy."

"Not all killers are sane, but this one is. Sane and methodical and patient. Remember I said the crime felt personal—the killer looked his victims in the face and shot them. Maybe losing a lawsuit was the final straw and he went back to take out everyone he lost to." It was thin, and her tone reflected that, but they needed to follow up.

Jerry pulled out his cell phone and hit a button. A second later he said, "Keith? Remember that case file you pulled, *George Andres versus Allied Accounting*? . . . yeah, that's it. Can you run all lawsuits where Andres was a plaintiff or defendant? Federal, state, and local courts. And get his current address and employer . . . I know it takes time, but send me what you find when you find it . . . Thanks, buddy." He hung up. "Okay, it's going, but it might take a while."

"Time is one thing we don't have on our side," Lucy said.

"I want to find this guy, but he's waiting a couple weeks between murders. We're still processing evidence from Garcia."

"Four weeks between the first two; three weeks between the second and third. He's cocky. He knows he's smart. He has someone else on his list, and I don't know if he can wait to target him."

Jerry stared at her and shook his head. At first she thought he was going to argue with her, then he said, "Damn, I really hope you're wrong about this, but I'm getting that itch that tells me we'd better find something, and soon, or we'll have another murder on our hands."

* * *

They met Susan Standish at the school where she worked near downtown San Antonio at three thirty that afternoon. She was in her classroom with another woman; all the children had left for the day.

"Mr. Walker, I hope you don't mind that I asked Gina to be here. She's my closest friend."

"Of course not," Jerry said. "Whatever makes you comfortable. And please, call me Jerry. This is FBI Agent Lucy Kincaid, she's assisting in our investigation into your husband's murder."

Lucy would much rather talk to Mrs. Standish alone. Friends and family meant well, but sometimes they didn't help a situation. Still, she understood grief, and she couldn't very well tell Susan not to have someone to support her.

"I'm Gina Clark," the woman said and extended her hand first to Lucy, then to Jerry. "I'm the assistant principal and have known Susie since she started working here." Gina towered over Lucy, who had never considered herself short. Compared with the petite Susan, she seemed even taller. "Let's go outside—there are tables we can sit at a bit more comfortably than these." She waved her hand toward the low tables and tiny chairs.

The tables were under an awning, and flies buzzed around the garbage cans, so they stayed far from the lunch remnants.

"You have news?" Susan asked. "When you called this morning, I didn't know what to expect, because you didn't tell me why you wanted to meet."

Jerry said, "There was another victim who was killed in the same way as your husband. We believe they are connected."

"Another victim? That makes three people? Dead?" Her voice increased in pitch with each question.

Gina squeezed Susan's hand and urged Jerry to finish.

"Do you know a chef named Julio Garcia? He worked

at one of the convention hotels on the Riverwalk—Sun Tower—and lives in Bulverde, north of the city."

She was already shaking her head. "I don't think so. Does he have a child at the school? There's three families of Garcias here, no relation, and two years ago I had a Garcia girl in my kindergarten class."

"His son goes to another school."

"He had a son? That's awful. Poor child. His wife . . . what she must be going through." Her voice cracked.

Jerry said, "We have a few follow-up questions."

"Do you have any suspects?" Gina asked. "Witnesses? Anything?"

"That's why we're here," Jerry said. "We're pursuing several lines of investigation because no witnesses have come forward."

"What about evidence? Like, DNA or fingerprints?" Susan asked.

"We're processing every shred of evidence we have, but so far nothing has matched in our databases," Jerry said. "Can you think back, in the days and weeks before your husband was killed, did he say anything about being followed? Maybe having an encounter with a stranger? Could have been at the store, or a gas station, or even work."

She shook her head. "Billy was working so many hours—he wasn't even home during the week because of the job in Houston. That's where the work is, even this long after Harvey, the good-paying jobs are there."

"What about you?" Lucy asked. "Have you seen anyone in your neighborhood or where you shop that has paid you undue attention? Anyone who made you feel uncomfortable?"

"Like how? Like a jerk who whistles at me?"

"Like any way. Someone you noticed even if you don't know why you noticed them."

She sighed. "You're asking me about vague maybe events from months ago. I really don't know."

Jerry said, "We've worked through several simulations that tell us the killer acted quickly. Your husband may have known the person who killed him. At a minimum, he didn't feel initially threatened."

"Are you saying that someone we know did this?" She shook her head. "No. I told you that when we first talked. Billy would give you the shirt off his back. He was big and had a gruff voice, but he was gentle as a puppy. Isn't that right, Gina? When he wasn't working, because in construction sometimes work was tough to find, it's seasonal sometimes, he would come into the classroom and read to the kids. Everyone loved him."

"Your husband had a couple altercations after he'd been drinking," Jerry began, but Susan cut him off.

"Those were minor. They were misdemeanors and the other guys involved were just as guilty. We paid the fines, everything is fine!"

Lucy didn't want the widow to become agitated. She said, "We understand that, Susan, and no one is placing any blame on Billy for what happened to him. We're simply looking at everything in Billy's past, even things that you might not think are important. If he was sued for any reason, even if there was no merit to the lawsuit. If he had a confrontation with a neighbor or co-worker. Think back, even back to high school. He played football, correct? Did he have a rivalry that maybe went from friendly to violent?"

"I can't believe you think this is Billy's fault!"

"We don't think—"

But Susan was irate. "People make mistakes, and now it's okay that he's killed for it?"

Lucy's mental antenna twitched. "What mistake are you thinking about, Susan?"

"I'm not thinking about anything!"

Jerry glanced at Lucy and gave her a nod. Good, he'd sensed the same thing she had.

Lucy said, "You said that he was *killed for it.*"

"That's not what I meant. You're putting words in my mouth."

"Susan, three men are dead, three women are widows, and two children are orphans. Julio Garcia's wife is pregnant; her daughter will be born without a father. We are asking *everyone* about anything odd, no matter how trivial you think it is. Maybe Billy didn't even do anything, but someone took offense, or made a mountain out of a molehill. What mistake were you thinking of when you spoke?"

Susie bit her lip. "It was an accident, and it was so long ago no one could possibly hold a grudge."

Lucy didn't say anything. She stared at Susan until the woman looked down at her fidgeting hands.

Finally, she spoke. "Billy was a high school senior. We'd just started dating—I was two grades younger. Billy and his best friend Joey were doing donuts in the mud after a storm, out past Calaveras Lake. A few of us were there, and we were all cheering them on, it was wet and dirty and fun . . . but . . . Billy lost control of his truck and it collided with Joey. They weren't even going that fast, but Joey's truck flipped and he was pinned down. Broke his back and lost his football scholarship for college. Billy was sick over it, and Joey's parents hated him after that. I don't think Joey hated him, but they haven't spoken since Billy tried to talk to him at the hospital. I heard Joey's had some problems with drugs after that, painkillers, but my mom said she saw him at the mall a few months ago and he looked good. I just don't really know what he's doing or anything."

"What's Joey's last name?" Jerry asked.

"Adkins," she said.

CHAPTER TEN

Monday Late Afternoon

"Good instincts," Jerry said as they left the school and headed to Olmos Park where Teri James lived. "Though I don't think this long-ago event is going to lead anywhere."

"Neither do I, but asking her these questions and getting her to think about any past slights may lead to a suspect."

Jerry called his office and asked them to locate Joey or Joseph Adkins, twenty-nine, graduate from South San Antonio High School eleven or twelve years ago. He said to Lucy, "We'll talk to him."

"If they had once been best friends like Susan said, maybe he knows of someone else whom Standish upset."

Jerry turned into Olmos Park. Lucy lived in the middle of a curving street close to the main park; the Jameses lived on the far west side of the community. She hadn't realized when Sean bought the house that the area was considered elite for San Antonio.

"I had a case here the first year I was an investigator," Jerry said. "Basic greed. Husband killed his wife for her money. Lots of money in here."

She hesitated, then said, "I live down that street." She pointed.

"Not on a federal salary," he said.

"My husband is a computer security expert. Businesses and governments pay him a lot of money to break into their systems to test their security."

"Do you talk to him about your cases? Like this one?"

She could lie and say no, but she didn't lie well. One former FBI agent had been livid when she'd shared information with Sean, but there was no prohibition against it. "Sean's sharp. He sometimes sees things I miss because I'm so close to the case. Talking things out can help."

"Jeanie, my wife, is like that," he said. "She's a mechanic for the US Air Force, stationed at Lackland. She's logical and damn smart."

"She must have an interesting job. Has she been deployed?"

"Twice, early in our marriage. Glad she's staying here now."

"My brother was army, and Sean's brother was a marine."

Jerry pulled up in front of a modest home across from the park. It was one of the smaller homes in Olmos Park, but was well maintained and had great curb appeal. They got out and walked up the brick that led to several steps and a porch that wrapped around down one side. A swing and several chairs, plants, and a small table decorated the area. Jerry knocked on the door. Teri James, like her husband, was an accountant, but she worked for herself out of their home.

She answered the door a moment later. She was a tall, willowy woman with shoulder-length dark-blond hair and bright-blue eyes. She wore little makeup and had flawless skin. "Please, come in. I made coffee."

Some survivors needed to do something—like make coffee, serve cookies—to ground themselves.

"We'd love a cup," Jerry said. "This is FBI Agent Lucy Kincaid. The FBI is assisting in this investigation."

"Agent Kincaid," Teri said with a nod.

"You can call me Lucy," she said as they followed her inside.

The house was decorated in a traditional style with large pieces of furniture, walls painted different colors that complemented the fabrics—mostly hues of burgundy and tan. Everything was perfectly placed. The coffee table, for example, had a large picture book about the history of San Antonio on one side and a flower arrangement on the other. The furniture was expensive but not ostentatious.

The dining room was comfortable and appeared to be used regularly, unlike many formal dining rooms. A tray with a coffee carafe and china sat on a buffet. Teri carried it to the table.

"How do you like your coffee?"

"Light and sweet," Lucy said.

"Black," Jerry said. "Thank you."

She poured the coffees, put the cups on saucers, and placed the coffee precisely in front of them. Then she sat. "I had hoped you had information about my husband's murder, Deputy, but I saw on the news this morning that someone else died and the police have no leads. They didn't say it was the same person, but it was clear from the report that it's a similar crime. The reporter suggested that this was the work of a serial killer. I find that rather— unlikely, wouldn't you think?"

Jerry said, "We haven't released the information yet because we're waiting on confirmation from the coroner and from the crime lab on ballistics, but yes, we believe it's the same person. Though *technically* by the FBI definition this is a serial murderer, we haven't ruled it as such."

"Is that why the FBI is involved?"

"No, Mrs. James. We asked for the FBI's assistance because of their experience in these type of crimes and their resources."

Jerry seemed irritated by the question. Was that because of his animosity toward the FBI?

"Do you really not have any leads? Steven was killed over three weeks ago."

"We're following up on every thread that we have," Jerry said, "which is why we're here now. Based on our analysis, we believe that the killer may have stalked your husband during the days or weeks leading up to his murder. Did he say anything to you about anyone making him feel uncomfortable? Anyone he may have had words with?"

"Steven was a calm, serious professional. He was also quiet. I wouldn't call him introverted, but he was often wrapped up in his own thoughts so he didn't always pay attention to what was going on around him. Absentminded, to a degree—though when it came to his job, he never forgot anything. More . . . reserved, you would say."

That confirmed the notes Jerry had from his meeting with Steven James's boss and co-workers earlier in the month. Meticulous in his work. Never raised his voice or became visibly angry.

"So exactly what are you saying? That he never said anything to you?"

"That he wouldn't have noticed."

"What about you?" Lucy asked. "Did you ever get the sense that you were being followed—either alone or when you were with your husband?"

She sipped her coffee, frowned. "I think I would have noticed. I honestly can't think of anything or anyone who seemed out of place."

"Did anyone other than you or Mr. James's employer know that he was out of town on business?"

"Our neighbors. Friends—I went out with a few women that Wednesday night. I think I may have mentioned that?"

"Yes," Jerry said. "I have their names. We believe that the killer may have specifically targeted your husband and knew when he was returning from his trip."

"I don't see how that would be possible. That's not the kind of information that I would post on social media, and Steven didn't have social media accounts."

"But several people could have known he was expected home late Friday night."

She frowned. "I suppose. But they'd be friends, I can't imagine someone we know killing Steven."

"We have to pursue every possibility until we can rule it out," Jerry said.

"But if the media is right and this is the work of a serial killer, it could just be that he was in the wrong place at the wrong time, right?"

Did she believe that or did she want to believe it? Lucy wondered.

"At this point, anything is possible, but we need to go through the lives of all three victims," Jerry said. "I know it's uncomfortable, but it's important."

"Anything I can do to help," she said.

"Your husband and his employer were named in a lawsuit four years ago. It was thrown out by the judge. The plaintiff was George Andres. Does that name mean anything to you?"

"Andres?" She seemed surprised to hear it. "I'm not sure. Four years ago? I vaguely remember the case, but don't know that I remember his name. Steven didn't talk much about it, he was irritated because of the time and energy he had to spend to prove that he hadn't done anything wrong. I think it had something to do with an internal audit of the plaintiff's company. I don't remember any details."

"We can get them from his employer. Do you know if your husband felt threatened at any time?"

"He didn't say anything to me. I know they were pleased that they had the case thrown out and the plaintiff had to pay filing fees. Steven is, as you can imagine, frugal. Oh—I don't know if it was that case, but there was a time about then that Steven came home upset because his boss had been verbally attacked. William—William Peterson—is the founder of Allied and in his seventies. He's still on the board but doesn't take clients. He was named in some lawsuit and was required to give a deposition, and the plaintiff was there and screamed at him. I only remember this because William had a health scare shortly before this, and Steven was concerned about his health. He thought of William more as a father or favorite uncle than an employer."

Jerry made a note. Then said, "Your daughter Abigail was at a volleyball camp when your husband was murdered. How is she handling everything? It's only been three weeks."

"It's been difficult, as you can imagine. Especially since she was gone for six weeks this summer for summer camp. She hardly saw her father at all before he was killed, and I know it deeply bothers her. They are—they were—very close. But she's going to school, her grades are adequate, and volleyball seems to give her a focus that is helping her grief."

Teri spoke so matter-of-factly that Lucy wondered if she was seeing a counselor to help deal with this tragedy.

"Does she go to Olmos High?" Lucy asked. It was the local public high school. Sean was undecided about where to send Jesse next year. Olmos had a terrific reputation and good test scores, but Sean thought a private school might have better security and some had more advanced classes. Lucy reminded Sean that Jesse wasn't him, and that just because Sean was bored in school didn't mean Jesse would be.

Mrs. James shook her head. "Victory Academy."

Lucy had heard of it—an expensive private school not too far away. Sean had already rejected it because even though it was a good school academically and virtually every graduate went on to college, he thought it was overpriced.

"Why spend as much for high school as for college?"

"Abby might have some information—" Jerry began, but Mrs. James was already shaking her head.

"She was gone. She left early Friday morning. And she'd only returned from camp two weeks before school started. I don't want her to have to think about this any more than she already does."

"Agent Kincaid has worked with young witnesses," Jerry said. The statement was true, but Lucy didn't know how Jerry knew that. "She will be extremely sensitive to her emotional state. We need to cover all the bases, and maybe Steven said something to Abby, or showed concern about her security if he thought he was being followed."

"I see. Well, could we arrange a time here? So I can prepare her?"

"Of course. When does she come home from school?"

"She has practice until six."

"Why don't we come back tomorrow evening?" Jerry suggested. "After dinner?"

"She has a game tomorrow, and I don't want her thinking about it all day. Wednesday would be better. I'll talk to her tomorrow night, and then seven thirty Wednesday evening would be fine."

Jerry made a note. "Thank you, Mrs. James."

*   *   *

After soccer practice, Jesse followed Brian off the field. Brian had had a bad practice. He was probably the single best player on the team—he was fast and had the best footwork of anyone Jesse had played with. But today he screwed up basic drills, and when the coach was talking he wasn't paying attention and they all had to run an extra lap. It wasn't just Brian—but Brian was the leader of the team. So when he didn't pay attention, no one else did. Some coaches kept the players longer; Coach Ron dismissed them early because they were pathetic, told them to get their head on straight before Wednesday. Somehow that was worse than extra drills. Jesse hated to disappoint his coach, but he was also preoccupied with Brian.

"Brian," Jesse called out.

"Fuck," Brian muttered.

"What's going on?" He glanced around, made sure no one could hear them. Sean wasn't here yet.

"You need to leave me alone. I can't believe you told Michael I was talking to a stranger. And then you guys hunt me down yesterday? This is my brother we're talking about! What am I, a little kid?"

"You're acting like it."

"Fuck you."

"What was with practice? You're the golden boy. You didn't even get the basics down."

"I'm just tired. I don't need a mother hen like your privileged white ass pissing around me."

Jesse had no idea what to say. He had no idea Brian thought of him like that. "We're friends, Brian." He wanted to be mad, but he was more upset than anything.

"Friends don't rat each other out. Friends don't follow friends."

"When they think their *friend* is screwing up, yeah they do."

"Leave. Me. Alone. And don't you say a word to Michael. I talked to him last night, everything is cool, okay? He has enough shit to deal with without your paranoid sissy-ass getting him wound up."

"What's wrong with Michael?" Was Michael going through something, too? And not telling Jesse? Did he think he wouldn't understand?

Brian rolled his eyes. "You're an idiot, Jesse. I don't know why you come over all the time. You're not one of us, you never will be. You should be grateful. You got a big house and a ton of money and parents and you want to slum it with the orphan boys? Really? Well boo-hoo you. Leave me the fuck alone. Don't come over. Michael is just using you because he's scared if he doesn't hang with you that Sean won't come over anymore, that he'll forget about us. I told him it didn't matter, he lives in a different world. I mean, as soon as you came around, Sean didn't, you know? Because now he has a kid, he doesn't need a bunch of orphans. And we don't need him."

Brian pushed Jesse and walked away. Jesse let him go. His eyes stung. He was mad and wanted to fight back, but he couldn't. He had nothing to say. He didn't know any of that stuff. And it made sense. Michael hated him at the beginning, and Jesse didn't think he really liked him, but Jesse was trying, and Michael was just humoring him. It all made sense.

He stared after Brian, then froze. The same dark-brown muscle car from yesterday, one of those older sedans that was all souped up, stopped at the curb. Brian got into the passenger seat. Almost without thinking, Jesse pulled out his phone and zoomed in, taking a couple of pictures. There were two older teens in the car, and they looked mean. One of them looked like the kid Brian had talked to—the one Michael thought might be his brother. Now

Jesse had pictures. But were things really cool between Brian and Michael? Or was Brian lying about that, too?

He knew he shouldn't judge people by how they looked—his uncle Kane looked mean, too. But this was different. These guys looked mean and acted like they were all-that, in their muscle car with loud music and tattoos.

Why did Jesse even care? Brian didn't.

He did care. He didn't want Brian to get in trouble, and he didn't want him to join a gang. It would break Sean's heart, and it would hurt Michael.

But Brian was right about one thing. He wasn't one of them.

He would send these photos to Michael and let him deal with Brian. Michael hadn't wanted Jesse around in the first place, he'd made that clear, and Jesse had ignored his wishes.

No longer.

Lucy was getting ready for bed late Monday night. They'd had dinner together, but both Sean and Jesse were quiet. No one wanted to play a game—Jesse said he had homework and went to his room early, and Sean went to his office to write a proposal for a jewelry store chain to improve their security. Rogan-Caruso-Kincaid Protective Services, the family business Sean worked for, had been contacted by the chain when they found an internal breach that enabled a staff member to steal small pieces that weren't initially missed. It was partly an inventory problem and partly a security problem.

Sean finally came up to the bedroom. "You look tired," Lucy said.

He fell back on the bed. Bandit came over and licked

his hand, earned himself a scratch behind the ears, then went to his dog bed in the corner.

"Jesse lied to me today."

"What about?"

"Does that matter?"

"Yes and no."

He looked at her with a frown.

She said, "Well, if you asked if he was interested in a girl you saw him looking at and he denied it, that's one thing."

"It's not about a girl." He didn't say more, and Lucy sat on the edge of the bed.

"Have you asked him?"

"What do I say? I know you're lying to me about something, what?"

"Now I'm confused."

Sean sat up. "I picked him up from soccer. He was preoccupied. I asked, how was practice. He said fine."

"Okay. Maybe he was reprimanded by the coach. Maybe he had a bad practice and didn't want to talk about it."

"I asked him why he was on the far field when he knows I pick him up at the main entrance. I got there and no one was there. I was a little freaked. He then said practice sucked and they got done early and he was just walking around to blow off steam and why did I care?"

"O-kay," she said, not quite understanding what Sean was getting at.

"That's exactly what I did to Duke. When I was up to something, I always turned it around back on Duke. Because he would get so angry, talk about my attitude and lecture me, and forget that he almost caught me doing something that was against the rules."

"Jesse is a good kid. You were too—"

"Not really. I mean, I didn't join a gang or shoot up heroin, but I did a lot of illegal shit before I was eighteen."

"You don't think Jesse is doing anything illegal?"

"I don't know. But he was evasive and I know all the tricks. And then he was texting Michael but made sure I couldn't see his phone. I almost grabbed it out of his hand to see what he was doing, but I froze." He stared at the ceiling. "I want to trust him. I *do* trust him. But I guess—I knew if I caught him in a lie, or doing something he knows he shouldn't, I would have to punish him, and at that moment I didn't have it in me. I know I need to be a dad—I need to set boundaries and expect certain behavior—but after everything he's been through this summer, how I failed him—"

"Stop."

"Luce, you don't understand."

"You have never failed him, and I never want to hear you say that again, okay?"

She made him look at her. "Jesse *is* a good kid, and if you think he's lying or being evasive, then you need to trust your instincts. He's thirteen. He needs boundaries and expectations. You are not your father, you are not Duke. More important, Jesse is not you. You are going to build up all the possible things Jesse could be doing—but whatever it is, it's probably not the worst thing you can think of. So you need to talk to him, just be honest. That you expect answers. I remember there were some things I just couldn't talk about with my mother. But I had brothers and sisters who *were* brothers and sisters, not guardians, not a second parent. You'll have to feel him out, and see if the secret is something you can live without knowing, or if it is potentially trouble."

"I don't know how to do that."

"You do. Maybe just sharing something from your childhood would help him see that whatever it is he's going through, he's not alone." Lucy paused. "He's worried about you, and maybe he doesn't think you can handle whatever's bothering him."

"He shouldn't worry about me. I need to be stronger for him."

"You need to be *you*, Sean. You are exactly what that boy needs. We're all figuring this out as we go along. Jesse has a lot of anger inside—mostly about Carson Spade."

"So do I."

"But you're not letting it out. You don't want Jesse to see it because you don't want him to take it the wrong way. But maybe you both need to talk about it. Let him know exactly how you're feeling, so he wants to share with you how he's feeling."

"Do you think it has something to do with the boys' home?"

Sean evidently wasn't listening to her.

"With Michael?" Sean continued. "They've been talking all the time, and Michael has been through hell and back. It's not that I don't want Michael talking about it, but if he needs to talk to someone, it should be me. Or Father Mateo. Kane would come up for any one of those boys if they needed him."

"He would. But Jesse is a Rogan, just like you, just like Kane. He may not have been raised as a Rogan, but some things you're born with. Michael has been through hell, but he's also a teenager, just like Jesse. Jesse doesn't have a lot of peers as friends. From moving from Orange County, to going into witness protection, to moving to Sacramento, then moving here—all within the last eighteen months—he hasn't kept any of his friends from his childhood. He needs peers. And maybe he connects better with Michael and the boys than kids in his own school right now. And the soccer team—he loves the team."

"True."

"That doesn't mean you shouldn't talk to him. Just don't go into it thinking that it's all bad, okay? Go in with your eyes *and* ears open."

"You're so smart, what did I ever do to deserve you?"

"I have no idea," she teased and kissed him.

"I love you." He smiled. "Are you tired?"

She wrapped her arms around his neck. "What did you have in mind?"

"It's a beautiful night. Want to go for a swim?"

"I can never say no to the pool."

He kissed her nose and pulled her out of bed. "I know."

CHAPTER ELEVEN

Tuesday Morning

Joey Adkins was the IT manager for a major company in downtown San Antonio. His record was clean: not even a parking ticket. They knew he had a permanent handicap placard for his vehicle; when they met him they knew why. He was in a wheelchair. It was highly unlikely—unless he had been faking his handicap for years—that he had killed anyone in the manner that Standish, James, and Garcia had been killed.

"It's not every day I get both local and federal cops in my office," he said. His office was ergonomically set up to accommodate his small electric chair, which he maneuvered with ease. He had several high-end computers at his work space, and a secondary desk with multiple disk drives laid out.

"Thank you for taking the time to talk to us," Jerry said.

"You said it was about Billy. I know he was killed a few weeks ago—two months? I didn't go to the funeral. My brother told me about it."

"You and Billy were friends."

"A long time ago."

"And you were in an accident together."

"Together?" He shook his head.

"We read the incident report after Mrs. Standish told us about it. You and Billy and another boy were driving four-wheel-drive trucks in the mud and your truck flipped on a rock when Billy cut you off."

He snorted. "Yeah."

"That's not accurate?"

"It's accurate—but he cut me off on purpose because of that lying girlfriend—*wife*—of his."

"Why didn't you tell the police?"

"Because I can't prove anything. Little miss perfect Susie Boswell. Cheerleader, all petite and sweet. Billy told me later when he thought I was dying that he was sorry he believed her. But I was done. I told him if he stayed with her, we were no longer friends. He chose her. I'm over it."

He didn't sound over it. He sounded angry and bitter. Lucy said, "What did Billy believe?"

"Susie and I went out first. But I saw right through her after about three dates. She was downright mean. You'd never know it. She was all sugar and spice and everything nice, but she would say mean things. Like, well, Ginger was this really nice kid who had a serious weight problem. Susie would go up to her at lunch and say maybe she should cut back on the carbs. In her sweet little southern belle voice. Or Bernie who had a stutter. She would mimic him in class and make it worse. My mama didn't like her from day one, and I should have listened to her."

"What happened before the accident?" Jerry asked.

"Susie told Billy that I had cornered her in the girls' locker room after practice and kissed her. Tried to convince her to leave Billy and come back to me. Which was bullshit." He glanced at Lucy. "Excuse me."

"Did something happen?" Jerry asked.

"Yeah. I had started seeing a girl, Rose. Really liked her. She was on the cheer squad with Susie. Susie made her life miserable. She didn't like that I had called her out on her shit, pardon my French. I tried to tell Billy that Susie was trouble, but he fell for her, hook, line, and sinker. She was the prettiest girl in school, and Billy was a good guy—a great teammate, a great friend until he got with her. But Billy wasn't the sharpest tack. First, he's very trusting. And second, Susie was the first girl he slept with. First and only. You might think I'm lying through my teeth, but I ain't. Like I said, we were friends. Anyway, the Thursday practice before that weekend, I had enough. Rose came to me crying. Wouldn't tell me why, but I got her to confess that Susie had spread a vicious lie about her, in her attempt to break us up. To this day, I don't know what it was. But I did confront Susie in the locker room, told her that I had enough with her, and if she so much as looked at Rose the wrong way, I would tell Billy that he wasn't her first—she'd flat-out lied to him that she'd been a virgin when they slept together. I know—because I slept with her, and I knew she wasn't a virgin then. I'm not proud of it—believe me, I wish I'd just hunkered down and ignored her in high school, stayed off her radar. Because anyone who got on her bad side, stayed there."

"Are you saying that Billy intentionally flipped your truck?" Jerry asked.

"No. I'm saying that he was angry with me and he intentionally tried to damage my truck. It was my brother's, and I wasn't supposed to be driving it in the mud, and I didn't want any damage. I overcompensated and didn't see the rock. Flipped right over. It was a freak accident, all because of how I landed."

"Is that how you were paralyzed?" Jerry asked.

"Indirectly. And I'm not fully paralyzed. My back broke, and I went through physical therapy but the pain was intense. I went through two surgeries over the last ten years, which helped the pain, but made my mobility worse. I can walk short distances with a cane, go to physical therapy every week, but it's not going to get much better. I'm working on building my endurance so I can walk my daughter down the aisle on her wedding day."

"Daughter? You're a little young to have daughter getting married."

"She's five. Rose and I got married two years after we graduated. We have a daughter, Mary Anne, and a two-year-old son, Grant."

Lucy remembered what Susan Standish had said about pain pills. "Were you ever addicted to pain medication?"

He snorted. "Susie told you that, right? I'll bet she did. A bitch from beginning to end."

"You didn't answer the question," Jerry said.

"No, I wasn't. My doctor wanted me to stay on the meds because I was in pain, but they made me fuzzy and I knew there was no way I could go through college like that. After three months I quit. I got my AA at SACC in computer science. Worked myself into this position here. Dealt with the pain. Still do, but like I said, the last surgery really helped."

"I graduated from SACC," Jerry said. "Criminal justice."

"You always want to be a cop?" Joey asked.

"Yes. My dad and my grandfather were Texas Rangers."

"Well, I always wanted to play football in college and go through ROTC like my brother and join the air force. That was all taken away from me. And Billy still married her. I don't know what she said, but I don't care anymore. I haven't cared for a long time."

He looked from Jerry to Lucy.

"So why are you two here? To see if I waited eleven years to kill him?"

"More or less," Jerry said, much to Lucy's surprise. "And to ask you if there is anyone else who might have wanted Billy dead."

"Other than Susie?"

"Why would she?"

"Hell if I know. Why does she do anything that she does? Look—Billy was a good guy. Got a little mouthy when he was drinking and would walk into fights because like I said, not the sharpest tack. But he was kind. Some of the guys from school went down to Houston after the hurricane and helped people get out of their flooded homes. Billy was one of them. If someone was having difficulty making their mortgage, he'd give them whatever he had. Never expect it back. I miss having him as a friend—there was a group of us in high school who hung out, and now they hang out with me, or they hang out with Billy, but I told Billy that if he stayed with Susie, we were through. He stayed, and the only time I've seen him since is when we were at the same function—a couple times at weddings, and last year at our ten-year high school reunion. And other than a hi, hello, we didn't talk." He paused. "I'm sorry he's dead."

"So there's no one else you can think of."

"Like I said, I wasn't really much into his life. Maybe he pissed off someone, though it probably wasn't on purpose and he may not have even realized it. But let me tell you this—at the reunion last year, one of my friends made a comment to a small group of us that Susie was prowling."

"Which means?"

"Just what you think. That she was interested in men not her husband. And while Billy might not be sharp, and he might be forgiving, and he might believe all her sweetness and tears—if he caught her cheating on him, he would walk out."

"Do you know this for a fact, or is this just a rumor?"

"Rumor that I believe."

"And no one told Billy?"

"No one would. No one would want to hurt him like that. Even me, even after what happened our senior year, I wouldn't hurt him like that. It would be out of spite. Let him find out on his own."

Jerry didn't say anything for the short drive back to BCSO. In the parking garage, he sat in the car, the air-conditioning blowing on them both.

"You believe him," Lucy finally said. "Though there is no evidence of anything he said, you believe him."

"He was bitter, but not overly so. He was seventeen and his life as he knew it was essentially over."

"And he built something new," Lucy said. "He has a wife, two kids, good job. No criminal record."

"I don't think he had anything to do with murder. We'll run his brother, the one in the military, just to make sure nothing pops, but why now? Why eleven years after an accident?"

"And you believe Susan Standish is having an affair."

"I think it's something we need to find out about, don't you?"

She sighed. "Yes." She really didn't like people all that much right now.

"Problem?"

"No. We need to know if it's true, and if maybe her lover wanted that insurance money more than she did. She might not be involved, but that's not to say she picks lovers who share her nonhomicidal values." But she could be involved. Why kill three men? To cover up a crime of greed?

"If we believe Joey Adkins, those values are off-kilter," Jerry said. "Damn, both times I interviewed her I saw exactly what I expected to see. A grieving wife, a pretty young teacher with big blue eyes and tears."

"And that may be exactly who she is," Lucy said. "I'll tell you this: I've always been a good judge of character, and interrogation is one of my strengths. I didn't see anything that would suggest that Mrs. Standish was involved in her husband's murder. She may be having an affair, but that doesn't mean that she wanted her husband dead."

"Let's find out."

"How? Ask her?"

"Yep, straightaway I want to ask her. See what she says. But Ash says he'll have his computer model ready to show us right after lunch. So let's get a bite in the cafeteria and head over to the crime lab."

CHAPTER TWELVE

Tuesday Afternoon

Lucy had known Ash Dominguez since her first joint investigation with SAPD, and she had never seen him so excited over a case.

"I'm so glad you're here," he said to Lucy and Jerry when they walked in. "This is the coolest computer model I've ever done."

"We're itching to see it," Jerry said.

"Oh—and the ballistics are back, and the same gun was used in all three murders. So there's that."

"Nice to have the confirmation."

"Look," Ash said and pointed to a huge screen on the wall. "I got IT to bring in a big screen. I need you to see this in all its glory."

He flicked off the lights, leaving the lab in semi-darkness. He kept talking. "This program is the best program I've ever worked with. It's truly amazing. Worth every dime."

"We're not on the budget oversight committee, Ashley," Jerry said, getting irritated. "Just show us what you found."

"Right. So, I input all the facts for each crime. The nonvariables. Position of the body, relationships with the surroundings, the like. Then I input the autopsy results—every identified injury and cause of death. The computer runs through every possible scenario from first attack to after death—like if the body was moved. Then I went in and made logical additions—not adjustments. We can't change facts, but we can change assumptions. Like, for example, we know that Julio Garcia was fatally hit on the back of the occipital lobe. Based on the angle and the force, and evidence on the body and the ground, I can make the assumption that he was squatting when he was hit."

"Okay," Jerry said. "Can you just do it?"

"I wanted you to know the methodology. Because in court, they'll want to know."

"And you're an expert witness," Lucy said. "You don't have to explain to us, we already stipulate to your expertise."

"It's just—well, so exciting to actually see it. I didn't go so far as to extrapolate how or why the victims got out of their vehicles, but from first blow to death, I know exactly what the killer did. Ready?"

"I've been ready for ten minutes, Ashley," Jerry said.

"Okay. Okay." He was practically shaking with anticipation as he pressed a couple of keys on his computer, and the simulation went up on the big screen.

The technology was amazing—the victims looked like people, and Ashley had input the height and weight of each victim, so everything was proportional. The killer avatar was less distinct. There was a core, but shading to indicate that the killer could be taller or shorter.

"This is Billy Joe Standish," Ash said, his voice low. "From the grease on his fingers, we believe he was hunched over an engine—a car, not a truck. Based on the angle he had to have been leaning over something short, but not squatting."

As Lucy watched, the same excitement grew in her—this was almost exactly how she'd pictured the scene when she did her spontaneous demonstration on Saturday. But a sick dread filled her at the authenticity—and brutality—of the simulation.

"I set it at half speed, so you can more clearly see the attack," Ash said. "And—"

"Quiet," Jerry said.

A generic car had its hood up. Standish was leaning over the car, his left hand near the grille, his right hand reaching for something in the middle of the engine. The killer—who could be between five foot six and six feet tall, according to the simulation—hit him on his upper back, just below his neck. The weapon depicted was an octagon-shaped steel mallet. Standish stumbled. His knee hit the bumper. Another blow as he was turning caught his lower back, and he fell to his knees. He stumbled and a third blow hit his stomach. He was down, but the edge of the road had a slope, and he slid away from the road. The killer followed and hit his hands hard into the ground as Standish was trying to stand. That brought him back down and he rolled over to his back, clutching his hands together to his chest. The killer tried to then hit him in the stomach again, but Standish put up his arms in a defensive posture. He was hit twice in the left arm, then grabbed the handle of the mallet with his right hand. They wrestled for the weapon and Standish had it for a short time but didn't have strength to fight back.

The killer reached into a utility belt or pocket and used a Taser on stun mode to shock Standish enough to drop the mallet. The killer picked up the mallet and hit him in the groin, then pulled out duct tape and taped his mouth.

Ash paused the simulation. "I don't know when the mouth was duct-taped, but this seems to be the most logical point."

"Just keep it going," Jerry said, his voice rough.

Ash cleared his throat and pressed PLAY.

The killer then pulled Standish's right hand away from his groin and slammed the mallet down on the hand three times. Standish reached over with his left hand, and the killer hit it three times. The victim lay there a moment, writhing in pain, pulling his arms to his chest, and the killer hit him once more in the stomach and again in the groin. The victim reached for the mallet, and the killer hit them again, then slammed the mallet into his abdomen. Then he stood on either side of Standish, his feet on either side of his hips, pulled a gun from his lower back, aimed, and fired. The bullet hit Standish in the face, just to the right of the nose. The killer holstered the weapon, reached down, ripped off the duct tape, then walked away.

Ash said, "Two minutes, fifty seconds from first blow to death."

"Next," Jerry said gruffly.

Steven James had no wounds on his back. Ash had made several assumptions, because there was no known reason for Steven to get out of his car.

Steven is facing his killer. The first blow is to the groin. He's now down to his knees, and another blow hits in the chest, a golf-club-like swing with the mallet. Now he's on the ground, curled into a fetal position. The killer kneels over the body, one knee on each side, and holds down one hand. Ash paused it again.

"Julie really did extraordinary work. When I started putting this together, she sent me more data—she found very faint bruising on James's wrists. He was wearing a long-sleeved button-down shirt, and we think the killer held his wrist down, causing the bruising."

Neither Lucy nor Jerry commented, and Ash hit PLAY again.

The killer hit the right hand four times, then the left

hand four times. No restraint, as Lucy had thought at the beginning. The pain could easily have incapacitated the victim.

Next, the killer duct-taped Steven's mouth, stood up, hit him twice in the chest—cracking his ribs—then again in the groin. The killer then stood on either side of the victim and fired the gun into his face. Removed the duct tape. A second later the killer had a Taser in his hand and Tasered Steven James through his shirt, then walked away.

Ash paused and said, "I don't know where the Taser was—in a pocket or on the ground. I think it was on the ground, but computer probability is only fifty percent. Did it fall out of the killer's pocket? Did the killer go back and get it, but had brain matter on his hands, and that ended up in the wound? I don't know."

"But it was postmortem, according to Julie," Lucy said.

"Yes, and there *was* brain matter on his shirt at that location. It's *possible* blowback could have reached there—there are a lot of factors. But from the distance and the angle and the evidence we gathered at the scene, I believe it came from the Taser itself."

"Good. Next," Jerry said.

Julio Garcia was squatting. Ash's demo had him looking at a tire on a car. The killer brought the mallet down. Julio didn't know, or didn't look back, but fell over—instantly killed.

Ash paused the demonstration.

"What?" Jerry snapped.

"I'm extrapolating something here, so bear with me. Rate of decomp is a science, but it has so many factors that when someone dies we might be able to give the hour, yet not the minute. But certain things happen in the body. I think—and this is something I don't think will hold up in court, if I was forced to testify—that the killer was expecting him to fight back or get up or something. So when he didn't, I think the killer hesitated here, for at least a minute, maybe trying to decide what to do."

"Which would confirm that he knew that Julio was dead instantly," Lucy said.

"Exactly."

"Just play it," Jerry said.

The killer paced on the screen, then dragged Julio's body away from his car. Dropped it.

"This is the only body that was dragged," Lucy said. "In Standish's simulation, we assumed he was dragged, but he fought back, and that was a natural progression of his resistance."

"Based on the evidence at the crime scene and on the body, that's the most likely scenario," Ash said. "Watch this."

On the screen, the killer pulled Julio's hands above his head. He hit them half a dozen times. Then he hit him in the stomach twice and the groin twice. Then he Tasered him in the side, pulled out a gun, and shot him in the face. The killer walked away, then came back and put duct tape over the victim's mouth, then pulled it off.

"Why did he walk away?"

"I just put that in there. I don't know that he did or didn't, I just wanted to make it clear that the killer put the duct tape on *after* he shot Mr. Garcia."

"It's a stage," Lucy said.

"What do you mean?" Jerry asked.

"It's clear here. Everything with Julio Garcia had to match the first two victims, down to the duct tape and the Taser—even though Garcia was dead and couldn't scream or fight back. He's setting the scene so that we see the same things that we saw at the other crime scenes."

"We have matching ballistics," Jerry said. "We know that it's the same gun that killed these three men, and therefore the same killer."

"But the killer is setting a stage, like theater," Lucy said. "He wants it to look the same way. Maybe because he thinks we're idiots and can't figure it out, maybe there's another, more personal reason for him to do so. Whatever it is, this is a setup. An act. Like he's directing a play. Close the curtain on the body, then cut, the end of the act."

"Now you're talking nonsense," Jerry said.

Lucy tensed. She knew what she was thinking, but maybe she wasn't explaining it well. "We should consult a profiler."

"No. I'm not going down that path of bullshit again."

She was taken aback. In the days that she'd been working with Jerry, he never swore. He appeared to be what he was—a polite, good-old-boy, diligent, and respected deputy investigator. But mention a psychological profile and he lost it.

"I don't know who you worked with before, but I have someone I explicitly trust who can give an honest appraisal. Help us narrow down what this killer is thinking."

"No," he said firmly. "We follow the evidence. The evidence will lead us to the killer. I'm not going to deal with a bunch of theoretical garbage that will delay our investigation." He turned to Ash. "Anything else?"

"No—I've gone over the crime scenes and evidence twice and haven't found any unidentified hairs or fibers. The killer wore gloves—we found no prints, and I looked at everything I believe the killer may have touched. The killer wore some sort of low-heeled boots, but the footprints were too indistinct to get a pattern to narrow down a manufacturer, or a precise size. The prints were found at the Garcia crime scene, but the first crime scene was too rocky, and the second crime scene was a parking lot."

"This is good work, Ash, thank you," Lucy said. "Can you please email it to me? I want to review it again."

"Of course. And I'll shade it—meaning, the areas that

are incontrovertible based on physical evidence will be identified, and areas where I made logical extrapolations of data will be identified."

Jerry said, "Ash—I want you to go over everything again. The scenes of the crimes were problematic because of the locations, but the killer touched the victims. He had to in order to remove the duct tape. To get close enough to stun. He dragged Garcia twenty feet, maybe there's sweat, hair, fibers, *something*. You're the best CSI we have in San Antonio. You will find something."

Ash opened his mouth, closed it. "Yes, sir. I'll go back and look at everything again, with an assistant. Maybe I missed something . . ."

"You didn't miss anything, but you might not have seen it yet. This demonstration is good, but it doesn't give us evidence."

"I'm on it. It's my number one priority right now."

Lucy and Jerry walked out. She was about to tell him good job for lighting a fire under Ash—stroking his ego was sure to get him to spend far more time than he should on the case, considering his workload. She agreed, the killer *had* to have left something behind. They might not be able to match it to anyone until they had a suspect, but finding the evidence was half the battle.

But Jerry spoke first.

"Now, don't get your panties in a wad because I don't want to consult some shrink."

"That's not what profiling is, Jerry. It's taking known human criminal behavior and looking at an unknown subject and helping narrow down an investigation. Because right now we have squat."

"We have more than we had before—we have Susan Standish as a possible adulterer, and we can and should track down her lover because maybe he has a clear motive."

"Possibly for Standish, but the others?"

"We follow the evidence."

She wouldn't be able to get through to him, but she planned on consulting her brother Dillon on her own time.

Because something felt so weird about this entire case that she couldn't help but wonder if they were missing something obvious—simply because they saw only what the killer wanted them to see.

Although Lucy and Jerry didn't see eye-to-eye on criminal profiling, they did have the same sensibilities about interviewing. After a brief discussion, they opted to visit Susan at her house. No friend to lean on, no one to raise objections if they had to get tough with her. Not that they planned to play hardball—that depended on Susan's answers.

Her car was in the driveway; there was a carport attached to their double-wide. It was a nice-looking place, clean and newly painted, dwarfed by the land it sat on. Plants and flowers overwhelmed the porch that ran along the length of the trailer.

They walked up four steps and Susan opened the door before they knocked. "Deputy. Ms. Kincaid."

"Agent Kincaid," she corrected.

"Right. Sorry. I don't remember making an appointment."

"We have a few more questions for you, and we were in the area," Jerry said. "We wanted to look at the crime scene again," he lied smoothly.

"Oh. Okay. I'll—well, come in. Excuse the mess."

The trailer wasn't messy, but it was cluttered—furniture a little too big for the space, pictures hanging from virtually every available wall, knickknacks and collections of dolls, crystal figurines, a whole rack of souvenir spoons hanging next to a rack of souvenir mugs. It almost made Lucy claustrophobic.

Two large, old dogs looked up from their beds in the middle of the living room, without much interest in the visitors.

"Please, sit," Susan said, motioning to the couch. "Can I make y'all some coffee?"

"No, thank you, ma'am. We won't be here long. We're going back through all our evidence, talking to friends and family again. We tracked down Joey Adkins."

"Oh?"

"He's married with two kids. The IT manager for a major San Antonio company."

"Oh. I guess I didn't know that."

Why did Lucy think she was lying? Why would she about something so unimportant?

"Did you attend your husband's ten-year high school reunion last fall?" Jerry asked.

"Um, yes?"

"You're not sure?"

"Of course I'm sure. I just don't know why that matters."

"I don't pay much attention to rumors—you know how some folk are—but there was a rumor that came up more than once during our investigation. So I have to ask—were you cheating on your husband, Mrs. Standish?"

She stared at him and blinked. She hadn't expected the question. She was stunned, and she was guilty. Something in her eyes, the way they shifted slightly down, looking for an answer that wasn't there. A moment too long before her response.

"Of course not," Susan said. "I would *never.* I loved Billy Joe. He was my soul mate."

"I need to follow up on these accusations, Mrs. Standish. Because maybe one of your other suitors might think getting Billy Joe out of the way would earn him a permanent spot in your bed."

She jumped up, hands on her hips. "Is that what Joey said? That I was cheating on Billy? You tell him he can go to hell, that's what you can tell him!"

No reaction to the plural *suitors*. Had she honestly not heard it? Jerry had made himself clear, Lucy thought.

"Mrs. Standish," Lucy said as she assessed the woman. She wasn't certain she was playing her right, but it was a gamble worth taking. She kept her voice firm and slightly superior in tone. It would sound more judgmental that way. "I need you to listen to me carefully. It is a crime to lie to a federal agent. I need you to answer Deputy Walker's question truthfully. Were you having an affair?"

"I—I—" She looked to Jerry, her eyes immediately tearing up. "Why are you doing this to me? I just lost my husband! He's dead, and I miss him every day. Why would you dredge up past mistakes?"

That's what she called Joey Adkins's "accident." A mistake.

"Why don't you sit down, Mrs. Standish," Jerry said, all nice and sweet. "Can I get you some water?"

"Thank you. Thank you *so* much, Deputy."

Unbelievable.

Not unbelievable. She's trying to play you. Well, she's trying to play Jerry because he's a man, and she's used to getting her way with men.

Lucy stood in front of the woman and stared. She didn't have to muster much acting skill to freeze a look of disappointment and disapproval on her face. Susan fidgeted.

Jerry came back with ice water. "Thank you *so* much," Susan said with a nervous smile, looking right up at Jerry with wide, wet eyes.

Lucy resisted the urge to roll her eyes. This was becoming ridiculous.

Susan drank. "Now. What is it I can do for you?"

"Telling the truth is a start," Lucy said.

The tears returned. "I have. I don't know who would have hurt my husband."

"Susan—can I call you Susan?" Jerry asked. "I don't think you killed your husband. But I need to investigate his case fully. You understand that, right? Because you've already filed the claim for your insurance, and I'm sure you can use the money, what with having to live on your lone salary. But the insurance isn't going to pay until I finish my report, and I can't finish my report until I interview everyone even tangential to this investigation."

"I—But I didn't kill my husband. I swear, Deputy, I didn't. I miss Billy so much."

Ironically, Lucy believed her. At least, Susan believed that she missed him.

"I know you do," Jerry said in a fatherly tone. "But he worked a lot, and he was gone more than he was here, wasn't he?"

She sniffed and nodded. Jerry handed her a tissue, which earned him a bright smile.

"So I need to know anyone you were romantically involved with. Maybe you broke it off. Maybe they were upset because they knew you loved your husband. Sometimes, people we think we know and trust, we really don't know very well."

Susan bit her lip and looked down. She didn't say anything. Lucy waited. Jerry waited. She still didn't talk. Was she trying to think up a lie?

"Mrs. Standish," Lucy said in a stern voice. "I can subpoena phone records, and I will do it and interview every person you have spoken to in the last year. Ask them if they were sleeping with Billy Joe Standish's wife while he was still alive. How many are going to say yes?"

"You make it sound so bad."

"We need names, we need them now, or I'll be getting that warrant first thing in the morning."

"Carl. But he would never hurt Billy Joe. He loved him like a brother."

Lucy had to bite her tongue to keep from saying anything.

"What's Carl's last name, Susan?" Jerry asked nicely.

"Franklin."

"And when did you and Carl get involved."

"I've known Carl since high school. We've been friends forever."

"You've been sleeping with him since high school?"

"Oh no! Of course not. Just—a few months ago. May. Billy Joe was gone for a whole month and it just sort of happened."

"Is it still happening?"

"Sometimes."

"And before Carl?" Lucy asked.

"Ricky Johns."

"Was he upset when you broke it off with him?" Jerry asked.

"We didn't exactly break up."

"Does he know about Carl?"

"I don't think so," she said slowly. "Is that all? 'Cause I'm real tired right now. It's been a long day."

"Agent Kincaid?" Jerry asked. "Any more questions for Mrs. Standish?"

"In the last year, who else besides Carl and Ricky did you have sex with?"

"It wasn't like that."

"Who?"

"It was just *one time*."

"Who?"

"Andy Kernick. But he doesn't even live around here, he was just here visiting for his little brother's high school graduation, and one thing just . . . well, you know how it is. Andy and I went out in high school and we were old friends. He's in Birmingham now, works for a big pharmaceutical company. And, well, you know, he might be married, too, so it was just that one time."

"Thank you for your time," Jerry said and stood up. "We'll let you know if we have more questions."

"And you can file your report now? Because I have repairs I need to do. I never had to pay for repairs before, Billy Joe was so handy with everything."

"We're almost done, I'll let you know."

Lucy walked out first. In the car she couldn't even speak.

Jerry drove away and called his office to ask for current information on Carl Franklin and Ricky Johns, then called his boss to talk about how they might be able to get a search warrant. She said they'd talk in the morning because right now an affair wasn't going to do it. He hung up.

"Unbelievable," he said.

Lucy didn't know if he was referring to Susan or Lucy playing hardball. "I saw that she was looking to you for validation, so I decided to be tough."

"I know. Good call."

She relaxed.

"You okay?" he asked.

"Yes, why?"

"Because you had a look on your face I couldn't quite read. And you were shaking."

"Was not." Was she?

"Well, I'm a keen observer of human nature, and you appear to be as well, but maybe we don't always see in ourselves what we see in others."

"She made me angry."

"Me too. Carl Franklin is her husband's best friend. I

interviewed him after the murder. He was genuinely grieving. I don't think he could have faked that kind of grief. But he could have killed him and the grief was guilt. If that's the case, it won't take much to push him over into a confession."

"Then why James and Garcia?"

"Why indeed. But we need to pursue this angle. She lied to me. Maybe not outright lied when I first talked to her, but an affair is a pretty clear motive for murder, and she didn't even hint to it."

"No amount of money could replace Sean," she said.

"Your husband."

"Yes. I'm sure he has a life insurance policy because—well, his line of work. His company would have it on everyone. But I've never asked, and I don't care. My life would never be the same without him."

"You don't seem the cheating type."

"I didn't know there was a cheating type." She'd met far too many people who thought extramarital affairs weren't a big deal.

"Maybe there isn't, but it seems your empathy for poor Billy Joe was real enough."

"It was." She glanced at him. "You and your wife have a good relationship?"

"Yes. I've never cheated. I almost did once. The first time she was deployed. Got myself into a prickly situation with a fellow officer. As it came clear to me that our mutual flirtation meant something more to her, I realized what I was doing. I transferred. It was inappropriate and I love my wife. I told her about it. My guilt was so strong, even though I never acted on it. It was a momentary weakness that I caught in time. I know some men, married and single, who play around with the badge bunnies—oh, I'm sorry, that's probably not very sensitive of me."

"I'm a big girl."

"Well, I just ignore it. I go home to Jeanie every night, and very much happy to do so. I would never hurt her. And I can't see how Billy Joe didn't know what his wife was up to."

"Maybe he did," Lucy said. "Maybe he'd figured it out and confronted one of the men who was intimate with his wife. And it ended badly for him."

"If he was the only victim, I'd be right there with you on that scenario. But it doesn't fit."

"It doesn't," she agreed. "But we're going to have to follow through. Follow the evidence, right?" she said, repeating his words.

He didn't respond. He didn't have to.

By the time they got back to BCSO it was after six, so Lucy gathered her notes and went home. They would talk to Susan's lovers in the morning.

"Home early," Sean said when she walked into the kitchen.

"It's nearly seven." She kissed him. "Something smells amazing. I hoped you saved some for me."

"We haven't eaten. I just made stew."

"Stew? Really?" He would never cease to amaze her.

"It was easier than I thought. You throw everything into the pot and it cooks."

"I think it's more complicated than that. Let me take a quick shower and change." She ran upstairs. The meaty stew had her stomach growling, reminding her she hadn't eaten in hours.

Her phone vibrated in her pocket. It was Brad Donnelly.

"Hey, Brad."

"Sorry, I meant to get back to you yesterday, but got swamped. I really hate being in charge."

"You're good at it."

"I'm better in the field. There's so much damn paperwork I want to scream. This was supposed to be temporary. It's been over a year. Anyway, I didn't call to complain. Nineteen seventy-six Chevy Chevelle, registered to Lee Sanchez, on East Santiago. I'll send you his stats and address. Lee is a cousin of Jaime Sanchez, more or less keeps his nose clean. Did a stint for possession with intent more than ten years ago. Was out working on an oil rig last year when Jaime was killed."

"How old is he?"

"Forty-two."

"The two kids I saw in the car were early twenties, tops. Maybe late teens."

"I don't remember if he has kids. Do you want me to look into it?"

"No, it's probably nothing."

"What did I say? Trust your gut. How's this—see the car again, call me and I'll dig around."

"Fair. Thanks."

"How's Sean these days? I had drinks with Nate a couple weeks ago, he told me what went down, that Sean got custody over Jesse's rich grandfather."

"They're adjusting. Sean's a good dad—I wish he'd see it in himself."

"And he has you. Win–win. Let me know if you need anything, and don't be a stranger."

"You're the one who was a no-show for our Fourth of July party."

"Work. Being in charge you'd think nine-to-five, right?"

She laughed. "You would never be happy working nine-to-five."

"True. Next party, call me."

Lucy cleaned up and went downstairs. Jesse was texting on his phone at the table in the breakfast nook. "Do I need to put your phone in jail?" Lucy said.

"What? Oh, no, sorry. Didn't know dinner was ready."

He put his phone in his pocket. Lucy couldn't very well ban phones from the dinner table—in an emergency she had to be reachable—but she and Sean had agreed that with Jesse here, they had to set the example, so phones could only be answered if they were in the middle of a case.

Still, she popped hers in the charger and put the ringer on so she'd hear it.

Sean put the tureen down and Lucy's stomach growled. Jesse laughed. "I totally heard that."

"I smell good food and I can't help myself," she said.

They had a nice dinner and Jesse seemed more relaxed and open than he had over the last few days. He talked about soccer and school. He got an A on his first essay for English, and a B+ on his second algebra test. He had a big project in history coming up, but he'd already started working on it.

Maybe her conversation with him helped, she didn't know. But the more normal and predictable their life, the better for Jesse, so she hoped to be home for dinner more often.

After dinner, Jesse and Sean went to play video games, which was a good bonding activity for them. Maybe because Sean was so young—he'd be thirty-two next week—he still loved playing. Maybe it was something he'd never grow out of. He and Nate often played at night over the Internet, two grown men wearing headsets and chatting about everything from the game to cases they were working.

Lucy went into Sean's office because he had the best computer in the house. She had already sent Dillon a message that she wanted to Skype tonight. It was eight thirty her time, so nine thirty in Washington, DC.

Dillon answered almost immediately. "Hello, baby

sister," Dillon teased. "It's always good to see you when we talk."

Lucy leaned back in Sean's desk chair. Not only did he have the best computer system, he had the most comfortable chair. "How are you?"

"Good. Relaxing. Kate is in New York on a panel interviewing FBI candidates for the next two weeks. She's not relaxing. I don't think she likes big cities."

"DC isn't exactly suburbia."

"But Georgetown has a quiet sensibility. Close to the city, but with a neighborhood feel. However, I'm going to fly up there for the weekend. Take Kate to a show, do fun things."

"Are you going to see Max when you're there? Tell her I said hi."

"Actually, I was planning on doing just that. I wanted to see how she was adjusting with all the changes in her life."

At the beginning of the year, Maxine Revere, a reporter who also had a cable crime show, had uncovered new evidence into the murder of Lucy's nephew Justin. Together Max and Lucy had solved the case and the murders of four other young boys spanning twenty years. Lucy hadn't liked Max at first, but by the time they were done she'd grown to respect her. She was unlike anyone else Lucy knew, and while Lucy wasn't certain she 100 percent trusted the reporter, she admired her tenacity. Dillon, on the other hand, had developed a friendship with Max and had helped her uncover answers about what happened to her mother more than a decade ago.

Dillon continued. "When you sent me a message that you wanted to call, I assumed it's for work—calling just to say hello to your brother doesn't need an appointment."

"I know, I should call more."

"Alas, Jack has usurped me as your favorite."

"Not true," she said. "I have no favorites."

"That's what you *say*, but actions, sis."

"You trying to make me feel guilty?"

Dillon grinned. "It's so easy. Now tell me about your case."

"Possible serial killer."

"Possible? Two or more murders with a cooling-off period?"

"Technically, yes, a serial killer."

"Why don't you give me the scenario?"

"First, I'm working with the sheriff's office. My partner scoffs at behavioral science. There's a deep disdain there that I can't figure out yet. I'm working on it."

"I've faced it many times since I became a forensic psychiatrist. There's nothing you can do except do a good job and hopefully people will come around. He's likely a cop who believes in evidence, experience, and procedure."

"Yes, but he also trusts his instincts—and they're good. So I'm hoping he'll come around and allow us to formally consult the BSU. But I wanted to pick your brain, unofficially."

"Pick away."

She explained the three murder victims, the time line, what was done to them. "There are some differences in the process. For example, the first victim was beaten more extensively than the second and third. The second victim was stunned *after* he was dead. And the third victim was killed with the first blow to the back of his head, yet the killer went through the ritual of the beating and shooting. The ME confirmed that the first blow killed him instantly and everything done to the body after was postmortem."

"And the marks match up?"

"Yes—same type of hammer—probably a mallet, steel head. Same gun. Ballistics came back on all three bullets as being fired from the same weapon. The forensic analysis says that the first victim went down fighting, but no one in his circle had any visible injuries after the attack. The second victim was the only one who didn't have a blow to the back."

"Suggesting he either knew or wasn't scared of his killer."

"But the other two men—they turned their back on their killer. We think, based on evidence found on the first victim, that he may have been helping with someone's car."

"A trap?"

"That's what we think. So he may or may not have known the person, but felt secure enough to turn his back on him and look under the hood or squat by a tire. Based on the angle of the first two blows, we believe the first victim was bent over a hood and the third was squatting."

Lucy took a sip of water and continued. "What really gets me is the gunshot to the face. The killer stands with one foot on either side of the victim. We believe the first two victims were incapacitated from the attack, and the third was dead—and he or she shoots the victim in the face. Almost straight down. That tells me he was looking in the victim's eyes, as if he wanted the victim to know that *he* was killing him. That it was personal. A vendetta or vengeance or . . . I don't know. It's just so cold. When our crime scene investigator ran through a simulation, the first thing that came to mind was that it was a stage—like a setup for a play. When you watch all three men killed, it was as if each of the blows was planned, whether necessary or not."

Dillon didn't say anything for a long minute, but Lucy could see him thinking and reviewing notes he'd taken while she talked. He finally asked, "Was the third victim more or less beaten than the first two?"

"About the same as the second, which was less than the first. Except the second had cracked ribs—I don't know if that means that he was hit harder, or if it was because of where the mallet landed on his body."

"And these men are upstanding citizens? No criminal record? No sexual assault accusations?"

"Nothing in the system. Which isn't to say that they are all innocent. The first victim had been in bar fights, misdemeanors, he's rougher around the edges but no jail time and people generally liked him. He was known to be a good employee with a strong work ethic. The second victim an upstanding accountant, reserved, respected. We know that even respected people can have dark secrets. But the third victim? I don't know him as well as the first two because we just started looking at his life, but everything we've learned so far is that he's a hardworking family man. His wife is eight months' pregnant and his mother moved in when she broke her ankle. Not one person has said he has done anything improper, and he has a clean record. He seems to be exactly as he appears: a devout family man who works hard to provide for his pregnant wife and mother."

"And he was killed instantly? That would take a lot of force."

"Julie, our assistant ME, explained that it wouldn't—the angle that he was hit and where he was hit at the base of the skull sent his occipital lobe into his brain stem. I might not be explaining it accurately."

"I know what you mean. It's very difficult to accomplish on purpose, though someone with skill and training could do it."

"Like in the military?"

"Perhaps. But it has been known to happen on accident. There was a bar fight once where the bartender laid out a drunk patron with a baseball bat—the man had been beating up another guy. The bartender didn't mean to kill

im, he was just trying to stop the attack. He didn't even
it him that hard, but it was the right angle."

"We think it was an accident. Based on the first crime
cene, attack from behind, get them on the ground, smash
heir hands—which would prevent fighting back—shoot
hem in the face."

"You mentioned something about duct tape?"

"Yes. The killer duct-taped the victims' mouths at some
oint, then pulled the tape off and took it with him."

"To keep them from calling for help?"

"Possibly. But the last victim was already dead. He
vasn't making any noise, yet the killer used duct tape on
him as well."

"I agree—that is very odd."

"It's not a sexual crime, even though the groin area
vas hit. I mean, it *could* be sexual and the killer is attack-
ng other parts of the body to hide it, but it doesn't feel
hat way to me. The hands . . . that's unusual. But what is
eally bothering me is shooting the victim in the face.
Looking him in the eye and killing him. Obliterating his
dentity."

"Like you said, it's cold." Dillon paused, then continued. "Cold, calculating, premeditated. The killer does not
have any remorse, does not care about the victims. The
killer wants their face to be the last thing the victim sees.
Or it's a way of dehumanizing the victim. 'You're nothing, you're no one.'"

"We haven't figured out how the men are connected. If
they're not connected, then they should connect to the
killer."

"Or one connects to the killer—but he is killing men
who remind him of his primary target. In fact, none of
them may be connected at all, and he's killing men as a
surrogate for his true target."

"The killer stalked them. Knew when they would b
alone."

"So they somehow showed up on the killer's radar."

"Exactly. They don't know each other, don't go to th
same church, stores, their kids don't go to the same school
they don't have the same doctors or live in the same neigh
borhoods. But there must be a place where the killer picke
up their scent."

"You don't need me on this, Lucy. I think you're abso
lutely right."

"Maybe it's just I miss you, big brother."

"I miss you, too."

"But seriously—I'm not trained as a behavioral scien
tist. You are. I'd like you to talk to my partner. I just have
to convince him that we can benefit from psychological in
sight."

"Your insight is as good as mine."

"Don't humor me. You've been doing this a lot longer
and you have that M.D. after your name."

"Just means I went to school longer."

She rolled her eyes and laughed. Dillon was always
humble.

"Seriously, if anyone can convince my partner, it's you."

"I'll talk to you off the record anytime you want, Lucy
but if you need an official profile, you're going to have to
go through channels."

"I will. Thanks, Dillon."

"Now—no more murder. Talk to me about you, Sean
and Jesse."

Lucy leaned back and they chatted about family before
Dillon ended the call to talk to Kate.

"Give her my best."

"Always." Dillon smiled.

Lucy leaned back and immediately her mind returned
to the crime scenes.

Cold.

Calculating.

Planned.

You don't matter.

That's what the killer thought. The victims don't matter. They're not important. They're nobody.

They're not important. The murders are not important. Then why? Is this really a thrill killer? Someone who kills just because it's fun? Then why the theatrics? Why the beating? The duct tape? The Taser burns? None of that led to death.

It was an act, Lucy thought. The idea grew on her.

The murders were an act, the crime scene the stage, the killer the writer, the actor, the director.

If it's an act, who is the show for?

CHAPTER THIRTEEN

Wednesday Morning

Lucy and Jerry had an appointment with William Peterson, Steven James's boss, first thing Wednesday morning. At seventy-eight years of age, he no longer worked on accounts, but served on the board and came into the office four mornings a week.

William was physically fit and played both tennis and golf, as evidenced from photos and trophies in his immaculate glass office overlooking downtown San Antonio and the Riverwalk.

"Detective, I hope this meeting is good news."

Jerry introduced Lucy, and they sat down in the informal sitting area next to his desk where four comfortable leather chairs faced one another. "We're still gathering information and weeding through witness statements, sir, but it's been a difficult case because of the lack of physical evidence."

"I read a disturbing news report that there was another victim. And his wife is pregnant?"

"Yes, sir."

William sighed, removed his glasses, and took a moment. Lucy didn't know if he was praying or simply trying to absorb the tragic news.

He gathered himself and said, "What else can I do for you? Anything, though I don't know how I can help."

"Just a couple of follow-up questions," Jerry said. "Initially, we believed that the victims were random, that they may have been killed spontaneously. However, we are exploring the idea that the killer knew the victims' schedules, where they would be and when. Who had access to Mr. James's schedule?"

William stared at him. "You think one of *my* people could have done this?"

"That's not what I'm saying. But someone may have known when he would land at the airport, and either they knew his route home and were waiting, or they followed him from the airport."

"Which could still mean it was random."

"Yes, sir. We're not ruling that out. But based on all three cases, we believe that the killer had at least some knowledge of these men's lives and routine."

William said, "Anyone on staff can access anyone else's schedule. It's on a shared system."

"Do you share that information when someone calls in?"

"We would tell clients if someone was out of town, but not their itinerary."

"Mr. James was in California meeting with a client all week? ForceCom?"

"Yes. They are a telecommunications company relocating their billing and customer service departments to Texas from the Silicon Valley. Steven was particularly adept at the complex tax issues that such a move creates."

"And anyone at that company would know that he was there and when he was leaving."

"I suppose. Though there are more than five hundred employees and I doubt that they would all have access to the information. I still don't understand what you're getting at."

"That a limited number of people could have known when he was returning from his trip. It's a finite pool, and a pool we can question."

That wasn't plausible, but if they had a list of names, they could compare those names with lists created from the other victims and see if anyone matched.

"I see. I will give you the CFO's contact information and you can work with them to find out if there was a security breach."

"I appreciate that."

William took a small moleskin journal from his pocket and made a note.

"George Andres," Jerry said. "He filed a lawsuit against this firm and named Mr. James personally. The suit was dismissed, but it was contentious. Did Mr. Andres threaten anyone here? Specifically Mr. James?"

William shook his head. "He was a thorn in my side for years, but that lawsuit was uncalled for. My attorney wanted me to settle, but I refused—largely on principle. When one frivolous lawsuit gets a settlement, more come. It's a slippery slope, and on this I was willing to take a stand, whatever the cost. We were vindicated. Mr. Andres wrote letters to the editor, to us, to the state and federal licensing boards—but eventually he stopped, and I haven't heard from him in more than a year."

"Did he threaten Mr. James in any way?"

"He threatened everyone he believed crossed him. He threatened lawsuits and bad publicity, but never physical injury. I don't like the man, but I cannot see him killing anyone."

Jerry made the note. "You told me when we first met that Steven didn't have a life insurance policy."

"He didn't feel there was a need. We have a policy that all employees receive one year's salary in the event of death. And his daughter, poor Abby, she was taken care of by her mother."

"What happened to her mother?"

"It was ten years ago—eleven next January, I believe. A weather-related accident coupled with alcohol. Multiple fatalities."

"The first Mrs. James had been drinking?"

"No—another driver. He was killed as well, took Mrs. James and a family of three with him. A tragedy."

"Did you know Mr. James at the time?"

"Only professionally. We'd worked on an audit together for a major corporation with headquarters in multiple states. I learned to admire and respect him through that project, and when he contacted me—and several other companies—about relocating from California, I created a board position for him here. So he would have more than just a job—he would have part of the company. I wanted him that badly. I had hoped . . ." He sighed.

"What, Mr. Peterson?" Lucy prompted.

"I'm semi-retired. I'd planned on having Steven take my position on the board within the next year."

"Could anyone have been upset about that?" Lucy asked. "Someone who might have wanted the position or felt they were better qualified?"

"No one was better qualified. And everyone here knew when I hired him eight years ago that I was grooming him. Except maybe Steven himself. He could be . . . oblivious at times. Not in his job, of course. He was meticulous. But he didn't come here to replace me. He came here because it was a good position doing what he liked, and he missed his wife. He thought it would be easier for him and Abby to adjust if he started fresh."

It had been a long shot—especially since the promotion wasn't imminent—but it was worth asking.

William continued. "Steven was a brilliant accountant. A good man. And his world revolved around his daughter. She'd been having nightmares after her mother died, and the move seemed to be good for her."

"So the first Mrs. James had a large life insurance policy."

"I wouldn't know. But you do know who her family was?"

"No."

"Bridget's maiden name was O'Connell. Her family was from Montecito, a wealthy community near Santa Barbara. They had old money, back to turn-of-the-century holdings. Land, mostly. Steven explained once, but I honestly don't remember the details. I know that Bridget was the only heir. There are other branches of the family, but Bridget's parents, when they died, left her millions. Her estate was vast, and half of it went into a charitable family trust, and the other half went to Abby. My partner, Joyce Witherspoon, specializes in estate planning, and while Abby's trust is managed by a law firm in California, Steven hired Joyce to audit the trust. The last report on Abby's trust was that it had grown to over fifteen million dollars."

"They don't live lavishly," Lucy said. "They have a nice home in a good area and Abby goes to a private school, but they don't live like they're worth millions."

"Of course not—Steven was frugal. And he felt strongly that it was Abby's money. They lived on his and his wife's salaries. And Abby can't touch her funds until she's twenty-one, except for schooling and a small monthly allowance."

"Does Steven's death change any of the terms of Abby's trust?" Lucy asked.

"No. We manage her estate, but we don't control the funds."

"I don't see how that works," Jerry said.

"We oversee the accounts. Audit regularly, make sure the funds are invested conservatively. That was the way Steven set it up—he was not a bull in the marketplace. He believed in the tried-and-true method of steady growth, and our clients loved him for it. But Joyce knows far more about the estate than I do. I would suggest you talk to her."

"Is she available now?" Jerry asked.

"I'll walk you down to her office and we'll talk to her secretary." He rose. "You don't think that Steven's death had anything to do with Abby's inheritance?"

"We haven't ruled anything out," Jerry said.

Lucy couldn't imagine that a trust that couldn't be accessed until Abby was twenty-one was the motive behind Steven James's death . . . especially when there were two similar murders.

But like Jerry said, they hadn't ruled anything out. And greed was always a powerful motivator.

Joyce Witherspoon was in a client meeting, but her assistant set up an appointment with them for tomorrow morning. Might be nothing, but investigations were often baby steps. Checking out everything to see where it might lead.

Jerry drove to Helotes, a suburb west of San Antonio, where George Andres lived. Lucy's last case had brought her out here, and she'd become familiar with the area.

"I was reading over Andres's cases last night," Jerry said. "He won a civil suit against a restaurant for food poisoning sixteen years ago, cleared a quarter million dollars. Since, he's spent at least that on nine different lawsuits, seven of which were thrown out, one he settled out of court for an undisclosed amount, and one went to trial and he lost."

"It's like he won one case and is looking for reasons to sue."

"Or he's just a jerk. Defending lawsuits is expensive and takes a lot of time. That's why so many companies settle. They weigh the cost of settlement with the cost of fighting."

"But that increases the number of lawsuits," Lucy said. "If each case was decided solely on the merits of the case, and not settled just because it's cheaper than going to court, fewer frivolous lawsuits would be filed."

"Tell that to the lawyers and insurance companies," Jerry mumbled.

George Andres lived at the end of a cul-de-sac in a fifteen-year-old development. Bikes and basketball hoops over garage doors told the story of a family neighborhood. Though Lucy wasn't enamored with the architecture or tract-home feel where every house looked the same with slight color variations, she could appreciate the safe community, the cheaper properties filled with growing families, and the good schools.

George Andres certainly didn't fit the profile of a resident. He was divorced, in his fifties, and as soon as Lucy stepped onto his porch, she had a feeling he might have the personality of Mr. Wilson without the nice wife.

There was literally a sign at the edge of the property that said:

STAY OFF THE GRASS

Another sign leading up the walk:

PROTECTED BY A-WATCH SECURITY

And of course the standard plaque over the doorbell:

NO SOLICITORS

The yard was immaculate—expertly trimmed trees, the

ground half rock and drought-resistant plants, the other half a perfectly manicured lawn. His car wasn't in the driveway, but a man like this would probably store it in the garage.

They approached the door. In the corner was a security camera. "Who is this guy?" Jerry said.

He knocked on the door, then held his badge up to the camera.

A moment later the door opened. They could barely see Andres with the security screen.

"Mr. Andres?"

"Yes. Who are you?"

Jerry showed him his badge. "Investigator Jerome Walker, Bexar County Sheriff's Office. This is FBI Special Agent Lucy Kincaid. We'd like to talk to you for a minute."

"About what?"

"Steven James."

"You'll need to talk to my lawyer. The lawsuit against Mr. James was erroneously dismissed last year."

"We're not here about the lawsuit. We're here about Mr. James's murder."

"Saw that on the news. That has nothing to do with me."

"We just have a few questions."

"I have nothing to say. If you have questions, you can send them to my lawyer and then I'll answer them."

This was ridiculous. Could this disagreeable man have killed Steven James in cold blood? Planned it? Probably. Executed it? Lucy didn't think so. But she knew better than to judge a killer on the surface.

"Mr. Andres," she said with a half smile, "we truly only have a few questions, and attorneys are expensive. It doesn't cost us anything but time, but for you it could be pricey."

"Not if I sue you for false accusations!"

"We haven't accused you of anything. We simply want to understand what led up to your lawsuit and whether you harbor ill will toward Mr. James."

"Because he's dead," he said flatly.

"Yes."

He grunted. "At least you're honest."

"I'm not going to lie to you, Mr. Andres. In fact, we could clear everything up in five minutes right now so that our bosses will be satisfied we've done due diligence, or I can tie up your lawyers for days responding to questions. It's your decision."

"Five minutes. And if I don't like the direction of the conversation, then it's over."

"Fair enough. May we come in?"

She wanted to look at where he lived, what he did with his time.

"You have to take off your shoes in the foyer."

"Well, for shitsake," Jerry mumbled.

"We can talk outside," Andres said.

"We are happy to take off our shoes," Lucy said with a smile.

Jerry grumbled again but left his boots in the foyer. He wore black socks with bucking broncos. Lucy grinned at him. He glared at her. Andres was oblivious.

They sat in the formal dining room. The house was sparsely furnished and very clean. No carpets, only tile—which was nice in the hot summers, but with no carpet why take off their shoes? To each his own, Lucy thought.

A portrait over the mantel showed Andres and his family. For a moment Lucy felt sorry for him. He had once been married, and his wife was lovely—he also had two girls. In the picture they were about three and five. They would likely be in college, or older, now. Had he always been this way or had his cleanliness and suspicion grown since the divorce? His picture was formal, but he was smiling and looked almost happy. Unlike the sour fifty-year-old who sat in front of them now with thinning gray hair perfectly gelled back.

"Five minutes," Andres said.

Jerry was uncomfortable here. He seemed almost afraid to touch anything. Lucy smiled at Andres. "We reviewed your lawsuit and saw that it was dismissed by the judge. According to records, there was a verbal altercation between you and Mr. Peterson after the judge's statement, and Mr. James intervened on the behalf of his employer."

"I'm positive he bribed the judge. I can't prove it."

"It would be difficult to prove," she said, humoring him.

"Exactly. Especially with cash."

"Did you have any contact with Mr. James after that day in court?"

"No. He sent a courier to return my files. I want nothing to do with Allied or anyone there."

"Fair enough. So you haven't seen Mr. James, even in passing. At a store or restaurant?"

"No."

"According to DMV records you own a 2017 Lexus."

"Yes."

"Do you own or drive any other vehicles?"

"No."

"What do you do for a living, Mr. Andres?" He was home on a Wednesday morning, which was odd.

"I worked for a telecommunications company until last March when a workplace accident required me to go out on disability."

"I'm so sorry."

He seemed surprised by her empathy, and nodded his appreciation of her concern.

"Were you home Friday night?"

"No."

She wasn't expecting that answer.

"What were you doing?"

"Is it important?"

"Yes."

"Is this the last question?"

"It depends on your answer."

"I was in Baton Rouge this weekend. My youngest daughter is a freshman at LSU and it was parents' weekend. I drove out there Friday morning, returned Sunday afternoon."

He looked over her shoulder to the portrait Lucy knew to be on the wall. She glanced at it, too. When she looked back at him, she felt pity. This was a man who'd lost his family long ago, and probably didn't even know why.

"Your family is lovely. What is your daughter studying?"

"She hasn't decided. She's very bright and has talked about law school. My oldest daughter is in her last year at Texas A and M. We fully expect her to graduate magna cum laude in biochemistry."

"You should be very proud."

"If that is all?"

"Where did you stay in Baton Rogue?"

"Embassy Suites downtown."

"Thank you for your time."

He walked them to the door. Jerry struggled to pull on his boots while standing. Lucy stepped into hers, zipped up the sides, and shook Andres's hand. It was soft—extremely soft. There were no bruises, no cuts, no calluses.

This was not a man who could have pummeled a man to death or shot him in the face.

They left and Jerry sped off. "Piece of work."

"I feel sorry for him."

"His alibi will be easy enough to verify. Dead end."

"You didn't think he was the killer, did you?"

"I didn't know what to think. Take my boots off. Really."

"I like your socks."

He glared at her. "I suppose you did well back there."

"Suppose? Is that your idea of a compliment? If we had to jump through hoops and exchange questions through lawyers, it would take days—if not weeks. We were there for less than fifteen minutes and we know he didn't kill these men."

"Sorry, it should have been a compliment. I reckon I'm just tired of cheaters. A cheating wife, a guy cheating the system."

"Being a cop you see the worst in people—but sometimes the best."

He sighed. "Usually the worst. At least it's a line to scratch off, but it doesn't bring us any closer to finding out who did this."

They returned to BCSO and went to the cafeteria to eat lunch, fortunately missing the rush. By the time they were done, Carl Franklin was in the building. Jerry was surprised when the deputy told him.

"What happened when you went to his place?"

"I found him at work—he's an electrician. I did exactly what you said—told him that you needed to talk to him about the Standish homicide, at his convenience, and would he prefer to come in this afternoon or have you come out? He said he'd come in right away—I think he thinks that you've solved it."

"Good work," Jerry said. "What about Johns?"

"He's out of town."

"Convenient," Lucy said.

"He works for a computer company and has been installing cable up in Amarillo for the last two weeks. Doesn't get back until Saturday. The owner said that he's happy to send you his work schedule if you need it. He does have a record—served three months in jail for a second DUI after crashing his car into a fence. Boss said he's been sober ever since."

"Get his work records—when he was on and off. It's nearly sixteen hours round trip," Jerry said. "Be difficult to manage without someone wondering where he was. Also find his contact information. Even if we confirm his alibi, I want to talk to him."

"I'm on it, sir," the deputy said. "Mr. Franklin is in interview two."

"Thanks."

Lucy followed Jerry down the hall. He knocked, then entered the room. Carl Franklin was a pleasant-looking man with a thick five-o'clock shadow, rough hands that said he worked hard with them—but no visible cuts or scrapes. He stood when they entered, his baseball cap in his hands.

"Thank you for coming down," Jerry said. "This is FBI Agent Lucy Kincaid. We're working together to find out what happened to your friend, and two other men who were more recently killed."

"I saw the news. Are you sure it's the same guy?"

"Yes."

"The media is saying it's a serial killer. We don't have serial killers in San Antonio."

That certainly wasn't true. The area had just as many notorious killers as most cities.

"Mr. Franklin," Jerry said using a fatherly tone, "when I talked to you nearly two months ago, after Billy was killed, you said you didn't know anyone who would have wanted him dead. You were upset, said you were his best friend."

"I was—we were friends in high school, but in a large group. Over the years, you know, people go, but Billy and I stayed close. He was a good guy."

"I believe that. He did have a few problems with his drinking."

"Yes, sir, he did, but he wasn't a mean drunk. Like I said, the bar fights were usually over stupid shi—stuff, like football. Nobody disses his Cowboys, you know?"

"Right. And I confirmed that with the people involved in the altercations. Did you know that Billy had a life insurance policy?"

"A what? Well, I don't know that I knew, but I'm sure he did."

"Why? It seems odd that a twenty-nine-year-old would have a life insurance policy."

"'Cause his dad owns an insurance business. He sells life insurance, so I'd guess he told Billy after he got married that he should have some."

That was easy to verify, Lucy thought.

"Do you know how much the policy was for?"

"No, why?"

Jerry didn't answer the question. Instead he asked, "You and Billy were good friends. You probably talked about things, right?"

"Sure. We hung out a lot, though he's been working in Houston a lot over the last year so, you know, not as much."

"You're not married, right?"

"No, sir. I had a girl that I asked, but she didn't want to get married and up and left town to go to college, though she was twenty-five. I haven't found the one, you know?" He smiled awkwardly, glanced at Lucy, then looked down as if he was embarrassed.

"You talk to Billy about your girl troubles?"

"Sure, I guess."

"And does he talk to you about his girl troubles?"

"Billy? He's married, he don't really have girl troubles."

But he wasn't looking at either of them. He was wringing the cap in his hands.

"Carl," Jerry said, "did Billy ever tell you that he thought his wife was having an affair?"

Carl turned beet red. This guy couldn't lie to save his soul, Lucy thought. "Uh, no, sir."

"Do you know if Susan was having an affair?"

"Susie?" His voice rose an octave.

"Billy's wife."

"I—I—well, you know, I—might have—a couple times—I just, I like Susie, and Billy sometimes is so busy, and it didn't mean anything, I mean, it did, I really like her, but she's Billy's girl, and I told her we couldn't continue, and we didn't, but then we was drinking and Billy was gone all week and it happened again and I felt right bad about it, but Susie said it was fine, Billy wouldn't know, because I love Billy like my brother, and I know I shouldn't have, but Susie is so dang pretty, and she's all alone out there in the middle of nowhere."

"I see," Jerry said.

"How long did the affair last?" Lucy asked.

"Affair?" His voice rose again. "It was just, well, a few times."

"When was the last time?"

He blushed an even deeper red and couldn't look Lucy in the face. He turned to Jerry. "Last weekend—well, she was so upset on Saturday, after she heard about the murder on the news, that she called me and I went over to console her and you know, it happened again."

"And Billy had no idea," Jerry said.

"No, sir. I feel real bad about it."

"Do you know if Susan had any other special friends?" Jerry asked.

"She had a lot of friends, everyone loves Susie—oh. You mean, like, friends with benefits."

"Yes."

"I'm sure not. She wasn't that kind of girl. She's a sweetheart, really. She teaches kindergarten, you know, and she's so good with the kids."

"You can't think of anyone else that Susie had a relationship with—other than you or her husband."

He shook his head, eyes wide. "Really, no. Why?"

"We're looking for a motive. There doesn't seem to be any reason for anyone to kill Billy, yet he's dead. And we learned this week that his wife was having a few affairs."

"A few? Like, for reals?"

"Yes, Carl, for real. And you're telling me you didn't know about any other men in Susan's life—maybe someone who wanted Susan all to himself."

"And kill Billy? No, no! That would be insane."

"And Billy never said anything to you about suspecting his wife was having an affair."

"No, no, never."

"Just for our notes, where were you this last Friday evening? Say, from eight until midnight?"

"I did a job out in Bandera that ended about six, then I went to this cowboy bar out there with some old friends, stayed until nine, was starving, so drove over to my grandma's house in Kerrville—it was sort of on the way home— and she is the best cook ever. Crashed there 'cause I knew I shouldn't be drinking, and my grams has this great still for moonshine. I had nowhere to be."

"When did Susan call you about the third victim?" Lucy asked.

"I was back in town, at my house—maybe five or six. She said she just saw a news segment and was freaking out, so I went over and, you know, stayed for a while."

His alibi would be easy enough to check out. But more than that, Lucy didn't see this guy as a killer. This all couldn't be an act.

The crime scene was a stage, the killer acting . . . acting like what? A serial killer?

The thought came, rattled around in her head, then faded away. Maybe the killer was an actor, maybe he was playing out a movie in his head with himself as the villain, taunting the cops. But Lucy just didn't think Carl Franklin was the guy they were looking for. And by the expression on Jerry's face, neither did he.

CHAPTER FOURTEEN

Wednesday Afternoon

Their coach called a five-minute water break and Jesse welcomed the breather after the intense footwork drill they'd just finished. Out of the corner of his eye he saw Brian talk to Coach, then grab his gear and leave.

Jesse walked over and asked, "Coach, where's Brian going?"

"Said something about a school project, but he knows he's supposed to tell me before practice."

"I gotta go."

"Not you, too, Rogan."

"I'll be right back."

Coach didn't look happy. He looked at his watch. "I'll give you ten minutes, if you're not back, you're hoofing an extra mile."

"Yes, sir."

Jesse pulled his phone out of his bag and called Michael as he followed the path Brian had taken to the other side of the park.

"Yeah," Michael said.

"I need you here. Practice. Brian just left."

"Shit. Okay, I'm coming. Where?"

"He's heading toward the west entrance."

"I'll be there in five minutes."

"It's fifteen minutes even if you run."

"I'm taking Father Mateo's car."

"You don't have your license."

"Sister Ruth is at the store, Father is doing some devotional thing at the church, no one will know. Just shut up about it." He hung up and Jesse fumed. Michael was going to get into serious trouble.

Fortunately, the park wasn't far from St. Catherine's, but Jesse didn't want Michael to get caught. What if he was wrong? What if Brian really did have a school project to do? They were on a select soccer team and practices were rigorous, but school came first. Coach expected good grades and if you got anything less than a C in any class, or lower than a 2.5 GPA, you were off the team.

Brian was standing in the parking lot on his phone. "Brian," Jesse said when he caught up with him.

Brian looked scared. "What the hell?"

"Why'd you leave?"

"It's none of your fucking business, Jess."

"It is if you lied to the coach."

"Go away. Please, just go back to practice."

"What are you into?"

"Nothing! Shit, Jesse, just leave me the fuck alone."

The same dark sedan Jesse had seen outside of the gang house pulled into the parking lot. Brian looked momentarily panicked, then hissed, "Get out of here *now*."

"I know what's going on, Brian." Jesse didn't, but he and Michael were guessing it had everything to do with his brother. "You found your brother—or your brother found you. But he's in a gang, Brian. You can't do this."

"You don't know what you're talking about."

Three gangbangers got out of the car. They all had tattoos, probably gang tats though Jesse couldn't really tell what was what. He was scared. But he stood with Brian.

"Who's your friend, Bri?" one of the guys said.

"Just on my team," Brian mumbled.

"You have a name, kid?"

Jesse didn't respond.

"Let's go," Brian said and started toward the car.

"Don't leave practice," Jesse said, not knowing exactly what he should say or do. He didn't know if Michael would be able to help. He should have called Sean. Why didn't he call Sean? But Sean was at least twenty minutes away, maybe more in traffic. Why did he think he could handle this on his own? He was in way over his head.

"Just go, Jess."

"Jess," the guy said. He put his arm around Brian. "A friend of yours?"

"From soccer, Jose. He's nobody."

"Nobody's a nobody. You want to come?" Jose asked Jesse.

"I don't want Brian to get in trouble for leaving in the middle of practice." He sounded a lot tougher than he felt.

Jose and the others laughed. "Told you to quit the team, Bri. Who needs this shit? Be here, be there, do this shit, do that shit." He looked Jesse up and down and smiled. But there was nothing friendly about the grin. *This* was Brian's brother? He looked mean as they came. But not as mean as his two friends who were circling around Jesse.

"*Tal vez deberíamos iniciar al chico blanco, darle una lección que no olvidará,*" one of the others said and they all laughed.

"Don't, Jose," Brian said. "Jess, go back to practice."

"He a *soplón, amigo*?"

"No," Brian said. "Just a *niñito. Vamos, vamos, José.*"

"Settle down, kid," Jose said. "Shit, you're antsy. What's the problem? He trouble? He looks like trouble."

"Let's just go. I have to be back by seven."

"Really. You still have a fucking curfew?"

"Come on, don't."

Brian glanced at Jesse and he saw fear in Brian's eyes. Fear and worry and confusion and Jesse couldn't let him get into the car with these guys. What were they doing? It was four thirty on Wednesday afternoon and they convinced Brian to leave soccer? For what? Brian loved soccer. He said soccer was his ticket out of here and he might have a chance to go to college.

"You'll get back when I say so," Jose said. "Get in the car."

"No," Jesse said. His heart was beating so hard he almost didn't hear himself speak.

Then he saw a gun tucked in the waistband of one of the gangbangers.

"Stop, Jesse. Please," Brian pleaded with him.

Jose walked up to Jesse and stood in his face. "What you looking at, punk? You one of those kids at his group home?" He looked him up and down. "Nah, you're just a pussy. Why you hanging around with pussies like Jess, Bri?"

Jose sucker-punched Jesse in the stomach, grabbed him by the neck, and hit him again. Jesse couldn't talk if he wanted to. Tears burned behind his eyes. He hated that he was scared, hated fearing he was going to die. Hated that he felt helpless and that he couldn't fight back.

"You stay out of my fucking business or I'll gut you, you fucking pussy. I see you again, you're ended. Stay away from my brother."

He pushed Jesse to his knees. Jesse fell over. His chest hurt and he couldn't move if he wanted. He looked up as Brian climbed into the car and the four of them drove off, burning rubber as they left.

He took a deep breath. Damn, he hurt. He didn't want to go back to practice. But he had to. He had to go back. He couldn't help Brian, and he was scared. What if Brian never went back to St. Catherine's? What if he joined Jose's gang? What if they made him do something he couldn't come back from?

Jesse forced himself to sit up, but he needed to catch his breath. He was shaking so hard he put his head between his knees. He wished he'd fought back. Wished he had the courage that his dad and Uncle Kane had.

"Jesse. Jess!"

He looked up. Michael had in fact taken Father Mateo's car. He parked right in front of Jesse and jumped out.

"What happened?" Michael demanded.

"He left with them."

"What are you talking about?"

"Brian. He left with Jose and two other gangbangers in the brown Chevelle. They had guns. Tattoos. I don't know what they meant, but they were on their arms and necks and they just . . . I don't know. Brian's scared, I know he is. He looked scared, but he still left with them."

"What happened to you? You're hurt."

"I'm fine."

"You're not fine."

Jesse shook his head. He would *not* cry. "Jose punched me. I wasn't expecting it." He tried to breathe deeply and it hurt.

"This has to end."

"And what about Brian? He'll be put in the system. He'll run. We can't—we can't let him go into the system."

"Of course not. I'm going to confront him tonight. You need to be there."

"He doesn't want to see me."

"He has to see you. He has to see that we're united."

Jesse looked up at Michael. He remembered everything Brian had said, and wondered if it was true. If Michael was just humoring him.

"Maybe it should just be you, Michael. He'll listen to you."

"You know that game *good cop, bad cop*?"

"What?" Michael wasn't making any sense.

"I am the bad cop. I have to tell him the truth. You need to be his friend."

"He doesn't like me. He doesn't want me around."

"Of course he likes you. Everyone likes you. Remember what I told you last week? Family makes us weak. He's weak around Jose, but he will listen to me. We have to be united, Jesse. You and me. And he needs to know that if he doesn't cut ties with Jose, we will go to Sean. We will go to Kane. Kane will come if I call."

Michael put out his hand and helped Jesse up. Jesse winced. "Are you sure you're okay?" Michael asked him.

"Yeah." He walked around and stretched. It hurt, but he needed to go back to practice. "Michael, what if Brian wants to leave . . . but Jose won't let him? What if he's already threatened Saint Catherine's?"

"Did you hear anything?"

"He knows about the house. Called it a group home. He might know who everyone is." He jogged in place and winced again. Damn, he was sore.

"You're really hurt."

"Just bruised. I'll be fine."

"You should tell Sean."

"Tell him what?"

Michael didn't say anything.

"That's what I thought."

"Tonight, can you get out?"

Jesse just stared at him. "Yeah. Right. Escape Sean's fortress."

"Make an excuse."

"Okay. I'll think of something. But I don't know that Brian will be back at seven. Jose thinks his curfew is stupid."

"When he comes home, I'll call Sean, tell him I need help in math. He'll come, you tag along."

"Fine," Jesse said. "Get Mateo's car back before anyone notices it's gone. You're not even fifteen. How do you even know how to drive?"

"We learned a lot of things when we were slaves."

CHAPTER FIFTEEN

Wednesday Evening

Lucy had considered walking to the James house—it was only a few blocks away—but figured that wasn't professional. This wasn't a social call; it was an interview. So when Jerry offered to pick her up, she agreed.

He was early, and Lucy invited him in. He took off his hat and looked around. "Nice place."

"Thank you."

Bandit bounded down the stairs. Lucy was surprised it took him so long. He greeted Jerry with a frantically wagging tail. Jerry stooped over and scratched the golden retriever's ears. "Fierce watchdog, I see."

"The fiercest," Lucy agreed.

He walked over to the picture that took up the center of the dining room wall. Sean had commissioned it—a shot of their cabin outside Vail, Colorado, on their honeymoon, taken from a drone. She and Sean were standing on their deck just after sunrise, about to kiss, Bandit at their side. The colors were so vibrant, and the peace radiating from the photo calmed her in ways she couldn't explain.

"Colorado?" he asked.

"Yes. That's where we went on our honeymoon."

"Newlyweds."

"I guess. Almost a year."

Sean walked in from his office. "Hello—Jerry, right?"

"You must be the computer expert husband."

"That's me. Sean Rogan."

"We have a few minutes before we're expected, would you like coffee?" Lucy asked. "I made a pot."

"Sounds good."

The three of them went into the kitchen. Sean pulled out a beer. "I'd offer you one, but you're working," he said.

"Rain check?"

Sean smiled. "Anytime."

Sean was being friendly. Was he assessing Walker? More info through kindness? Did he know something that Lucy didn't? Though Leo hadn't gotten back to her with any information about Walker's previous cases with the FBI, Sean was resourceful that way. But he would have told her.

Lucy poured coffee, doctored hers, and handed Jerry his mug black. They sat at the island and Sean leaned against the counter.

"I called Marissa Garcia's sister," Jerry said. "We're meeting them tomorrow morning, at Sandra's house. She convinced Marissa to stay with her for a while. The funeral is Saturday. I just don't think we're going to get anything from her. I talked to Garcia's boss, there's been no problems at work. Maybe we talk to his colleagues in the kitchen, but it feels like a long shot. We have nothing. We have a cheating spouse, a wealthy teenager, and a grieving pregnant woman. Maybe there're individual motives, but one singular motive?" He shook his head. "I don't see it."

"I talked to my brother last night."

"The army brother?"

"Another brother. Dr. Dillon Kincaid, a forensic psychiatrist who consults with the FBI. He has credentials a mile long, but more important, he's the smartest guy I know."

"Hey," Sean said with a mock frown.

Lucy blew him a kiss. "I really think we should officially consult with the BSU. I know you don't hold much weight with psychology, but Dillon knows what he's doing."

"Lucy," Jerry said, shaking his head. "I may be stymied now, but in no case that I've worked has psychological profiling given me anything that good police work didn't. And we talked about this—I'm not going to be diverted from an organized investigation chasing down some rabbit hole because a shrink says the killer is a one-armed man with daddy issues."

She resisted calling him on his bias. With as much calm as she could muster, she said, "Just today we used psychology—psychological profiling in action. With George Andres. I assessed him and found a way to get him to talk. And you, with Carl Franklin, getting him to spill everything without so much as breaking a sweat because you could read him."

"That's police work. Knocking on doors and asking questions and assessing witnesses and suspects right in front of us."

"Andres would never have talked to you, and I think you know it. And I don't think Carl would have been as forthcoming about his affair with me, a woman, because he was embarrassed."

"You have a way with people, I'll give you that, but that's being a good cop—not a shrink who pulls things out of the air just because it sounds good."

"If you just—"

"No. Because we talk to him and if I disagree with his

assessment he'll pull rank and you'll ice me out. I'm not walking away from this investigation."

"Dillon can't. He's not FBI. He's a private consultant who is authorized to work with the FBI. I can make the call, it'll be—"

"No. Every damn time the head shrinks come in they screw things up. Your brother's probably a good guy, might be smarter than anyone I know, but I don't trust your process. This isn't against you, Lucy. I've liked working with you, you're sharp as a tack. But I'm not giving up control to some shrink who isn't on the ground, who hasn't interviewed witnesses, who is looking at pictures and reports and making some academic determination that the killer is a white male between the ages of thirty-five and forty-five whose daddy beat him with his belt."

Lucy was trying to keep her blood from boiling over. "That is not profiling. I talked through the case with Dillon. I thought about it yesterday, after watching Ash's simulations, but talking through it with Dillon, I realized this is theater. A show. The killer is setting the stage. The real question is for who? For the victims? The survivors? The police? It's an act, every time, yet he's compelled to make sure the end looks the same, even the victim who died with the first blow."

"Nonsense."

"We're missing something and having an objective eye will help." Lucy glanced at Sean, who was watching the exchange while biting his tongue. She was grateful he didn't interfere.

"Then I'll bring in a task force of objective cops to look at the evidence again. But no way in hell am I turning this case over to the FBI. And if you have a problem with that, you can walk away, because this is still my jurisdiction, and your boss already promised they wouldn't pull rank and take the case. That's the only reason you're tagging along."

That made her angry. "I'm doing more than *tagging along*," she snapped.

"That's not how I meant it."

"Yes it was. I am going to finish this out. I'm not walking away because you're being a jerk."

She was stunned that she had actually said that.

"I didn't think you would, but we're still not calling the shrinks."

She was getting nowhere with him. She thought for sure that Dillon being *not* FBI would be a bonus, that Jerry would listen.

She grabbed her gun, badge, and phone off the small kitchen desk and said, "It's nearly seven thirty. We'd better go."

Abigail James was a tall girl who looked like she'd suddenly grown six inches and didn't quite know what to do with her body. She sat awkwardly at the formal dining table in sweats and a volleyball T-shirt with her high school emblazoned across the front in green and gold, her long blond hair braided down the back, still damp from a recent shower.

"Teri said you had some questions for me. About my dad."

"Yes," Jerry said. "I hope that's okay. We know that this situation is difficult."

"It's okay," she said. She picked at her fingernails, which were all short. "I just—I don't know who could do something like this to my dad."

"We're putting together a time line of your father's days and weeks leading up to his murder. The weekend before he left for his business trip, what did you do?"

"We went shopping for school supplies—school started Monday. He had to go on the business trip—he wanted to reschedule it, but I told him it was fine. He postponed it a day so he could be here when I got back from my first day at high school. Dad never really liked shopping. I told him we could order everything online, but he wanted to make a day of it."

She looked off, not really focusing on them.

Teri took her stepdaughter's hand and squeezed. "He always did what we wanted to do, even if it made him uncomfortable. Hold on to those memories, sweetheart."

Abby nodded. "We had fun. Went shopping all morning, had lunch, did some more shopping. Sunday we hung around the house."

She got up and walked across the room, looked at a photograph of her, her dad, and Teri on the hutch. "I just wish I had more time with him." She looked down at her hands and took a deep breath and slowly let it out.

"Abby," Lucy said, "did your dad say anything to you during your day together that you were concerned about?"

"I don't understand." She turned back to face them, but didn't sit down. "We just—it was just like always. Dad was a good listener. But he didn't say anything was bothering him."

"We believe that whoever killed your dad might have followed him. That he knew where your father would be and when."

"Like, that he was coming back from a business trip?" she asked.

"Exactly. And sometimes when people are followed, they have a feeling that they're being watched, even if they don't see anyone."

"My dad didn't say anything about that. We talked about high school—I'm a freshman—and I talked to him about volleyball. Tryouts were the week before school started, and I made the team. He was happy about it—my dad doesn't really get sports. He was all about numbers.

He said there was peace in knowing that there was only one possible answer, that two plus two would always equal four. But he promised to come to all my games and said I'd have to explain the rules to him. But then—I saw he'd bought a book about volleyball and took it with him on his trip."

The more Abby talked, the more upset Lucy became. Someone had taken a good father from his daughter. The unfairness to the tragedy just hit her. Maybe because Jesse was about the same age and he, too, had lost a parent.

"Did your father ever mention to you about feeling threatened or scared? That maybe someone was angry with him? It might not have been about work," Jerry added. "Maybe a neighbor or someone at church or the store."

"Dad didn't go to church," Abby said. "And really, everyone liked my dad, but he didn't socialize a lot. He liked working and he liked being home."

"Outside of your family, who knows that your mother left you with a sizable trust?"

Both Teri and Abby were surprised by that question. Teri said, "What does Abby's trust have to do with this?"

"We don't know that it has anything to do with this case, but it's one more angle we have to look at," Jerry said. "It's our understanding that the trust can't be touched, aside from a monthly allowance, until Abby is twenty-one—even in the event of her father's death."

"That is true," Teri said.

"Why would someone k-kill my dad for my money? They can't get it—I can't even get it. I don't want it. If I could have my dad back, they could have all my money, I don't care about any of it!"

Teri looked over at Abby, then back to Jerry and Lucy. "Deputy, it seems that this line of questions is not getting anyone anywhere. It's clear to me that my husband's mur-

der was a random act of violence, or someone's sick head.
You're upsetting Abby."

"I'm okay," Abby said. "Really. I want to find out what
happened. I want to know. I miss him so much and it
doesn't seem fair."

"It isn't fair," Lucy said. "And we will find out what
happened to your dad. I'd like to show you both a few pictures. If you can tell me if you have ever seen these people
before."

"Are they suspects?" Teri asked. "Are you actually
showing my daughter suspects?"

"No. But they may be connected to Steven's death. We
just don't know how yet."

Jerry looked at Lucy oddly. She hadn't discussed this
with him because she'd just formulated the idea this afternoon.

"I want to," Abby said. She sat back down, closer to
Lucy so she could more easily see the pictures.

Teri sighed. "Very well."

Lucy had photos of everyone involved, even remotely,
on her phone. She quickly added them all to one folder,
skipping Steven James's photo, and then turned her phone
to show Abby. Teri stood behind her stepdaughter to see
better. Lucy started with Susan Standish.

No reaction.

She went through Susan's two current lovers, then her
onetime lover from Baton Rouge. Then Billy Joe Standish.
"I saw him on the news," Teri said. "He was killed before
Steven. The reporter said it might be the same person."

"Yes," Lucy said. She flipped to his friend Joey Adkins.
Nothing.

She showed George Andres, Julio Garcia, and Marissa
Garcia.

"Wait," Abby said.

Lucy's heart skipped a beat.

"Go back."

She did, and Abby looked carefully at the picture of Julio Garcia. She bit her lip. "He looks familiar but I don't know why."

Teri studied the picture. "We saw it on the news this weekend." She turned to Lucy and Jerry. "That must have been it."

"I guess," Abby said.

"Think, Abby. Do you recognize him? Other than seeing his picture on the television?"

"I—I don't know. Maybe. But . . ." She shrugged.

Lucy didn't want to push her too hard because sometimes memories could be led down the wrong path. If she recognized him, Lucy hoped that it would come to her, but she decided to push a little.

"He was a chef at a hotel on the Riverwalk. The Sun Tower. Do you go to the Riverwalk?"

"All the time," Abby said. "Well, I used to. My dad's office is down there on West Guadalupe. Sometimes after school I'd meet him and we'd go for ice cream. My dad was so serious all the time, but he loved ice cream. Mint chocolate chip was his favorite."

Her voice was strong, but tears burned in her eyes.

Lucy pulled the phone back. "If you think of anything, please call us." She slid over her card.

"Wait," Abby said. "I've seen him."

Lucy looked down at her phone as her screen faded. She pressed the HOME button and turned the phone to Abby. "Him?"

"Yes, like all the time. He walks a dog."

Teri stared. "Are you saying my husband's killer is a neighbor?"

"No," Lucy said. "This is my husband. We live a few blocks over. We have a golden retriever."

Abby smiled. "I thought I recognized you, too," she said, "but I wasn't sure. You run sometimes in the park."

"Not as much as I should. My San Diego–raised body doesn't like running in Texas humidity."

"I was born in California. In Santa Barbara."

"Beautiful up there."

"Do you miss San Diego?" Abby asked.

"Sometimes. The weather, yes. The beaches. My family. But I like San Antonio." She assessed Abby. "You miss it?"

She shrugged. "I guess sometimes, too. My grandpa died a couple years ago, I never really knew my grandmother. I don't have anyone there but some cousins I don't know who are older than me. And my uncle—my dad's brother—is in the navy, stationed out of San Diego, but he's not there most of the time."

Lucy didn't have in her notes that Steven James even had a brother.

"If that's all?" Teri said. "Abby has school tomorrow, and it's been a long day."

Lucy and Jerry stood, thanked them for their time, and left. Jerry drove Lucy back to her house.

"I hadn't thought of showing photos," he said. "But it didn't get us anywhere. She may have thought Julio looked familiar, but unfortunately, cross-race identification can be sketchy."

"Excuse me?"

"A young white girl may think that all adult Hispanic men look alike. So he looks *familiar* but she never really saw him."

Witness identification was notoriously a problem, and one of the easiest things for lawyers to refute in court.

"Except, he worked less than a mile from where Steven James worked. What if Standish did a job in the same area in the last year? What if somehow the Riverwalk connects the victims?"

"That's a stretch, Lucy."

"Did you talk to Steven's brother?"

"No. He was deployed on a ship somewhere in the Pacific Ocean. He was granted hardship leave for a week and was here for the funeral, but there was no reason to interview him."

"Maybe James called him. Talked to him about whatever was bothering him."

"I'd think the brother would have reached out to us if he knew anything."

"Maybe he doesn't know that he knows something."

He sighed and pulled up in front of her house. "I'll find out where he is and go through the channels to talk to him, but I think it's a waste of time."

"We have to pursue every thread we have until it ends."

"True. We'll show Marissa and her sister the photos, see if they recognize anyone. But at this point, I don't know which end is up in this investigation."

Lucy didn't, either. She wanted to work through the crime scenes again and talk some more to her brother Dillon. But Jerry had put his foot down.

He'd put his foot down at officially bringing in a profiler, but unofficially . . .

Lucy would have to tread carefully.

Because at this rate, they would never solve this crime, and that would increase the chance that there would be another victim.

CHAPTER SIXTEEN

Wednesday Night

Sean was surprised to get a call from Michael at seven thirty. Lucy was in the middle of an interview with her temporary partner—though Sean wasn't sure he liked him much after his piss-poor attitude—and Jesse was in his room. He'd been quiet and sore after soccer. Sean asked if practice was bad, and Jesse simply said, "Tough." He said he wasn't hungry and went to shower and Sean wondered if the coach had yelled at him. Sean had never participated in team sports. His parents never put him in anything, and in high school he was too angry to commit to a team. He just wanted to do his own thing.

The first thing Jesse asked to do when they came back from California after his mother's funeral was to find a soccer team. Brian's team had a position for him, and though it wasn't in the neighborhood, Sean didn't mind driving him to and from. It was a competitive team so they didn't have regional boundaries. Jesse tried out and made it. Sean was so proud of him, and Lucy felt strongly that team sports, especially soccer—which Jesse loved—were a great way for Jesse to adjust to living in a new city as well as make friends with similar interests.

But Sean had never seen him so down after a practice. It had only been a month, but still—Jesse was unusually tired and sullen.

He shook it off and answered Michael's call. "What's up?"

"I need math help. I have a test tomorrow."

"Ask away."

"It's geometry. It's complicated. Father tried to show me, but he made it worse, now I'm completely confused."

St. Catherine's was more than twenty minutes away, and Sean had just been on that side of town picking Jesse up an hour ago. But Michael rarely asked for help in anything, and Sean didn't want to say no. "Okay. I'll come over. Thirty minutes?"

"Thank you." He hung up.

Sean went upstairs to tell Jesse he was going out. "I won't be long—and Lucy should be home in an hour or so."

"I'll come with you."

"You look tired. You should go to bed early."

"I am, but I want to go. Unless you don't want me to come."

Why would he think that? "Of course not. We'll bring Bandit and make it a party."

Jesse got out of bed and winced. A small moan escaped.

"What's wrong?"

"Nothing."

"That's not nothing. Did you get hurt?"

"Just got hit with the ball. I wasn't paying attention and it knocked me down. Totally took the wind out of me. I'm fine, just feel stupid, and the coach yelled at me for not paying attention."

That could explain his moodiness, but Sean wasn't sure. "Maybe Lucy should look you over when she gets home. She's an EMT, and she has a lot of experience taping up bruises and cuts between Kane, Jack, and me."

"I'm fine. I promise. But I'm glad we don't have practice tomorrow."

Sean was still adjusting to this whole parenthood thing, and he didn't want to make something from nothing, but he didn't want to miss something important, either.

Sean was glad he had Jesse's company, even though Jesse wasn't chatty. They pulled up at St. Catherine's, and Michael met them at the door. They went to the family room where Frisco and Tito were playing games. When Bandit saw them, he ran around the couch three times at high speed. Sean whistled and Bandit stopped, then looked up at him with anticipation of playing.

"Can we take him out back?" Frisco asked. "We won't let him get in the pool." Bandit loved to swim, but driving thirty minutes in a car with a wet dog wasn't fun.

"Sure," Sean said, and the two boys grabbed a baseball that was in a basket by the door and ran out with the dog.

Jesse spread out his own homework. Not for the first time, Sean reflected how much he loved his kid. He might not have raised him, but Jess was a Rogan. His son. And he was certainly a better kid than Sean had been. Jess cared about school, he wanted to do well. He played sports, made friends easily, and was friendly. That was because of Madison. Genetics may have played a part in it, but Madison had raised Jesse and he'd turned out well.

Sean wished everything had been different. He loved having Jesse living with him, but not how it happened. In an ideal world, Madison would have left Carson, moved to San Antonio, and bought a house in the same neighborhood so Jesse could have both parents nearby. But he'd lost his mother, and Sean knew exactly how that felt. The burning rage. The deep, unspeakable sorrow.

Sean shook it off. It was foolish to dwell on the past. He had to find a way to move forward, to make sure Jesse felt loved, safe, and happy.

"Here's the study guide," Michael said and handed Sean a green sheet of paper. They went over it for the next thirty minutes. Sean loved math, so it wasn't a hardship for him, and Michael caught on quickly. His problem seemed to be memorizing the formulas because Michael was a kid who had to understand why. Sean had been the same way. So Sean explained why the formulas worked, and gave some history as to how they came about.

Paolo ran in. "I heard you were here, Sean. Can you help me with something?"

"Math?"

"No, the computer isn't working. Please? I have to type this essay for English and I think I lost everything and I don't want to do it again."

Sean glanced at Michael. "You good? Any more questions?"

"I think I understand."

"You'll do fine on the test."

Sean got up and walked out with Paolo. The computer was upstairs in the study area, though most of the boys used the larger family room to do their homework. Paolo was chatty, and Sean sat down to fix the computer, listening to Paolo talk about school and Father Mateo and what he'd had for dinner.

Michael waited until Sean had left the room, then said to Jesse, "Let's go."

"Where?"

"Brian is in Father Mateo's office. He came in an hour late and didn't call. Father is at the hospital giving last rites to a parishioner, and Sister Ruth told him to stay there until Father came home."

"You told Paolo?"

"I had to do something, Jess. When Brian was late, I called a meeting with everyone and told them what was going on. They need to be careful. I can't let Brian's mistakes hurt anyone else. So I messed with the computer and told Paolo to come in at nine and tell Sean something was wrong. We don't have a lot of time—I don't know how long it'll take Sean to fix it."

They walked through the kitchen to the small office in the back of the house. It had its own entrance and looked more like a principal's office than anything—except that there were a bunch of religious things all over, and Jesse noticed a picture on the wall with the boys, Father Mateo, and Sean standing in front of the house. It reminded Jesse that he should have told Sean from the beginning what was going on. It was clear that Brian, Michael, and Jesse were out of their depth.

Brian was doing his homework at the desk. His face was red and damp from crying. He looked up as soon as the door opened.

"You can't be in here," Brian said and sniffed.

Michael closed the door behind them. "This has gotten out of hand, Brian."

"Go away."

"Jesse is hurt. What would you be saying to Sean now if Jesse had been shot? If he had died?"

"I told him to stay out of it!"

"It's Jose, isn't it?"

"You don't understand. Just leave me alone, Michael."

His voice cracked and Jesse wondered what he'd already done. But he didn't say anything. He sat down because his stomach still hurt from being punched. In the shower he'd noticed a big bruise, and he wasn't surprised because it *really* hurt.

"Is this the path you want? You want to join Jose's gang? To kill? Did you like killing for the general? Did you like hurting other people?"

"I hate you."

"Hate me. Leave. Go and join Jose and his gangbangers and you won't live to see eighteen. You know the truth and yet you betray us!"

"Hey," Jesse said. The emotion and intensity made him very uncomfortable. He didn't really understand why Michael wanted him here, the whole *good cop, bad cop* conversation not making much sense. "Brian, I'm okay, really. But they had guns. What do they want you for?"

"Jose is my brother. You can never understand. He's blood. He's family."

"The same family as your father who sold you," Michael said, his voice low and filled with quiet rage.

"Jose didn't know."

"Lie to yourself all you want, Brian. I don't care. But you are putting everyone here in danger. You don't care about me or Jesse, fine. But Tito is innocent. Frisco and Kevin and everyone else. They have a chance for more. For better than what we were all born in. And you would bring the violence back to our door?"

"No. I won't. I promise, it's not like that."

"What is it like?" Jesse asked quietly. "What does your brother want from you?"

Brian clung to the question like a life preserver. "He just wants to be a family again."

"Then why hasn't he petitioned the court to be your guardian?" Jesse asked.

"He has a record—he doesn't think he would be allowed."

"You know, my dad can move mountains," Jesse said. "If you really want to live with your brother, Sean can probably make it happen."

Brian paled. "No. You can't tell him."

"Why? This is your family. Sean understands family."

"He wouldn't understand. Because of Jose's record, he would think—"

"Fuck that," Michael said. "You are making excuses. He has a record and he carries a gun, what does that mean? He's already back in the gang life. He's living in Saints territory. He doesn't care about you, he cares only because you're young and stupid."

"Screw you."

"You need to leave, right now," Michael said. "I will not risk everyone here because you are weak and stupid."

"No, Michael, don't," Jesse said. Was he serious? Would he really force Brian to go? "We can fix this."

Brian closed his eyes and fought with tears. "I—I—"

"Tell me what's going on," Michael said. "Tell me the truth, right now, or I will call Kane and he will find it for me."

At the mention of Kane's name, Brian shook his head. "Please no. Kane would kill my brother. He's the only family I have left."

Jesse didn't know what to think about this conversation. Why would Michael call Kane? Why not just tell Sean? Or Father Mateo? Would Kane really kill someone?

Jesse knew the answer to that. He'd been in Guadalajara when Kane, Sean, and others came down to rescue him and take his stepfather into custody. But they wouldn't kill in cold blood. Not without a threat. Without a reason.

Michael stared at Brian. Brian looked from him to Jesse. "Jess—I'm sorry about today. I didn't mean for any of that to happen, and I was scared."

"I know," Jesse said. "I'm not mad at you."

"I don't know what to do, Michael! I want Jose to have the same chance I had—but he doesn't understand that there are options outside of the gang. He calls them his family. Says I am family, too, that I need to be with him."

"He knows there are options, but he doesn't want to take them."

"They'll kill him."

"He's not scared of the gang," Michael said. "He's a part of it. If he was scared, there are ways to disappear. You and I both know that. But that would mean hard work and sacrifice, and Jose only believes in himself and the gang, in violence and money and drugs. Tell me the truth: What does he know about Saint Catherine's?"

"Just that it's a group home run by the church. I didn't tell him everything."

"But he knew about the general."

"He was in prison, he couldn't come for me."

"Do you think he would have? Do you really believe he would have rescued you and taken you away from the life?"

"I—I—"

"If you can't be honest with yourself, you can be honest with no one."

"I don't know," Brian whispered. "I want to believe, but . . . I think he would want me with him, in the Saints."

Jesse leaned forward and put his hand on Brian's arm. Moving made his chest hurt, but he tried to conceal the pain. "We're here for you, no matter what. Okay?"

"What's he up to?" Michael demanded. "What do you do with him and his gang?"

"Just stuff."

"Drugs? Guns?"

Brian slowly nodded.

"Is that what you want?"

"No," he whispered.

"Are you sure? Are you sure you don't want the gang life?"

"I don't. But . . . he's my brother."

"Grow up. Stay away from him. That is your only choice if you want a life."

"I don't know how. He expects—" Brian stopped talking.

"What does he expect?"

"My help."

"You cross that line, there is no coming back. Before you had no choice. Now you do."

"I don't know how to stop. I don't—he knows where we live."

"Did he threaten you?"

"Not me." Brian looked at the picture on the wall.

"Fuck!" Michael kicked the desk, the sound loud in the small room. "Why didn't you tell me? From the beginning?"

"You can't fix everything, Michael. But I can do this. To protect everyone. He saw you, Michael! When you were following me. He knows who you are and what you did last year. He thinks you're a traitor. But I can protect you! If I do what he wants, I can protect all of you."

"You are not responsible for me," Michael said.

"This has gotten way out of control," Jesse said. "We have to tell Sean."

"No—Jose is part of the Saints," Michael said. "He has the power of the gang behind him. Alone, Sean can't defeat them. We can't let him get on their radar. We have to figure this out."

"I'll leave," Brian said quietly. "I'll go to El Paso and blend in. I'm good at that."

"I'm not letting you run away."

"But you said—"

"I know what I said. But if you're willing to fight for what you have, for what we have here, then tell me the truth, right now. Do you want to be part of the Saints or do you want to live here? Are you willing to give up Jose? Because he will not change, and you know it. In your heart, you know it."

Brian was crying again, but he wiped the snot and tears away with the back of his hand. "I am so sorry about all this. I didn't know what to do when he found me. He's my brother, I wanted to try . . . but I'm scared, Michael."

"I have an idea, and it will work—but there's no going back, Brian. You have to cut all ties."

"I will. I promise, Michael."

"Tell me everything about what you've seen. I need to know where the drugs and guns are. If the police raid the house and find Jose with anything illegal, he will go back to prison. He's on probation. He doesn't get another chance."

"You want me to send my brother back to prison?"

"I want *my brothers*—and that includes you—to be safe. You brought Jose and the Saints into our lives again. You have to help get them out. Or you go with them, and I pray you survive."

Brian looked to Jesse, as if begging him for another answer. Another idea.

"Michael is right," Jesse said. "We do this or we call my uncle Kane and let him take care of it."

Brian took a deep breath, put his head in his hands. A moment later he looked up. "You are right. I can't risk Father Mateo, Tito—everyone. I will help. The Saints have a house on East Santiago Street. That's where they package drugs for distribution. They get new shipments late Friday afternoon, package them all night, and their distributors come by and collect for the weekend. I've never seen so many drugs in one place—not even when we were mules."

"I need the layout, quantities, anything you remember. And you have to make sure Jose is there tomorrow—and you're not."

"I can do that. But they have a lot of guns, a lot of people."

"That's why I'm going to call the DEA. I know exactly what to say to get them to act. Listen to my plan. We won't have a second chance."

CHAPTER SEVENTEEN

Thursday Morning

Joyce Witherspoon, William Peterson's partner at Allied Accounting, was a crisp sixty-year-old wearing a professional gray suit with clean, white tennis shoes.

"I'm so sorry I couldn't meet with you yesterday when you were here," she said after shaking their hands and sitting behind her desk. Jerry and Lucy took seats across from her. "With Steven gone . . . we're juggling a lot, even nearly a month later. His shoes will not be easy to fill."

"You haven't replaced him?" Jerry asked.

She shook her head. "We hired someone to help, but it's not someone of Steven's caliber. He had a true gift—you know how someone can play music by ear, or a great athlete who breaks all the records? Steven intuitively understood accounting at a level I've never seen. And he loved it. I know, sounds weird." She sighed. "I miss him."

"Mr. Peterson suggested that you would be best able to explain how Abigail James's trust works," Jerry said.

"Yes, I audit the trust. It's managed by the longtime O'Connell family attorneys—a firm in Santa Barbara. I can give you their contact information. But because Steven believed in checks and balances, he hired me—through Allied—to audit the trust every two years."

"Did Mr. James have any say over the trust or how the money was disbursed?"

"Yes and no. The trust was managed by the law firm and the money invested in a conservative manner. Once a year, Steven would analyze the investments and suggest changes. The partners in the firm would then vote on any changes, with the primary goal of protecting the trust for Abby's future. So he could offer changes, and he had a vote on whether they were implemented, but he couldn't unilaterally make any changes."

"And Mr. James didn't receive any money from his first wife's death?"

"Is that relevant?"

"Honestly, Ms. Witherspoon, we're facing dead end after dead end. So we're going back into the lives of all three victims to see if there is anything that may connect them, or any motive for their death. So far, we have nothing."

"I don't put much weight on the media, but press reports floated the idea that this was the work of a serial killer."

"Trust your judgment on that, until you hear an official statement from the sheriff's office," Jerry said.

"I am privy to Steven's finances. He has always been extremely frugal. The O'Connell money—family money, I guess you would say—all went into the trust. But everything that they bought during their marriage—the house in Santa Barbara, a vacation home in Hawaii, cars, jewelry, art—that was left to Steven, even if it was bought with O'Connell money—aside, of course, from certain specific bequests. He sold the Santa Barbara home and bought the house here in Olmos Park. He retained the Hawaiian home and goes there once a year for two weeks. I believe he put the jewelry in a safe-deposit box for Abby to decide what to do with when she's older. He made a very good salary here, more than enough to support his family."

"But he had no life insurance policy, which seems odd," Lucy said. "From a fiscal point of view, wouldn't he want his wife and daughter protected?"

"Like I said, he was frugal and he had no debt. The trust will provide for Abby's living expenses—there is a provision that if Abby is orphaned, the trust will increase her allowance in order to provide her day-to-day living expenses. And everything purchased during the marriage is now the property of Teri. I also believe Steven has in his will that Teri gets the house here, and Abby will have ownership of the Hawaiian house. But I'd have to double-check."

"So," Jerry said, "there's no way that if Steven James dies, anyone else can get their hands on Abby's money."

"No. Abby herself can't even make decisions on expenditures until she's twenty-one—if she needs funds, she applies with the trustee. Education will be paid for. The trust pays for her private high school. There have been too many times when young people are persuaded by unscrupulous people to part with their money. For example—I audited a trust where, on his eighteenth birthday, a boy signed over half his trust to a so-called charitable organization to save the Amazon forest. He'd been conned by a young, unscrupulous woman—a long con. She was in high school, and she and her older sister came up with the plan. She dated him for a full year. It was a sadly brilliant scam, and the women were never caught. When Abby's twenty-one, she'll control half the trust, and when she's twenty-five she'll control the entire trust."

"What about her guardian? Could Mr. James have changed the terms of the trust?"

"No. The basic terms were set by the O'Connell estate—

such as the age at which Abby would receive the money. Abby's stepmother, as her guardian, would fill Steven's role on the board of the trust until Abby is twenty-five, where she will then serve as her own advocate. But again—it's one vote out of five. Three are partners with the law firm who handles the trust, one is Abby's great-aunt—a woman as frugal and responsible as Steven. When Abby's grandfather died, she became the matriarch of the O'Connell family. Abby's grandparents had one daughter, Bridget; Abby's great-aunt had one son who has only one child, about Abby's age. There's a few cousins, but I don't know much about them. They all live in California."

"And the family was on good terms with Steven when he moved to Texas?"

"As far as I know. Until Abby's grandfather died, they went to visit often. Abby spent a large part of her summer in California. As the auditor for the trust, I've never found the law firm or Abby's aunt difficult. In fact, just the opposite."

"Thank you for your time, Ms. Witherspoon."

"If I can help in any way, please let me know. Steven James was a quiet soul, but he left a large footprint and I will always miss his friendship."

"Another dead end," Jerry said.

"I feel we have more insight into Steven James as a person. He's rather the opposite of Billy Standish on the surface—Steven is quiet, frugal, reserved; Billy was loud, rough, prone to getting in fights when drunk. But both were well liked among their peers. I suspect Julio was the same."

"So this killer is targeting nice family men?" He shook his head. "There are a lot of nice family men out there, Lucy."

"I'm not saying that's the reason—in fact, it likely isn't. It just adds to the confusion as to how the killer is choosing his victims. Three family men who are well liked, even if they had some problems. Julio financial problems. Billy family problems. Steven—well, there don't seem to be any specific issues in his life. So why them? Why not a man who beats on his kids or is a slacker at work?"

"Because they're randomly chosen. Maybe they weren't stalked. Maybe the killer was on the prowl, saw a lone male, and targeted him," Jerry said. "It's the only thing that fits."

"If that's the case, he has to have a partner. Because otherwise, why would the men get out of their car? They did it to help someone—the grease on Billy's hands attests that he touched the engine of a car that wasn't his own."

"And maybe he *was* specifically targeted and the others because the killer had a taste for killing."

"Which brings us back to Mrs. Standish's two lovers—known lovers. Carl Franklin doesn't have it in him to kill anyone, and Johns has an alibi."

"Yeah—and we confirmed it this morning. No way he drove from Amarillo to San Antonio on Friday. He worked all day, was off at six—he couldn't have made it here until well after midnight. And he had breakfast with one of his co-workers at seven thirty Saturday morning—in Amarillo. I checked the airlines just to cross it off—he didn't fly under his name, at least. Neither guy is all that good . . . or bad. Just normal folks, with secrets—this secret being they were screwing around with their friend's wife."

Marissa was at her sister's house when Lucy and Jerry arrived at eleven that morning. Sandra was doting on her, and brought out water for everyone, and juice for Marissa.

"I don't want Marissa to get upset," Sandra said firmly. "If she does, you'll have to leave."

"We understand," Jerry said. "We just want to follow up on a few things."

Marissa nodded. "I want to help."

Her voice was quiet. She looked tired and completely drained of energy.

"Mrs. Garcia," Jerry said kindly, "we think that your husband may have been followed in the days or weeks leading up to his death. Did he say anything to you? Did he show concern that someone was harassing him?"

Marissa shook her head. "He said nothing. But he wouldn't. He wouldn't want me to worry about anything."

"Would you mind looking at some photos and telling us if you recognize any of the people?"

"Is one of them a suspect?"

"No. They're people who may have also been victims— or related to the victims—of the person who killed your husband," Jerry said. "We are working nonstop to find this man, and this could be important."

She nodded and looked at her sister, who sat next to her and took her hand.

Lucy scrolled through each of the photos—she'd already taken Julio's out of the array. With each one, Marissa and Sandra shook their heads. They didn't recognize any of the people.

"Is there someone else he may have confided in?" Lucy asked Marissa.

"Me." A short, fit man of about forty walked in. "I'm sorry I'm late. I'm Robert Vallejo—Sandra's husband. And Julio's friend."

"Did he say something to you?"

"Sandra, I'm going to take these officers to the back, okay?"

Sandra nodded.

Marissa looked worried. "Why? Why can't you talk in front of me? I need to know what's going on."

Sandra took her hand. "Issa, remember what the doctor said. She doesn't want you to stress."

"What do you know, Robert?" Marissa asked. She shifted uncomfortably on the couch.

"It may be nothing," Sandra said. "Let him talk to the police and if it's nothing, we don't need to worry you. If it leads to something, I promise I will tell you. Okay?"

Silent tears fell, but Marissa nodded, and Robert led Jerry and Lucy into a home office. It was a family room that had been converted into an office with a separate entrance, two desks, and a small conference table. "It was so much cheaper to set up our real estate company here," Robert said. "It helps that Sandy is my best friend as well as my wife."

He motioned them to sit at the table.

"I take it that Julio shared something with you that may relate to his murder."

"It might. Sandy and I have been talking all week about what to do with this information, and Sandy said I should tell you. She loves Marissa so much, and Marissa made her promise not to say anything. But I didn't make that promise. But I beg of you—please don't talk to Marissa about this, not unless it is absolutely necessary. She is thirty-four weeks' pregnant. The doctor wants to postpone labor if at all possible for at least two more weeks. Marissa has been in pre-labor before—both with Dario and with this baby—and stress is a mitigating factor. Dario was born a month premature, but he was five pounds and had healthy lungs. The doctor says this baby isn't yet four pounds."

"Unless we absolutely have to, this will remain confidential and a part of our investigation," Jerry said. "We don't want to trouble Mrs. Garcia any more than necessary."

"That's why she's here—Julio's mother is difficult, and she's grieving. She's not a bad woman, she's just—well, let's just say that no woman would be good enough for her perfect son. And I say this with love, because Julio was damn close to perfect. He was the finest man I know. I remember when Julio came over for their first date— Marissa was still living with us. You know her parents died when she was a teenager, Sandy raised her and Anna. I'm an only child, but Issa and Anna are my sisters in every way but blood."

He took a deep breath. "Anyway, Julio and Marissa had met at the hotel where he still works. She was a maid, Julio had started in the kitchen. I liked Julio immediately. He was a good man, a religious man, worked hard. Everyone loved him. He only had eyes for Marissa." He paused.

"Robert?" Jerry prompted.

"This is very difficult to discuss, because I feel like I'm betraying Julio and Marissa."

"But you think it is relevant to our investigation."

"Yes. Yes I do." He took a deep breath again, let it out. "Marissa is a good girl. In this day and age so many young people turn to drink or drugs or sex—casually. I'm not disparaging them, it is part of society now and chastity isn't promoted as a virtue. But to Marissa it was. When we learned that she was pregnant—this with Dario, nearly seven years ago—and she and Julio weren't yet married— they were engaged, not married. We. Well. We didn't judge her because we knew they loved each other and things happen. But it wasn't like that. Marissa was depressed and withdrawn and would talk to no one. Julio's mother didn't make it any easier, accusing Marissa of trapping her son. I finally confronted Julio because this was so unlike Marissa, and I needed to know that he was going to continue to do right by her. This sounds old-fashioned, but Marissa *is* old-fashioned. I wanted what was best for her, and she was so unhappy.

"Julio broke down. His best friend—his longest childhood friend—raped her. Full disclosure—he didn't tell me who until recently. He only said it was someone he trusted, a friend. Marissa didn't tell anyone until she learned she was pregnant, which was more than two months after the rape. Julio convinced her that he would claim the baby as his, that they would never speak of it again. I told him they should file charges, to punish this man for what he'd done. Julio wanted to—but Marissa refused. I told Sandy—I had to—and Sandy tried to convince Marissa to change her mind. But she—both of them are stubborn. Marissa almost miscarried at four months, and that's when we had an agreement never to bring it up again. Julio cut this man out of his life, took Dario as his own son. It is his name on the birth certificate."

Lucy said, "Why are you telling us this now? Did Julio have a confrontation with Marissa's rapist? Does this man know Dario is his son?"

"Dario was a month premature, the man had left San Antonio for work, and because Julio had cut him out of his life, there's no reason that he would have thought the baby was his. If he heard about Dario, he would have assumed the child was Julio's."

"Except?" Lucy prompted.

"This man was gone for years. Julio saw him in his restaurant, at the hotel, a month ago. They had a confrontation. Julio regretted it. He hit the man, had to tell Marissa that he'd seen him. He has never lied to her, he couldn't start now. Marissa is terrified that her rapist will find out Dario is his son and take him from her. She thinks no one will believe her."

"No one is going to take Dario from Marissa," Lucy said firmly. "You need to tell us who he is."

"I will. But you must promise not to tell him anything about Dario's paternity."

"It won't come from us, but could he suspect that Dario is his son?" It could be a motive for murder. At least one of the murders.

"I honestly do not know. But Julio was very concerned about the altercation, and while he didn't lie to Marissa, he downplayed it." He took a deep breath. "His name is Christopher Smith, the grandson of the owner of Sun Tower, where Julio worked. Chris left San Antonio to start up another hotel, then returned and Julio was concerned because he didn't want Marissa to run into him—that's why Julio told her he was in town. It's the only thing that has happened in their lives that could—possibly—lead to . . . to *this*. This senseless murder. I hope it isn't so, but you need all the information."

"Did Smith threaten Julio?" Jerry asked.

"I don't know. Julio didn't say anything to me about threats, just that he'd seen him at the hotel and they fought. Julio wanted him to leave. I don't know what he planned on doing, I told him to just ignore Chris. But Julio—he's a man of honor, and Chris hurt the woman he loves."

CHAPTER EIGHTEEN

Thursday Early Afternoon

"You're quiet," Jerry said as they drove to the Sun Tower Suites. "We've done nearly a dozen of these interviews this week, and you've always had an opinion. You think he's lying?"

"No," Lucy said.

Melancholy, she supposed, would be the right word. They didn't say anything to Marissa after talking to her brother-in-law—Lucy wanted to talk to her about the rape, but the woman was eight months' pregnant. The stress of discussing it wouldn't be good for her or the baby. But at some point—if Chris Smith had anything to do with Julio's murder—she would have to give a statement.

"We're going to have to talk to Smith."

"Not yet," she said.

"Why not? He has motive—if we believe Vallejo, then Dario is his kid. Something like that could set something off. And remember—Julio was killed with a blow to the back of his head. Everything else was just window dressing."

"There may be a motive to kill Julio, and there may be a motive to kill Standish, but it's not the *same* motive. And if we take what we know as gospel, they are the *moral victims*. Standish's wife cheated on him with at least three men. Julio's best friend raped his fiancé. We *know* that the same killer killed these three men. Even if we discount the consistent MO, they were shot with the same gun."

"I agree, but that doesn't mean don't question Smith. His name came up, there was a confrontation, and Julio is dead."

"Vallejo said that Julio saw Smith in the hotel. If they did have an altercation, someone there must know about it. Let's find that person—or persons—and that gives us another reason to talk to Smith."

Jerry didn't say anything for a moment, then nodded. "I see what you're getting at, but we already have a reason. If this guy is guilty, I don't want him to get off."

"Guilty of killing Standish and James? Because why? He may have a motive for killing Julio—Julio lied about the paternity of Dario—but what would be the motive for the others? We would have to find a connection between Smith and the other two victims before we go there."

"There could be a connection."

"Yes, but the best case right now is to pursue his altercation with Julio, and if we bring up the reason, then it'll tip him off."

"To what?"

"What if he *doesn't* know that Dario is his son? I don't want him to learn it from us. He could make Marissa's life hell."

"He raped her."

"Oh, come *on*," Lucy said. "We both know rape is going to be almost impossible to prove after seven years. He could sue for a paternity test, then sue for custody. I'm not going to give him that option. He doesn't need to know any of this, which is why we find an actual witness to the fight between Smith and Julio. With Vallejo it's hearsay with no one to corroborate because Julio is dead. We find a witness, we have reason to talk to Smith and ask for his explanation, his alibi, maybe learn something if we play this right."

This time, Jerry was silent.

"What?" Lucy finally said.

"I'm not arguing with you. We do it your way. It's just—I don't know. There's something different in your approach with this."

"I have investigated dozens of sex crimes." She hesitated, wondering how much she should share with her temporary partner. She really didn't want to talk about her past now. It wasn't professional, or appropriate. Maybe later, if it would help, but right now she wanted to think about how to nail Chris Smith. A seven-year-old rape—even with the ten-year statute of limitations on most sexual assaults in Texas—would be difficult to investigate. Especially if Smith was aware that they were looking into it. But if he didn't know . . . if they could get something they could follow, a conflicting statement, someone else who might know the truth, then she could pass it on to SAPD Detective Tia Mancini. Tia was one of the best cops in the division, she specialized in sex crimes, and she knew how to build a case to satisfy the DA.

And how and when to talk to Marissa Garcia.

But that was later. If Smith was guilty of multiple homicides, rape was the least of his worries. If he was innocent of murder, then Lucy would follow through. There was no way she could let him get away with it, not as long as she had a badge to investigate.

"Lucy? I see you thinking, but you're not talking."

"I want to bump this over to Tia Mancini with SAPD."

"A sex crimes detective."

"If we learn Smith didn't kill Julio, I want to pass on what we know."

"Marissa Garcia hasn't filed charges."

"And maybe she won't. Maybe she wants to forget. But she'll never forget, it will stay with her forever, made worse now that the man she sees as her soul mate and her protector is gone. Who else has Smith assaulted? Sexual predators don't usually stop with one victim. Tia will find his other victims. Someone will have evidence. There is strength in numbers."

"Slow it down," Jerry said. "One case at a time. Let's find out if Smith is a possible suspect for murder, and then go from there."

"Of course. Murder has a much longer sentence, and Texas has the death penalty."

It didn't ultimately matter what Jerry wanted to do. If Smith wasn't guilty of murder, Lucy would bring everything to Tia. She didn't need his approval or his permission.

But she did want his blessing, so she shelved the topic until they had more information.

Sun Tower Suites was a convention hotel on the Riverwalk, smaller than some of the larger chains, but nicer in many ways with large rooms, a pair of five-star restaurants—one with a view of the city—and one of the nicest gardens that was the backdrop of many weddings, receptions, and special events. It was pricey, but never seemed to be lacking for guests.

They spoke to the head of security first, a large beefy former cop named Vince Paine. Jerry knew him from the job, and they chatted a few minutes, then Jerry said, "We talked on Saturday, you confirmed Garcia's time here, no disciplinary actions, well liked."

"He was. Very much, especially among his staff."

"In the last couple of weeks, were there any problems? With a guest or staff? Even if it was minor—nothing that would go on his record—was there any verbal or physical altercation?"

"That doesn't sound like Julio. He was a peacemaker. Never raised his voice, as far as I know. And any physical altercation would almost certainly result in termination, except under extraordinary circumstances. Why? Did someone say he was in a fight?"

"We're talking to everyone who knew him. His brother-in-law thought he'd had a disagreement with someone, didn't say specifically that it was work-related. We're trying to run it down."

"I didn't know Julio well, but I knew him well enough to know he wouldn't instigate a fight. You can talk to anyone on the catering staff—they know him best—or even the folks in the main kitchen. He was well respected."

"We'll be talking to everyone, if you can direct us?"

"Start with his assistant, Mitchell Duncan. He worked closely with Julio. If there was anything wrong, he would know."

Having security escort them to the kitchen where Julio worked as head chef of catering helped give the vote of confidence to their investigation, and Mitch was more than happy to talk about his boss. Mitch was in his fifties, bald and portly, with a smooth baby face. He called over another cook and gave him instructions, then motioned for Jerry and Lucy to follow him to a small office that had Julio Garcia's name on the door.

"I'm still in shock," Mitch said. "Julio was a good man, a great boss, devoted to his family. Anything I can do to help find out who did this to him."

"We appreciate that," Jerry said. "This was his office?"

"Yes, though he spent very little time in here. Mostly to talk to vendors or the catering manager about upcoming events. He was a great chef—it takes skill to run a catering kitchen, where you may need to prepare five hundred identical meals to be ready at the same time. And he could present a low-budget buffet with the same class as a high-end wedding banquet. Honestly, he'll be hard to replace."

"You haven't replaced him?" Jerry asked.

He shook his head. "It's not my skill set. Just managing this kitchen this week has raised my blood pressure. I was his assistant, but that didn't mean I did what he did. He ran the kitchen. I managed staff, mostly. Made sure everything was done to his specifications, directed traffic, so to speak. Julio didn't have a mean bone in his body—if an employee wasn't pulling their weight, was habitually late or something like that, I took care of it. Julio sometimes—well, he had a big heart. He believed every sob story. Me? First time, I get it. Second time, they're on notice. Third time—sorry, you're out. Julio would have given people a hundred chances, then apologized for firing them."

"How long have you known Julio?"

"Since I started here three years ago. He'd just been promoted to head chef, catering, and I replaced him as the assistant. But he was able to put his footprint on the kitchen, and we shifted responsibilities so he could focus on the food, and I could focus on production. I loved that about him—he listened and adopted new procedures in order to streamline the process and increase quality. And I made sure he had the staff to do it."

They knew that Julio had worked for Sun Tower for nearly eight years—since he'd graduated from a culinary school in the city.

"Were you working Friday night when Julio left? He clocked out at eleven twenty-three that evening."

"I left at ten. We had a wedding reception here, but once dinner was served most of the staff left. Julio and I stayed, and half a dozen others, for the dessert bar. Everything was done, it was just a matter of setup and teardown. Julio has been working extra hours—he doesn't mind doing the grunt work as well as running the kitchen. But he was prepping for a breakfast we had for Saturday. I know he wanted the extra hours because of the baby." His voice cracked. "I called Marissa the other day. Just to tell her I'm so sorry. It shouldn't have happened."

"Did Julio seem preoccupied lately? Worried about something? Did he express concern for his safety?"

"I don't know what you're getting at."

Lucy clarified. "Did his attitude or behavior change in any way over the last few weeks? Did he confide in you about anything, work-related or personal, that might have bothered him?"

"I don't know if I feel comfortable talking about this."

"It's important," Jerry said. "Even if it has nothing to do with what happened to Julio last week, we need to build a time line of his days."

"About a month ago, maybe five, six weeks? A week or two before Labor Day, I know that. Julio came in late. He's never late—I wouldn't have even said anything to him, except that he was—well, not himself. He was tense and looked really angry about something, and he's not a guy who gets mad easily. I get a slow driver in front of me or an idiot who doesn't go at a green light, I'm pissed. I'll honk, rant about it later. Julio, no. He'd just assume that the driver was preoccupied or being safe. He always gave people the benefit of the doubt—I have to be the bad guy when staff is trying to get away with something. So when he came in, sort of heated and his shirt untucked, I was surprised. I asked him about it. He wouldn't say anything, not then."

"But?" Jerry prompted.

"That night—most of the crew had gone home, and he was sitting in his office just staring at the wall. I came in with a couple shots of whiskey. Put one in front of him and said, 'Can I help?' That was it. Just let him talk. He said he might be fired because he punched one of the executives. I didn't believe him, said so. He then said it was Chris Smith, who of course I'd heard about—he's the grandson of the owner, learned everything about the business here, then moved to Arizona to open the Sun Tower there. Managed it for a few years, just returned. What I didn't know was that Smith and Julio had gone to school together—you wouldn't think it, you know? A rich white kid and an eighth-generation Hispanic Texan. But apparently they met playing baseball when they were little kids, and were friends ever since. I guess not anymore. I asked why he hit him, and he wouldn't tell me. Not the whole story. Said something happened right before Smith left for Arizona. He hadn't spoken to him since, and when he saw him he lost it. Those were his words. I know he was angry, and he was worried—because Marissa is pregnant, and his mother has been sick. Julio keeps his problems to himself, but Marissa had a difficult first pregnancy and he was worried about this one."

"Did anyone see the fight?"

"I doubt it. No one came to talk to Julio, I asked a week later if he was reprimanded or something, and he said no, and Smith was going to open a new hotel in Florida. But Smith is still around, so I don't know when that's going to happen. It's not like I'm in the loop about corporate decisions."

If Julio knew that, then he must have talked to Smith or someone else after the altercation. And it was odd that Smith didn't report it. A sign of his guilt? Or because of their lifelong friendship?

"Is there anyone else here whom Julio talks to regularly? Someone he trusts and confides in?" Lucy asked.

"Everyone likes Julio, he is—he was—a good guy. But he didn't have many close friends, outside of his family. I know he's close to his brother-in-law. Bob—Rob, Robert, that's it. Maryanne Sanchez is in charge of housekeeping—she's been here forever, and she was Marissa's boss when she worked here, before her first kid was born. I know they're still friends—like *socialize outside of work* kind of friends. Maryanne has a grandson Dario's age. One of the bartenders—he's a cousin to Julio, Julio got him the job, they sometimes have a drink together after work."

"Do you know his name?"

"Peter Garcia. He might be Julio's nephew—the son of his oldest brother or something. I really don't know, he has a huge family." He paused, then said, "I doubt he'd have told Peter anything private. He's a good kid, has been going to college part-time and working and has a private bartending gig on the side, but he's still a twenty-three-year-old with a penchant for girls and parties and fun. Julio was a good influence on him—I mean, Pete has a solid work ethic, don't get me wrong. But I don't see Julio sharing anything sensitive with him. Maryanne though? Yeah. They're tight. She's Dario's godmother."

Jerry thanked Mitch for his time, and he and Lucy stepped out. She suggested that he talk to Pete the bartender and she talk to Maryanne.

Jerry was skeptical. Did he not trust her to interview a witness alone? She said, "If Maryanne is close to the Garcias, and she's been here since Marissa worked here, she might have more information, but she'll feel more comfortable talking to a female cop than a male cop. Plus, I speak fluent Spanish, if language is a barrier."

It was clear Jerry didn't want to let Lucy do it alone, but he couldn't find a good excuse. "We meet back here in the lobby in thirty minutes and talk to Chris Smith, agreed?"

"Yes."

Relieved, Lucy talked to the security chief and found Maryanne in the middle of inventory on the twenty-first floor. She showed her badge and handed Maryanne a card, and said that she was cleared by security to talk to her about Julio Garcia's murder. At the mention of his name, her eyes dampened, but she held her chin up and motioned for Lucy to follow her to a room. "It's vacant, but hasn't been cleaned yet," she said. "We'll have privacy."

When Maryanne closed the door, Lucy said, "You don't seem to be intimidated to talk to me."

"Why should I be? I didn't do anything wrong. It's about time someone came here asking questions. Julio has been dead a week tomorrow. A *week*. His funeral is on Saturday, and the man who killed him is still out there."

Lucy raised an eyebrow. "Do you know who killed him?"

"No," she said, arms across her ample chest. "But I don't think the police much care, otherwise they would have been here asking questions."

"My partner did talk to management, and we have been asking questions, but an investigation like this takes time."

"Hrumph."

Lucy decided not to try to justify how they approached this investigation, because it was too complex to easily explain.

"Mitchell Duncan, Julio's assistant, said you were Julio's closest friend in the hotel. Is that true?"

She looked momentarily flustered, then nodded. "I suppose it is. I love him like a son. And Marissa like a daughter." She took a deep breath. "I went over a couple times to see her, her sister takes good care of her. She's like a zombie. She needs to take care of that baby girl."

"Did Julio tell you about an altercation he had with Chris Smith? Five or six weeks ago?"

Silence, but it was clear that Maryanne knew exactly what Lucy was referencing.

"It—it was obviously minor. Julio wasn't fired, so it was clearly not a serious fight."

"That's not what I heard."

"From who?"

"Maryanne, I want to find out who killed Julio. I want justice for his family and to put a killer behind bars. That is my job. Help me do my job. What do you know about the argument between Julio and Chris?"

"Do you know who Mr. Smith is? He is the owner's grandson. He is wealthy and powerful and if there was no reprimand, it was not an important argument. Julio and Chris had once been friends. They played baseball together, went to the same high school."

Lucy wanted to be forthcoming and tell her what she knew about Marissa and her first pregnancy, but that would be severely violating the confidence and discretion that Robert Vallejo asked for. It might come out at some point, but not from Lucy, not until she could be guaranteed that Chris Smith couldn't—or wouldn't—come after his victim and her son.

"Mr. Duncan told us of the fight, and he was clear that he didn't know why. We know that Julio and Smith were once friends, but that they had a major falling-out and didn't speak for the last six or seven years. So you know what their falling-out was about?"

"How would I know?"

"That's not an answer."

"Are you interrogating me?"

"I'm trying to find out who killed Julio."

"The news says it's a serial killer. Mr. Smith may not be a nice person, but a serial killer? That is preposterous."

"Why don't you believe Mr. Smith is a nice person?" Lucy said.

"He is my boss's boss. I can't talk about him. Do you want me to be fired? Do you know that Sun Tower is one of the few companies that has a retirement savings account for housekeeping staff? I'm not going to risk that talking about gossip and innuendos and hurting people who have suffered enough. You find out who killed Julio, that is your job."

"If people won't talk to me, how can I find out?"

"There is evidence, there would have to be something."

Lucy was about to argue with her, but she realized that there might very well be evidence of the fight. A security tape, maybe. Why didn't security know about it? Where had the fight occurred? She didn't even know exactly what date or where. But she had an idea.

"Maryanne," Lucy said quietly, "I know you are trying to protect Julio and Marissa, and I respect that. Let me ask you this in a different way. Have you met Chris Smith?"

She fretted. "Yes," she said.

"When was the first time you met him?"

"Years ago. When he was little. I've worked here for nearly thirty years, ever since Mr. Smith—Richard Smith, his grandfather—bought and renovated the Tower. He is a great man."

"The grandfather."

"Yes. He retired, now a management company runs the hotel, but he still owns it and has a stake. Semi-retired I think they call it? Where he is still involved?"

"Yes, semi-retired. And is Chris Smith involved in running the hotel?"

"Not here. He opens other hotels. He left and he wasn't supposed to—" She stopped herself.

"He wasn't supposed to come back?"

"He's leaving again. They are opening a hotel in Florida, and he will be there. It was delayed because of the hurricane, but he will be leaving soon."

"Does it matter, now that Julio is dead?" Lucy asked bluntly.

The blood drained from Maryanne's face.

"Yes it matters! Of course it matters!"

"Why?" Lucy asked. "Help me help the Garcia family."

"Understand this: Nothing you can do can help. But you can make everything worse. I do not like that man, but he would not kill Julio. I don't see him killing Julio, no matter what happened between them."

"What if Julio threatened to expose him for a crime?"

Maryanne stared at her. She knew what had happened to Marissa, and she was stunned that Lucy knew.

"Some crimes cannot be proven," Maryanne said quietly. "I need to get back to work."

Lucy gestured toward the business card Maryanne held tight in her fist. "If you want justice for Marissa, call me. I can help."

Lucy was late meeting Jerry. "The nephew was a dead end," Jerry said. "Young kid, upset about his uncle, but he doesn't know anything. Doesn't know about a fight or a disagreement."

"Maryanne knows, but she's not talking."

"Maybe we should bring her in, compel her to talk."

"She's scared of losing her job. She's also worried about the repercussions to Marissa. She confirmed that she heard that Chris Smith was going to Florida to open a hotel, that it was delayed because of the hurricane." Lucy paused. "She doesn't like Chris, but she has known him since he was a child, and doesn't see him as a killer."

"That means squat."

"Just repeating what she said. But if we can find a connection between Chris and the other victims, we might have something here. We need to find out when he returned to town. The exact date."

"That should be easy enough. We'll ask him, then confirm. But if he was in town for all three murders, he goes way up on our suspect list."

Chris Smith had an office on the executive floor. There was no name on the door, but that didn't surprise her—he wasn't usually in this hotel. He voluntarily let them in his office. "My security chief said you wanted to talk about Julio Garcia's murder."

"Yes, if you have a minute," Jerry said respectfully.

"Of course. Everyone here is upset—he was well liked and respected. My grandfather is going to his funeral Saturday."

"Not you?"

"I—no."

"Why not?"

"It's not important."

"It might be."

Chris wasn't an idiot, and he looked from Jerry to Lucy and back to Jerry. "I'm going to flat out tell you I didn't kill Julio. I'm not stupid, I know what you're getting at. Everyone knows that Julio and I used to be friends and now we're not. I'm really sorry he's dead—we had a falling-out, but in no way did I want anything bad to happen to him."

"We have a witness who said that you and Julio had a disagreement that resulted in a physical altercation a few weeks ago. What was that about?"

Chris stared at them. "None of your business."

"If it was serious enough to come to blows, it is our business, now that Julio is dead," Jerry said.

"Look, I'm getting ready to leave for Florida. I'll be

there at least two years. That's my life now, getting new hotels off the ground. I can't help your investigation."

"So what you're saying is, you're the only person who has had a disagreement with a well-liked, well-respected employee—a disagreement that resulted in a physical fight—yet the employee wasn't fired or reprimanded. Why didn't you turn him in? Your security officer said that there is a zero tolerance policy for fighting."

"That's my business."

"Now it's our business."

"No, it's really not."

Jerry was getting agitated. Lucy had buried her anger. She was good at that. She had to be, or she'd never be able to do the job. In a cool, calm voice she said, "When did you leave Phoenix? That's where you were living for the last few years, correct?"

He was surprised at the change of questions. "Um, August."

"August what? This is important, Mr. Smith. What day did you return?"

"Um—it was about a week before Labor Day. My grandfather's seventy-fifth birthday was September first, I was here for that. I flew in the morning . . ." He turned to his computer, typed, and said, "I came back Sunday, August twenty-fifth, on Southwest Airlines, arrived at eleven twenty a.m."

Lucy wrote it down. Standish was killed in early August, and James killed the Friday after Smith returned. She wanted Chris Smith to be guilty, but he would have to be here for all three murders . . . unless he had a partner, which just didn't seem to fit.

"Before you returned, when was the last time you were in San Antonio?"

"Why?"

"We're putting together a time line, Mr. Smith. It's important."

"Last Christmas, for a week or so. I can get you the exact days if you need them." He paused, looked from one to the other. "You know, I've screwed up in my life, I've done many things I've regretted, but I've never killed anyone. Even when I was drinking, I never killed anyone, though God knows I could have."

Jerry asked, "Are you an alcoholic?"

"Yes. Sober seven years this December. It's why I originally went to Phoenix, to check into rehab."

Those in an addiction program were often very open about their process, Lucy knew from experience in interviews. One of the tenets of most programs was to admit to the addiction without hesitation. Had his alcoholism been a contributing factor to Marissa's rape? It certainly wouldn't be the first time alcohol fueled violence—nor was it an excuse.

She pulled out her phone and said, "We'd like you to look at some pictures and tell us if you recognize any of the people."

"Why?"

"Because we're in the middle of a murder investigation and if you want to help us find who killed your former friend Julio Garcia and left his two children fatherless, we would like to know if you recognize any of these people," Lucy snapped. She didn't want to lose her cool—if she lost it, she wouldn't be able to get it back.

He nodded.

She flipped through the photos slowly, carefully watching Smith's reaction. Nothing on Standish or any of the people connected to him. Nothing on Steven James or the people connected to him. When he saw Julio's picture, his face fell, and when he saw Marissa's picture the blood drained. He was visibly shaking. "You cannot possibly believe that Marissa had anything to do with what happened to Julio."

"But you know her."

"Of course I know her! She used to work here in the hotel. It's how she and Julio met. We used to double-date and—" He stopped. "Look, I've read the news, seen the reports. I know you're looking for a serial killer."

Jerry said, "We don't know what kind of killer we're looking for, other than he shoots his victims in their face as if they are nothing to him. Not a father, not a husband, not a friend."

Smith rubbed his eyes. "I wish I could help you. I really do. But Julio and I didn't talk. Yes, we had a fight, and no, I didn't report it because it was personal and no one's business. I told him I was here temporarily, that I was going to Florida."

"Why would he care about that?"

"It's personal."

Lucy bit her tongue. It wasn't personal; Smith had committed a horrific crime and Julio didn't want him anywhere near him or his loved ones. She wanted to be angry at Julio for not reporting this guy, but she understood that deep down he was terrified of losing his family. The system didn't always work. And sometimes it failed those who were the most vulnerable.

"I can't accept that answer," Jerry said. "Your friend was murdered, you had a fight with him only weeks ago, and you can't tell me what it's about?"

"I'm not going to, and honestly, you can't make me. It's personal, it's between us, and it's over. I had nothing to do with Julio's murder, I'm sincerely sorry that he is dead, and if I had any information that would help you find out who killed him, I would give it to you. But I don't."

"Where were you Friday night between ten p.m. and midnight?"

At first he looked confused, then he shook his head. "Shit. You're really doing this." He turned to his computer again, typed, turned back to them. "I was here, at the hotel, until nine p.m. working. I can give you a list of a dozen people I spoke to or who saw me. I left just after nine for home—my mother's house, in New Braunfels, where I'm staying until I leave for Florida. I got there shortly after ten. It's a gated community, there should be a log—they maintain pictures of every vehicle entering and exiting, time-stamped. She was awake, and we talked for a bit, and I went to bed shortly after eleven. I had an early-morning meeting back here at the hotel—I was up by five, at the hotel at six to work out at the gym, showered, then had my business meeting at seven thirty a.m. My grandfather was there."

"Thank you," Jerry said, making note of everything he said. "When do you leave for Florida?"

"Next week. Thursday."

"Leave a way for us to get in touch with you if we have additional questions."

Smith nodded. He looked oddly dejected and sad. Lucy had no sympathy for him. Regret for a crime—if that's what this attitude was—didn't negate the crime. Too bad his guilt didn't motivate him to confess.

Jerry and Lucy walked out. "A complete waste of time," Jerry said. "Unless he flat out lied to us about the dates—which we'll be able to easily track—there's no way he could have killed all three men."

"Following the evidence is not a waste of time," Lucy said. "But I still think we should consult—"

"Drop it, Kincaid. We go back to the *facts* that we know, reexamine all evidence and witness statements, see if we're missing anything from any crime scene, and go from there."

"And if we're still back here with no viable suspects, no motive, and no road to follow will you at least *consider* an off-the-record conversation?"

Jerry didn't say anything, which Lucy took as a win. Because they had nothing, and she feared another victim was right around the corner.

CHAPTER NINETEEN

Thursday Afternoon

Sean was trying not to be an overprotective parent, but realized that it probably wouldn't happen overnight—if at all. Such was the nature of his world. He and Lucy led dangerous lives, and Jesse was still a kid, barely thirteen.

He had soccer practice Mondays and Wednesdays, and those days Sean let him go to the field with another parent of a kid on the team who was at the same school. He'd done a full background on the family; the kid's dad was an SAPD cop, and his mom was a nurse. They were good people and Sean had them over for a BBQ at the beginning of the school year just to get to know them. Sean picked Jesse up at the field when practice was over.

The other days, though the junior high was only a mile away, Sean opted to pick him up. There were only two routes to get home without going way out of the way, and if someone *was* watching his kid, it would be easiest to grab him walking or biking home.

Sean had thought a lot about how to fix the situation, and realized that it would never be "fixed." Jesse was a Rogan. There were many benefits to being a Rogan, but that also meant there would always be a bull's-eye on his back. Kane wanted to take him for a couple weekends of "training"—and Sean knew exactly what that meant. Sean wasn't comfortable with any form of military-style training for his son, not now. But Jesse did need to learn self-defense and situational awareness, and because they had guns around the house, gun safety was an absolute necessity.

Kane would be the best guy to teach Jesse the ropes, but Sean wanted to be there to limit how far Kane went. Lucy was right: With Kane, everything was black-and-white. Maybe Jack would be the better option—Jack had a similar background to Kane, but he wasn't so rigid in his view of how things worked. He would be more respectful of Sean's wishes to limit the kind of drills he put Jesse through.

Sean didn't mind picking Jesse up from school—he actually liked it. He hadn't been around to teach him to walk, but in a couple of years he'd teach him how to drive. He hadn't been around to help with his homework, but he'd be around to help him with college applications. He wasn't in his life on his first day of school, but he'd be there giving him advice on his first date. He'd watch him graduate from high school, see him pursue his own dreams. Sean was trying to look at the positives and not dwell on everything that was denied him for the first thirteen years of Jesse's life.

He got to the school early and waited in the long line of cars—other parents, mostly moms, who picked up their kids. Sean didn't mind being a stay-at-home dad. He had a job, he was lucky that most of the time he could do it from his computer. He already had a backup for when he traveled—he and Lucy had made a lot of friends in the nearly two years they'd lived in San Antonio. If Lucy couldn't pick Jess up, they had Nate, Brad, Tia, or Jesse's soccer friend. Jesse also had his own Uber account. It wasn't like he always needed a police escort, but Jesse would always be protected.

Kids poured out of the school. Jesse was usually in the middle. He was friendly, and though it was a new school and a new city, he had adjusted better than Sean would have. The soccer team meant instant friends with a common hobby. Plus, Michael had really stepped up to help Jesse feel comfortable with his new situation. They'd been practically inseparable last night. It was good for Jess, but also good for Michael to know that there wasn't just hate and violence in the world. That there were good people and good kids who did good things.

Jesse didn't immediately come out of the main entrance. Sean wasn't concerned at first. Jesse could be talking to a teacher, picking up an assignment, using the john. But he kept a close eye on the double doors, and the surrounding area. He inched his Jeep up as cars in front of him left, giving him room. He was in front of the line when he finally saw Jesse emerge from the building.

His relief was short-lived. Something was wrong. Jesse was walking slowly, like he was in pain. His right arm was stiff across his stomach, and he wasn't chatting with anyone. Someone waved to him, and he lifted his arm to wave back, then winced.

Dammit, what happened?

Sean jumped out of his Jeep and watched Jesse as he approached. When Jesse caught his eye, Sean saw him try to mask the pain. Sean strode over and took his backpack from him. "What happened?"

"Nothing."

"Jess, tell me."

"I did. I'm just bruised."

"From soccer yesterday? Lift up your shirt."

"No, stop, I'm fine."

"You're not fine. You look like you have a broken rib. I know. I've had a broken rib."

"In the car," Jesse mumbled.

Fair enough. Sean tossed his backpack into the back and jumped into the driver's seat. As soon as Jesse sat down, Sean motioned for him to lift his shirt.

The left side of his chest was purple and black.

"We're going to the hospital."

"I'll be *fine*."

"You're not fine. If it's broken it can be serious. You could have internal bleeding. Why didn't you tell me you were in so much pain?"

"I thought it would get better."

There was really nothing to do for a broken or cracked rib except to make sure that there was no internal bleeding or sharp edges that might cause problems down the road. Pain meds, minimal activity, and breathing deeply were important.

He drove to the emergency room. Jesse didn't object again, which told Sean he was in serious pain.

It didn't take long before they were called back, which was a small blessing because Sean was going stir-crazy. He wanted to call Lucy, but he also knew she was working this difficult case and he didn't want her attention divided. If it was serious, he'd call her.

First Sean filled out paperwork. Then the nurse took Jesse's vitals. Told him to take off his shirt and put on a gown. Then they waited longer and a tech came in to take Jesse for an X-ray. Then they waited again. Finally a doctor came in moments before Sean went to hunt him down.

"Hello, Mr. Rogan, Jesse. Soccer injury? Usually I see broken legs, sprained ankles, the occasional concussion. You a goalie? Get kicked diving for the ball?"

"No, sir," Jesse said. "We were doing a drill. I was distracted and the ball hit me in the chest."

"Huh. Get the wind knocked out of you?"

"Yes, sir."

"Let's see. I'm just going to lift up the gown, okay?"

"Okay."

As soon as Sean saw the bruises in the harsh hospital light, he knew they weren't from a soccer ball. He had been in enough fights to know that the small, circular bruises were caused from a punch. Two punches. Sean looked at Jesse's hands. They were clean. He hadn't fought back.

"Tell me when it hurts," the doctor said as he pressed different parts of Jesse's stomach and chest. As he neared the bruises Jesse showed signs of pain.

"Well, okay, young man, let me show you what's going on here." He pulled up the X-ray on the computer. "You have a hairline fracture on rib seven here, right where it connects to the cartilage. The bruising is caused by the ball, not the cracked rib—you can actually have a cracked rib with no bruising, believe it or not. Fortunately, there is no sign of internal bleeding, and there are no bone spurs or anything to impede recovery. Everything else seems to be just fine."

He looked at Sean, Sean's hands, then Jesse. Did the doctor know this wasn't a soccer accident? Did he think that Sean had hit Jesse? Sean wanted to argue at the unspoken charge, but didn't. He had to talk to Jesse one-on-one and find out exactly what happened.

But he'd lied to him. Jesse had lied to him about something important and Sean didn't know how to fix this. Punish him? Ground him? Sean had lied to Duke all the time about where he was and what he was doing, and Duke had grounded him repeatedly and Sean had ignored him. He realized, not for the first time, that he had been a problem kid growing up.

Maybe he owed Duke a bigger apology than the one he'd given him. Coming into parenthood with a ready-made teenager had to be one of the hardest things to do. Sean would be more confident going back to Mexico and fighting the drug cartels.

"There's nothing to do for the injury, medically speaking. I'll write a prescription for ibuprofen—stronger than over the counter. We don't tape most rib injuries because it can inhibit deep breathing, which creates other problems. No sports for the next four to six weeks. Go to your regular doctor for an X-ray in four weeks and she can clear you if you're healed. You're a young, healthy kid. I don't see future complications, but you'll want to take it easy for a couple of days."

"Thank you, Doctor," Sean said.

"I'll leave the 'scrip and sign the papers while you get dressed." He left the cubicle, pulling the curtain closed behind him.

"I told you it was nothing," Jesse said. He slid off the gown and started to pull on his T-shirt, then winced.

Sean helped him with his shirt. "I've had broken ribs and cracked ribs and it hurts like hell. Are you sure a ball did this?"

"You don't believe me?"

No, I don't.

"Jess, you can tell me anything."

"I want to go home."

"Dammit, I need you to be honest with me!" Sean was about to lose it, and he didn't want to. Not here, not at home, not ever. But he was on edge, and Jesse lying to him was going to send him over. He didn't know how to deal with this.

"I'm not lying!"

But he wasn't looking him right in the eye. He *almost* was, but not quite.

"Why don't you trust me?"

"Why don't you trust *me*?" Jesse countered.

"I've been beaten before. I know what a fight looks like. If you're in trouble, if someone is bullying you—"

"Stop. You're wrong."

Sean wasn't wrong. Maybe about the circumstances of the fight, but he wasn't wrong that Jesse had been attacked. He didn't know how to get Jesse to tell him the truth.

CHAPTER TWENTY

Thursday Night

"I'm sorry I'm so late," Lucy said when she came in well after nine. "Jerry and I have gone around and around about this case and we're getting nowhere."

Sean was sitting at the island in the kitchen nursing his third beer. He tried to listen—Lucy was clearly frustrated with the lack of evidence on her case—but he was only half listening.

"Hey," she said and put her arms around him from behind. He didn't realize how much he needed her right now. He'd been so tense since the hospital that his head ached.

He leaned back on the stool, closed his eyes, and let Lucy support him. Just for a minute. Just to clear his head.

She kissed the back of his head and hugged him tightly. "Talk," she said.

"Jesse. He lied to me. A big one, and I don't know what to do about it."

She kissed him again, then walked around to the counter and poured herself a glass of red wine from a half-empty bottle on the counter. She sat next to him and took his hand. He stared at his beer and told her about the

cracked rib, about how when he saw the bruises this afternoon he knew that Jesse had been punched. "If someone
is bullying him, at school or at soccer, why won't he tell
me? This isn't just a couple of guys roughing it up—I
know, I've been in enough fights in my life. He had no defensive wounds. None. He just let someone beat on him,
and now he's out of soccer for at least four weeks. I called
Michael because Jesse has been talking to him so much,
see if Jesse said something to him, but he said he didn't
know anything about it."

"And?"

"Michael knows something and he's not telling me. I
called Jesse's coach tonight and asked about practice on
Wednesday. He said Brian left early and Jesse went after
him, missed thirty minutes of practice. What are they up
to? Were they fighting each other?"

"Brian? I don't see that," Lucy said.

"I can't help but think this has something to do with all
the time Jesse has been spending over at Saint Catherine's.
Last night Michael called me for help in math. I'm happy
to help, you know that, but I had a feeling that he didn't
need it. It was like the mistakes he made were almost de-
liberate. I didn't think about it at the time, but I haven't
stopped thinking about it this afternoon. Michael isn't
talking, and Jesse isn't talking, and I'm at my wit's end. I
don't have to know everything, but when someone hits my
son hard enough to crack a rib . . . I'm not going to sit back
and let it go."

"What did Jesse say when you confronted him?"

"I haven't."

"Why not?"

"He didn't waver in his explanation to the doctor. I
asked him if he was really hit by a ball, and he said yes,
accused me of not trusting him. But I *saw* the bruises.
What if the doc thinks that I'm the one beating on him?"

"That's ridiculous," Lucy said.

"Not really. I had CPS down my throat once when I got in a fight. I was fifteen, and Duke dragged me to the emergency room after I got in a brawl with three guys who were bigger, but stupider, than me. If it wasn't for Duke's friends in law enforcement, I might have been thrown in foster care and Duke into jail."

"Different situation."

"Not really—the nurse called them because Duke and I were yelling, and I was out of control, and she thought Duke beat me." Sean shook his head. "He probably wanted to, but he never laid a hand on me."

"You and Duke had a much different relationship than you and Jesse. You're different people. And you're not the same person you were as a teenager. Why didn't you tell Jesse you know?"

"Because I don't know what happened! I only know it's not what he said. I need more."

"You could ask. Tell him what you think, ask him to fill in the holes."

"I don't know if I can handle him lying to me again. I just want to find out what happened, then I can talk to him."

"Whatever it is, consider that he might have a good reason."

"I have. But that still doesn't justify him lying."

"Of course it doesn't. Have you eaten?"

"I wasn't hungry. Jesse went to his room when we got home. I brought him a sandwich. Tried to get him to talk. He wouldn't. Said he had homework and I left."

"I'll make you something."

He looked over his shoulder at her with concern. "Really?"

"Stop it."

"There's leftover Rib House on the bottom shelf."

"I can use a microwave just fine." She walked around the island to the refrigerator and pulled out the leftovers, then the doorbell rang.

"I'll get it," Sean said and checked the security pad on the kitchen desk. "It's Leo Proctor. Were you expecting him?"

"No. I asked for a favor, but I assumed he would call."

Sean walked to the front door and let Leo in. "Sorry for coming by so late," he said. "I've been working on this counter-terrorism case all week—twelve-hour days—and this is the first time I could break free."

"Anything to be concerned about?"

"Some scumbag stole RPGs from Lackland last week. I've been working with the MPs and SAPD to track them down. We recovered every piece and arrested every person involved, but today it's been a mountain of paperwork."

"Beer?"

"Love one."

Sean liked Leo, the FBI's SWAT team leader and member of the counter-terrorism squad. He and Lucy had worked together on a couple of cases, and Lucy trained under him in hostage rescue.

Leo sat at the island while Sean retrieved two beers. "Can I dish you up leftovers?" Lucy asked.

"No, thanks. I ate at the office—we brought in hoagies, and I'm still full. But you're on my way home, so I thought I'd tell you what I heard about Walker. Better in person."

"It could have waited until tomorrow."

"I won't be here tomorrow. Taking the day off after this long week. Going fishing up past Spring Branch with a couple buddies. Camping a couple of nights along the river. Drink beer, not think about work."

"Sounds good," Sean said.

"Somehow I don't think you'd have the patience to sit still and fish."

"Probably not."

"Your brother, on the other hand, he'd be good."

Sean laughed. "True."

Lucy put a plate in front of Sean, and had a smaller plate for herself. She sipped her wine and said, "Did you learn anything?"

"Yep." Leo sipped his beer. "Barton boys. Kidnapping, murder."

"Kids?" Sean asked.

Leo nodded. "I wasn't involved with the case. It was handled by a task force led by SSA Grant Stocum."

"I don't know him," Lucy said.

"He's not here anymore—transferred a few years back to God knows where. Might have even left the bureau. Good riddance. I didn't like him, he didn't like me. He was a ladder climber. I wouldn't say he was a bad agent or a good agent—his clearance rate was solid, but that's because he cherry-picked his cases. And with the Barton case, he put the blame on his team—not on himself. One of the task force members was Emilio. Everyone likes Emilio, who never says shit about anyone, so when Emilio didn't have a kind word, I knew I was justified in not liking the prick."

"Emilio must have been a rookie back then."

"Yep. About six months in at the time. Basically—the Barton brothers, six and eight, were kidnapped by their aunt on their way to school. Walker got the initial call. Because it was sensitive and timely where every minute counted, the FBI was brought in fast—I doubt Walker made *that* call, but from folks in the know, he was fine with it until Stocum took over and iced Walker out. There were a lot of accusations tossed around. Walker believed that this was a volatile situation, they had to act quickly, while the FBI called in a profiler who took the information that this was a family dispute and decided that the aunt wasn't a danger to the boys, that they should negotiate for their safe return, find out what the aunt wanted, the whole nine yards. That time would help de-escalate."

"Aunt?" Lucy asked. "Not a noncustodial parent?"

"Yeah. The older sister of the mother. Stocum ignored Walker, then kicked him from the investigation when he went off the reservation. Can't have two people calling the shots. Stocum followed protocol, but the profile was wrong or misinterpreted, and the boys died—murder-suicide. Walker was suspended when he decked Stocum. I heard through the grapevine that he developed a drinking problem—I just didn't know why. Now I do. He's cleaned himself up and is one of the best investigators in the sheriff's office, but yeah, he does not like us much."

"It makes so much more sense now," Lucy said. "He has complete disdain for the Behavioral Science Unit and criminal profiling. But we need it on this case."

"It's that bad?"

"Three victims, no connection. If the MO and ballistics didn't match, I wouldn't think that the same person killed them. But it's looking more and more like we're dealing with an actual serial killer, and if so, we need to put together a bigger task force, more resources, and develop a deep profile."

"No motive?" Leo asked.

"Not collectively. I suppose there are individual motives, especially for the first and third victims, but nothing really solid. Plus, we learned that the first wife lied to us." Lucy realized Marissa Garcia had also lied—a lie of omission—by not telling them about Julio's confrontation with Chris Smith. But Lucy really didn't blame her.

"Sounds juicy," Leo said. "And guilty."

"She was cheating on her husband, and not with one guy. Plus, we believe she manipulated her husband into ramming a friend's truck in high school, which inadvertently paralyzed his friend. So maybe she's into something else we haven't found—Walker is all over it. He really didn't like how she attempted to manipulate us. And there's an insurance policy on her husband."

"Money," Leo snorted. "Number one cause of divorce and murder."

"And I suspect if we didn't have two more victims, Leo would have pushed harder on Little Ms. Sweetness and found out about the boyfriends on the side. But that still doesn't tie her to Standish's murder. Then, four weeks later, another guy gets killed, also on a Friday night, late, this one coming home from a business trip. There's less motive to kill him—pillar of the community, teenage daughter, lives here—in Olmos Park. Frugal, well-liked accountant. The only real motive would be that his daughter is independently wealthy. Super wealthy."

"The teenager?" Sean asked.

"She's fourteen, her mother was from an old-money family in California. When her mother died, Abigail was awarded a substantial trust. But no one can access the money until she's twenty-one. We've found no dirt on James at all. Then the third victim." She sighed, rubbed her eyes. She'd lost her appetite and rinsed off her plate.

"Something different with Garcia?" Sean asked.

"His wife is eight months' pregnant. He is a hardworking family man. But we learned that his best friend may have raped his wife a few months before their wedding. I haven't interviewed the wife yet, the information is secondhand. But it's clear from what we know that the boy Garcia raised is the child from the rape. There was a fight between the men a few weeks ago, and while we don't know whether the rapist found out the truth about the child's paternity, if he did that is motive."

"For Garcia to kill him," Sean said through clenched teeth.

"Or for the rapist to kill Garcia if he thought his former friend lied to him all these years. You know as well as I do that after seven years it's going to be difficult if not impossible to prove a rape. We interviewed the guy, and I want him to be guilty, but his alibi for the first murder is solid. Jerry already confirmed. Impossible for him to have been in San Antonio. The third murder—his former friend—is a looser alibi, but it's still pretty good. He's staying at his mother's house while he's in town."

"Are you investigating the suspected rape?" Sean asked.

"I called Tia Mancini when I was driving home. She's very interested and is going to do some preliminary work."

"She's good," Sean concurred. He rinsed his plate and stood behind Lucy, rubbing her back. She was tense. This was a tough case, but with this added assault, he knew she was twisted up inside.

"So three victims," Leo said, "no connection, each where there is a motive—weak, maybe, but present."

"But it's three *different* motives. Adultery, daughter's trust fund—unless James has a secret life we haven't found out about yet—and a seven-year-old rape. But the victims *were* the victims—I mean," Lucy corrected, realizing that she was overtired and not speaking clearly, "the victims were the ones who had a motive. Standish, one of his wife's lovers; Garcia, the man who raped his wife. If Abby James was the one who died, the trust reverts to the larger family trust and most of the money goes to charity. At least, that's what I got from the paperwork. It's extensive."

"I can take a look at it," Sean said.

"Maybe that would help—because it's written in complex lawyer-ese."

"I see why you want to consult BSU," Leo said. "There's no one motive—unless the guy is a nutjob."

"Most serial killers are not legally insane," Lucy said. "He has a reason—it might not make sense to us, but he has a very specific reason for killing these people. They may be a surrogate for someone else, or they may have slighted him in some minor way that he exaggerated in his head. We have no similar murders in other jurisdictions. The murders feel like a setup—everything just how the killer wants it, a show. For us. I can't shake that feeling. But ultimately, it's the shot to the face that tells me the killer truly has ice in his veins. He—or she—looked the victim in the eyes and fired. Each victim—except Garcia, who was already dead when he was shot. It takes either rage or cold to shoot a person in the face. To look them in the eye as you pull the trigger."

She should know. She'd done it. Her rapist—the man who had kidnapped her and had others rape her in front of a video camera—she'd killed him in cold blood. She did not regret it. Cold had seeped into her bones. Filled her with icy rage. People say that anger is hot, but for her it was the cold that enabled her to kill an unarmed man.

But she hadn't shot him in the face. She'd emptied the revolver, all six bullets, into his chest. Why? She hated him. His arrogance. His borderline insanity. She *should* have shot him in the face.

"Luce," Sean whispered in her ear.

"I'm fine," she said, and cleared her throat. "When I first caught this case, I thought revenge. It felt like revenge. But revenge for what? None of these men have done anything to warrant killing—unless we haven't found it. And the killer is becoming bolder. Killing faster. Four weeks, three weeks . . . do we have two weeks now? One? Tomorrow's Friday and I feel like we're no closer to finding a suspect than we were two months ago. That's why I want to consult with BSU, but Walker has put his foot down."

"You're a criminal psychologist," Leo said. "You understand profiling."

"I studied, but I'm not a criminal psychologist. I don't

do this full-time. My brother Dillon has years of experience. BSU employs a dozen people, all of whom have more experience than me. Fresh eyes can open up an investigation."

"You could consult alone, go around Walker."

"I didn't want to go that route, but I may have to."

She really didn't want to go over Walker's head—not when they had been getting along fairly well. But they were stymied, and she couldn't figure out a way to get inside this killer's head. Couldn't figure out why.

Leo finished his beer and stood up. "I'm going to head home. Thanks for the beer, I'll see you on Monday—can't wait to relax and not think of idiots who steal military weapons or serial killers who shoot people in the face."

Sean walked him out and Lucy cleaned up the kitchen. There wasn't much to do, and she was done by the time Sean returned.

He pulled her into his arms and kissed her. "Talk."

"I'm fine."

"This is hard for you."

"I'm just frustrated."

"That's not what I meant."

She knew what he meant; she didn't want to talk about it. "I'm okay. Seriously—we'll deal with any fallout later, but it's not going to impact this investigation." She kissed him. "I have my case, you need to focus on Jesse."

"He's asleep—I just checked on him. So it's you, me, and—well, not Bandit, because my traitor dog is on Jesse's bed. He knows it's the only piece of furniture I won't kick him off."

"I've been thinking about Jesse's situation. Maybe Brian knows what's going on."

"You've been thinking? Between analyzing your case with Leo and dinner?"

"Ha. Seriously, the coach said Jesse went off with Brian,

right? Maybe Brian is the one in trouble, or the one who knows what's going on with Jesse."

"Brian doesn't get in trouble. He's always been a responsible, quiet kid. Michael is still . . . well, edgy. I worry about him."

"And you always will. After what he went through, what he had to do to survive, you wouldn't be human if you didn't worry."

"You think it's Brian?"

"It's the logical place to start. But not tonight. It's nearly eleven, and we need to call it a night. We're both exhausted."

"I'm not *that* exhausted."

She raised an eyebrow. "Oh?"

"I mean, I'd like to go to bed . . . but I might not be able to go right to sleep."

He smiled and played with her hair.

"Let's see about that," Lucy teased and led Sean up the stairs.

CHAPTER TWENTY-ONE

Friday Morning

Lucy woke up at dawn and went to work early. She read every press report as well as the FBI file on the Barton kidnapping and murders. It had been an awful tragedy, but she couldn't tell from the reports whether the agent in charge of the investigation had done anything wrong. Profiling was usually accurate—but it wasn't 100 percent. And much of profiling was dependent on accurate information about the crime, the victims, and the perpetrator. And in the Barton case, they didn't have time to develop anything more than a superficial analysis.

She could understand why Jerry had disdain for the FBI and profiling, but it was *one* case that had ended badly, and there was no way of knowing whether the outcome would have been different if they had handled it differently.

Rachel came in at eight and, after putting her belongings in her office, walked over to Lucy's cubicle. "I heard you were in at six this morning."

"I wanted to read some old files."

"Related to this investigation? The murders?"

She hesitated, then decided she had to be forthcoming. "The case Walker worked on with the FBI ten years ago.

I needed to understand why he has put up a stop sign into asking BSU for a profile."

"And did you learn anything?"

"The case was a tragedy all the way around. I don't know who was to blame, if anyone—I think the profile, which isn't in our files, may have relied on misinformation or incomplete information. But the whole thing ended in less than twenty-four hours. Walker caught it, the FBI came in, the profile was rushed because it was the kidnapping of two minor children, and the boys were killed in a murder-suicide a day after they were grabbed by their aunt. In that time Walker was kicked off the task force because he and the lead agent butted heads."

"What does that have to do with now?"

"I don't want to go over his head."

"I hear a *but*."

"We need a psych profile, and we need it soon. The killer isn't going to stop with three now that he has gotten away with it." *Or she.* "I feel like the killer is giving us a message. Setting the stage. Take the Taser hit, for example. The first victim, based on a reenactment, fought back and may have gotten away or the upper hand when the killer Tasered him in the stomach to get him down, then shot him. And why use duct tape at all? That puts the killer very close to the victim. Then remove the duct tape?

"We could argue that the killer didn't want anyone to hear . . . except Jose Garcia was dead at the first blow, and still the killer went through the motions. The beating, the duct tape, the Taser, then shooting in the face. No need—except to make the crime scene *look* exactly like the first two crime scenes. If the killer left Garcia after the fatal blow, we would never have connected his murder with the first two."

"If you need my authorization, you have it. Make the request."

"I want to call in my brother—Dr. Dillon Kincaid. He consults with the FBI and I've already been talking to him, off the record. But I need BSU to formalize it."

"Whatever you need, do it. Don't worry about Walker. He has his own baggage, and if he can't see the value in consulting with experts, that's his problem."

"I want to set it up and inform him that it's happening, see what he does. He might just avoid it, and I'm okay with that—but we need a direction because everything else has led to a dead end."

"And you think another body is going to drop."

"I know it. Unless we find him first."

Lucy spent all morning going through proper channels—and cutting a few corners—to get a BSU-approved consult with Dillon. She sent all her notes and the files to the BSU district liaison and received a confirmation that *Dr. Dillon Kincaid and a BSU agent will be available to consult via video at 2 pm ET.*

That was one p.m. locally. She considered all her options, and decided that if she asked Walker to come here, he would be in enemy territory—in his mind. She didn't want to blindside him completely. So she brought everything over to the sheriff's office and set up the equipment in the small conference room that they had been using. She then texted him and asked him to meet her as soon as possible, but didn't say why.

Lucy didn't like confrontation, and she grew even more tense as she waited for Jerry.

He walked in at five to one, handed her a Starbucks coffee. "The coffee here is crap, and you drink more than I do."

"Thank you," she said. She took a deep breath as he eyed the small video screen. "You and I agree that we're dealing with a serial killer, albeit not a traditional killer."

"This isn't new."

"And as every road we've traveled has ended us nowhere but back at square one—and we spent all afternoon reviewing every file, every piece of evidence, and have no more leads—I think it would benefit us to consult with fresh eyes. I honestly considered doing this on my own, at FBI headquarters, but then you would think I was taking the case, and I'm not."

"Nor would I let you," he said, his voice low and rough.

"I want full transparency here. Dillon is my brother. I asked specifically for him because he doesn't work for the FBI, but often consults for the FBI. We need more information about this killer. Criminal profiling isn't going to hand us a name, but it *will* give us information that can help us evaluate the crime scenes in a different light. If we can't figure out *why* the killer is targeting *these specific men*, we'll never be able to find him until he makes a mistake. I don't want to face another victim if we haven't done everything humanly possible to stop him."

She sighed, then continued when Jerry didn't say a word. "I get it—you had a bad experience on the Barton case."

"What the hell do you know about that?"

"I'm a cop. I learn things. And I can't say whether the profile was right or wrong, or whether Stocum—who is no longer in our office—screwed up and those two little boys could have been saved. *I don't know.* I wasn't there. But you're a good cop and I trust your judgment. You think it was a screwed-up investigation, I trust your assessment. But that doesn't mean that a profile in this case can't help us."

"Dammit, Kincaid! You went over my head!"

"Yes and no," she admitted. "I did set this up, but I want to do it here. I want you to participate. Go ahead and leave, I'll talk to BSU and see what I can learn. But I would much rather you be here because you know this case backward and forward and might think of things to ask that I don't. I sent the files to Dillon this morning. I want to hear what he has to say. And your experience and insight will be invaluable."

"Don't placate me."

"I'm not. All I want is for you to hear him out."

"And what happens if you agree with him and I don't? If I think he's full of horse shit and you think he's speaking gospel?"

"Talk about borrowing trouble."

The video chat beeped. "You can go," she said.

He didn't budge.

Lucy turned and answered the chat. A second later, Dillon's face appeared on the large computer screen she'd brought in. He was in his home office, and Hans Vigo was sitting next to him, on the edge of the screen. "Hans," Lucy said, "I didn't expect you."

"I saw your request, and since I had other business to discuss with your brother, I opted to take the consult."

"Are you back in BSU?"

"No, still stuck at headquarters, but spending more time at Quantico teaching. Might be permanent. I have five more years until mandatory retirement, and spending that time at Quantico is sounding better and better."

Hans had been seriously injured two years ago when Lucy had been going through the FBI academy, and though he didn't complain, she didn't think he was 100 percent. He'd started in a field office, then went to BSU, was the assistant director at Quantico, then moved over to headquarters to liaison with regional offices. He'd been out in

San Antonio last summer, and Lucy always liked working with him. Hans had been her mentor, and was one of Dillon's closest friends.

"Where's your partner?" Dillon said.

"Right here." She looked over at Jerry, who was standing out of the way of the camera. She moved her chair over slightly and pulled up a chair for Jerry. "He just got back from getting me coffee." She held up the cup.

"Good partner," Dillon said.

Jerry glared at her, then blanked his face and sat down next to her. "Deputy Investigator Jerry Walker, Bexar County Sheriff's Office," he said.

"Dr. Dillon Kincaid, forensic psychiatrist. Lucy's brother, as I'm sure she's told you. This is Dr. Hans Vigo, assistant director with the FBI."

"Not as glamorous as it sounds," Hans said. "Like I just said to Lucy, I'm looking forward to going back to Quantico permanently."

"Y'all have worked together before, I take it."

"A few times," Hans said. "I was down there last year when your local congresswoman was under investigation. Then I worked with Deputy Marcus Bellows on follow-up—know him?"

Jerry was surprised, but masked it pretty well. "Yep. We go way back."

"Good cop," Hans said. "You have a lot of good people down there."

Lucy wanted to kiss Hans. Dillon must have filled him in on the situation with Jerry and his animosity to psychology. Having that local connection would help put Jerry at ease.

Dillon said, "We know you're deep in this investigation, so I'm ready to jump in. Both Hans and I have read the case files and witness notes, and watched the simulations that your forensics unit put together—amazing stuff, really.

I looked at the methodology, and I might suggest a couple minor changes in the assumptions, but the bulk of the analysis is accurate. We don't need to rehash the crime scenes—but was there anything that came up today that changes where you are in the investigation?"

"We're nowhere, if that's what you mean," Jerry said. "What we know is that the crimes would never have been connected if they didn't present the same way and if the same gun wasn't used. We may in fact have ourselves a random serial killer."

"Definitely a serial killer, at least by the definition. But there is nothing random about these murders," Dillon said. "Each victim was selected with a purpose."

"Which is?"

"That, we can't determine with the information we have. When Lucy and I talked the other night, she floated the idea that this was an act, that she felt that the killer was setting a stage. I think that's a good analogy. He—or she—wants you to see the crime scene in a specific way. It's nonsensical on the one hand, right? The shattered hands, the beating, a Taser that was unnecessary, at least in two of the murders. The order of attack was different with each victim, yet the wounds matched up more or less in the end. Beating, hands shattered, Taser to the side, bullet to the face. Each victim found on his back. Each victim shot in the middle of his face, obliterating his identity. But there was no question as to who each victim was—their vehicle, registration, wallet, ID, and prints all pointed to their identity. There was no attempt to conceal the body. There was no passion to these murders."

"Back up," Jerry said. "What the hell do you mean by *passion*? Sex crimes?"

"Not that kind of passion. I mean to say, the killer didn't take particular joy in killing these men. No overkill."

"The hands were overkill," Lucy said.

"True—and it's odd. And because it's odd, it was the first thing we all looked at, right? Trying to figure out what it means. And my professional opinion is that the hands mean nothing."

"Then why?" Lucy said.

"Go back to your initial gut feeling—that the killer is creating a scene. Who studies that scene? Cops. You look at the crime scene and come to conclusions based on the evidence. You see shattered hands, you think a thief, a man who can't keep his hands to himself, or rage. But there was no rage in these murders. None of the murders took longer than three minutes. Attack, kill. The shattered hands and the duct tape were props, for lack of a better word."

"And the Taser," Lucy said.

"Actually, I think the killer needed the Taser with the first victim, Standish. He fought back and might have been on the verge of getting away—or getting the upper hand on his assailant. The Taser put him to his knees, and then another blow had him back down. The biggest change I would suggest to your analysis is that I think the first murder was more violent—that the killer was hurt in the fight, and would have shown signs of injury."

"There was no physical evidence on Standish or around the crime scene," Jerry said. "No DNA, no hair or unidentified fibers."

"I'm not surprised. The killer wore gloves, and he came prepared, down to the type of clothing he wore. This was an extremely well-planned murder. All of them were. Getting back to the Taser, because the killer used it on the first victim—he had to use it on all future victims. In some ways, the killer is mimicking the first kill."

"But is it?" Lucy asked. "Can someone kill so violently his first time? With no hesitation or mistakes?"

"Good question, and most of the time I would say no.

This time—I can't honestly say. I think, but I would not swear, that Standish was the first time for this killer. Something happened in the weeks or months before the first murder that triggered the killer. Something happened where he went from anger and frustration with his own life to murder."

"That's true in just about any crime," Jerry said. His disdain was there, in his tone, and Lucy tried not to react defensively.

"Absolutely," Hans concurred. "And doubly true for a serial killer. A guy who robs a bank—he might be thinking about it for a while, but it isn't until he gets to that *all is lost* moment, like when his girlfriend leaves him or his wife kicks him out or he loses his job—that's when he acts. But a serial killer has had the urge to kill for a long time. They have fantasized about killing for a long time—definitely for months, but often for years. I worked a case early in my career where a guy killed nine women over the course of two years, and when I interviewed him, we learned that he had been thinking about killing women for more than twenty years before he had the courage and opportunity to do so—he'd been fantasizing since he was a teenager. But to go from fantasy to action, it is almost always a very specific event or series of events that lead to the first kill."

"What is stumping me," Dillon said, "as well as Hans, is that we don't have the why. In most serial killings we can look at the victim pool and see the why. But this time it's not clear. There's no connection between the victims. While they were all married, and they are all in the same relative age group, that's not enough to say that those two similarities were factors. In that case, it appears random, but the killer singled them out for a reason—therefore, they are not truly random."

Lucy said, "I've suggested the killer stalked his victims, that he knew their routine."

"That's a good assumption. They were not spontaneous kills—they were planned kills. The killer knew their routes home, and planted himself on each route to lure the victims to the side of the road. The Standish case in particular proves that because he had grease on his hands from a vehicle. But the biggest takeaway here—the key point that Hans and I agree on—is that the killer is uniquely cold. This is a coldness that cannot be hidden. He would be polite, respectful, follow all the social norms. But people who know the killer would probably call him or her introverted, quiet, intelligent, aloof, possibly antisocial. This is not someone who likes people in general, but he can function in society. He or she has at least some college education, above-average intelligence, organized not just as a killer, but in his personal life. He may have friends, he may be married, but he keeps his friends at a distance and is cool with his spouse. However, the killer can play whatever part is needed—true sociopaths are masters of understanding character and psychology, so they can step into a variety of roles with ease. They can't stay in the role forever, but they can play the part. That makes these sorts of killers extremely difficult to track. The BTK Killer, for example, appeared to be a mild-mannered, churchgoing, loving husband and father—we learned that he was a brutal killer whose own arrogance in taunting the police helped with his identification and capture. But here—this killer is setting the stage for the police, leaving bread crumbs, if you will, to follow. But he does not want to be caught.

"This killer is arrogant to the point that he or she thinks that he is better than most people, because he's either smarter or better looking or morally superior. Some serial killers want to be stopped, they have an inner battle between right and wrong. They know that what they are doing is reprehensible, but they almost can't help themselves. So they make mistakes, or drop clues on purpose, hoping that the police will stop them . . . but also hoping they can continue for as long as possible. This killer does not want to be caught. He fully intends to get away with murder."

"Excuse me," Jerry said, "you talk a good game, Doc, but how can you possibly make that deduction? I'm not saying he wants to be caught or doesn't, but how can you make a blanket statement that he's cold and aloof in his day-to-day life? That he went to college? That sounds like psychobabble."

Lucy winced, but neither Dillon nor Hans was fazed. "I understand your skepticism," Dillon said, "and that's going to help you in this case. I think you need to look more closely at Steven James and the people in his life. He absolutely knew who his killer was. The others *may* have known the killer, and they weren't scared—hence turning their backs—but James faced the killer and likely talked to him. Why did he pull over? It was the most populated of the three crime scenes. The parking lot itself was empty, but it was near open businesses. Was he meeting someone there? A client? A friend? How did he communicate with them? We know he called his wife when his flight landed, but that was the only call he made after he de-boarded the plane. Had he planned something before he left California?"

"Dillon makes all good points, and I concur," Hans said, "but I also want to suggest that even the gunshot to the face—which is cold, calculating—was part of the scene. To make us question motive versus opportunity, to steer our investigation into a specific direction."

"I see that," Lucy said, "and it was completely clear after watching the simulations. But Jerry and I reviewed how each crime scene was approached and investigated, and it wouldn't have made a difference. Jerry had the first two solo—and there's nothing he did or didn't do that I would have done differently."

"But it wasn't a robbery. If it was a robbery-homicide, it would have been investigated differently. The focus would be elsewhere because robbery would be the obvious motive. But these murders were staged as a brutal attack, no obvious motive, and you dug deep into the lives of all three victims. You uncovered things about them and their families. What you have learned may not make sense now . . . but it will when the next body drops, simply by the law of percentages."

"Next body," Jerry said bluntly. "Aren't we here doing this song and dance so there won't be another victim?"

"In a perfect world," Dillon said, "but the next victim is already selected. The only thing I'm one hundred percent confident about is that the murder will happen on a Friday night, and that the victim will be male."

"Why Friday?" Lucy asked.

"I think because the killer would be missed other days. By an employer or family. This killer is extremely smart. But very smart people can trip themselves up in their own brilliance. When you find this person—and while I lean male, Hans leans female—"

"Why?" Jerry interrupted.

"Because a male killer isn't going to hit another guy in the groin, unless the killer was sexually assaulted as a child or teen," Hans said. "That's my expert opinion. But this doesn't read like a sexual crime."

"Except," Lucy said, "the groin *and* hands were attacked. It could be a symbol of being touched. An explicitly sexual response."

"That was my guess," Dillon said, "but it's still a guess because we all agree that everything about the crime scene is staged, and I'm wondering if the sexual overtones are here with purpose, not because the killer was previously abused."

"You were saying something, Doc," Jerry commented. "That when we find this person, male or female . . ."

"You won't get them to confess. They will look you in the eye and lie. They are so cold, so collected, a lie detector would be iffy—and I wouldn't offer it up. Even if you present them with irrefutable evidence of their guilt, they will calmly deny that they had anything to do with the crimes. You're not going to rattle them. You need an absolute airtight case against them because they will go all the way to trial without hesitation. There's no doubt in my mind that the killer wants at least one of these people dead—likely for a selfish reason—or perhaps all of them. But because of the theatrics, the forensic bread crumbs, it very well could be two murders are covering up the true motive for one."

"That will make it damn difficult to explain to a jury," Jerry said. "Airtight case might not even do it."

"When you get to that point, I will be happy to be an expert witness. Hans and I discussed it, and we aren't going to put this in writing. Generally, when we create a profile we want to give local law enforcement the most information possible, so that when you're in the field you can use what helps and disregard the rest. And considering there are a couple huge factors—such as the gender of the killer—that are still unknown, we don't want it to leak. Meaning, if we put it in writing, and you arrest a suspect, they could have access to the report in the discovery process. If we get something wrong—which is certainly possible—they may latch onto it and divert a jury's attention. So we're calling this an informal consult, and Hans gets to deal with the paperwork on that because BSU hates when we don't dot *i*'s and cross *t*'s."

"Any questions," Hans said, "call me. Anytime, day or night. Dillon is going to be unreachable until Monday morning."

"Oh—I forgot you were meeting up with Kate," Lucy said. "I hope we didn't keep you too long."

"My flight doesn't leave for ninety minutes, and Hans already agreed to drop me off at the airport."

"You've given us a lot to think about," Jerry said, "but we still don't have a suspect, and you're telling us another body is going to drop."

"I wish I could say you have time—but you don't. Tonight, next week? Most likely. There's a very specific plan and he wants to complete it—is compelled to finish it. The killer thinks he's smarter than any cop, and if you haven't interviewed him—such as he's only indirectly connected to the victims—then he's watching somehow. Following the news, reading papers, crime blogs. You might consider releasing misinformation to lure him out—but again, be careful how you do it, because this killer will smell a trap. And, like I said before, go deeper into Steven James's life. There's no doubt in my mind that he personally knew his killer."

Lucy thanked Hans and Dillon, logged out of the videoconferencing system, and turned to Jerry.

"You blindsided me," Jerry said. "You had no right to set all that up without my approval."

"You had no intention of giving me approval. I get it, Jerry—you were burned by the FBI in the past. I don't fault you for being skeptical now. But we need all the help we can get, and there are not two more qualified people than my brother and Hans."

"We had already determined that James knew his killer because he wasn't attacked from behind—based on evi-

ence. We already determined that the killer was cold,
alculating, and planned each murder—that isn't new in-
ormation. It doesn't take a rocket scientist to think the
iller is arrogant and aloof. Sometimes I think you people
hrow out words to make you sound better, when we
earned nothing new."

"You're right—this is all information we've been work-
ng with, but presented differently, and it makes me look
t each interview from a different light. We went through
verything last night; I'm going through each crime again,
very statement, using the profile that Dillon and Hans just
hared. It's not complete, but it's solid."

She didn't think that Jerry was truly angry with her—
e had asked questions, some of them edged with antago-
ism, but he was paying attention. Thinking. That was one
f the key points in getting a good profile, so that when
ou saw something in an interview or at a crime scene, it
ook on the appropriate meaning. Helped with the direc-
ion of questions.

She spread out her own notes again. "You were trying
o reach Steven James's brother. Did you?"

"We're working on it. We've made contact with his CO
nd he's working on a time to set an interview, but they
re doing maneuvers in the South Pacific and have been
adio silent. He'll contact me as soon as Trevor James is
vailable."

Jerry rubbed his eyes. "Okay, I'll go through all this
with you. Again. Because right now we have no one left
o interview, no evidence to analyze, nothing but dead
ends. But if you're right and the killer knows his victims—
specifically Steven James—then the connection is here
nd we just have to find it."

They were deep into the files again when Jerry's phone
vibrated. "It's Ash." He answered, put the CSI on speaker.
"What do you have?" he asked.

"I found something. Two things."

"Spill."

"The killer was in Garcia's car. I should have figure that out earlier, but because it presented so much like th first two murders, I didn't spend as much time on his ve hicle as I should have. There is evidence that a gas can wa placed on the floor of the passenger seat. Trace evidenc left from the bottom of the can includes gasoline, dir and grass cuttings. Small amounts, but enough to test an compare with other samples."

"Back up, Ash," Jerry said. "Garcia could have put a ga can in his car."

"Yes, and I need to go to the Garcia house and inspec it. I can easily test whether the dirt and grass came fron their yard to rule it out. But I don't think it's his. First, th samples were relatively fresh. Gas evaporates at a specifi rate, and since there was no gas can found at the scene we can surmise that if it *was* his gas can, he removed i prior to going to work on Friday. My computer analysi says it would have been completely evaporated over tha length of time. But I have another reason—there were sev eral small rocks embedded in the floor mat that I con firmed came from the side of the road leading to the park."

"What if," Lucy said, "the killer was allegedly walk ing back to his car with a gas can and flagged Garcia down? Asked for a ride? The gas station was only a mile away. I would be so realistic that Garcia would believe it."

"Possible," Jerry said. "So Ash, you're saying that you can find out where the dirt and grass came from?"

"I can test it against samples we collect. First thing we do is rule out Garcia. Then find me samples, and I can tell you definitively."

"That's great. Thanks."

"I said there were two things."

"I thought that was two."

"The other is even bigger. The duct tape. So duct tape is sticky. It picks up everything, right? And we thought the killer took the tape because it might have his fingerprints or DNA on it. But the sticky also *leaves* a residue. What was difficult was to extract and differentiate trace because of contamination. I just don't have the tools here. But I remembered that since the FBI is assisting, I could use the FBI lab. I sent everything I could obtain from the mouth and face of the victims to the FBI lab and asked that they rush it. It helps that I worked with their lab before, they know me, and, well, I kind of name-dropped your name, Lucy. You have a lot of friends over there."

"Drop my name anytime if it gets results," Lucy said.

"And I just got their report. It's amazing what they can do. They separated out grease, dirt, fibers, and specific cleaning chemicals. I pooled together the commonalities from all three crime scenes in order to establish what was left by the duct tape. I have a specific soil—it matches what I collected from the floor of Garcia's car—and a specific cleaning product that I can use to test against other samples if you get me a suspect. Plus, on the first victim there is a cotton fiber that doesn't match anything else on the victim. I think it was on the very end of the duct tape— you know how the end kind of rolls up just a bit? It's likely from a carpet, and the thread count suggests carpet from a motor vehicle. But the soil is unique and easy to identify."

"I could kiss you," Jerry said. "Damn good work. I'm going to send a deputy with you to go to the Garcia house— you're not a cop, you do not do it on your own. We don't know who's involved or how much they know of our investigation, so we're doing safety first, got it?"

"Yes, sir, I'm ready to go."

Jerry jumped up and ran out of the room. He returned a minute later and said, "This is great. Tangible evidence. I told you, Lucy, we follow the evidence, we'll catch the killer."

CHAPTER TWENTY-TWO

Friday Evening

Brad Donnelly didn't want to work late tonight. Not that he had anything important to do, but he'd been working late every night and he wanted to go home, have a couple of beers, watch the Astros on TV. They had a serious chance at another World Series victory. He didn't have a serious girlfriend, and the girl he had been seeing wasn't working out, so he was avoiding her calls. Truth was, he was closer to forty than thirty, and maybe should be thinking about settling down, but there was no one special, no one who came close to giving him that jolt.

He was working near-frantic on paperwork so he could leave at five without guilt. At quarter to five, his personal cell phone rang. It was a blocked number, but that didn't much matter—he had informants, cops, friends who didn't have caller ID.

"Donnelly," he answered.

"I have information on the Saints." The voice was low and male.

Brad perked up, but was immediately suspicious.

"Who's this?"

"You remember that the Saints fell apart after Jaime

Sanchez was killed. Most of the gang went to prison o
were killed."

"I don't work gangs."

"You are DEA, are you not?"

"Point?"

"The Saints are rebuilding. A new, younger crew. Several of the Saints were released from prison recently. A
large shipment of drugs arrives this evening and will be
repackaged and sent out to the streets. Thirteen Oh Eight
East Santiago Street. But if you don't act fast, they'll be
gone."

"I need something more than your word."

"You have acted on less. Your window is seven to nine.
Too early, the drugs won't be there. Too late, and the drugs
won't be there. If you miss them, they'll move—you know
how this works, Donnelly."

The voice was calm and deep . . . but it sounded
strained. Was this a trap? He didn't see that—he hadn't
gotten in the face of anyone for a long time. He couldn't,
being the boss. *Temporary* boss.

"What's your name and how do I reach you?"

The caller hung up.

Brad stared at the phone. There was something familiar . . . but more than that, it was the connection between
Sanchez and the Saints. Sanchez wasn't a member of the
Saints, but it was absolutely true that they fell apart after
he was killed—because of a coalition under the general
that Sanchez had put together. Very few people knew that.

The voice wasn't Kane Rogan, but he was one of those
people who understood where Sanchez fit in with the
Saints and how they had operated then—and he might
know about distribution. But why wouldn't he call him
himself? Why would he give Brad's private number to
someone who refused to identify himself? If he didn't, he
might still know what's going on.

Brad called Kane and was surprised when he answered the phone. Kane never answered his calls, or anyone else for that matter. Brad had expected to leave a message.

"What," Rogan answered.

"Rogan?"

"Who else?"

"You never pick up your phone."

"Then why did you call me?"

"Are you in town?"

"No."

"Did you give my number to someone with information about the Saints' new distribution network?"

"If I had that information, I would call you myself."

"I got this odd call and he said something that made me think of you. It wasn't anything specific, just a feeling. And the caller understood that Sanchez wasn't a Saint, but that when he died, the Saints and the coalition he built was crippled. That's not information most people put together, even after the raids last year. The voice was familiar, but I couldn't place it—I think he was trying to disguise it."

"You think I would disguise my voice." It almost sounded like Kane was laughing. "What's the intel?"

"A house on East Santiago. The Saints were divided after all that shit with Nicole and Tobias. They were spread thin. If it's true that the core is back together, and that they developed a new distribution network, I might have a chance to shut them down before they get a foothold."

"The core? That was the intel?"

"Yes."

"Names?"

"No."

"Sounds like a trap."

"I'd think so, except I haven't been working the Saints. That's all under SAPD now. My unit will come in when asked, but I trust the people running the gang unit with SAPD. Carmine Villiarrosa is in charge."

"He's clean."

Of course Kane would know that, Brad thought wryly.

"You sure it didn't come from them?"

"No. Carmine doesn't play games."

"If I was there, I'd check it out with you, but I'm four hours away."

"I wasn't asking for help, just trying to figure out what is so damn familiar about the caller. It'll come to me."

"Take backup."

"I'll ask Carmine for an assist. The caller made it sound like it was tonight or never."

"Could be moving. Could be a rival organization. Could be a diversion. Could be a trap. Watch your back."

"Thanks for picking up."

"I suppose you could say I'm turning over a new leaf."

Kane hung up. Brad had never thought that guy would settle down, but he had a girlfriend now, and he was spending more time in Texas than he was in Mexico, which was a good thing—at least in that Kane was less likely to get his head blown off here.

Brad called Carmine. "What have you heard about the core Saints getting back together?"

Silence.

"Can you talk?" Brad asked.

"One of your snitches talking?"

"Not really. But it sounds like you're on it."

"Just surprised. It's been done quietly, and you haven't been involved in gangs in over a year."

"I had an anonymous call twenty minutes ago. Tried to track it down because it felt weird to me—core Saints back together, a couple guys out of prison, and a location of their new distribution center. Smack in the middle of the mission district."

"Mission? My people have said they're out in the county, cooking meth. We haven't been able to find their house."

"I have an address."

"Have you checked it out?"

"On paper—East Santiago, owned by a management company. Don't have rental agreements in the system."

"East Santiago—well I'll be damned. You think your intel is good?"

"I was hoping you could tell me. After walking into a trap or two, I need more info before I sweep in. But this caller—he got under my skin. Said tonight was a big score, be there between seven and nine or lose everyone."

"There might be some truth to that. I've been tracking two Saints who came back from the border last night. My people couldn't get shit on them, we had to let them go, but there's been a lot of movement, a lot of young members."

"Young? Like teens?"

"Teens, younger. You know the drill—it's exactly how Jaime Sanchez operated."

Michael.

The call was from Michael Rodriguez. Now it made sense. He'd sounded like Kane because Michael knew the system nearly as well as Kane. How the hell did he know what was going down with the Saints?

"It's yours," Brad said, "if I can come along for the ride."

"I don't know how fast I can put together a raid."

"I can give you four people."

"I can work with that, pull a small team together. Between the two of us, we'll have enough. Be here in one hour. I'm going to send a scout now to check it out, get the lay of the land."

"Do you have list of the Saints you've been tracking? Particularly their core and the new parolees. I want to look at it. I have an idea, but need to look at names."

"I'll shoot it over to you. But don't be late—if your intel is solid, we can deliver a huge blow to the Saints before they get back to full power."

Brad waited for the email from Carmine and quickly dealt with the rest of his paperwork. He was about to toss a note when he did a double take.

1976 Chevelle. East Santiago. Lee Sanchez.

The car Lucy had him run because it had been in the neighborhood of St. Catherine's. Her gut said something was off . . . and now he gets a call about the house on East Santiago. That the Saints are getting back together, and he thinks it's Michael.

The kid knows something.

They were going to have a long talk tomorrow about this anonymous caller bullshit.

How the hell is Michael involved? What is that kid up to?

Michael was a tough kid who had been to hell and back, but if it wasn't for him, Brad would be dead. He wasn't going to say anything to Carmine—or anyone else for that matter—but he sent Kane a text message.

I'm nearly certain Michael Rodriguez is my anonymous caller. I'm talking to him tomorrow—all is a go for tonight with SAPD.

A moment later Kane responded.

Keep me in the loop.

CHAPTER TWENTY-THREE

Saturday Morning

Lucy needed more coffee.

It was five in the morning and she had poured one cup on her way out the door, but that was long since finished and she needed the caffeine. But most coffee shops weren't even open yet.

Victor King had been found beaten and shot on a remote road overlooking Canyon Lake, in Comal County north of Bexar. King's neighbor called the park ranger's office after his dog showed up limping, with an open wound and trailing a leash. The rangers searched the area and found King's body just after midnight. The rangers called the sheriff's office. As soon as the deputy from Comal saw the pummeled hands and gunshot to the face, he called his boss, who called Jerry's boss, who called Jerry, who called Lucy. They were on scene less than eight hours after the murder.

At least Jerry wasn't so angry about yesterday that he iced her out completely.

"One week," he said. "One week, not three. He's escalating."

"Could be," Lucy said. "But this is different."

"Want to bet the slug is fired from the same gun?"

"I'm not saying a different killer. The victim is older—fifteen years older than the next oldest victim. The first three victims were in their car. This one was walking his dog. If he walked his dog the same time every night, the killer had to have known that—and in this remote area, the neighbors would notice a stranger, wouldn't you think?"

She remembered what Dillon had said.

"The only thing I'm certain about is that the next victim will be a male and killed on a Friday night."

"We need to talk to the neighbor who found the dog. Others in the area."

"Is he single?"

"Don't know—no one mentioned a wife. But someone could have seen something—the victim was found only a thousand yards from his house."

"Can we get the body to our morgue?" Lucy asked. "Julie and Ash have worked on all three victims, they should have this."

"Yeah—my boss already worked it out with Comal County. Ash is on his way, and their coroner will transport to our morgue. It's nice when the two sheriffs are friends, makes my job a lot easier."

They walked to King's house. A deputy was standing on the small deck.

"Where's the dog?" Jerry asked. "We want to check him for evidence."

"My partner took him to the vet, sir. He was injured."

"How so?"

"He was limping, and the neighbor noticed he wouldn't put his paw down. Thinks his leg might be broken or sprained. There was some blood around his ears. Who would hurt a dog?"

The same person who would bludgeon a middle-aged man.

"Deputy, make sure that the vet knows to collect and preserve any evidence from the animal," Jerry said.

"He's aware the dog was at a crime scene," the deputy said.

"Where's the neighbor?"

"It's the couple to the west—Mr. and Mrs. Brown. A victim counselor is sitting with them, they were shaken when they learned their neighbor had been murdered."

"Thank you." Jerry led the way to the neighbors' house—the houses were set far apart from one another, with trees and shrubs giving more privacy. It was actually nice up here, Lucy thought—a good place to live. Half the area was privately owned, the other half a state park. Wasn't Leo camping someplace near here? She thought it was farther to the west, where the Guadalupe River comes into the lake.

The counselor was Rebecca Guiterrez, a petite psychologist with a soothing voice and comforting manner. She asked to speak to them before they came into the house.

"The Browns are in their seventies, both retired, and they've known the victim for more than thirty years—since Mr. King moved here with his wife. They aren't taking this well, so please consider what information you share."

"We'll be sensitive," Jerry said.

"I'd like to sit in as well—I work with the sheriff's department here, as well as the smaller police departments. They'll need someone when you all leave and they don't know what's going on. I can be their conduit for information."

"Fine with us," Jerry said.

"Thank you."

She led them into the living room. The Browns sat on their couch together, holding hands. There was iced tea and coffee on the table.

Mrs. Brown started to get up. "May I get you something? Fresh coffee?"

"I'll get it, Mrs. Brown," Rebecca said. "You sit down, okay?"

"Thank you, sweetheart. You have been so kind."

Rebecca went into the kitchen. Jerry said, "Rebecca said you've known Mr. King for a long time."

Mr. Brown nodded. "We've lived here since we built this house in the 'seventies. Victor and Margaret—Margie died three years ago, cancer. They moved in when they were married. Our kids were a bit older, our daughter babysat for them for years. We became friends. When Margie died, we had Victor over at least twice a week for dinner. Found him a new bridge partner, another widower. We'd played bridge with Victor and Margie every Thursday for as long as I can remember."

"I can't believe someone would hurt him," Mrs. Brown said.

Rebecca came in with fresh coffee, and Lucy was immensely grateful. She accepted the mug and sipped. Strong. Just what she needed.

"I'm from the Bexar County Sheriff's Office, and Agent Kincaid is from the FBI. We believe that Mr. King was killed by a suspect who has taken the lives of three other men over the last two months. Have you seen or heard anything in the neighborhood that made you suspicious? An unfamiliar car? A stranger walking by?"

They both shook their heads. "People don't come up here much—the state park is too far, and there's no thoroughfare. One way in, one way out," Mr. Brown said.

Mrs. Brown looked up at him. She was trying to say something with her expression.

Lucy needed to know exactly what she was thinking. "Mrs. Brown? Do you know of someone who may have wanted to hurt Mr. King? Has anyone threatened him lately?"

"No, of course not," she said, but didn't look Lucy in the eye.

Mr. Brown rubbed his eyes. "This is so difficult for us right now."

"We understand that," Lucy said. "Victor was your friend."

"He was like family," Mrs. Brown said, her voice cracking.

"It's very important that we know everything about his life. Was he still working?"

"He was only fifty-five. That's why losing Margie was so hard on him, he expected to have her into his retirement."

"What does he do for a living?"

"He and Margie were both teachers at the high school. Margie taught advanced math, but had to leave because of cancer treatment a few years before she passed, and he teaches American history and government. I don't think he was even thinking about retirement, he enjoyed his job and loves working with teenagers."

"Does he have children? Brothers or sisters?" Jerry asked.

Again, that look.

"Natalie is thirty, also a teacher, married to a doctor. They live in the Dallas–Fort Worth area, visit at least once a month. They have a beautiful baby girl, Maggie—Margaret, after her mother, who was born on Margie's birthday the year after she died." Mrs. Brown's voice cracked.

Rebecca said, "Can I get something, Mrs. Brown?"

She shook her head.

"Natalie is the only child?"

"No," Mr. Brown said, then nothing more.

"Was Victor estranged from his other children?"

"He has a son, Garrett. A year younger than Natalie. He's not a bad kid."

Most adults didn't call twenty-nine a "kid," or lead with "He's not a bad kid."

"Is he local?"

"Garrett has had a difficult time holding down a job," Mr. Brown said. "Victor would have been happy having his son live here, but Garrett didn't want to do anything, just thought he could live here rent-free and not lift a finger to help."

"Now, he has his issues, but hear what you're saying, honey—Garrett wouldn't hurt his father."

Mr. Brown didn't look as confident as his wife. "All I'm saying is, Garrett was really angry when Victor told him to move out. This was after Garrett lied about losing his job, then stole from him—stole from his own father."

"When was this?" Lucy asked.

"Two, three months ago. End of the school year, so I would guess mid- to late June."

"Thank you," Jerry said with a glance at Lucy. It was clear that he was thinking exactly what Lucy was thinking, which is what Dillon had said yesterday:

"Something happened in the weeks or months before the first murder that triggered the killer. Something where he went from anger and frustration with his life to murder."

"You're thinking, and I don't know what," Jerry said. They were in Victor King's house searching for any evidence that would give them a motive, as well as where they could find his son, Garrett. "It's clear as day that everything your shrink brother said is pretty accurate. And the evidence supports it."

"I don't know."

"We find Garrett King and talk to him."

"Would he kick a dog? Hit a dog with a sledgehammer?"

"I've seen worse." Jerry glanced over at her. "So have you, I reckon."

He wasn't wrong. Lucy hated this case. The victims were all good men who worked hard and had people who loved them.

"Why kill Standish, James, and Garcia?" Lucy said. "It's so . . . senseless." And the theatrics. The cold-blooded murders.

Jerry went down the hall and Lucy started looking through Victor's desk, which was in a small open den off the family room. He had pictures of his students all over the place, and a prominent picture of his wife on his desk, where he could always see it. She was lovely, even as she aged. A framed picture of the family on vacation when the kids were teenagers showed the four at a happier time.

A son, killing his father. It made her stomach churn. Families could love passionately—and they could hate just as passionately.

She looked through his well-used desk calendar. The corners were frayed as if he stuffed it in a briefcase or backpack every day. In small, perfect block letters he kept a detailed accounting of his time. Doctor's appointments, school holidays. The first day of school the last week of August was boxed in red with a star. He had staff meetings and after-school appointments; a plumber came out the week before school started. Bridge with the Browns and a guy named Eric Lopez, every other Thursday night. He had tickets to see the Astros for their last home game of the season—next week. Three months ago a contractor came for "deck replacement." One week was marked off.

The week after that he had an appointment with "James @ Allied" and indicated he needed to bring "tax, retirement, insurance."

That couldn't be a coincidence.

King had an old computer, but it wasn't turned on. He was pretty old-school about his desk—such as the physical calendar—so she searched for an address book. She found it in the top right-hand drawer. Everything was organized. Some pages had business cards stapled to them. She flipped through slowly and found Steven James's business card.

There was nothing for Julio Garcia or Sun Tower, but she nearly jumped out of her seat when she saw the name *Bill Standish, contractor—deck* with his contractor's license number written below.

"Jerry," she called out.

A minute later he walked into the small den. "No sign of forced entry," Jerry said when he entered, "though his son probably had a key. I found where Garrett has been living. Downstairs has its own entrance, a bathroom and family room. Pullout couch. A bunch of his stuff is there. I called in for a warrant. I think we have cause, the house isn't in his name and the neighbors said he wasn't living here, but I don't want that bastard getting away with this if he finds himself a slimy lawyer who can twist around what's what."

"I agree," she said. "I found a connection."

She showed him both the desk calendar and the address book. "Nothing this year about him going to Sun Tower and Julio Garcia isn't in his address book, but both James *and* Standish are—it appears James was his accountant and Standish rebuilt his deck."

"Well, I'll be damned."

"Still doesn't explain why."

"Does there have to be a reason? Maybe the guy has a screw loose. Maybe he's off his meds. I had a case a few years back where this kid, twenties, was the sweetest girl you could ever meet—until she thought she was cured and stopped taking her pills. She attacked her sister with a baseball bat."

"These murders were well planned, not the spontaneous act of someone who is mentally unbalanced."

"Maybe he has a reason," Jerry said. "Like your brother said—if the victims aren't connected, the killer is connected in them in some way. And right now, we have three of four after just a few hours. I already put out a BOLO for Garrett King."

"We should call William Peterson and see what exactly Steven James did for Victor King—what kind of motive there might be for Garrett to target him."

"Maybe he cut him out of his will or something." Jerry looked at his watch. "It's still early, not even seven in the morning. I'm famished. Want to get breakfast and then we can call on Peterson?"

"There's one more thing in this address book we should follow up on—before he slips away." She turned a page to face Jerry. It listed Garrett King and his current address—which had been written over a space with multiple white-outs.

"Well, dammit, I'm going to be grouchy without food."

"I have energy bars in my glove compartment."

"Not helping."

Unfortunately for the case, but fortunately for Jerry's stomach, Garrett King wasn't at his apartment in downtown San Antonio. Jerry called in a deputy to sit on the place and he and Lucy met at a chain diner down the street.

After coffee, pancakes, and bacon, Jerry said, "I owe you an apology."

"You don't."

"I jumped down your throat yesterday when you called me on the carpet for letting the Barton case cloud my judgment on this case. So far, everything you and your shrink brother have said has made sense. It's common sense, but yeah, I can see the benefit of understanding the psychology behind a crime. And for a case like this—if King is guilty, the jury is going to have a hard time connecting the victims. His father, sure—wouldn't be the first time family turned on each other. But why the others? We have to make sure the DA has a solid case to take to court. Your brother talks smart, but also in plainspeak. He must be good as an expert witness."

"The best," she agreed. "I'd like to interview Garrett King. Dual interrogation."

"Because you're psychic or something now? Tell if he's guilty by looking at him?"

"Not psychic, but interrogation is something I'm good at. Dillon says the killer won't break—he'll be cold, calculating, uninterested in the proceedings. Arrogant and confident that he will get off. That may be the case. We need to figure out before we go in whether he'll respond better to a female being the good cop or the bad cop."

"Like George Andres and Susan Standish."

"Exactly."

"I'm good on the fly. Tag team it is."

She glanced at her watch. "Would you mind if I took a couple of hours?"

"Family?"

"My stepson's soccer game. It starts at nine, and I should be able to make it before halftime."

"There's not much we can do. We have people looking

for King, someone sitting on his apartment, we don't know where he works. I'll call you when we bring him in. Plus I like to keep my suspects on ice for a while before the interview, so no need to rush back."

CHAPTER TWENTY-FOUR

Saturday Mid-Morning

Sean didn't know how to talk to Jesse. He'd gone to school Friday, come home, and disappeared into his room. Was he avoiding Sean because he felt guilty about lying? Or was there something more going on?

On Saturday morning Jesse had a soccer game. He was benched, but he needed to be there to support his team. He looked miserable as they drove over to a field across town.

"Lucy might not be able to make it," Sean said. "She was called out early this morning because there's another victim, but she said she might be able to slip away."

"Same guy?"

"They think so. She just texted me and said they have a suspect, so let's hope they can wrap it up this weekend." Sean didn't like that two of their weekends had now been taken over by this investigation. He didn't fault Lucy for working so hard—she loved her job, and she was good at it—but he found himself relying more and more on her advice and wisdom about how to raise Jesse.

Parenting—especially when you came into it when the kid was already half grown—was *damn* hard.

"I'm sorry, Dad," Jesse said quietly when they pulled into the parking lot.

He was going to come clean. Tell him what was going on.

"I know."

He waited.

Jesse sighed. "You're disappointed. That I can't play."

What?

"No," he said. "I'm sorry because I know *you* want to play. And it's good for you to be here and support your team. But don't apologize for getting hurt. That wasn't your fault, right?"

He hesitated, then said, "Right."

Dammit, he wasn't talking. He was sticking with his original story. Maybe Sean should have confronted him earlier with what he knew.

His cell phone rang. It was Brad Donnelly. "Hey, I gotta take this. Go join your team, I'll be out there before the game starts."

Jesse left the car as Sean answered.

"Hey, Donnelly. What's up?"

"I need to talk to Michael Rodriguez today. I tried calling Saint Catherine's but there's no answer."

"What's going on?"

"I'm pretty sure he called in an anonymous tip yesterday related to the Saints' new distribution network. I had a team that followed up on the tip with SAPD and damn, shut it down. Missed a few people, and now I'm really worried about Michael. Did you know that Jose Torres is out of prison?"

"I don't know who that is."

"Yeah you do. He's Brian's brother."

In the far reaches of his mind, he remembered that Brian had a brother, but he didn't know much about him.

"Aren't you supposed to be notified when family is released?"

"Doesn't always happen. He got out two months ago. We sent a scout to do surveillance yesterday to confirm the tip—I was suspicious because of something the caller said that reminded me of Kane, so I called him, thinking it was one of his people. It wasn't. Then I pulled the list of all the known Saints gang members. At first I didn't put two and two together—but the scout returned with a photo of Brian going into the house with Jose, and I realized Torres was out of prison. But neither of them was there when we raided. Is Brian missing?"

Sean looked out at the field. Brian was warming up with his team. Michael and the rest of the boys from St. Catherine's were in the bleachers with Sister Ruth.

"No. I'm with him now."

"Jose wasn't in the house. I know you have an affinity for those boys—I do, too. But Jose is bad news. He did extra time because his attitude got him into more trouble behind bars. If Brian has been initiated, you've got to get him away from those boys."

"I know what's going on." Michael was trying to save Brian. And somehow, Jesse was involved. Shit shit shit! How could Sean protect any of them if they lied to him?

"Sounds like you know more than I do."

"Michael's trying to get Brian away from his brother. That means he's been following him, found out about the house—tipped you off." With Jesse. That's why Jesse and Michael had been spending so much time together—they were partners in this . . . this *intervention*.

"I trust Michael," Brad said, "he's never going to be one of them, but he can be ruthless and reckless, and you know it. Worse, do you realize what the Saints will do to him if they find out? That house was new—just started up when Jose got out. That means very few people know about it.

He's going to think Brian betrayed him—or he knows about Michael. And get this—Lucy had me run a plate last week. Said it was a car that looked suspicious around Saint Catherine's. I didn't think anything of the owner, a distant cousin of Jaime Sanchez, and the address is in the general area of Saint Catherine's. But—it's the house we raided, and the distant cousin who owns the car? He's working a long-term job in Houston. Seems he let the Saints back in, but didn't stick around."

"I have eyes on all of the boys. I'll find the truth."

"Are you at Saint Catherine's? I'm heading there now."

"No. Brian has a soccer game at Houston Park on Guadalupe. The boys are here watching him."

"I'll be there in twenty. Until we know where Jose and the rest of the gang are, Brian and Michael are both in danger. I'm sending you a recent photo of Jose—and also, I talked to Kane late last night when I put everything together. He's flying up now, should be landing soon."

"Thanks, Brad."

Sean hung up, jumped out of his car, and opened his trunk. He pulled out an extra gun and ammo, concealed everything with a light windbreaker. Then he called Nate Dunning, his closest friend in town who, fortunately, was on FBI SWAT and one of the few people Sean trusted explicitly.

"Want to watch a soccer game?"

"Sure, I guess. When."

"Now. And bring extra firepower. We might need it."

As soon as Sean caught Michael's eye, Michael knew that he knew the truth. Sean didn't wait for him to approach, but went right over to Sister Ruth.

"Ruth, we may have a situation. Can you keep the boys here with you? In the stands? My friend Nate Dunning with the FBI will be here soon and he's going to sit with you and keep an eye out. I need to talk to Michael."

"Sean, what's going on?" Ruth asked, concerned.

"Brian's brother was released from prison and is back with his gang."

"Should we go home?"

"Not until I can get you protection there. Where's Mateo?"

"He's visiting local nursing homes with a group of parishioners. I can try to reach him—"

"No, it's better that he's out now. I'll talk to him later."

Sean looked at Michael and didn't say a word. Michael followed him to a spot under the trees behind the bleachers. Sean could see the entrance to the parking lot from their location.

"Tell me everything," Sean said.

"What do you know?"

"So you can lie to me? Like Jesse has been?"

Michael straightened his spine. "I told him we could handle this on our own."

"You can't. You're playing with fire and putting your own head on the chopping block. Dammit, Michael! You were responsible for taking out Jaime Sanchez's operation and sending half the Saints to prison. Those who scattered, where do you think they went? Back to the Saints. You think they're going to forgive you? You're not that stupid."

Michael glared at him. "Brian knows he made a mistake, we're fixing it."

"You should have come to me."

"You don't know how to handle these people. I would have called Kane if I thought it was necessary. Instead, I called in a tip to the DEA."

"Donnelly called me. He figured out that it was you."

That surprised Michael.

"You're playing with fire. The raid was a complete

success—except that Jose Torres wasn't captured, and they think a handful of his gang slipped out with him. He's going to know that either you or Brian made that call and he'll come after you. Maybe you're prepared to fight and die, but what about the others?" Sean swept his hand to the stands, where the seven other boys living at St. Catherine's were excited to watch Brian and his team compete. "You saved them only to condemn them. And you dragged Jesse in with you."

Michael glared at him. This kid did not back down. Sean admired his tenacity, his deep sense of right and wrong, but worried that his stubbornness would get him hurt. Or worse. "Jesse is the one who saw Jose with Brian in the first place," Michael said. "He's the one who got pictures and told me. I figured out it was Jose and we confronted Brian. I was prepared to expel him, but he came around, he understands what is at stake, and he's mine to protect."

"And you're *mine*. Dammit, Michael, you're not alone and you need to stop acting like you're the only one who cares about these boys. I care. Lucy cares. What about Mateo and Ruth? Do you think Torres is going to give a priest and nun a pass? And while you *think* you had a plan, your plan sucked. You need more than an anonymous call to shut down this operation."

"Jose was supposed to be there," Michael said quietly. "Brian made sure of it. I don't know how he disappeared."

This kid was so smart and so stupid all rolled into one.

"Who hit Jesse? I want the truth."

"He told you?"

"No. He lied to me. I think to protect you and Brian. What the fuck happened? He has a cracked rib and I know what taking a punch looks like."

Michael took a deep breath. "Wednesday Brian skipped out on the second half of practice to meet Jose. Jesse chased after him. It wasn't just Jose, but a couple of his thugs. Jesse tried to talk Brian out of going. Jose punched him. He doesn't know who Jesse is, Brian swears that he told Jose that Jesse was just a friend from soccer. I will protect him."

"You can't even protect yourself, Michael. Don't give me that look—why didn't you trust me? What have I done to make you not trust me?"

That surprised Michael. "I will always trust you. But you are not in this battle. You're not like your brother."

"What the hell is that supposed to mean?"

"You have something to lose."

Sean stared at him. He thought he understood Michael—but he didn't, not until that moment. "Because of my family?"

Michael nodded.

"*You* are my family, Michael."

"Jesse is your family."

This was a conversation they needed to have, but not now. Nate pulled up in the parking lot and Sean motioned for him. "We're going to have a long talk when this is over, Michael—because it's not over. Nate's going to stick with the boys for the duration. Donnelly is on his way, and Kane is flying in from Hidalgo."

"You called Kane?"

"Donnelly did. Because he's the one who figured this out. And dammit, you are going to come clean completely, because you just put a bull's-eye on everyone at Saint Catherine's. Brian may have started it, but I could have extracted him from that without you getting involved. I may not be Kane, but never underestimate my ability to get shit done."

CHAPTER TWENTY-FIVE

Saturday Late Morning

Lucy made it to the soccer game just before halftime. She was surprised to see both Nate Dunning and Brad Donnelly there—Nate was sitting with the boys from St. Catherine's, and both Brad and Sean were clearly working a protection gig.

She walked up to Sean and kissed him. "What's going on?"

"Long story short: Brian's gangbanger brother is out of prison. Michael turned him in to the DEA—but he slipped away."

"Does he know Michael turned him in?"

"We're assuming that he does."

"This is what Jesse has been keeping from us," Lucy said.

"Yes."

It was clear now. Michael had a knack for instilling loyalty in people. It's how he had led the boys at St. Catherine's during their darkest hour. It's how he kept them alive. They trusted him. Jesse trusted him.

But Michael was still a kid, and he was not bulletproof.

Sean continued. "I haven't had the chance to talk to

Jesse. He's with his team." He paused, glanced at her. "Kane's on his way."

"It's that serious?"

"Brad thinks so. I have some ideas on how to draw Torres out."

"You know why Jesse didn't talk to you, right?"

"No. I don't. I should have been the first person he came to."

"He wants to be strong like you and Kane."

"Like Kane."

"Excuse me?"

"Michael essentially said that if he thought this situation was serious enough, he would have called Kane. That I have too much to lose."

"Don't take that personally. Kane is a warrior to Michael."

"That kid—I don't know what to think."

"You love him. He trusts you, Sean—but he's been solving his own problems for years. It's not going to be easy for him to change."

"But now Jesse is involved. I just—damn, I don't know what I'm doing wrong."

"You're not doing anything wrong."

Brad approached before Lucy could say anything else. Sean always took things personally, and she had to get him to see what was really going on.

"Hey, Lucy, thought you were working."

"I am. I'm waiting for a call that our suspect has been located."

"Status?" Sean asked Brad.

"I have two agents patrolling. No sign of Torres."

"Do you think he would show up here? At a soccer game?"

Brad shook his head. "I think he's going to hang low

until he can hit hard. Does Brian know what his brother was in prison for?"

"I don't know," Sean said. "We were focused on the boys' parents. I can tell you the fate or disposition of every mother and father of those boys, but not siblings. I should have seen this coming."

"*I* should have seen this coming," Brad said. "You're not a cop, Sean. I had all their files. I should have tagged Jose Torres."

"I have an idea," Sean said.

"I'm listening."

"I want all the boys in my house. I have the room."

"You can protect them there, but they have to go to school. They can't live there forever."

"Michael and Brian will remain at Saint Catherine's. Jose is going to be looking for them, and he'll think that a house with a nun as the only adult will be easy pickings."

"Bait."

"It's the only way. This can't drag on for weeks or months. We don't have the manpower to watch them all twenty-four seven. We lay a trap. It's the only way we can protect them. But we keep this information tight and contained. I know your house is clean, but I can't risk anyone getting wind of this."

"The two agents I have with me today I trust with my life. We'll keep it small and sharp. Plus we have Kane and Nate, right?"

Sean nodded.

"Good. I'm waiting for intel back on Torres and the two others that slipped away, then we'll figure out a solid plan."

Sean looked down at his phone. "Kane just landed. He'll be here before the game is over."

*   *   *

Lucy left just as Kane arrived at the soccer field. "Where's she going," he asked Sean in lieu of *hello*.

"Back to work. Murder suspect has been located."

"What's the plan?"

For now, it was him, Brad, and Kane. Michael was back in the stands with Nate and the boys, and Brad's two agents were patrolling the park.

Sean told Kane what he wanted to do—split up the boys and set a trap for Torres.

"And when that fails?" Kane asked.

"It's a good plan."

"He's not going to walk into a trap."

"Not if it's obvious."

The last thing Sean needed right now was Kane completely taking over. He would lose all respect from Michael and Jesse. They both saw Kane as a hero, a warrior—and he was. Sean loved and admired his brother more than anyone on the planet. Sean couldn't compete with that. He hadn't even been able to protect Jesse and Madison in his own house.

Maybe he should listen to Kane. Kane knew a hell of a lot more about this shit than Sean did.

"Bait is a good idea," Kane said, "but we need more intel about Torres. Who he runs with, what he's done."

Brad said, "He was in prison for possession with intent and manufacturing meth. Because he fled the scene, resisted arrest, and shot a cop—not fatally—he was tried as an adult at the age of fifteen. Given five to ten. Served seven—three in juvie, four in max. Ties to the Saints through his father, who was killed in prison. I dug around last night into senior's life—he was killed after the boys were rescued."

"Shit. So retaliation. And Torres probably knows that."

"Good bet."

Sean said, "According to Michael, Jose enticed Brian with dreams of being a family again. That they were brothers, bonded for life, and Brian had some sort of obligation to him. Michael said Brian has come back into the fold, but we need to verify that. This is his big brother—he has an idyllic image of him. He might be humoring Michael because Michael threatened to call you."

Kane stared at him. "What the fuck does that mean?"

"All those boys, include Jesse, see you as their savior. You fought for them and you won. Take no prisoners. I get it—you're a hero."

"I'm no fucking hero."

"To them you are. No one can compete with that."

"Donnelly, check the perimeter," Kane said without looking at the agent.

Brad didn't even object to the order, just turned and walked away.

"Spill," Kane said.

What could Sean say? "I'm glad you're here because I'm out of my depth with this bullshit, but the fact remains that Michael and my son see you as the only one who can fix this. They had every opportunity to tell me what was going on, but they didn't. They thought they could fix it themselves, and if they couldn't, you were waiting in the wings."

"This is what I do, Sean. So your nose is out of joint because they don't see you as a killing machine? Damn, you're an idiot. You're just as much a hero to those kids as I am."

"Jesse lied to me! Torres punched him in the gut and cracked his rib and Jesse lied about it. He doesn't think I can keep him safe."

"That's bullshit."

"I couldn't! His mother died because I couldn't keep

them safe. And deep down he knows that, and that's wh
he didn't tell me what was going on this week. And her
we are."

"I'm going to tell you this once, Little Rogan. Jack an
I were there, in the house, two of the best-trained merce
naries working today, and we couldn't keep any of yo
safe. Get it? You were also a target. Are you so dead se
on feeling guilty that you don't remember that Carso
Spade put a fucking million-dollar price on your head? D
you think that I didn't feel exactly what you're feeling whe.
I woke up and my little brother was missing? That
couldn't protect *you* when you asked for my help?

"Get over the damn pity party right now, Sean, because
we don't have time for it. I don't know what's going throug
Michael's or Jesse's head right now. And neither do you
We'll set them straight. But right now, I need you com
pletely focused. You are the fucking smartest guy I know
but if you keep second-guessing yourself we're going to
fail, and I'm not about to lose any of those boys—not Mi
chael, not Brian, and certainly not Jesse."

Sean wanted to hit Kane—and he wanted to hug him
He did neither. His emotions had been a wreck for the las
two and a half months since Madison had been killed, anc
it was true—he had been holding on to the guilt because
it was something tangible.

But he had to let it go. He had to find a way to let it go
and forgive himself.

"What's your plan?" Sean asked.

"I was special forces. No way am I coming up with a
strategy without more intel. First thing: We get those boys
out of the line of fire, they're sitting ducks here. Put Donnelly's people at Saint Catherine's with them. Then I'm
talking to Brian, and no one is going to be in the room with
me."

"Kane—"

"I'm not going to beat him, but he will wish I did when I'm through. And I'll know what we need to know to find Jose Torres and put an end to his threat, once and for all."

Sean wished there was another way, but Kane was right—moving the boys into his house would split their protective detail, and everyone wanted to keep this operation as tight and controlled as possible. But Kane liked Sean's idea of getting the younger boys as far from potential danger as they could. He called a friend, Father Francis in Hidalgo who'd served with Jack in the army—known as Padre to his closest friends, not because he was a priest, but because he had been a former seminarian when he first enlisted. He joined the priesthood when he left the army.

Padre had helped rescue the boys eighteen months ago, and would do anything to help them now. Better, the boys would feel safe with him. He ran a summer camp for fatherless boys, and the facility—located halfway between Hidalgo and San Antonio—was currently vacant. Sister Ruth packed up all the boys—except Brian and Michael.

They were still at the boys' home as they worked through their plan. Kane had gone off with Brian. Sean was worried—the kid might say anything to avoid getting in trouble. Brad was in the dining room talking with Michael about how he'd put the connections together. Nate was escorting Sister Ruth and would return in a few hours, while Brad's two agents were watching the house outside. That left Sean alone with Jesse in the family room. Jesse sat glumly in the corner of the couch, still in his soccer uniform.

Sean sat next to his son. "I'm sorry," Jesse said, not for the first time. "I should have told you from the beginning."

"You didn't trust me."

"That's not it."

Sean had absorbed what Kane told him. "Then why? Because I don't get it, Jess. You put yourself in danger and didn't come to me for help."

"I—I didn't think it would get this far. Michael promised we'd come clean if we couldn't get Brian out from under his brother's thumb. We thought if you and Mateo knew what Brian was doing, that he would be sent away. And—I guess I wanted to prove to Michael that he could trust me. That I'm not this soft kid who can't do anything. But I am. I don't know how to fight back. I don't know how not to be scared."

"I can help with the first. But the second—we all get scared. Do you think that Kane is fearless? He's not. The difference is that he knows how to manage the fear. I see why you look up to him—he's practically a superhero."

"So are you, Dad."

"No. I'm just a worried father who doesn't know what he's doing. I knew when I saw the bruises that they weren't caused by a soccer ball, and I knew you'd lied to me about it. I wanted to confront you then. I didn't—but if I had, I would have known about Michael's insane plan to give the DEA an anonymous tip. I didn't because I was scared. I don't know how to do this parenting thing. I second-guess every decision I make."

"I'm really, really sorry I lied. I didn't want you to worry."

"I worried more because I knew someone hit you. I just didn't know who or why or why you wouldn't tell me." Sean considered what Lucy had told him earlier this week. "You know," he said, "I grew up in an unusual family. There were a lot of us, but we weren't close like Lucy's family. I was fourteen when my parents died. Duke left the army to become my guardian. I was an angry kid. Angry

hat my parents were dead and I couldn't save them. Angry that Duke was so hard on me. I got in a lot of trouble.
I should have been in juvie, but Duke had a lot of friends.
Every time he got me out of a situation, I doubled down. I
don't know if I had a death wish or just wanted the world
to know I wasn't happy. I lied a lot, and every time Duke
called me on it he tightened the screws and I fought back.

"In hindsight, we were both wrong. But Duke didn't
know anything more about being a father than I do now."

"But he wasn't your father. He was your brother. That
had to be weird."

Astute, Sean thought. "Maybe. Duke had his own issues with our parents, and with Kane. Kane has always
been this way. It's like he was born a warrior. He joined
the marines right out of high school. He left because he
doesn't take orders well and formed his own soldiers-for-
hire group. He's gone down some dark paths . . . but
everything he's done, the good and the bad, he's done for
the right reasons. When I was a teen, I didn't do things for
the right reasons. I did them because I could, because it
pissed off Duke, and because I was angry. I don't want
you to go down that path. I know you have a lot of anger
right now, and I don't blame you at all if part of it's directed at me."

"You? Why would I be mad at you?"

Sean was about to tell him when Jesse continued. "I
guess you're right. I *am* angry. I'm angry that Brian's
brother used him and manipulated him and made him feel
guilty so that he snuck around and actually considered
joining the gang. I'm angry that I couldn't fight back when
Jose hit me. I'm mad that you didn't stand up to my grandfather, that you let him make you feel bad about what
happened to my mom, when it wasn't your fault at all. I'm
angry at myself that I didn't tell you, because I do trust
you, Dad. More than anyone. You've never lied to me,

you've never said a bad word against my mom even though
I know what she did to you, that she lied to me and she
lied to you and to everyone else who ever asked who my
father was. And I know she knew what Carson was doing
with the drug cartels and just looked the other way. I mean
I look at what happened to Michael and the others and I
get so mad that Carson and my mom were a part of that."

"They weren't—that wasn't Carson's operation."

"You can say that with a straight face? They might not
have been part of the people who *actually* hurt Michael
and Tito and the others, but they were part of the people
who hurt kids *like* Michael. Or is there a good drug cartel? A drug cartel that doesn't hurt people or kill them or
force them to do things they don't want to do? Did Carson
work for a *good* cartel?"

Jesse was going from slow burn to full boil. "No," Sean
said quietly.

"See? So they can pretend that they didn't know what
was going on, but that was because they *chose* to ignore
it. And then Carson wanted you dead. And he might have
said that he wanted you dead because you were in my life,
but he *really* wanted you dead because you took down his
illegal business and he got in trouble. And my mom—I
can't even tell her I'm so mad at her because she's dead. I
can't yell at her or ask her why or say goodbye."

Tears were streaming down his face and Sean pulled
him into a hug. He was so tense, his body shaking with
emotion as he fought the tears.

Sean didn't know what to say, and maybe there was
nothing to say.

"L-lucy," Jesse said, "s-she said to forgive th-them. I
c-can't. I try. I c-can't."

"It's okay. It's okay."

Sean took a deep breath, then extracted Jesse's arms

nd looked into his face. He wiped the tears from his
heeks, held his head. "I promise you, Jess, that we're
oing to get through this. We'll find a way to forgive Mad-
son. She loved you, I know that and you know that. We
oth have to let it go."

"Can you forgive Carson? Tell me the truth. Can you?
After he wanted you *dead*?"

"For that? Yes. He's not the first person who wanted me
dead." *Don't lie to him, Sean. He'll know. Don't lie about
our feelings.*

Sean took a deep breath. "Lucy is amazing, and I love
ter more than my life. But if you want the truth, I will
tever forgive Carson Spade for putting you and Madison
n danger. Never. And I'm okay with that."

Jesse sighed, his whole body relaxing, and he hugged
Sean again.

Sean closed his eyes and absorbed the love coming from
ais son. "When this is all over, and when your rib is healed,
we'll start basic training."

"Basic training?" Jesse leaned back and wiped his face
on his shirt. "What's that?"

"Self-defense, boxing, karate, whatever you want. I'll
teach you how to use a punching bag—it's a great way to
work out frustration, and it's good exercise. I taught you
basic gun safety, but you should know more than how to
be safe with firearms. I can teach you, but I think Nate
would be better. He has a lot more experience, and he's
part of SWAT. I would have loved to learn how to shoot
with SWAT."

"That would be fun."

"You will be scared in your life—that's a given. But I
never want you to feel helpless again."

Sean knew exactly how that felt—when he couldn't save
his parents after the plane crash. When he couldn't save

Madison after she'd been drugged. The former made him angry, but the latter was different . . . he froze. Feared. Second-guessed himself. Doubted.

No more.

CHAPTER TWENTY-SIX

Saturday Afternoon

It was nearly two when Lucy arrived at the sheriff's office. Garrett King was in a holding cell—he'd been well on his way to drunk when a deputy located him at a bar near his apartment. They had him drinking coffee and sobering up all afternoon, and Jerry felt he was ready to talk.

They executed a warrant on his apartment and truck while he slept off his drunk. That he'd started drinking early in the morning seemed suspicious at a minimum— kill his dad, drink off the pain.

Except for Dillon's voice rattling around in her head. That the killer would be cold. Calculating. Arrogant.

Profiles could be wrong. Look at the profile in the case Jerry Walker had worked that resulted in a murder-suicide.

Jerry walked into the small room they were using, which was now cramped with people working—going through statements and records and information gathered from Garrett King's apartment. "Bingo," he said.

"You found the gun."

"No. But I found one more connection. Remember how the Browns said Garrett was fired a few months ago? Guess where he worked."

Lucy was tired, but she didn't need to guess. "Su▮ Tower."

"In the catering kitchen."

"He's connected to all four victims." It was loose, b▮ Garrett King was the only person they had identified wit▮ a connection to all four victims. Now to prove he had motive to kill each of them.

"We haven't found any physical evidence yet," Jerr▮ said, "but I sent a search team to the area surrounding Vic▮ tor King's house. The neighbors say Garrett keeps od▮ hours, can't tell when he comes and goes. We're goin▮ through his phone and computer now, but I'm having hin▮ brought over from holding."

"I'm ready." She wanted to face the man who had de▮ stroyed so many families. She didn't know what she ex▮ pected to see—remorse? Guilt? Gloating? Or the cool calm arrogance she expected from this organized killer?

They went downstairs to the interview rooms. Garret▮ King was already sitting in one, video camera on in the corner, clutching a water bottle. His clothing was dishev▮ eled and he looked exhausted. When Lucy and Jerry walked in, he glanced up at them. His eyes were red and he smelled like body odor and beer.

"My dad is dead. Why am I here?"

"Drunk and disorderly," Jerry said, sitting down.

"I wasn't."

"You took a swing at the deputy who found you. He just▮ wanted to talk to you about your dad, and you took a swing at him."

"I thought he was lying to me."

"We're sorry for your loss," Lucy said in her most sym▮ pathetic tone as she sat directly across from him. While she could play bad cop well, it was clear that Garrett was far more intimidated by Jerry. He was an imposing cop, and he'd already hauled him into holding. It was best for her to be the sympathetic one. And based on the little they had gathered about his background, he had probably gone to his mother for support and encouragement. It wasn't until after his mother died that his father was firm about Garrett finding—and keeping—a job.

"Thank you," he said and sniffed.

"When was the last time you saw your dad?" Lucy asked.

"Couple weeks ago. We—we had an argument. I'm sure Mr. and Mrs. Brown already told you that. They didn't like me much."

"Families argue," Lucy said. "I have six brothers and sisters and I've had some huge fights with them over the years. My dad was in the military, and he was a great dad, but you couldn't disagree with him about anything. His word was law."

"Yeah, I get that," he grumbled.

"What did you argue about?" Lucy asked.

"Look, I made some mistakes. I borrowed money without asking, and I said I was sorry, that I would repay him, but he didn't believe me. So I didn't talk to him for a while. But . . . I went over there on Labor Day, you know, to just talk to him, ask him for a little help . . . did you see my apartment? It's shit. It's a shitty apartment and I can't think let alone sleep with all the noise, and I just wanted to move back in, for a couple months until I got a regular job."

"I completely understand," she said. "And he didn't want to help?"

"Said that I was almost thirty and needed to stand on my own two feet. But he had all that space—he let me keep stuff there. Why not live there? Why should I pay six hundred dollars for the shit of an apartment when I could give him the six hundred?"

"And he didn't want to take rent?"

"I didn't get that far. I just—I can't believe that the last time I saw my dad, we fought. I wish—damn. Damn!" He pounded his fist on the table.

"Do you know who might want to hurt your dad?" Lucy asked.

"No one. I mean, he was cheap and all, but he was a nice guy, you know?"

"So no one threatened him? Did he have problems with any of his neighbors?"

"No. They're all old-timers. A couple people have vacation cabins nearby, come up on weekends and stuff. But no problems."

"Can I show you some pictures? Tell me if you recognize any of these people."

"Okay."

Garrett hadn't asked for a lawyer. He hadn't asked any questions about how his dad was killed—he was told he was attacked and murdered while walking his dog, but given no details.

Lucy had printouts of everyone she'd shown the other families, but she only wanted to show him the victims. She pulled out Standish.

"Do you know this man?"

He scowled. "Yeah. He worked on my dad's deck. I could have done that work, I don't see why my dad paid him a ton of money for something I could have done for half the cost." He frowned. "Did he kill my dad?"

"No," she said. "He was murdered eight weeks ago."

"Oh. Well. That's too bad."

She showed him Steven James. "What about him?"

He shrugged. "I don't know him."

"His name is Steven James. He's your father's accountant."

"Oh—yeah, I know him. I mean, I don't *know* him, but he was my dad's *estate planner*." He rolled his eyes. "My dad was always cheap, but he got cheaper after he hired that guy."

"When was that? This year?"

"Two or three years ago. Right after my mom died. My mom handled all the money in the house. She was really smart, a math teacher and everything, and Dad had never been that good with money. So he hired that guy to help him with tax stuff."

"And you've never met him?"

"No, why would I? But my dad thought he was brilliant. He told my dad to put more money into his retirement account, which was ridiculous because he had like a great *pension*, you know? He's been a teacher forever, why did he need to save more money?"

"More for you?" Jerry said.

"That's not what I meant. But James enabled my dad, you know? Enabled him to be cheaper than he already was."

This guy was clueless. He had no idea that Jerry had been baiting him. If he was guilty, wouldn't he have been suspicious?

He knew the other victims. No one else knew all three victims.

She showed him a photo of Julio Garcia. "Do you know him?"

"Well, yeah, of course. I worked for him for like six months."

"At Sun Tower?"

"Yeah. Until I was fired. I screwed up *one time* and they fired me."

"When was that?"

"July. Why? What's going on here?"

Now he was suspicious.

Lucy laid out the three pictures, then added the DMV

photo of Garrett's dad. "These four men were all killed by the same person."

He stared, his brows furrowed. He was confused . . . or a good actor.

It took an actor to set up those crime scenes. Was he playing them like he had been playing them with the murders?

"That sucks," he said.

Jerry slammed his fist on the table. "They were beaten to death and shot in the face."

Lucy wanted to tell Jerry to tone it down. So far, Garrett was chatty.

"I'm sorry," Garrett said.

"Where were you last night?" Jerry said. "Start at eight p.m. and go from there."

He blinked. "Home."

"Alone?"

"So?"

"You were drinking in a bar at ten this morning. We were at your apartment before eight to tell you about your dad, but you weren't there. Where were you?"

"I was standing in front of Home Depot trying to get a day labor job. Rent's due on Tuesday, man. I got there at seven. When I didn't get hired, I went to the bar for a bite to eat. Drank a bit too much because I hadn't eaten much. I didn't mean to hit the cop."

Lucy slid over a pen and tablet. "Can you write down exactly where you were? Who you talked to?"

"Why? Why—you don't think I killed my dad, do you?"

He stared at the four pictures and then what Jerry had said came clear to him. "All four of those guys are dead?"

"Yes, Garrett," Lucy said. "The same person killed all four of these men."

"Not me. I have never killed anyone. Ever. I didn't."

"We need to verify your alibi, and then we'll talk again, okay?"

"I need a lawyer, don't I?"

"Do you?" Jerry asked.

"Yes. Yes. I think I might. Are you arresting me?"

Jerry picked up the pad, looked at the one line Garrett had written. "I'll be right back." Then he walked out.

Garrett looked at Lucy. "Where's Justice?"

"We're looking for justice, for your dad and all these men."

He blinked, confused. "No. My dad's dog. His name's Justice. Is he okay? You said my dad was walking his dog. Justice is *my* dog, but I couldn't keep him in the apartment. And Dad loved him, said he would keep him. Justice would have protected my dad. I mean, he's a Lab, he's friendly, but he wouldn't let someone hurt him."

That was odd. "Justice is at the vet. He has a broken leg and might need surgery for internal bleeding. He was hit with, we believe, a sledgehammer."

Tears leaked from Garrett's eyes, and Lucy didn't think it was an act. "He's going to be okay, right? I mean, it's not serious, right? Who would hit a dog? He's a Lab, he's the friendliest dog on the planet."

And that's when Lucy knew that Garrett wasn't a killer, no matter what the evidence said.

"I'm having a difficult time believing that Garrett killed these four men," Lucy said when she and Jerry were alone in their small conference room.

Jerry slammed his fist on the table. "He knows all four victims. He has motive. Julio fired him. James was encouraging King to be more frugal, which may have led to King kicking his adult son out of the house. Standish took a job that Garrett King thought he should have gotten. His dad cut him off. He's a spoiled brat."

"It's his dog."

"People can be cruel to animals. Isn't that Serial Killer 101?"

"The dog was hit with the same weapon that the killer used on his victims."

"Maybe he didn't realize what he was doing."

"The killer was cold and ruthless. He shot the victims in the face."

"Maybe the reason that he shot them in the face was because he was picturing his father. Maybe leading up to it."

It was an idea . . . and actually a logical deduction based on psychology, because it was often easier to kill or dehumanize people you didn't know or didn't know well than it was to kill someone you loved, or had a love–hate relationship with, like Garrett and his father. But Lucy didn't think that Garrett King was smart enough to execute such a well-planned murder spree, and she said as much.

"It's possible," she said, "but Garrett is not ruthless or smart."

"It's an act. You were with me on this. When we searched King's house. When we talked to the Browns. Garrett King matches the damn *profile* you begged me to consider."

"First, that was preliminary and verbal. No one can make a solid profile on limited information. And second, King does fit it . . . to a point. But he's not cold or calculating, and I'll bet he barely passed high school."

"And the profile could be wrong. I'm not letting him go because he doesn't line up in all those shrink boxes. He's a whiny, entitled brat who—just like the profile said—was dealt a severe blow when his father cut him off."

"I don't see him meticulously planning four murders over the course of two months."

"Maybe the first three were him building up to killing his father, who was his real target."

That was certainly possible, and she acknowledged as much.

"And Standish," Jerry continued, "he was a big guy. He knew Garrett, he fought back. And if he saw Garrett broken down by the side of the road, he'd probably stop to help."

Reasonable assumption.

"We didn't get a confession. Being nice cop sure didn't help, and now he wants a lawyer."

She considered what Garrett had said at the beginning of the interview—she was playing it friendly to get the most information. As soon as Jerry started getting confrontational, Garrett clammed up. There was no way the DA would prosecute without at least *some* physical evidence. The gun, the mallet, trace . . . they needed something.

Jerry knew all of this, so she didn't tell him. She simply sat down and began to go over the facts and evidence they *did* have.

"Garrett Ronald King, twenty-nine, an unemployed contractor, has been arrested this morning, only hours after his father, Victor King, a history teacher from Canyon Lake, was found murdered. Stay tuned to Channel Five for details as they come in," the reporter said on the news.

Lucy was livid. They should have kept this under wraps—until they had something solid to share—but someone had leaked King's arrest to the media.

They should never have arrested him. That put them on the clock—they had seventy-two hours before he had to be arraigned and if they didn't find something solid, he would be released. And then he could disappear, especially if he was guilty.

And though Jerry didn't agree that he might *not* be guilty, he was just as furious that the report had been released.

"Dammit," he muttered.

"But you think he's guilty."

"Yeah, I do, but on the off-chance we can't build the case, we're going to have to let him go, and that'll embarrass the sheriff and my department. I told them to keep it under wraps for the weekend while we finish executing the search warrants."

Assistant Sheriff Jimenez walked into their small conference room. "Before you come storming my office, you should know it wasn't leaked on purpose."

"How did it happen? We have no physical evidence tying him to any of the murders. And he wasn't arrested for murder—he was arrested for drunk and disorderly, just to keep him in lockup for a couple days while we keep digging. So how?"

"A reporter had been talking to the PIO about another case and picked up on the search warrants coming in. He eavesdropped on a couple cops, then saw the arrest report for Garrett King—didn't see it was for the D and D—and he knew through the PIO that the fourth victim was identified as Victor King. He ran with it, though fortunately he didn't connect it to the other three murders—yet."

"Well, shit," Jerry muttered. "We should never let reporters into our house."

"If we have the right guy, we're fine."

"We do."

Jimenez looked at Lucy. "You concur?"

Lucy didn't say anything. She wanted to support Jerry, but she couldn't lie about her opinion.

"I don't know," she said finally. "I won't go so far as to say he didn't do it, there's just a few things that aren't matching up. We have a lot of work ahead of us."

Jerry stared at her. It didn't matter that she'd hedged, he expected her to support him 100 percent.

There would be no reasoning with the man, unless she found irrefutable evidence of Garrett's innocence. Yes, there was a chance Garrett was guilty. Lucy could see him killing someone in a rage—spontaneously. He was certainly no saint. But planning four perfect murders? Because until Victor King was killed, Garrett's name hadn't even come up in the investigation. Sun Tower hadn't mentioned him as a disgruntled employee. Susan Standish hadn't mentioned that he'd harassed her husband. Nothing.

If he had an alibi for just *one* of the murders, he would be cleared. No matter what they might find. It wouldn't even take a good lawyer to get him off—anyone with a brain would see that four murders + same gun + same MO = same killer.

Unless he had a partner. Someone smarter, savvier than him.

It was a possibility. But who would trust this man with their identity? He was a wild card, and wild cards notoriously talked when they were arrested.

When push came to shove, Lucy didn't believe that Garrett King—who had been a solidly mediocre student, who couldn't hold down a job, and who blamed everyone else for his problems—could have executed this killing spree.

Jimenez looked from Jerry to Lucy and back. "I'll talk to the sheriff and we'll get the media to eat some crow, but find something, and fast, because this is spiraling out of control and the last thing we want is a bull's-eye on our back for the media to take aim."

*   *   *

"I can't believe you don't see it," Jerry said after Jimenez left. He paced the small office, seeming frustrated by the lack of space. "The guy is connected to all four victims. He has motive for each. Standish took a job he thought should be his. James encouraged his father to stop supporting him. Garcia fired him. His father cut him off. The kid is a mess. So he doesn't fit neatly into the profile your brother cooked up, he *does* fit the key components. Your brother said he wants at least one of the people dead, and possibly all of them. He wants his father dead the most, the others are just people who wronged him, and he was working himself up into killing his father. Patricide isn't easy."

Lucy agreed. "We need something solid. I also can't discount that while there was a lot of conjecture in the profile, there was something clear that Hans and Dillon agreed with—and that I have been saying from the beginning. The killer is cold. Methodical. Organized. Drunk Garrett is none of the above."

"And Dr. Kincaid said that he wasn't writing this up because there wasn't enough information to give a clear profile and he didn't want to screw a conviction."

"That's not exactly accurate—"

"Listen, keep your theory to yourself. Talk to me, but if it leaks out to the press that we have doubts about this arrest, whichever slimy-ball defense attorney takes King's case will use that against us in court."

"Other than my boss—and she will understand the sensitivities of this—it stays here."

"You tell your boss, she might just pull this case."

"She won't. You need to trust me."

He was torn, but just shrugged. "I'm going to follow up with the cops executing the search warrants. We're searching the areas around the crime scene for additional evidence, and Ash is at the vet collecting evidence from the dog."

"Is the dog okay?"

"Broken leg and the vet's keeping him overnight to monitor his other injuries. Minor surgery to close a wound. The vet wants to keep him calm and sedated and make sure that there's no other problems. The dog may have bitten the attacker. Not serious—he couldn't find any skin or blood in the dog's mouth—but there were some fibers embedded between teeth. That's why Ash is there, to protect the chain of evidence. Plus we might get lucky and swab the mouth for human DNA, but Ash said that it wouldn't last long in a dog's mouth, and could be easily contaminated."

"Still, that's terrific," Lucy said. "A piece of clothing the killer wore? That's something we can possibly trace, or find the match."

"You want to come and supervise the warrants?"

"We should interview Mitchell Duncan about Garrett King's termination. He might remember something important that he didn't before—it was three months ago, he may not have thought to mention it to us."

"Agreed." Jerry glanced at his watch. "It's three thirty—I'll call him and see when he can meet."

"I'll call William Peterson and see what he says about Steven James's relationship with Victor King, and what might have set Garrett off."

"Good—he'll want a warrant, I'll talk to the DA and make it happen." He left, and Lucy called Peterson. Jerry was right—he couldn't release specific client records without a warrant—but he did say he couldn't recall anything odd about the account. "We have weekly staff meetings to go over clients and their needs, and as far as I know everything related to King was standard retirement planning. His wife had always done their taxes and he didn't feel qualified to do so when she passed, so he hired Allied. It's a smaller client than we usually take, but I vaguely remember that one of our clients referred King to us."

"If you could ask that the files are copied, I'll let you know when we have the warrant and can pick them up."

"I'll have them ready first thing Monday morning."

Lucy loved working with private citizens like William Peterson who didn't make their job difficult. The warrant was to protect law enforcement, Allied, Victor King's privacy, and Garrett King's rights, and she certainly didn't mind going through the process.

She called Rachel and filled her in on the case. When her boss didn't immediately respond, Lucy thought she'd screwed up.

Rachel finally said, "It sounds like you don't think this guy is guilty."

"Does it?" She was trying to be impartial.

"I've worked with you for nearly a year, Lucy. If you think someone is guilty, you make the case, even with minimal evidence. If you think someone is innocent, ditto. You're hedging. What are you not telling me?"

"Did you read my memo about the profile?"

"The unofficial, unwritten profile that we can't use."

That really sounded bad, Lucy realized. "Here's the thing. I interviewed Garrett with Jerry. Garrett is a spoiled, self-absorbed, overgrown kid who is mad that his dad cut him off and won't let him live rent-free at home. He can't keep a job. He drinks too much. There is nothing about him that says that he's organized or has above-average intelligence. There's nothing that says to me that he can plan out these four murders and leave not one shred of physical evidence at any of the crime scenes. And Justice is his dog."

"King's dog?"

"Yes—he said that his dad was taking care of the dog because he couldn't have him in the apartment. Garrett has problems, and his life is a mess, and I don't particularly like him, but I don't think that he would hit his dog so hard as to break his leg."

"He has motive."

"He does. He knows all four victims, though he claims to have never met Steven James in person. Julio Garcia fired him three months ago, and that may have been the trigger—coupled with the fact that his dad hired Standish to build his deck when Garrett has a contractor license."

"Motive drives this case. I read all your reports, and each victim may have had another enemy to fear—there are other motives out there, from Mrs. Standish's lovers to Mrs. Garcia allegedly being raped. But Garrett King is the only one who connects to all four victims.

"And," Rachel continued, "in my experience, when a life is cut short by death, be it murder or accident, secrets have a way of coming out. Most of those secrets have nothing to do with the death, but they may embarrass surviving family, or show the victim in a better—or worse—light. I worked a case in Phoenix where a divorced woman was killed in a hostage situation. She was a respected trauma nurse who went to church every Sunday and sang in the choir. In our follow-up we learned that she had an extensive porn collection and more dildos and vibrators in her bedroom than I've ever seen outside of a sex shop. We kept the information private, but all her belongings were ultimately handed over to her family—the porn collection I personally gave to her sister, and suggested that she decide whether the parents and grown children needed to know about it.

"Everyone has secrets, Lucy. And they come out—especially in an investigation as deep and detailed as this. Doesn't mean those secrets led to murder."

Sadly, true. Lucy had once wondered what people would learn about her that she didn't want them to know, if she suddenly died. In the past, there was a lot she kept hidden. Since she met Sean, much less. Because Sean knew everything about her.

But Jesse's mother had secrets, and when she died those secrets were exposed, and the poor kid had to figure out how to come to terms with what he now knew about his mother, and how he remembered her before she died.

Lucy said, "I took something different from the profile than Jerry took. Namely, that the killer is so cold, so calculating, so organized that he will not break. Even if confronted with hard evidence, he will remain calm. His arrogance will shine through. And the fact that we all believe, based on the crime scene, is that Steven James knew the killer. Garrett King said he never met him."

"And King could be lying about that."

"But he didn't lie about Garcia and Standish."

"Maybe because there were witnesses."

"Maybe I'm overthinking this."

"I'm playing devil's advocate, Lucy. Do the work. The answers will come. Just keep an open mind. Garrett King may in fact be guilty of murder—and kicking his dog. I believe in psychological profiling, but not to replace hard evidence. Find the evidence, the rest will follow."

CHAPTER TWENTY-SEVEN

Saturday Evening

Lucy texted Sean and said she'd be late, but she would leave if he needed her. He called her back immediately.

"We're covered. Ruth and Nate left with the boys to go to Padre's camp outside Corpus Christi. Kane's with Brian and Brad's with Michael, both trying to get answers and information."

"How's Jesse?"

"Better. We talked, and we're better."

Lucy was relieved. She'd been so worried about both of them. "You need me, I'll be there."

"I know. Just nail that guy. Four murders and Nate said he nearly killed a dog."

"If he's guilty, I'll prove it."

"If?"

"It's still not settled."

"When you are on your way home, call me—I don't know where I'll be, and I don't want you walking into a situation."

"I will. Be careful. I love you."

"Love you, too. And Jesse says lock him up and throw away the key."

She ended the call and smiled, then re-sorted all the information they had and looked at it on the wall.

She couldn't discount what Dillon had said, about the personality of the killer—or that they needed to focus on Steven James's life. She stared at the time line of the murders, the methodology, the names of everyone they'd interviewed.

Susan Standish was an actress through and through. She could cry at the drop of a hat, but there was not an ounce of remorse in her petite little body that she had cheated on her husband, and Lucy didn't feel any real grief from her. But Billy Joe had been dead for seven weeks when Lucy first talked with her. Ditto for Teri James, whose husband had been dead for three weeks. Would that be enough time to process grief? Or was that her personality? As reserved as her husband? The only spouse she'd met who truly grieved was Marissa Garcia, because Lucy and Jerry had been the ones who told her about her husband's death. A week later she was still grieving, holding her life together by a thread.

Lucy didn't want to think about what would happen if she lost Sean. Three weeks, seven weeks, a year . . . she didn't think that she would ever be the same. There had been times when he'd been in danger, where the thought of losing him had first paralyzed her, then mobilized her. But he'd survived, and she hadn't lost him.

She just couldn't think about it without a twinge of panic in her stomach, so she pushed it aside.

Chris Smith was also an actor, just like Susan Standish. If Lucy believed what Marissa's brother-in-law said, Chris was a rapist and liar—he had clearly called Jerry and Lucy out on their questions. He was right, he was under no obligation to answer them, and they didn't have enough evidence to compel him to answer. He hadn't seemed violent—and he had an aura of remorse. But rapists were rarely remorseful. Was he more upset that he'd lost his friend than the reasons why? Had his alcoholism played a part in his past criminal acts? Did he even remember? He definitely needed a more thorough review.

But neither Standish nor Garcia was part of Steven James's life in any way. Steven James had a relatively small world. His wife, his daughter, his brother, his co-workers. They'd met Peterson, Witherspoon, and Steven's personal assistant. They were all of above-average intelligence, professional, helpful. None appeared particularly cold, but that was something—as Dillon said—that could be masked for a time. His wife Teri was formal. The immaculate house, proper etiquette, cool demeanor. But what would be her motive? According to Joyce Witherspoon, no one—not even a guardian sitting on the trust board—could touch the money in Abby's trust account. And if Abby died, most of that money went to the family trust. Even Abby couldn't designate someone else.

Or could she?

Lucy made a note to get a copy of the paperwork on Abby's trust to see if there was a motive there. It was a long shot, but absolutely worth looking into.

Lucy reviewed the notes from each of their interviews, both her notes and Jerry's.

Jerry had written something after the conversation with Abby and Teri James at their house on Wednesday.

Tension between Abby and stepmom???

That was it. What did that mean? Lucy hadn't noticed anything specific. She closed her eyes and thought back to the interview. It had been brief, ultimately unnecessary. They hadn't learned anything. They were all sitting at the table . . .

No. Abby got up. Why did she get up? She got up and didn't sit back down until Lucy showed her the photos.

Lucy replayed the scene in her head and realized that

Abby didn't like being touched by her stepmom. It was after Teri put a consoling hand on Abby's arm that the teenager got up and walked to the hutch, focusing on a photo of her with her dad and stepmom. It might not mean anything—teenagers could be prickly, and often had a difficult time with grief and emotions. Or it could mean that there was tension between them, as Jerry had sensed.

She put the notes up on the board and was about to review the statements from the California company that James had been visiting the week before his death when Jerry came in. "We have Trevor James for ten minutes, provided the satellite connection holds up. It's early morning in his time zone, somewhere off the coast of Japan. We're using the computer room because they have some super wires or whatever."

Lucy followed him down the hall and around the corner. A screen showed Trevor James, a much younger version of his brother, sitting in a command center of sorts on his ship. The image was slightly off, but they could hear him clearly. "Thank you for taking the time, Lieutenant James."

"I'm sorry I couldn't call sooner."

"We're just following up on every possible lead into your brother's murder. We may have a suspect in custody, but there are some holes."

"Anything I can do to help. How's Abby? She and Steven were tight."

"She's holding up. Misses him."

"I'm out here for another six weeks, then I have a three-month leave. I already emailed Abby to see if she wants to spend Christmas with me in San Diego—it's where I'm stationed. She said she's looking forward to it, and wants me to come to San Antonio for Thanksgiving. She's a terrific kid, Steven did a great job with her. It was hard after her mom died."

"Abby was three?"

"Yeah—fatal car accident on Highway One on the coast. Five people dead, and Steven was a zombie. He loved Bridget. I know he's reserved and introverted—I was outgoing in high school, the athlete in the family; Steven was quiet and loved school. But Bridget brought out the best in him, brought him out of his shell. So does Abby."

"What about his new wife?" Lucy asked, now curious as to why Trevor was focused on Steven's first wife who had been dead for eleven years.

"I don't really know Teri that well. Steven seemed happy—I mean, I got the feeling that he would always miss Bridget, but he and Teri had a nice, quiet life. My brother—he was only thirty-nine, but he was born an old man. I say that with great affection. He liked being home, being with family, having a few close friends—no wild parties or risky behavior. He rarely drank, and if he did it was a lone glass of wine. I got all the wild oats to sow in the James genes." He smiled, but his voice was sad.

Jerry was about to sign off, Lucy could tell by his posture, so she jumped in with a question. "Are you familiar with Abby's trust fund?"

"That's not my area of expertise. Steve was the finance expert—which was ironic, because he doesn't really care much about money."

"Because he lived frugally?"

"But it's why he lived frugally. He was conservative in everything he did. Didn't drink to excess. Never lost his temper. If he didn't need something, he didn't buy it. He believed that money was for foundations—a house in a good neighborhood, a good education, savings for emergencies."

"Is that how he and Teri met? Because they're both accountants?"

"I don't really know how they met. Is that important?"

Jerry was staring at Lucy strangely. She ignored him. "Everything is important until it's not. I'm trying to see the big picture and understand why someone might want to kill your brother."

"I thought it was a random act of violence. Though Abby emailed me something about two other men dying in the same way."

"Four men, including your brother, were killed by the same attacker. And while we have a suspect, we are missing key evidence. A forensic psychiatrist who has consulted in the case feels that your brother knew his killer, because he was the only victim who was facing the killer when he was attacked, as if they were in a conversation. So we're digging deeper into Steven's life, trying to find anyone who may have a beef with him, or help us figure out if our current suspect has a motive."

Jerry was clearly growing more irritated with her questions, but Lucy was unfazed.

"Who couldn't like Steven?" Trevor said.

"What about Teri's family? Did they approve of the marriage? Or her ex-husband?" Lucy had seen a note from Jerry that Teri's ex-husband lived in Colorado, but no one had spoken to him.

"I didn't meet any of her family—no one came to the wedding, which was small and informal. I stood up for my brother, took a week to watch Abby while they went on a honeymoon to Hawaii. She was eight at the time—we had a blast. That kid is really smart. She has my athleticism, Steven's brains, and her mother's good looks."

"Who can we call who will know exactly how Abby's trust works?"

"Her great-aunt Abigail O'Connell Bridgeton. She's a tough old broad, just so you know, fierce, really. But sharp as a tack. She liked Steven because they thought the same way about wealth and money, but Steven and I came from a middle-class home with a nurse for a mom and a cop for a dad."

"They're not still around?" Lucy didn't recall hearing about other grandparents.

"My dad died in the line of duty when Steven was in college, I was in high school. My mom died of cancer two years after Bridget was killed—I think that, even more than the car accident, had Steven wanting to move away and start fresh. Look—I really need to go. I'm on duty in two minutes. Just tell me that Abby is okay."

"She's okay," Lucy said.

"Great. I'll try to call her later, next time I get a chance, just to make sure. I came out for the funeral, but I only had three days. I love my job, I love the navy, but it makes it hard to be there when your family needs you."

"Thank you for your service," Lucy said. "I know what you mean. My dad was career army."

The call ended, and Jerry said, "What was that? Tea time?"

"You said in your notes that Teri moved here after her divorce because this is where she was from, that her family was here. Why wouldn't her family be at the wedding?"

Jerry stared at her. "And this is important why?"

"I don't know. Rachel said something to me that in death, every secret is discovered, even if it has nothing to do with the death. Like Susan's affairs. So it might be nothing—but we need to know everything about the James family, focusing on Teri, Abby's trust, and who might benefit from Steven's death, and circling back around to his employer, clients, and colleagues. Teri was an accountant as well—she works from home, correct?"

"That's what she said."

"Just worth a look. And we should talk to her ex-husband."

"Why? We have a suspect, Kincaid. And you can't

possibly think that Teri James killed four men for n
reason."

"You made a note after our meeting with Abby and Ter
on Wednesday. You questioned whether there was tensio
between Abby and Teri."

"So? Stepmother. Abby lost both parents. It doesn't tak
a shrink to see that it is a heartbreaking situation for Abby.

"But you noticed something."

"I don't remember what it was."

"I didn't see it at the time—or didn't register the im
portance. But I have a good memory, and I replayed th
scene—Abby got up from the table right after Teri put he
hand on her arm. She walked away and didn't look at Ter
again. Didn't sit down until I showed her the pictures
Maybe it means nothing—like you said, tension betwee
parent and child who have no real connection except a
dead man. Or Abby is uncomfortable around her."

"That's a big stretch." But Lucy could see Jerry's wheel
turning as he mulled over her thoughts.

"And? I don't think that Garrett King hit his dog with
a sledgehammer so hard that he broke his leg. I know tha
sounds trivial, but there it is. And until we find solid evi
dence that he is guilty? I'm going to continue down thi
path."

Jerry wanted to say something more, but didn't. Instead
he said, "Mitch Duncan said we can come by the hote
anytime, so let's go. Jeanie is holding dinner for me."

Mitch was frazzled when they came by, and they waited a
good ten minutes before he stepped out, and ushered them
away from the office and kitchen. He said, "Do you
mind if we go outside so I can have a smoke? I hate this
job. I quit smoking eighteen years ago, and started again
after Julio was killed."

Jerry motioned for Mitch to lead the way.

Outside there was a covered alcove with benches and ashtrays, and no one else. It was warm and sticky, but not unbearable.

Mitch lit up and took a deep drag. He took care not to blow the smoke at Lucy and Jerry. "So you have a suspect."

"Garrett King. Do you know him?"

"King? That kid? He killed Julio? What the hell for?"

"According to his neighbors, Julio fired him three months ago."

"The neighbors are wrong."

"He wasn't fired?"

"He was, damn straight. I fired his ass. That kid—look, he wasn't a bad kid. Friendly and all that, did an okay job. But he couldn't be on time to save his life. Julio wanted to give him another chance, but how many fucking chances are we supposed to give people? He was late *twenty-two* times in six months. Not five minutes late, either. We're talking consistently thirty, forty minutes late. But when he screwed up entrées that delayed dinner at a wedding reception by a full hour and cost us a bonus, he had to go. I didn't even tell Julio until after I canned his ass. He agreed it was past time, but he reached out to help the kid find another job. Unfortunately, Garrett had burned a lot of bridges in the restaurant community, and Julio suggested he go back to construction. A little more flexibility, and his skills were pretty good—if he showed up."

"You fired him," Jerry said flatly. "Could Garrett have thought that Julio fired him through you? That it was his decision?"

"He could think it, didn't make it so. I doubt it, though. Garrett knew I ran the staff, and that Julio was a softie. I told him not to dare appeal to Julio, because I would go over his head if he so much as thought about it. Said if he got his act together and could hold down a job for six

months, I'd consider bringing him back on a probationar
basis. Haven't seen him since."

Mitch looked from Lucy to Jerry. "You don't reall
think he killed Julio."

"His father was murdered last night and his alibi wa
that he was home alone. We have to look at every possi
bility."

"Look, Garrett is a loser. I'm sorry, it's true. Some peopl
just can't quite make their life work. Not because they hav
shitty parents or no opportunities, just because they can
put two and two together. They don't connect their action
to consequences. They mean well, they're actually nic
people, but always think they can find an easier way to d
everything. That's Garrett. Honestly, I think the only thin
he truly cared about was his dog."

CHAPTER TWENTY-EIGHT

Saturday Evening

Brad and Michael returned long before Kane and Brian. It seemed that Michael had been keeping his ear to the ground ever since he returned from Mexico. He knew people, understood the business, and had been feeding information to the DEA through the anonymous tip line for more than a year. But because that tip line didn't lead to instantaneous response, this time he'd called Brad directly.

Michael had his head up. Proud, stubborn, no regrets. He was the bravest kid Sean knew.

"Michael," Sean said, "I'm proud of you in so many ways. But never do this again. I said we'd talk later, and now is later."

"I told you—"

"I know what you said. And you're wrong. Yes, I have something to lose. I could lose you because you're too stubborn to see how important you are to not only the boys here, but to everyone. To me."

Michael didn't respond, but at least he wasn't arguing. It was a start.

Brad said, "No more anonymous bullshit. I told Michael he can call me anytime about anything and I'll run an assessment. But—and I'm deadly serious about this Michael—I told you before, but I don't think you understand the ramifications. People like Jose Torres know who you are."

"I'm not scared of them."

"You should be, because if they think they can get to you, they will—and they don't care about collateral damage. So you have to be extremely cautious. But you have me, kid—me, Sean, Kane, Nate, Lucy—any one of us will drop everything if you're in trouble. But you have to recognize when you're in over your head. This time you were, but you didn't see it. Next time you will."

"Yes, sir."

Finally, Kane and Brian emerged from Father Mateo's office. Brian didn't have a bruise on him, but he was pale and his shoulders sagged. What had Kane said to him?

Kane said, "Head up, Brian. Tell everyone what you told me."

"I'm sorry." He looked down.

"None of that," Kane said. "Jose is your family, we all get that. Sean and I have a brother who made bad choice after bad choice, and in the end we couldn't save him. And as I told you, you get a pass this time. You came clean, and I know it was hard. Do you think I was lying about your brother?"

"No."

Kane looked at Brad. Brad said, "Brian, I pulled your brother's record, talked to people who know the truth. I told Kane what I found. And I'm really sorry, sorry he wasn't the man you thought he could be."

"I screwed up," Brian said.

"I said, no more self-pity. Tell them," Kane repeated.

Brian took a deep breath. "I got cold feet. I was afraid Jose would be killed, because he said last week that he would never go back to prison. That he would rather die

aking down pi—cops than go back. And I didn't want him
o die. So I told him to leave last night. He didn't even ask
ne why, just looked at me and I guess he just knew and
ne left."

"What did he tell you?"

"I wasn't his brother unless I joined the gang, and to
join I . . . I have to kill someone." He looked at Michael,
ears in his eyes. "He wants me to kill you."

Kane put his hand on Brian's shoulder. "The Saints
know all about Michael, where he lives, where he goes to
school. We have to get all of them, otherwise Michael is
coming home with me."

"No," Michael said. "This is my home."

"It's not up for discussion," Kane said. "I'm not letting
you die. I might be the only person who can ensure you
live long enough to enlist in the marines—if you still want
to when you're eighteen."

"I will not change my mind."

"Good. You may be a marine in your heart, but you
have a lot to learn—like trusting your team. And you need
to recognize that your team is not only you and these boys,
but Sean and Brad and me. We are part of the team, and
you can never do what you did and withhold information.
Ever. The key to being a good soldier, a great warrior, is
both training and information. We gather intel, then for-
mulate a plan, then execute the plan. That is the way to
survive. Understood?"

"Yes, sir."

"Now that I have information about Jose, his hangouts,
and his endgame, I've developed a plan. No one here is
going to like it, it's dangerous, but tactically—it's the only
way we're going to get Torres back behind bars. I promised
Brian here one thing: that we will do everything in our
power to take Torres alive. Brian knows he's not going to
reform, but I respect the fact that he doesn't want him dead.

And Brian understands that if the decision is between his brother and any one of you, that it's no decision, and he goes down. Right, Brian?"

"Yes, sir," he said.

"Good. We're on the same page. So Brian has unintentionally given us a game plan. He gave Jose inside information about the raid, and Jose was able to slip out. In the process, he didn't tip off how he knew, so my guess is Jose—while suspicious—will believe Brian when he tells him he killed Michael. Because that's the only way Jose will let him inside."

"How do we do that?" Brad said.

"We'll fake his death. Brian will call Jose, send him a picture, tell him he's scared. I want to use the church for this—no reason to let Jose into this house, and because of the gates we can control how he gets in and out. Jose will come, and we'll arrest him."

"You think it'll work?" Brad said. "What about the other two who slipped away?"

"My guess is that they'll come with Jose—we need a team inside the gates and outside, to block their escape. Nate will be back shortly, then we go."

"No," Brian said.

"We talked about this," Kane said sharply. "Your brother goes back to prison, or you and Michael will be living in Hidalgo until Brad can find them."

"Jose isn't going to fall for it. Yes, he trusts me sort of but he's not going to come here to look at Michael's body. He'll tell me to come to him, to just leave."

"I'm not putting you in the line of fire, kid," Kane said.

"But you know I'm right."

Sean had to agree with Brian. It's what he would do if he were Torres. "Kane—Brian is right. Torres will stay in the shadows after the raid last night."

Brad shook his head. "I can't let you send a fourteen-year-old kid into a volatile situation."

Kane assessed Brian, then nodded.

"No," Brad said. "Shit, Rogan! We don't use kids as bait."

"I don't like it, but I like less that the bastard knows where Michael lives. We can't keep this place under watch twenty-four seven. I get Michael and Brian out of here, Torres could still come by and make these kids' lives miserable."

Brian stood firm. "I want to do this. I want to make this right. I should never have told Jose about the raid—he would be in jail now. We would be safe."

"Or a cop could be on a slab in the morgue," Kane said, "because Jose wanted to go out the hard way."

"Shit, shit, shit!" Brad paced.

Sean understood that he was between a rock and a hard place. He was a federal agent, and if this operation went south and anyone was hurt, he could not only lose his job but be prosecuted. "Brad—Kane and I can do this without you."

"Hell no," Brad said. "Let me think."

"We don't have a lot of time," Kane said. "The Saints were dealt a severe blow last night—because they were already spread thin. The two who escaped with Jose need to be captured as well, or this cycle will continue. Brian knows where they will be—tonight. But after tonight, they could disappear or come after Michael."

"I want this to end," Brian said. "I started it, I need to finish it."

"You didn't start it," Kane said. "Your father did when he joined the Saints and raised Jose to be in a gang. Your father sold you to the general and your brother was part of that deal. Never forget that. He does not care what kind of life you have, as long as it is in service to the gang and his own selfish wants. But you can help end it. And there will be no guilt, no regrets. Whatever happens, hold your head up."

Brian nodded, but he was shaking. Guilt. Pain. Sorrow.

Kane looked at his phone. "Nate's almost here. We need backup—Brad, if you're in, you and Nate cover us. Hopefully, we won't need you. But if it goes south, there's no one else I'd rather have on my six."

"No," Brad said.

"Shit, Brad, we've been through this."

"Look—our goal is to arrest Jose Torres, right? So this is now *officially* a DEA op. I'm going to shut out SAPD and hope Carmine doesn't have my hide for leaving him out of the festivities, because I agree we need to do this lean and mean and fast, and no way could I get Carmine to agree to let Brian go into the middle of this. Hell, I don't want him to either, but we need confirmation that Jose is inside that house before we breach. I shouldn't even let *any* of you be involved—but I'll deal with the fallout later. One of the few perks of being in charge." His eyes rested on Michael. "We're a team," he said. "We'll watch each other's backs."

Sean took Jesse and Michael to his house. "I have to know that you'll stay put. Do not leave this house. Do not open the door to anyone, for any reason. Lucy will be home soon."

"I should be there, with Brian," Michael said. He had forcefully argued with Kane and stood his ground. Kane still said no, but clearly admired Michael's spine that he stood up to him. Sean didn't know if he, as a teenager, would have stood up to Kane so forcefully.

"You made your case, we explained why it is too dangerous, and you're going to stay put. No arguments. You trust Kane, right?"

"Of course," Michael said. "He has always lived up to his word."

"Then trust him now. Trust both of us."

Michael nodded once.

Jesse hugged Sean tightly. "Be careful. Please."

Sean looked down at his kid. "I promise. I have a lot to live for." He walked to the door. "Oh, and in case you get a stupid idea to leave this house and try to help, consider yourself under house arrest." He typed a security code into the keypad. "Every camera is on, and I'll be alerted if you so much as crack open a window. I trust you both—but I also know you don't sit out easily, Michael, and when we're dealing with a gang who wants you dead, no way am I letting you get in the line of fire. Either of you."

He walked out to where Kane, Brad, and Nate were out front waiting for him. "Did you put the fear of God into them?" Brad asked.

"The fear of Kane works better." Sean winked at his brother. "Not to mention my kick-ass security system."

They piled into two cars, Brad and Nate in Nate's truck, and Sean and Kane with Brian in Sean's Jeep. Brad had two agents meeting him near the house.

Kane turned around and said to Brian in the back, "You don't have to do this."

"What happens if I don't?"

"You and Michael will come live with me in Hidalgo so I can protect you, as I said, until Brad can build a case against Jose and the others. It could be a few weeks, it could be a few months."

"Or never."

"That's always a possibility, but Brad is a good cop, and he's motivated."

"But the others might not be safe."

"There's no reason that Jose would go after anyone else."

Brian didn't say anything.

"Brian, talk."

"I wouldn't think so, but I don't know. I just don't know and I couldn't live with myself if something happened to Father Mateo or anyone else because I made a mistake. I'll do this. I want to do this. But you promised—he lives."

"I promised I will do everything in my power to take him alive. But I'm not going to lose Sean—or you—or any of Brad's team—to do it. Agreed?"

Brian nodded.

Kane handed him a 9mm gun. This was getting into legally dangerous territory, but they didn't have much of a choice right now. Jose had already proven to be a threat to the boys at St. Catherine's, he'd beaten up Jesse, and he planned to put a hit out on Michael if Brian didn't kill him first. This was their only window of opportunity.

"You have the phone Sean gave you?"

He nodded.

"We'll be able to hear everything. It'll build the case for Donnelly, and give Jose proof that you did what he wanted. Be yourself, Brian—but be careful. Your brother is a smart bastard, and if he thinks you're screwing with him, he doesn't care if you're his brother. Understand?"

"Yes, sir."

"Remember the codes?"

"Yes."

"Then we're ready."

Brian knew of Jose's safe house in the event the Santiago house was compromised. They drove into the neighborhood and parked a block away. Brian slipped out of the car and Sean tracked him on his tablet.

"I hate this," Sean said.

"I don't like putting the kid in danger any more than you, but he will never live in peace if his brother is still out there."

"Would you really take Michael and Brian in?"

"Yes." Kane glanced at him. "They were mine the day we rescued them. I'm responsible for them, and I will protect them. Brian is going to need more help than Father Mateo can give him after this. I should have been here more; I will be here more in the future."

Sean hadn't expected that from Kane. That he took such responsibility for the boys who would have died if they hadn't found them. His brother had always been complex; this added more layers to him than Sean expected.

Sean was listening through the open mike on Brian's phone. He'd masked the app so that even if Jose inspected it, he wouldn't know he was being recorded. This was Brad's operation—he, Nate, and two DEA agents would breach the house. Kane and Sean were solely responsible for getting Brian to safety.

"He's there," Sean said.

Kane nodded and opened the car door.

They slid out and approached the house in the dark of night, dressed in black, mindful that there could be scouts, though Brad and his SAPD contact were certain that only three or four remaining gang members were at large.

"What are you doing here, little brother?" Jose's voice came through their com system.

"I did it." Brian's voice was shaky. He wasn't faking. He was scared and worried. But that fear would help sell the con.

"What did you do? Is there another fucking raid coming?"

"No. I hit him four times. I think."

Four. There were four people in the house. Good, Brian

wasn't so terrified that he couldn't remember to do what he needed to do.

They were all on earpieces, and Brad indicated that he and Nate were in the rear of the house. "On my cue," Brad said.

"Yes, sir," Kane said. Sean almost laughed, but it was a testament to how much Kane trusted Brad Donnelly that he was okay with letting him run the op.

"Hit who?" Jose said. "Brian, speak up!"

"M-michael."

"I don't believe you."

There was shuffling, here and there, voices in the background. "I did," Brian said. "Here." He must be showing Jose the phone with the picture.

"He's armed, Jose."

"Give me that," Jose demanded. "Smells recently fired, but that means shit. Sit," Jose told Brian.

"Where?"

"Anywhere, shit, do I have to wipe your ass for you, too? Let me see that picture again."

Another male voice said, "Holy fuck, he did it."

Another voice, "In the back, wow, badass."

"Where is this?" Jose demanded.

"At the church. In F-father Mateo's office. I—I told Father I needed something, he gave me the key, and Michael followed me because he was so mad at me and I shot him. Don't let them send me back to foster care. I want to stay with you. You said if I killed him I could be a Saint."

"You did, Jose," another voice said.

"I didn't think you had the balls to do it," Jose said.

Did he not believe him? That photo was clear as anything, and they staged it well. They'd all seen enough dead bodies and bullet wounds to know what it would look like.

"Welcome, brother," Jose said. "You are really a badass. Why are you crying? Shit, Bri, this kid was a fucking problem. You know that, right? You would have been fine with the general. When I got out I would have promoted you, you know that, right? You wouldn't have to live in filth anymore."

"You knew I was there? In that prison?"

"So fucking what? You know that this *puta* got our father killed, right? His father, our father, both dead because Rodriguez couldn't follow orders. Don't feel bad for what you did. True Saints don't have regret. Let's go."

"Go?" Brian said. "Where?"

Sean wished he had eyes in the house. It sounded like Brian was moving around, and he shouldn't be—he was supposed to find a seat and stay there then, when Kane and Sean breached, take cover.

"Little brother, you have a lot to learn. The first is to not ask questions. We are the last of the Saints, but we will be joining a bigger, stronger *Hermanos de la Muerte*. And you need to be trained for what's coming."

"But I thought we would be a family. You promised, Jose."

"We are! We are the *Hermanos* family, bigger, power-ful, and we will own this city. We now run the largest meth house in San Antonio. I am their top cook. You will have everything you've ever wanted. Money. Girls. Power. Re-spect. You will have it because you're my brother."

In their ears, Brad said, "I have enough, go, go, go!"

Brad and Nate were going through the rear; Brad's team was monitoring the perimeter, and Kane and Sean had the front.

Kane went in first—he always did. Because he was the warrior, Sean knew, and because he could instantly assess the threats in the room.

Sean's job was to get Brian out safely. He came in behind Kane.

They had the element of surprise, but they were dealing

with the remnants of a vicious gang who wouldn't think twice about killing any of them.

The house was small and cramped and had the foul stench of a former meth lab. There was no telling what kind of chemicals were in here that might create a bigger problem.

"What the fuck?" Jose screamed. "You betrayed me!"

"No," Brian said, but Sean didn't think anyone heard him.

Everyone was moving. Two started out the back. The back door burst in, where Brad and Nate had it covered.

"DEA! Hands up!" Brad shouted.

"Hands," Kane said to Jose and the gangbanger in his sight. He had his gun aimed squarely at Jose, but his eyes were on both.

Sean rushed to the right, right next to Brian. "Behind me," he ordered Brian.

The kid was terrified. He scrambled up, grabbed hold of Sean's shirt.

A gunshot from the back of the house, followed by three more. Brian screamed.

"Are you hit?" Sean asked.

"N-no."

Kane was assessing Jose. "Don't do it," he said. "Don't think. Down on the ground."

Jose slowly went to his knees, but he was looking to the side. Sean and Kane both followed his gaze. A fifth person emerged from the dark hall. It was a woman, and she had an AR-15.

Sean grabbed Brian and pushed him out of the house as gunfire rang out. He practically threw him over the edge of the porch and ordered him to stay. Then he went back, staying low. By the time he reached Kane, the gun battle was over.

Kane was bleeding. "Fucking bitch," he muttered.

"Where?"

"My arm. I'm fine. Get Jose. He's hit, but he'll live."

Nate came in, gun out, looking at the bodies. "One DOA, one injured in the kitchen. Donnelly called it in."

"Two DOA, one injured," Kane said.

Sean cuffed Jose. "I will kill you all," Jose sneered. "Starting with my traitorous brother. Brian!" he screamed. "You are a dead man walking!"

Kane kicked him. "Your brother is the only reason you're breathing."

"You should kill me now, motherfucker, because I will come back. I know who you are."

"I dare you."

Sean wished his brother didn't always act like the tough guy he was.

Brad walked into the living room. He had searched the rest of the house. "Stick to the plan, we're good. There's a shitload of illegal contraband in his place, not to mention supplies and chemicals to cook meth, enough to blow up the entire block."

Sean went back outside. Brian was right where he left him, huddled into a ball, his arms over his head.

"Hey. Brian. It's over."

"He hates me. I heard him."

"Jose isn't capable of love."

"I should have let you kill him. *I* should have killed him."

"No. You did the right thing." Sirens grew closer. "You're a good kid, Brian. Don't let your mistakes define you. Let the good define you."

Brian wrapped his arms around Sean and hugged him tightly.

CHAPTER TWENTY-NINE

Saturday Late Night

Kane was staying with Michael and Brian at St. Catherine's for the night. Not because there was another threat, but because he wanted to make sure they were okay after the events of the last week. He'd been hit in the arm, a through and through, and paramedics on scene had bandaged him up.

Sean had sat with Jesse long after his son fell to sleep. This could have been so much worse than it was. And they would have some fallout next week. Brad was taking the brunt of the blame for not following protocol, but one thing in law enforcement that Brad could use to his advantage was that in the end, justice was served. They got bad guys off the streets, they saved the life of a young boy, and they confiscated more than one hundred illegal guns. Brad was confident he would be able to track down the *Hermanos* meth lab with the information obtained from the phones of the five gangbangers in the house, and that would be another win for keeping dangerous drugs off the streets.

In the end, the people Sean loved were safe, and he could rest easier.

Lucy came home after midnight—nearly one Sunday

morning. She was exhausted and they went right to bed, but neither could sleep. Sean told her everything that happened, and she told him what was going on with her case. "We arrested Garrett King, but he didn't kill anyone."

"Then why did you arrest him?"

"Drunk and disorderly—that's the story. To build a case. A case that we can*not* build. I'm going to do something tomorrow that Jerry will be angry with, but I don't know how else to get him to see the truth."

"Which is?"

"I talked to the vet tonight. We can take the dog tomorrow or Monday and I'm going to bring the dog—named Justice, ironically—to the jail and see how he reacts to Garrett."

"Smart."

"Jerry isn't going to like it. I think he's coming around, after our interviews today."

She was tense, and Sean pushed back her hair as they lay in the dark. "What else?"

"I can't stop thinking about the case."

"That's not unusual."

"What's driving me crazy is that on paper Garrett King is the best suspect possible. He has a motive—however weak—to kill all four of those men. Standish because his father hired him over Garrett to build a deck. James because he convinced his father to cut Garrett off, make him live on his own. Garcia because he fired him—except he *didn't* fire him. His assistant fired Garrett, and Garcia had been helping Garrett find another job. So why would he kill him?"

"Wait, wait, wait," Sean said. He turned on the lamp next to the bed. They wouldn't be sleeping much anyway. "Garcia didn't fire him, so why is that a motive?"

"Garcia was the boss. In charge of the kitchen. But his

assistant—and we confirmed this with management—is the one who handles employees, including termination. And Garrett knows this because he *was* fired. So there's no real motive—except on the surface."

"Except that most people would think that if you're fired, your boss is the one responsible."

"But Garrett knows he's not responsible."

"I'm not talking about Garrett. I'm talking about anyone who didn't work at the hotel. Anyone who doesn't understand the structure of the individual work environment would logically assume that Garcia fired Garrett. Because Garcia hired him, and was his boss."

"Okay. And? Garrett has a good reason for wanting his father dead—he cut him off. There's not a lot of money involved, but Garrett had been living there, rent-free, and Victor King had a good job and retirement. We're getting a copy of Victor's will, but I think if Garrett splits the estate with his sister, they sell the house, et cetera—I'd guestimate that after taxes and expenses he'll clear a quarter million."

"That's a lot to kill for."

"But I don't see him hurting his dog." She sighed. "Who would frame him?"

"Wow, high jump."

"You said it yourself—it's logical to think that Julio Garcia fired him, and that's why Garrett killed him. But following that logic, Garrett would have killed Mitchell Duncan, the assistant, who rode him hard and actually *did* fire him."

"So we're looking for someone who would know about Garrett's problems with these people."

"His father would have, but he's dead. Maybe the neighbors, who seem to know everything about the family."

"Friends? Drinking buddies?"

"Garrett has a lot of drinking buddies. I suspect he's an alcoholic, or borderline. Spends a lot of time in bars."

"Could he be working with someone?"

"I thought of that . . . but if I were a cold, calculating killer I wouldn't trust a drunk. A drunk might talk, let something slip, turn me in for a reduced sentence."

"How did you learn about these connections?"

"Standish and James from Victor King's appointment calendar. Garcia from the neighbors who said that Victor had told them that Garrett had been fired again, and then through a search of Garrett's apartment we learned he'd worked at Sun Tower. We confirmed it when we showed Garrett the picture of Garcia. He flat out admitted it. And we know that the termination happened at the end of June—right before Victor met with James about retirement planning, and a few weeks before he hired Standish to rebuild his deck—which Standish completed before taking the job in Houston."

"Maybe it was someone connected to Victor who could learn all these details. Maybe Victor was the ultimate target, and Garrett is the scapegoat."

"So far, Victor King led a simple, happy life. He taught history in high school. Widowed three years ago. Has friends, has family."

She leaned back. "I feel like we're never going to solve these murders."

Sean turned off the light and kissed her. "Sleep. It'll come to you. It always does."

On Sunday they relaxed at the house all morning. Lucy desperately needed the day off to unwind, but she had to confirm her theory.

"When are you going to be home?" Sean asked after

they had a leisurely brunch. "I thought you had the whole day off. You haven't had a day off in forever."

"Two hours, tops. I talked to the vet and Jerry and we want to try something."

"You convinced Jerry to let the dog be a witness?"

"Something like that," Lucy said.

"The younger boys are staying at Padre's camp for a couple more days—they're having fun now that they know Brian and Michael are safe. But Father Mateo wants us to come over for dinner. Kane told him what happened, and I don't really know how he's taking it. But we'll make it right."

"I know you will, and I'll be back long before dinner, I promise."

She showered and dressed in casual clothes, then drove to the vet. They were closed on Sunday, but the vet met her there and agreed to follow her to the jail, then take the dog back with him. The dog was cleared to be released, but there was no one to take him so they were boarding him.

Jerry met Lucy at the jail. He didn't look happy, but he had agreed to this plan. He absently scratched Justice behind the ears, and the dog wagged his tail frantically. "Let's do this fast, Jeanie is already grumpy because I haven't been home much these last ten days."

"Jeanie and Sean both," Lucy said.

"This might not even work. This dog doesn't look like he'd hold a grudge."

"If King hurt him, he'll react."

"No court is going to accept this as testimony."

"We have the vet here observing." The vet was behind the one-way glass. Jerry and Lucy were waiting with the dog for a deputy to bring Garrett King in from holding. "We have to know if we should even be looking for another suspect. Because I keep going back to the fact that

Garcia didn't fire Garrett King, so there is no real motive for his murder."

Jerry didn't comment.

A deputy knocked and opened the door. Garrett King walked in, his hands cuffed in front of him. As soon as Justice saw his owner, he pulled at the chain, his tail wagging, limping as far as he could get.

Garrett walked right over to the dog and got down on his knees. He had tears in his eyes when he said, "Hey, Justice, I missed you."

The dog whined and jumped on Garrett, knocking him down, and licking him frantically all over his face and neck.

Jerry caught Lucy's eye and sighed.

"Back at square one," he grumbled.

"No, we're not," she said.

CHAPTER THIRTY

Monday Morning

Lucy skipped the FBI staff meeting Monday morning to go to the sheriff's office. She feared Jerry was still angry with her because she'd brought Justice, the dog, to visit Garrett in holding yesterday.

He wasn't. In fact, he had Garrett arraigned first thing in the morning and released on bail for the drunk and disorderly.

"He didn't do it," Jerry said.

"I thought we agreed on that yesterday."

"Yeah, well, that dog was so damn overjoyed to see him, and Garrett cried. Mitchell Duncan—if he was dead and Julio was alive, I'd think more that Garrett was guilty. But there's also evidence."

"What evidence?"

"The soil that Ash found in Garcia's car doesn't match any of the crime scenes. It doesn't match Garcia's property, King's property, or Garrett's apartment. There is a gas can at Garcia's house, in the garage, but it's clear it hasn't been touched in months. Garrett has no alibi—he was home, alone, for each of the crimes—but a lot of people are home alone late Friday night. We've found no physical evidence at his apartment or in his truck—no duct tape, no gun, no mallet or sledgehammer. He could have tossed everything after he killed his dad, but where? In the lake? Possible. But get this—I had Ash give his truck a rectal exam, and it's clear he hadn't been up at the lake in weeks. He analyzed layers of dirt or some such thing and said he hadn't been up recently . . . which makes me think that Garrett wasn't lying when he said he and his dad had a blowout over Labor Day weekend and that was the last time he'd seen him. We really are back to square one."

"No, we're not. I've also been thinking a lot about this. Sean said something that made me wonder—who would know about Garrett King? Who would know that he was angry with his dad, that he had been fired, that he was jealous his dad had hired Standish and not him? It could be someone close to Garrett—or close to Victor. And it got me to thinking what William Peterson said the other day—that Steven James didn't normally take small estates like Victor King's. Why did he take this one?"

"I already sent an officer to pick up the files, since the warrant came through. But I still don't see where you're going."

"Where are we on finding Teri James's ex-husband?"

"I have his contact information, I didn't think he could contribute anything. And you cannot be thinking that woman had anything to do with this."

"I think we should find probable cause to test the soil in her yard. We've been going around and around, and it might be as simple as this: We couldn't figure out how the killer knew where James would be since it's such a short drive to his house from the airport. I've driven the route multiple times. He passed the golf course on his way home—why did he pull in? We know that he called his wife and they spoke—she knew when he would be coming home, when he would reach the golf course. He has no other calls to or from his phone. I also want to talk to Abby without Teri James around."

"That's problematic."

"Not if I think she's at risk."

Jerry was thinking. "Okay, let's say I buy into this insane theory. Why? What's the motive? She doesn't control Abby's trust fund. She doesn't get millions of dollars. She gets an allowance, right?"

"And a seat on the board. But maybe their marriage wasn't as idyllic as we were led to believe. Abby might know that. And think of this: Every interview we've done, no one talks about Teri. It's like she almost doesn't exist, or has never connected with people on a personal level."

"You're going back to that shrink."

"That shrink? My brother? Yes. I am. The killer is cold and impersonal. Someone who doesn't make human connections. Someone with little empathy. And you saw it, that's why you wrote those notes about Abby's relationship with her stepmother. I've gone around and around and around and this is the only thing that makes sense. We know the killer doesn't have to be physically strong."

"Your brother leaned toward a male killer."

"And Hans, who has at least ten more years' experience than my brother, leaned toward a female killer. Not that I would discount my brother, but at a minimum, they couldn't conclude male or female. I'll bet she has researched serial killers and created this crime scene to make us think specific things. That's why it looks like a stage, like she set a scene. The bread crumbs Dillon talked about.

"I also spoke with Abby's great-aunt yesterday," Lucy continued. "She is a character, I'll say that. And she was absolutely forthcoming about Abby's trust. It's untouchable. *Except* . . . the guardian is paid to serve on the trust board. One hundred thousand dollars a year to advise and consult, plus ten thousand dollars a month for living expenses until Abby is eighteen."

"Over two hundred thousand dollars."

"Steven never took the money. The ten thousand a month he donated to a charity his first wife had founded to research rare diseases—Bridget's best friend died from a rare disease in high school. The hundred thousand he reverted back to the trust, minus actual expenses, which he billed separately. They never totaled more than fifteen thousand a year. He made a good salary at Allied and lived on it. But I have another theory."

"I can't wait."

She didn't know if he was being sarcastic. "I don't think Teri James has family here, or if she does they are estranged. I need to confirm that with Abby or her ex-husband. And I don't think that money is the primary motivator, though I'm sure it has something to do with her actions."

"Then why? If not for money, why kill her husband?"

"You've talked to her more than I have. She is cool, she is unusually neat and tidy, she works from home, alone, and doesn't appear to have much of a social life. I think the strain of trying to live a normal life with a husband and stepdaughter took its toll. She couldn't be herself—but she couldn't keep up the act."

"So she kills her husband? Why not just divorce him?"

"And maybe that's where the money comes in. Maybe she doesn't do all that well on her own, and wants the money to live on. Or maybe she couldn't accept that she couldn't keep up the charade. It could make her feel inferior, and that's something that would grate on her."

"Psychobabble again," he said, but surprisingly, his expression didn't match his words. He was rethinking the case. He would come around, Lucy was certain, except for one thing: evidence.

Jerry said, "We still have nothing tangible."

"Track down the ex-husband. Let's talk to him, see wha he has to say. Then I want to talk to Abby, after school before she goes home."

Roger Abbott was an asshole, Lucy thought after only a ten-minute conversation. But the conversation was gold.

"Thank you for taking the time to talk to us," Jerry said on the speakerphone. "We only have a few questions."

"I hope so, because I have work to do, and I really don't care what my ex-wife is doing."

"I have in my notes that you were married for five years."

"Yes. The divorce was amicable. We haven't spoken since."

"Have you remarried?"

"No. Not interested."

"You know that Teri remarried."

"I heard, I don't care."

Jerry made a face at Lucy that almost had her laughing.

"Teri said she moved back to San Antonio to be close to her family, but we haven't been able to find her family."

"Because they're all dead or moved away. She was born in San Antonio, but they moved to Denver when she was in high school, after her parents divorced. She came here with her mother, a cold bitch of a woman. Two peas in a pod, though Teri wasn't a bitch. She was just a cold fish. Still lives here, as far as I know—but I don't keep track of Teri's family. Her father moved to Florida or something. She never talked to him in the years we were together. Never even talked about him. She's an only child, never talked about aunts or uncles or cousins so I don't know what family would be left in San Antonio."

That in and of itself didn't mean anything—she could

have returned to San Antonio because it's where she lived as a child and she had fond memories.

"She's a self-employed accountant," Jerry said, "works out of her house."

Roger laughed, one disturbing bark of a sound. "Because she doesn't get along with anyone. She had a great job here in Denver for a CPA, but she blew it. She wasn't promoted, so she installed a virus into their servers and destroyed the business from the inside out. By the time they figured it out, the backups were also corrupted."

"And she wasn't prosecuted?" Lucy asked.

"They couldn't prove anything. She actually got a severance package from them. It took them years to rebuild."

"But you knew about it."

"Not because she told me, but when I heard about the accusation I thought, yeah, that's Teri. She would quietly destroy someone and not think twice about it. She doesn't need the credit. She just wants the job done. She probably hasn't thought about it since."

Lucy asked, "But you married her. Why? Doesn't sound like you two had a whirlwind romantic courtship."

Again, the barking laugh. "Romance? Who gives a shit about that? Teri and I were realists. We got married because it was convenient and helped us both out at the time; divorced for the same reasons. I was never home because I travel for work three weeks out of the month, mostly to Japan. She liked that. And she kept an amazing house. Spotless. When I had to entertain, it was always perfect. She liked to entertain, put on the big production. And she's smart and can hold a conversation with anyone about anything, which helped me with my clients. But when I was promoted to vice president and traveled less, she didn't much like having me home. And I didn't much like spending more than a couple nights a week with her.

We talked, agreed to divorce, split our assets, and went our separate ways."

Lucy couldn't imagine living that sort of life, and by Jerry's expression, he was befuddled as well.

"And you haven't talked to her since your divorce—ten years ago now?"

"Correct. Well, I wouldn't say I haven't talked to her at all. She came up six or seven years ago for business and we had dinner to address a few minor financial things that came up after our divorce. It was amicable. She may have said she was seeing someone, but I wasn't really paying much attention. Now I really have to go. Anything else, call my secretary and she'll set up an appointment."

He hung up before Jerry could say goodbye.

"What a jerk," Lucy said.

"We see all kinds in this job." He shook his head, rubbed his eyes. "Nothing there we can use. He might not give her a good character reference, but that's not going to convict her of murder."

"Time for me to talk to Abby. Alone. She'll feel more comfortable that way."

"Tread carefully, she's a minor."

"And if she's in danger, we need to get her out of that house."

An officer came in with a thick file folder. "The documents you requested from Allied." He dropped it on the table.

"Thanks."

Jerry immediately opened the file, but glanced at the clock. "Want me to read?" Lucy asked.

"Would you mind? I'm going down the hall to talk to Jimenez. See if she thinks we have enough for a warrant. I don't know—I don't see it."

"If we can get Abby to go on record, that might give us what we need."

"She would need a court-appointed advocate, just to do
everything aboveboard. We don't want a conviction jeop-
ardized because the defense thinks we pressured a minor."

Jerry stepped out, and Lucy started reviewing Steven
James's files on Victor King. There were a lot of financial
records—hardcopies of everything, with notes that the financial documents had been scanned into the system.
Every meeting was detailed—time, date, what they discussed, what Victor needed to do, and what James would
do regarding filings and transfers and the like.

And then she saw it. The two items that might give them
the warrant they needed.

First, Steven James met with Victor one day at his
house. It would be easy enough for Teri, who worked from
home, to overhear any conversation—but this meeting
took place two days after Garrett was fired. It was something that Victor might have discussed.

And second, everything on Allied's server could be
accessed with Steven James's password.

That meant not only King's records, but Joyce Witherspoon's audits of Abby's trust. While Teri might have access to joint financial statements, it was clear that Steven
James also had his own accounts, separate from his wife.

She called William Peterson. "Mr. Peterson, I'm sorry
to disturb you again."

"Did you get the files? I gave them to an officer who
produced the warrant."

"Yes, I did, thank you. Another question—can your IT
department run a log of every time Steven James logged
into the Allied server from a remote location? And provide the IP address, date, and time of that login?"

"I imagine they can—but why?"

"I have a hunch, and this may help us bring a killer to
justice."

"I'll get back to you."

Jerry walked in with Maria Jimenez. He didn't look happy. "We need more," Maria said to Lucy.

"I have more. Victor King was at Steven James's house end of June for a business meeting. Steven's notes say that he was bringing over documents, it was a Saturday. That gives Teri James proximity—she could know about Garrett's job situation, that he'd been fired, and make the logical deduction that Julio Garcia fired him. And she may have had access to Allied's records, which would include King's as well as her stepdaughter's trust."

"It still isn't enough."

"I'm going to talk to Abby. If she has any hint that Teri is dangerous, we'll have her sit down with an advocate and give an official statement. Enough to get us a warrant. At a minimum for her car."

"Why her car?" Maria asked. "GPS tracking?"

"No," Jerry said, "grease. It's hard physical evidence."

"With that, we can get a full search warrant."

"Make sure it's solid because we don't want this biting us in the ass," Maria said. "I'll talk to the ADA and give her a heads-up."

"Thanks, Maria."

"Just do it right, Jerry." She left.

"I have an idea," Lucy said, "and I need to enlist Sean's help to do it."

"I'm listening."

"Each murder was committed on a Friday night. Teri lives in Olmos Park. The people in Olmos Park are security-conscious. Many of them have security systems, including cameras. Sean knows a lot of the neighbors—he's friendly. He's also a security expert who has high government clearance for his job, so if he extracts and documents data, it will be far easier to get it admissible in court."

"I'm not arguing, I just don't see what you're getting at."